Dedication

— This one is for all the loving mothers in the
world. Blessed be.

Epigraph

"Lies aren't always bad. Sometimes they're the thing we need to keep going. To keep our enemies from knowing we're actually a threat. To protect ourselves and those we care about."

— Auryn Hadley,
Power of Lies (The Dark Orchid #1)

Adult Pure Blood Mages

Brendan Winters, (Enchanter, Dark Syndicate Boss)

Alvar Elofsson (Seelie Noble), Married to Estelar

Danny Erling (Warlock, Police Officer), from Mount Gambier

Johnathan Ryan (Warlock, Limestone Coast District Leader, Mayor), from Mount Gambier

Jaxon Hayes (Warlock, Police Officer), from New South Wales

High Magus O'Grady (Mayor), from New South Wales

Jessica Ó Máille (Clairvoyant)

Chester Rowan (Conjurer)

Teenage Mages

Neve Winters, daughter of Alannah & Brendan Winters

Jasper Rowan, son of Chester Rowan

Caitlin Maher, daughter of Monique Lane & Steve Maher

Fiona Ryan, daughter of Jessica Ó Máille & Matthew Ryan

Lorcán Ó Máille, son of Lucas Ó Máille

Kane Sheridan, grandson of Duncan Sheridan

Rónán Doyle, son of Danielle Sheridan

Other Magicals

Cara Hughes (Half-mage Shaman, Conservationist)

Jacob Bennett (Boggart, Dark Syndicate Spymaster)

Caleb Hawthorn (Fae- Endarkened, Unemployed)

Bridey Hawthorn (Fae- Endarkened), Caleb's older sister

Estelar (Elven Princess of the Seelie Court)

Erik & Elna Alvarsson, (Fae- Enlightened), twin children of Alvar & Estelar

Saoirse (Mermage Warrior)

Tyler Quirke (Half-mage Warlock, Police Officer), from New South Wales

Nick Patterson (Orc, Orchardist)

Ben Sanders (Weredingo, Vet Assistant)

Connor Foley (Half-mage Abjurer, Marine Biologist)

Bailey Dougherty (Half-mage Warlock, Bartender)

Bianca Oakley (Fae- Wood Nymph, Cabaret Singer)

Amy Smith (Dwarf, Metallurgist & Council Blacksmith)

Playlist

'Throne' by Bring Me The Horizon
'My Name is Ruin' by Gary Numan
'Jealous Sea' by Meg Myers
'Natural' by Imagine Dragons
'Dark Side' by Bishop Briggs
'Bottom of the Deep Blue Sea' by MISSIO
'Dressed to Suppress' by Metric
'The Therapist' by Foreign Air
'I'm a Wanted Man' by Royal Deluxe
'Risk' by Metric
'Turn Up the Stereotype' by RedHook
'This is My World' by Esterly, feat. Austin Jenckes
'Call My Name' by The Unlikely Candidates
'Used to the Darkness' by Des Rocs
'Say Amen' by American Authors, feat. Billy Raffoul
'Ocean' by Goldfrapp
'Glory Box' by Portishead
'Way Down We Go' by KALEO
'Under Your Spell' by The Birthday Massacre

Playlist available on Spotify.

The Cast of Characters

The Council of Mages, Fleurieu District

High Magus: Kieran Lane, Monique's father (Mayor)

Seat of Aether Mana: Alannah Winters
(Conjurer, Dress Maker)

Seat of Elemental Mana: Liam Winters
(Warlock, Police Officer)

Seat of Organic Mana: Ross Winters (Abjurer, Doctor)

Seat of Emotional Mana: Nora Winters, née Maher
(Shaman, Vet)

Seat of Energy Mana: Steve Maher (Alchemist, Pharmacist)

Seat of Names Mana: Monique Lane
(Alchemist, Council's Secretary)

Seat of Cosmic Mana: Lucas Ó Máille (Clairvoyant, Lawyer)

Seat of Physical Forces Mana: Matthew Ryan
(Warlock, Police Officer)

Seat of Matter Mana: Mr. Duncan Sheridan
(Alchemist, Pharmacist)

Seat of Senses Mana: Mr. James Maher (Illusionist)

Chapter One

Sixteen years following the events of Winter's Maiden 2

Glancing at her reflection in the bedroom mirror, Alannah cringed. She studied her cotton unicorn pyjamas and felt the beginnings of a mid-life crisis set in. *When did I trade in the black satin slips for these PJs? How am I only now noticing how frumpy I look these days?* With a bamboo brush and some concerted effort, she managed to tame her wild bed-hair. It had been another restless night.

The house was quiet when she made her way to the kitchen. The silence was unusual, but not alarming. Being a summer Saturday meant Liam was likely at the beach already, making the most of the surf. She turned on the coffee machine and looked across the open plan living space. Her daughter sat at the dining table, watching something on her laptop.

Neve was using headphones, which explained the lack of noise. But the sound of grinding coffee beans got her attention. 'Morning, Mum.'

'Morning, hun. I didn't expect to see you up before me on a Saturday.'

'You do realise it's nearly midday, right?'

'Oh shit! Really?' Alannah looked at the old grandfather clock, which she had recently acquired from an antique auction. 'Damn. I guess I overslept. Did you get yourself some breakfast?'

Returning her attention to whatever YouTube had to offer, Neve shook her head.

Alannah took her fresh brew to the table and sat next to Neve. 'You know, if you want me and your father to show more leniency, you are gonna have to start behaving responsibly. That means looking after yourself more.'

'Spare me the lectures, Mum. I get enough of those from Liam. Besides, I remembered to feed the cat.' Neve gestured at the ball of white fluff sleeping on the couch.

Sighing, Alannah returned to the kitchen. She threw together some avocado and cheese toasted sandwiches. 'Here, eat this.' She put one of the plates beside Neve's laptop, then sat in front of her own computer.

Sipping her coffee, she scrolled through her social feed. Not much engaged her foggy brain beyond some cat memes. She clicked like on a few and went to close her laptop when a news bulletin caught her attention.

'Mum, can—'

'Wait a sec, hun. Come look at this.' She opened the live video feed and gasped at the aerial footage.

'The Victorian Government has declared a state of emergency. Melbourne residents flock from their homes amidst the city's collapse.'

'Oh wow! Is that a volcano erupting?' Neve asked. 'It looks awesome!'

'The dormant volcanoes erupting from part of the Newer Volcanic Province. This disaster follows a series of earth tremors. Experts claim the odds—'

Alannah muted the sound. 'It's devastating is what it is. Don't forget I spent nine years of my life living in that city. I have friends there.'

Remorse filled Neve's bright green eyes. 'Shit! Sorry, Mum. Can you call to check if they're okay?'

'Now's not a good time to be clogging up the phone towers over there. I hope they've marked themselves as safe.' Alannah's hands trembled as she clicked over to Melissa's profile. Nothing. She looked at Emma's and Cole's next. *Damnit!* None of them had checked in.

'Mum?'

'Mm?' Alannah was too distracted to give Neve her full attention.

'Is it okay if Cat and Fi come over for a bit?'

'Yeah.'

Neve disappeared down the hall. Alannah switched between face-stalking her friends and watching updates on the disaster. The more she watched, the more uneasy she felt about the whole thing. The reports coming from the scientists only fed her suspicions. *Why is a dormant volcano with such low odds of current activity erupting in such a prominent place? Could this be the work of dark mages?*

The issue warranted some investigation, so she sent a quick email to Kieran Lane, the High Magus of her state. She included a link to the newsflash with the question: *Could this be dark magic?*

When Kieran did not reply within an hour, she grew impatient and rang him.

'Yes, Councillor Winters?' His curt tone was typical, even after years of working with her.

'Did you get my email, Your Honour?'

'I did.'

'And?'

A loud sigh crackled through the line. 'Why are you asking me about the goings on in another state? You know I don't have any jurisdiction over there.'

'Are you not the least bit concerned for them?'

'I sympathise, sure. But it's not like I can do anything. If High Magus Hanigan has need of us, I'm sure he'll be in touch. Now if you don't mind, I am in the middle of something.'

'Of course. Sorry to bother you.' Alannah hung up and flung her phone at the couch out of frustration. *Sixteen years on and I still haven't earned enough respect from the man.* Then it struck her. *If this volcano business is a dark magic conspiracy, they could hit South Australia. What if I can uncover such a plot and prevent devastation at our doorstep?* Surely *doing so would raise Kieran's esteem.*

With newfound enthusiasm, Alannah dialled her friend Monique.

'Hey girl, what's up? I hope Caitlin isn't causing you any grief.'

'What?' Alannah remembered the girls were over and hanging out in Neve's room. 'Oh right. No, she's fine. Have you seen the news?'

'No. Why? What's happened?' Monique's cheerful tone plummeted.

'A volcano in Melbourne. It's all over social media, so you should check it out. But listen, I was hoping you could hack into your dad's work files. I need some contact details for the magic community in rural Victoria.'

'You thinking foul play?' Monique was always more astute than her father, the High Magus.

'Yeah. Your dad's too stubborn to look into it, so I need to use some back channels to check it out.'

'I'll see what I can do.'

'Thanks.' After signing off, Alannah returned to checking on her friends. A little relief washed over her when she found Emma's update declaring she was fine and out of the danger zone. She continued to wait for news from the other two.

'Well, there goes my plan to fly under the radar.' Brendan huffed as he stuffed his phone back in his pocket. Zipping his small carry-on case closed, he became thankful for the decision to pack light.

'What do you mean?' asked Caleb.

'My flight got cancelled; something about a volcano in Melbourne spewing too much ash into the air. Now I need to magiport there, which sucks

'cause I'm not keen for High Magus Kieran to know
I'm in town.'

Caleb's big, dark, soulful eyes looked so
pretty when they grew wide with surprise. 'A
volcano in Melbourne? Are you for real?'

'Yup.'

Grabbing his own phone, Caleb became
engrossed in footage of the volcano erupting. 'I
didn't even know we had active volcanoes in
Australia, let alone under cities.'

'Hmph. We should have paid more attention
in school.'

Sardonic eyes peered over the small screen in
Caleb's hands. 'You were the one playing hooky all
the time. I kept my head down and got the work
done.'

'That's right.' Brendan cast wistful thoughts
back to their youth. Stalking around the bed, he
backed Caleb up against the wall. 'I'd almost
forgotten you were a nerd back then. Hm, I
wonder... would I have noticed your beauty sooner
if you hadn't buried your head in books so often.'
He brought a hand up to Caleb's face, tucking a
strand of long, black hair behind one of his pointy
ears. The proximity aroused them both, their dicks
tenting against each other.

The pitch of Caleb's voice lowered. 'Perhaps, but then I would have been nothing more than a distraction, a passing fad like all the girls you used back then.'

'Touché. Instead, your timing was perfect. You were like my life raft in a sea of despair.' Brendan drew Caleb's lips into a deep, passionate kiss. When the calendar alarm on his phone sounded, he groaned as he pulled back. After silencing the damn thing, his gaze returned to Caleb's mouth. Subconsciously, Brendan grazed the pad of his thumb along the bottom lip. 'Gods I'm gonna miss these sweet lips.'

Caleb's mouth curled into a mischievous smile. 'Jacob has pretty soft lips.'

'You sly fox,' Brendan laughed. 'You never told me the pair of you hooked up.'

'Sure I did. I told you about all the times I partied with him whenever I paid our hometown a visit.'

'You told me about the gangbangs, but you never related the details of being intimate with *him*.'

'My bad,' Caleb replied with a wry smile. 'I figured you'd assume we fucked.'

Brendan drilled into Caleb's soul with a stern expression. 'You know I don't like it when you leave me guessing. When I ask for details, I want *everything*. The who, the where, and most definitely the how. I am going to have to punish you for such insubordination.'

A slight moan escaped Caleb's lips as his eyes darkened with lust.

With a wicked grin, Brendan stepped back, breaking all body contact. 'I can see how much you want me right now, Thornsy. But you see, punishment is never about what *you* want.'

Caleb's eyes lowered. 'Of course. I'm sorry for offending you, Sir. What is my punishment?'

Seeing his submissive stance sent signals southward and tested Brendan's willpower. It would have been too easy to dish out a few lashings and take him then and there. But what he had in mind would be more fun in the long run, and it would give Caleb time to reflect upon his actions. 'No intentional sexual release until I return home. You will not touch yourself and you will not initiate intimate contact with anyone else while I am away. I'll let Bridey know the deal too, so she won't let you get off.'

Caleb gasped.

'What's wrong, Thornsy? Are you afraid of a little celibacy?'

'Not afraid, more… frustrated. I can't remember the last time I went so long.'

Closing the distance, Brendan reached inside Caleb's pants and gripped his erection. Then he leaned in to press his lips to Caleb's ear. 'If you think this is frustration, how do you think you will feel in two weeks?'

'Ah Gods!' Caleb gritted his teeth against the torture of Brendan's teasing touch.

'Will you be good for me Caleb?'

'Y-yes Sir,' he replied with a shaky voice.

'Good man. Now I want my goodbye kiss.' Embracing Caleb, Brendan kissed him with ardent fervour. Their passion rivalled anything Hollywood ever put on the big screen. He walked out sporting a massive smile and the boner to match. At least he could use magic to control the latter, although he didn't have time to hide it before finding Bridey in the parlour.

She glanced at his situation and grinned. 'Oh dear. Has my brother left you unsatisfied?'

'Quite the reverse, I assure you.' He dropped his case beside the chaise longue and straddled her lap. 'At least I can do something about mine, unlike Caleb. I have forbidden him from seeking relief for the next two weeks. Can I rely on you to police him for me?'

'Certainly, Sir.'

'Thank you, Bry.' The farewell kiss he shared with Bridey was much more savage, like a pride lion with his lioness. By the time he left, Brendan considered the merit of Caleb's suggestion: seeking out Jacob might prove necessary. The pickings in Gaeilge Shores were slimmer after the Council had exiled him. He was not even sure if Bianca would welcome him back in her bed.

EDM blared from Neve's speakers as she sat on her bed with the girls. She fastened her long, black hair in a ponytail and grabbed her laptop. Clicking NEXT on the photo slideshow, she gasped at the fine specimen.

Fiona flicked her red hair and squealed with delight, 'Oh. My. God. Dorian Pearce is so hot!'

'I know right! And you know what they say about vampire bites.' Neve licked her lips.

'Your parents would have a fit if they heard the two of you lusting after a vampire,' Caitlin scoffed as she adjusted her short plaid skirt. 'Especially your mum, Neve.'

Neve shot Caitlin a suspicious look. 'Why do you say that? I know Liam can be an arrogant arse, but Mum is more tolerant than most bloodline mages.'

'Didn't she ever tell you about her vampire ex?'

After scooping her jaw up off the floor, Neve questioned her blonde friend, 'My mum dated a vampire? I can't imagine her doing something so sordid.' A giggle slipped out as she thought of her mother letting a vampire bite her.

'She did. He was Dorian's late uncle, in fact. Austin was working for your great-grandmother, who was a lich. Under her orders, he tried to talk your mum into becoming cursed, which freaked her out, so she dumped his arse. But he went crazy and tried to force the curse on her. There was a big battle where your mum killed the lich, and Liam killed the vampire.'

'Wow! How did you know all this and how have I never heard anything?' Neve asked.

'My mum told me… she was there! I guess the memory is too traumatic for your mum to retell.'

'Hm, I guess.' Neve continued looking at the photos she had downloaded from her phone. She paused when one of the Rowan family filled the screen.

'Mm, Jasper!' Neve and Fiona chimed in perfect unison.

'At least our folks can't complain about his bloodline status,' added Fiona.

'Well actually… he is a massive slut. I heard he's already slept with half the girls at Gaeilge High,' explained Caitlin. 'And he is a senior! Good luck pinning him down for more than one night.'

Neve laughed. 'I'd gladly pin him down for a night.'

As if on cue, her phone buzzed with a message from Jasper: END OF SUMMER HOLIDAYS PARTY AT MY HOUSE TONIGHT. OPEN INVITATION.

Screaming, she threw the phone at her friends. Then using the breathing exercises Mum had taught her, Neve tried to calm her excitement. *Jasper messaged me! The hottest boy in town sent me a personal invitation!*

Fiona gave her a wicked grin. 'Looks like you might get your wish.'

'Will you give up your V-card to the rat? Don't you want your first time to be special?' Caitlin asked.

Neve frowned at Caitlin for throwing a wet blanket over her elation. 'With Jasper, it will be special.'

Caitlin sighed. 'To you sure, but not to him.'

'So?'

'So, you should hold out for someone who will treat you with respect, someone who appreciates you.'

'Ugh, why are you being such a drag, Caitlin?'

'Because I care about you, and I don't want to see you get hurt. What about Lorcán Ó Máille or Kane Sheridan? They are both hotties and they're nicer boys.' Caitlin grabbed one of the carrot sticks from the snack plate on the bedside table.

'They are in our year level, so they're way too young. Boys mature slower than we do, so you need to pick one at least one year older, two years is even better. Besides, I doubt they even look at girls that way yet.'

A loud crunch filled the air, then Caitlin grinned. 'Trust me, hun, they've noticed us. Don't forget mages grow up quicker than humans.'

Neve gasped. 'You like one of them, don't you? Alright, spit it out: who are you crushing on?'

Caitlin blushed, but kept her mouth shut.

'Oh, come on, Cat. You know we won't tell anyone. Your secrets are safe with us, right Fi?'

'Of course,' replied Fiona with an eager tone to equal Neve's.

'Okay. It's Lorcán. He is so… dreamy.'

Fiona cupped her mouth in her hands to hide the big smile on her face. But the joyous expression was still there when she pulled them away. 'Are you in love?'

Caitlin bit her lip. 'Hardly,' she scoffed. 'I don't even know how he feels about me. The attraction is purely physical at this stage.'

Fiona shrugged. 'Let's go to this party. Then you can both find out what the guys think of you. Plus, it would be a great icebreaker before we start senior high school on Tuesday.'

'True,' agreed Neve. 'So, the big question is, what should I wear?'

Liam hung up his surfboard beside the outdoor shower at the back of his house. Peeling off his wetsuit, he slipped under the warm water. He closed his eyes and basked in the stream cascading over his skin and seeping into his tight muscles. It was his favourite form of meditation. Then a scream followed by fits of giggles coming from an upper floor window broke his reverie. 'Curse that girl,' he muttered as he stepped out and grabbed a towel.

Wrapping the Egyptian cotton bath sheet around his waist, Liam stepped inside. He spotted

Alannah curled up on the sofa with Luna the cat purring beside her.

She was texting someone, tension swirling around her like storm clouds.

Is she oblivious to my presence, or choosing to ignore me? 'Who are you messaging?'

'Hm, what?' Alannah's attention remained on her phone.

Meanwhile, his own attention shifted to the sight of her curvaceous body in a skimpy summer dress. He had not seen her wear anything so revealing for years, and the design looked new. 'Who are you chatting to and why do they have you so worried?'

'Oh. It's Emma from Melbourne.' Alannah finally glanced at him, but she took little heed of his partial nudity, or his growing arousal. 'Have you seen or heard the news at all?'

'No. I've been at the beach all day. What happened?' He sat next to her, adjusting himself in a none-too-subtle way, although she did not notice.

Alannah showed him the footage of the volcano erupting in Melbourne.

'Christ! That's horrible. I'm so sorry, babe.' Leaning in, Liam kissed the crown of her head. At least she did not flinch when he did so. 'Are your friends okay?'

'Emma is. But we can't get hold of Mel or Cole.'

When his hand moved to her back, she stiffened. But he refused to pull away from his wife when she needed comforting.

'Neve's friends are here, by the way, so you should put some clothes on.'

So she did notice. Liam dismissed the thought as soon as it occurred. *Doesn't mean she cares.* 'Explains the squeals coming from upstairs.' He rose and headed into his room, closing the door with a little too much force. The last thing he wanted was for Alannah to feel pressured, especially at a time like this. *But what was she thinking when she put that damn dress on?*

Slumping onto the bed, he eased the towel free. He used it to contain the mess when thoughts of his last time with Alannah brought him over the edge. Then he threw it in the laundry hamper and fetched some clean clothes. Dressed in black cargo shorts and a tight, white surf brand t-shirt, he returned to the living room.

'Can I get you something to eat?' he asked as he fixed himself a snack in the kitchen.

'Just a coffee, thanks.'

Concern furrowed his brow. 'Have you eaten much today?'

Alannah glared at him. 'I'm not hungry, okay? What do you expect me to do? I can't exactly conjure up an appetite.'

'Jesus, Lana… I'm worried about you. I can tell you're not sleeping properly, and you've been losing weight again. Why won't you let me help you?'

'Because you can't. Let me work through my own shit, okay?'

'You could see your therapist again,' he suggested, trying to be supportive.

She snorted. 'You have no idea what my therapy entails, do you?'

'Not exactly, no. I know you said he uses unconventional methods. You tend to feel better after a weekend of therapy, and it's those results I care about.'

Neve chose the moment to interrupt. 'Mum, can I go to Naomi's house tonight?'

'Yeah I—'

'Wait,' Liam cut Alannah off. 'Will her parents be there?'

Neve shrugged. 'I dunno. Probably.'

'Unless you can get me confirmation from her parents the answer is no.'

'But *Dad*—'

'I won't hear it, Neve. I don't trust Jasper anywhere near you. Rowan boys don't exactly have the best reputation for respecting girls.'

Noticing Alannah's shiver, Liam kicked himself for reminding her of Clayton.

'*You're so unfair, Liam!* All my other friends will be there.'

'So not only are Naomi's parents unlikely to be there, but it sounds like a party. You are most definitely *not* going.'

She gaped at him. 'I hate you, Liam!' Storming off to her room, she slammed the door behind her.

'Fucking brat,' he cursed under his breath.

'Do you have to be so hard on her?' Alannah asked.

'Do you have to be so soft on her?' he retorted. 'She's only fifteen, Lana. Far too young to be going to parties and hooking up with boys.'

'She turns sixteen in July. Have you forgotten what we were like at her age?'

Recalling Alannah's reckless past, Liam paled. He dreaded the thought of Neve following in her mother's footsteps. 'I remember. That's the problem… especially if she's anything like you.'

He imagined thunder rumbling from inside Alannah as raging storm clouds burst around her. 'How. Dare. You.'

Startled, Luna sprang from the couch and skidded along the floor in her attempt to flee the room.

Shit! 'Lana, I didn't mean it like that. I'm concerned about her is all.'

'Right. Like you're worried about me. But there's nothing wrong with *you*, is there?'

Liam froze. 'What do you mean?'

Alannah sighed. 'Never mind.'

'No. I want to know what's on your mind. If I've done something wrong… or upset you somehow, I need you to tell me.'

'Do you really want to know what's wrong?'

'Yes. I do.'

A tense moment passed as Alannah studied him. 'You're a lousy lay, Liam. Sex with you is boring. It's why I stopped putting out for you. You don't do it for me.' Her words floored him.

Anger simmered away inside his nerves. 'So what, no sex is better than sex with me? Is that it?'

A malicious grin formed on her perfect face. 'Who said I wasn't getting any?'

Liam's heartbeat kicked up a notch.

'Would you have been so quick to suggest therapy sessions if you knew what they involved?'

Shaking his head, he denied what he was hearing, 'No.'

'Oh, yes, Liam. My therapist fucks me the way I like it because you can't.'

With his blood boiling, Liam took off in a mad dash for the gym where he pummelled the punching bag. 'Fuuuuck!'

Chapter Two

Alannah began to itch as fear and remorse prickled her skin. *I can't believe I confessed my affair to Liam. Not that I've seen Tyler in ages. But still.* The possibility of losing the comfort and security Liam provided terrified her. Despite their lack of sexual chemistry, she still loved and needed him. *Way to go, moron!*

An alert tone on her phone broke the fall of Alannah's downward spiral. Melissa's message said she was in hospital, recovering from minor injuries.

After replying, THANK YOU AND GET WELL SOON, Alannah updated Emma. *Still nothing from Cole, damn it.* Quite beside the fact he had been her first high school sweetheart, Cole had been one of her best friends. He had also married Emma, so anything bad happening to him would devastate Emma.

Argh! I need comfort from a friend. Picking up her phone, Alannah rang Cara.

'Hi hun. How are you?' Cara's tone was light and cheerful.

'Not great. Can you come over?'

'Of course. What's the matter?'

'I'll explain when you get here.'

'Okay.' The worry in Cara's voice rang out as she signed off.

Glancing down at her red summer dress, she sighed. *So much for showing you off to the girls.* Instead of meeting friends at the coffee shop, she had spent the day moping and messaging Emma. It was a shame because she was proud of her latest design. She changed into something more comfortable, wishing she had done so sooner. It might have avoided Liam's unwanted attention and the ensuing argument.

By the time the doorbell rang, the house had grown deathly quiet. Alannah was the only resident who bothered to answer the door.

Cara leaped inside and pulled her into a bear hug. 'Please hun, tell me what's going on?'

'Can we go to my room first?'

The nod Cara gave her told Alannah she understood the code for 'secret women's business.' With the door closed behind them, Cara perched on the edge of Alannah's bed and waited with a curious expression.

Alannah sat up against the headboard and sighed. 'Where do I even start?'

'Oh Gods, is it that bad?'

'There are a few different issues. I guess the easiest one to tackle is the fact a volcano recently erupted in Melbourne. One of my friends over there got injured and another is missing…' Her eyes began to water.

'Christ! If that's the easiest, I hate to imagine what else is going on.' She moved up to embrace Alannah. 'I'm so sorry hun. I did hear about the volcano, but I forgot you had friends over there.' Cara gave Alannah a few minutes to sob against her soft, warm chest.

When she was able, Alannah continued, 'The other issues are marriage problems.'

'Hm, I feared as much. What has Liam done now?'

'Actually, this time it's me. We had a minor disagreement earlier and, in my frustration, I kinda let something big slip: like the fact I've been having an affair.'

'*What?* When did this start happening?'

Guilt over not telling Cara was compounding with what she felt for cheating on Liam. 'About sixteen years ago.'

Her redhead mage friend sat there gobsmacked with wide brown eyes staring back at her. A minute later she snapped out of the daze. 'Who is he?'

'Remember Tyler?'

'The warlock from Sydney who looks like... *him*? The one you hooked up with one time and ran off with on your wedding day?'

'Yeah, him. Thing is, the hooking up kind of became a regular thing for us. And between rounds of wild sex, I would offload all the shit I was feeling over... *him*. It was like therapy for me.' Alannah could almost see the gears turning in Cara's mind as she put the pieces together.

'All those weekend retreats?'

Alannah nodded.

'Is Tyler married?' Cara asked.

'No. He and Sam are in a long-term de facto relationship, but she knows all about us. She even joins in sometimes.'

'Wow. I'm discovering a whole new side of you.'

'It's not new, Cars... I've always had this wild side. You might have seen it more if things had worked with... *him*. But since becoming a mother, I've tried to repress it for Neve's sake. And Liam never provided the right outlet for me, so I kept going back to Tyler.'

'How wild are we talking here?'

'At our kinkiest, Tyler and I are like Nick with you, or you with Bailey.'

Cara's relationship dynamics had become somewhat complicated since her split with Jacob. She lived the full BDSM lifestyle as a switch. When she wanted to top, she would spend her time with Bailey, otherwise she submitted to Nick. 'Let me get this straight: you like subbing to Tyler?'

'Yeah.'

'For the full works?'

'Ah huh.'

'I can see why you are incompatible with vanilla Liam.' Cara sighed. 'I wish I knew about this side of you years ago. It would have been fun to take you to the club.' Hope filled her eyes. 'You should bring Tyler the next time you see him!'

'So, the whole breaking my marriage vows thing doesn't bother you at all?'

Cara snorted. 'Hells no! For one thing, notions of monogamy are strange to me. I also think Liam is a dick who doesn't deserve you. I'm curious about Tyler, though. I always thought his resemblance to Jerk Face was uncanny.'

'There's a magic reason for them looking identical. Tyler is a doppelganger, or magic twin. He did some research and discovered one of the deities in his gene pool was Isis, Goddess of magic. While in utero he developed a mystical link with another mage. Anyway, I digress. Turns out if Tyler performs magic with his mystical twin, they enhance each other's powers.'

Cara had listened with a fascinated expression. When Alannah finished, she took a few seconds to process everything. 'So, um, has Tyler met his magic twin?'

'Yes, unfortunately. There was a whole dark mage conspiracy resulting in the summoning of an evil God from the Underworld. Tyler admitted to performing dark magics—of the soul tainting variety.'

'Damn. Has Tyler's soul recovered?'

'Yeah. But... *you know who* is still a dark mage.'

'So, what are you going to do about the whole Tyler and Liam situation?'

Alannah exhaled sharply. 'I don't know.'

Liam strode with gusto into the pub. Being a balmy summer night, it seemed like the perfect time to be slumming it with the common folk. It was not like he had a choice, anyway, what with the closure of the Sailing Club. The crowds parted like the Red Sea for him as he approached the bar. And he felt pretty chuffed at the attention he drew from these people who stood in awe of his greatness.

'What can I get you, Sir?' the humble bartender asked.

'Nothing but your finest cognac will do.'

'Indeed, Sir.' The bartender reached for the top shelf, then he poured the liquid gold with the greatest care.

As the glass slid across the bar, a pretty blonde lady from out of town sat beside him. 'You must be very wealthy to be drinking something of such quality.'

'Quite. I am like royalty in these parts.'

She laughed sweetly. 'Are you like a prince or a king?'

'More of a knight with very shiny armour and a great white stallion. Oh, how I love to ride my stallion.'

She giggled as if he had said something funny, but Liam did not understand why. He had not made any of his usual lame jokes. Then she placed a hand on his beefy arm and leaned in as if to tell him a secret. 'You could ride me tonight if you wish. I can be wild like a horse.'

Shocked, Liam observed the drink in her hand and wondered how many she had already consumed. 'No, my lady, I am an honourable man. And happily married too. I could never cheat or take advantage of a lady with alcohol in her system. Do you not see the golden halo on my head and my prissy angel wings?'

'Oh, yes sir. I do. Can you fly with those?'

'Alas no. I use them to prance about and create great gusts of wind

when my talking cannot fill the space with air.'

The girl tittered. 'You are so very funny.'

'Ah, but you have not yet heard me make with the puns. They tell me I am a master, and I even have a Diploma in Dad Jokes.'

Jacob sniggered at Brendan's mockery of Liam. 'And I bet his daughter hates the dad jokes.'

Brendan whirled around to glare at his captain across the table in a dark corner of Doyle Dougherty's Irish Pub. 'Liam has a daughter? With Alannah?'

All the blood drained from Jacob's face. *'Oh shit!'*

'Yeah, *Oh Shit*, about sums it up. Your job is to keep me in the loop, Red. How did you fail to mention my douchebag brother having a kid with my ex?'

'Neve is not technically Liam's. She's a Beltane baby.'

'Good. At least Liam hasn't bred. I can't bear the thought of miniature versions of him running around.' Jealousy rarely touched Brendan, who thrived in the polyamorous lifestyle. Yet he could not escape the years of resentment and sibling rivalry his father had nurtured. Knowing some *other* guy had sown his seed inside Alannah soothed Brendan. But then realisation hit: 'Wait! How old is this girl?'

'Fifteen and half. She starts senior school this year. I hear she is quite a looker and popular…' Jacob quit yammering as he noticed the change in Brendan's expression. 'What?'

'If my calculations are correct, Alannah's conceived her daughter at Beltane in 2023.' He watched as Jacob did the sums in his head.

'Yeah, sounds right. So, what's the big deal about *that* Beltane?'

'Alannah only had one partner.'

'How would you know th—' Jacob's eyes widened. 'Unless… *Oh Shit!*'

'They seem to be your favourite words tonight, Red. Unless you want another *Oh Shit* moment, tell me why I'm only finding out about my daughter when she is fifteen and a half.'

'I was advised to minimise intel about Alannah, for your sake.'

'Advised by who?'

Jacob bit his lip.

'Who are you loyal to, Red? Your Boss who is also your best mate, or…?' Brendan used a lethal tone, not to sound threatening but as a by-product of his anger.

'I'm loyal to you, I swear. I thought I was doing you a favour, avoiding the opening of old wounds and such.'

'Advised. By. Whom?' Brendan disliked pushing his weight around with friends, but desperate times …. Nothing instilled fear like playing the Syndicate Boss card.

'Lord Stirling, Sir.' Brendan could read the sheer terror on Jacob's face like an open Stephen King novel.

'Fuck!' The utter betrayal he felt at the mention of Caleb's code name devastated and infuriated him. While Jacob had been ignorant, Caleb knew how things played out at *that* Beltane. He knew Brendan was the baby daddy. 'Thank you for being candid with me, Red. Even if you are sixteen years late on the news.'

'I'm so sorry, Lord Jet. Do you wish to punish me?'

Brendan sneered at him. 'From what I've heard, you would enjoy it too much.'

Jacob's cheeks turned a shade of red matching his glamoured hair.

'No. I have no desire to touch you now.'

Disappointment washed over Jacob like a hailstorm, shattering his hopes like glass. However, something about the pleading in Jacob's eyes did Brendan in. 'But I suppose you could make it up to me.'

'Anything, Sir.'

'I want to know everything there is to know about Neve, Alannah, and Liam... starting with why the wanker is here instead of the Sailing Club.'

'Well, you were right about the closure. There is a private function on there tonight.'

'What's wrong with the liquor in his own house?' Brendan sent dagger glares into the back of Liam's head, wishing they were real knives. *Oh, but they could be.* Brendan almost knocked his beer over, startled at how dark his thoughts had turned.

'I see talking about her still gets you edgy.'

'Answer my fucking question, Red.'

'Right. They can't have alcohol in the house. Alannah went through an addiction phase several years ago. She's been sober for a few years now, but Liam doesn't want to take any risks.'

'Hm. What drove her to drink?'

Jacob shrugged. 'I don't know exactly, but I do know her marriage to Liam has been on the rocks for years. They hide it well in public, but as one of the few people she invites into her home, I've seen the signs.'

'You guys are still friends?'

'If you can call it that. Alannah doesn't let anyone past the solid walls she has erected around her soul. She treats her friends more like acquaintances, including Liam.'

'Curious.' Brendan did have a little experience with Alannah's defensive barriers. 'I've seen her behave that way in the past because she was afraid of her feelings for me.'

'No.' Jacob shook his head. 'This is completely different. What she did back then was more like hanging a curtain compared with the thick stone walls she has now. Alannah has changed a lot since you saw her last. She is much colder and meaner.'

Brendan struggled to keep a lid on his volcanic temper and Liam's proximity was not helping. *Liam did this to her. The arsehole needs to pay.* Needing a distraction from thoughts of vengeance, he changed the subject: 'Tell me more about Neve.' Listening to descriptions and stories of his daughter filled him with a longing to meet her. While business would only keep him in town a few days, he could arrange a change of plans.

Once she had calmed down from her fit of rage, Neve made plans to go to the party regardless. She took some time choosing her dress, a sleek black mini she had only worn once before. With a little makeup, the outfit made her look a few years older. She put some ballet flats in her clutch purse and threw her high heels out the window. With bare feet and ninja stealth, she climbed out after them. Magic would have helped, but her mana rings were in the ritual cellar. Putting her gymnastics lessons to use was easier than sneaking past her parents.

Thanks to the tree near her window, she made it to the ground with only a few minor scrapes. From there it was a short walk—slow and arduous in heels—to Naomi and Jasper's house. She breathed a sigh of relief when she finally arrived. Moonlight sparkled in the large windows covering Jasper's seafront mansion. Mum described the house as a modern eyesore, but Neve did not mind the light airy atmosphere of the place.

The deep booming bass of EDM rattled the glass as Neve opened the front gate. A rowdy group of older kids hung out on the front lawn. Ignoring several wolf whistles, she held her head high as she strode toward the front door.

The front room, a large living area, had become the dancefloor. It did not take long to spot her friends among the popular people in the middle. Pushing through the crowd and swatting groping hands, Neve reached the girls. They were dancing with Lorcán and Kane.

Fiona squealed at the sight of her. 'You made it!'

'Of course I did.' She hugged them all and smiled at the guys. 'Hi.'

Lorcán draped his arm over Caitlin's shoulder. 'We didn't think your old man would let you out.'

'He doesn't know I'm here,' admitted Neve.

'You are a naughty girl.' Kane waggled his brows.

'I hear it runs in her blood.' The warmth of a familiar voice stole the breath from Neve's lungs.

Turning, she came face to face with Jasper. 'Hi.'

He grinned at her. 'Hi Neve. I'm so glad you could make it.' Jasper's eyes scanned her body from top to toe, then up again. 'You look lovely tonight, my dear.'

Her pulse was racing, and her legs felt like jelly. 'Uh, thanks, Jasper.' She mentally praised him for looking so hot. He wore a tight, button-down shirt emphasising his muscular body. Messy looking blond hair topped off the look. It took all her self-control to avoid drooling.

'Would you like to join me for a drink?'

'I'd love to.' She began to follow him when Caitlin shot her a concerned look. With a reassuring smile, she mouthed the words 'I'll be careful' then continued.

Jasper led her into a kitchen of black polished marble counters and bright white cupboards. There was a tub of ice on the sink from which he retrieved a glass bottle and handed it to her.

She looked down at the red fizzy drink, then glanced up at him. 'What's this?'

'It's like a raspberry soft drink. Most of the girls love those things.' For himself he grabbed what looked like a beer.

'Does it contain alcohol?'

'A little. You can't taste it though.'

Apprehension gripped her as she hesitated with the drink. She'd never tried alcohol and after seeing what the stuff had done to her mum, she wasn't sure she wanted to.

'Relax, Neve. It's one drink.' Taking the bottle from her hands, he cracked the lid off using a metal gadget before offering it again. 'If you don't like it, I'll get you a cola.'

The smile returned to her face. 'Okay. Thanks.' She sipped the red drink and found Jasper was right: it tasted like raspberry soda, and it was delicious. 'Mm, yum.'

His eyes lit up. 'Told you. Come on, lets head outside where we can talk.' He took her out into the backyard.

On the patio a group of people stood around a table throwing balls into plastic cups. 'What are they doing?' Neve asked.

'Playing beer pong. It's a drinking game.' Jasper continued into the garden where he settled on a bench seat. 'How have you been?'

A bundle of twitchy nerves, Neve sat beside him. At least she could still see other people from where they sat. Instinctively she almost told him she was good. *Isn't it what people want to hear when they ask?* But when she paid attention to his expression, she could see genuine interest. 'Not great, to be honest.'

Jasper's eyes narrowed with concern. 'Why?'

She looked down at her hands. 'Things have been difficult at home again lately.'

'I'm sorry, Neve. Is it your mum or dad?'

'Both. Mum's been in a mood lately, and they were both fighting again today.'

'Ugh, parents suck.'

Neve gave a half-hearted laugh. 'Yeah. At least yours give you plenty of space and freedom.'

He sighed. 'It's not as good as you'd think. Sometimes I wish they would pay more attention. It seems like the only time they notice me is when I'm getting in trouble. But hey, the grass is always greener, right?'

'Totally,' she agreed. Neve found the raspberry fizzy easy to drink and as the volume lowered, her spirits rose. 'I'm looking forward to senior high school this year.'

He cringed with exaggeration. 'Really? I can't stand school.'

'Why? You're like the most popular guy there.'

Jasper gave her the greatest grin she'd ever seen. 'Is that so? I suppose there are some good aspects. But the schoolwork is a drag and some of the teachers are arseholes.'

'Are there any subjects you do like?'

'I suppose drama is okay. It is the one class where I can express myself.' He leaned closer to whisper, 'and it gives me a chance to practise channeling my attunement.'

Her interest piqued. 'Which is?'

'Emotions.'

She sucked in a breath. *Is he reading me now?* Thoughts of other ways he could use those powers occurred to her and she blushed.

Jasper brushed a finger across Neve's cheek. 'Right now, you have me wishing I could read minds.'

For a few precious seconds, she forgot to breathe. Then she let out an anxious laugh. 'I'm kinda glad you can't.' She skulled the rest of the drink to break their eye contact and regain some composure.

The moment she lowered her empty bottle, Jasper whisked it away. He dropped it along with his own empty one on the ground. Moving closer, he cupped her chin in his hand. 'You are the most beautiful girl I've ever seen, Neve.'

Wow. Just wow. He had rendered her speechless. As his lidded eyes zeroed in on her lips, she lost herself in their big, brown orbs, twinkling with specks of red and gold. *This is happening. I'm about to have my first kiss!* The world disappeared around her as Jasper became the extent of her awareness.

The sound of a throat clearing broke the spell. 'Well, well, well. This must be Jasper Rowan, self-proclaimed king of the school. Looks like we found him in his natural habitat: seducing a sweet, young virgin.' The insanely beautiful man's eyes locked with Neve's. At first glance, he appeared elvish thanks to his long, blond hair and pointed ears. But Neve noticed the golden radiance of his skin.

He must be an enlightened fae, and by the Gods he is stunning.

The enlightened guy's lips curled into a smirk.

'Who the hell are you?' Jasper demanded in a tone more venomous than Neve had thought possible for such a charming boy. 'And what gives you the right to barge into my house and interrupt me?'

Bells tinkled as a girl in an elegant gown sashayed forward. 'I am Elna, and this is my twin brother, Erik. We are the real royalty here. Our mother Estelar is an elvish princess. I'm sure you have heard of her.'

'Right,' Jasper scoffed, 'and what brought you out of the woods today?'

Erik shifted his gaze from Neve to Jasper. 'Do not mock us, *boy*. Do you not understand who or what we are?'

Released from his magnetic gaze, Neve took in the sight of the twins standing side-by-side. They looked almost identical. Aside from her feminine curves, only colouring distinguished Elna from Erik. Where Erik wore bright pink streaks through his blond locks, Elna had bright green. The neon wisps of hair were not the result of dye, but an extension of their main auras: outward displays of their personalities for all to see.

Jasper shrugged. 'You're fae, so what?'

'Are you unaware of the enlightened and our superiority? You should look us up, ignorant fool,' Elna chimed in. 'As for our right to be here. You did extend the invitation to *all* students of Gaeilge High. That now includes us. We thought tonight would be the perfect opportunity to meet our new subjects. Oh, and to knock you off your throne.'

Neve despised the tone they took with Jasper. *How dare they talk to him like this! In his own home, no less.*

Erik shot her a fierce look.

Shit! Did he read my mind?

'What is your name, sweetheart?' asked Erik.

'Neve. Neve Winters.'

A flash of recollection followed by respect showed in his eyes. 'Figures we'd find Jasper Rowan sucking up to the most powerful mage in the school. Would you like to join us for a drink, Neve?'

The extent of Erik's research impressed her, but not enough to shake her crush on Jasper. 'No thanks. I'd rather stay here and hang with my friend.'

Erik's expression transformed into pure, unadulterated shock. 'I doubt you would call him a friend if you knew what he had planned for you, sweetheart. You have offended me, Neve, and I don't take kindly to insults. I'm going to extend the olive branch this once because I understand you are young and naïve. Consider your options more carefully this time. Would. You. Like. To. Join. Us?'

With rage building to bursting point, Neve jumped from her seat and glared at Erik. 'I'm aware of Jasper's intentions, thank you very much. I am also okay with them. You, Erik, are a pompous buffoon. My answer is still no.'

'I see. If that's how you want it, consider the battlelines drawn. See you at school on Tuesday, Neve.' After scowling at her, Erik turned and strode away with Elna in tow.

Neve huffed. 'The nerve of those two.' She turned back to gaze upon an awestruck Jasper.

'Thank you for sticking by me, Neve. The way you stood up to them was incredible.' An impish gleam twinkled in his eyes. 'I'm curious, though: what did you think my intentions were?'

She felt her cheeks flush. 'I know what you're like with girls, Jasper, so it wasn't a stretch to assume you wanted in my pants.'

Jasper laughed. 'You, my dear, are a lot more fun and much wiser than I gave you credit for.' His eyes darkened with lust. 'So, about those pants of yours...'

Panic seized Neve's nerves. Jasper's proposition made his intentions clear. While she wanted him, Caitlin's voice whispered in her mind like the proverbial angel on her shoulder. *Damn it! I thought I was ready for this.* Instead of hinting at her cowardice, she flashed him a wicked grin. 'I do intend to give you what you want, but it's not gonna happen tonight. You, my dear, are going to have to wait.'

'Oh, so you want me to chase you more?'

'Don't guys like you enjoy the pursuit?'

He sucked in an audible breath. 'We do.'

'Then consider me your prey.' Leaving him slack jawed, Neve walked back inside to join her friends.

Chapter Three

'*Neve!*' Liam yelled, banging on her door. The little brat had locked her door again and he was five seconds away from kicking it down. 'Hurry up! We are going to be late.'

She pulled the door open and glared at him, dark circles around her eyes. 'Go on ahead. I can walk there myself.'

'How late did you go to bed last night?'

'Normal time. I had difficulty sleeping.' The defiant tone did little to mask her obvious lie.

But Liam did not have time to address the issue. People were expecting him, and he was not about to let his delinquent daughter spoil the day of fun he had planned. 'Fine. Whatever. I'll see you there.' *Well, I've dealt with one of the females in the house, now for the other.* He tapped on Alannah's door. Nothing. He knocked a little louder. Still nothing. Taking a chance, he opened the door. *Ah hell!* Alannah was sleeping, and he did not have the heart to wake her. After easing the door closed, he scribbled a quick note on the message pad, reminding her of their plans. *She probably won't want to come anyway.*

In truth, Liam was not ready to face Alannah yet. They had not spoken since her confession, which he still needed to process. So, he made his way to the beach party at the Sailing Club on his own.

Monique greeted him first: 'Hey Liam. On your own today?' Lounging on a folding chair, she watched Owen—her youngest—splashing in the shallows.

'Yeah, for now at least. The girls had a slow start today. I'm sure Neve will show up, since Caitlin and Fiona are here. I'm not so sure about Lana.'

'Understandable considering all the drama in Melbourne. I was so sorry to hear about her friends over there. Please send her my love when you see her tonight.'

'Will do. Where's Steve?'

'He headed out in the boats with a few of the other guys.'

Liam spotted the tell-tale specks of kayaks on the horizon. 'Thanks, Mon. I'll see if I can catch 'em.' After changing into his wetsuit, he readied his gear in the boatshed. From there, he set off to sea.

Floating free with the wind in his hair and the smell of ocean spray filling his senses, Liam felt at peace, at home. It was such a thrill to ride the waves. When the swell was too gentle, he would channel the elements and grow the curl to more exciting heights.

When he caught up to Steve, Lucas, Brock, and Jordan, he mucked about with them for a while. But as they headed back to shore, he told them he wanted more time.

'Don't forget to join us for lunch,' Steve shouted.

He laughed. *'Don't worry. There's no way I'm missing the barbeque.'* A few more waves later, Liam coasted for a while and let the serenity soothe his nerves.

'Are you okay, Sir?' The strange female voice close to his ear startled him.

Liam's kayak capsized in the panic. 'Christ!' It was nothing to worry about, though. He was a skilled kayaker and a strong swimmer. A moment later, he flipped the boat upright and climbed back in.

'Oh dear, I'm sorry. I did not mean to scare you. Did you sustain any injuries?' The woman who addressed him swam alongside his kayak. At a second glance, he realised she was a mermaid.

'I wasn't scared, just surprised. You came out of nowhere.'

'Technically I came from beneath the surface. I was keeping pace with you along the ocean floor for a while, but when you began to drift, I worried you were unwell. So, I came up here to make sure you weren't about to drown.'

Liam eyed her. 'You were following me? Why?'

The mermaid's cheeks turned pink, and for the first time, Liam noticed her beauty: a delicate oval face with high cheekbones and a heart-shaped mouth. Her brown, wavy hair fell around soft, bare shoulders. 'Your powerful aura attracted me. Then when I saw your face, I felt compelled to stay.'

It was usually a turn-off for Liam when women were so frank about their attraction to him. But the sincerity and innocence of the mermaid's admission appealed to his inner beast. His lips grew into a genuine smile. 'I'm Liam, by the way. What's your name?'

'Saoirse.'

'Mm. Such a perfect name.'

Another blush of colour. 'Why do you say that?'

'Because I always find the sea so liberating and it's your home.'

'Ironic then, how I often feel as though I live in a cage.'

He frowned at the thought. 'How so?'

'Family commitments keep me tied to this gulf. I would give anything to swim across the world, but my father is too ill.'

'I'm sorry, Saoirse.'

'Why do you apologise? It is not your fault.'

She is so sweet. 'It's my way of showing sympathy for you. It's hard to see the people we love suffering.'

'It sounds like you speak from experience.'

'Because I do. Do you have brothers and sisters to help? Or a husband?'

A small giggle slipped out. 'I have siblings, yes, but I don't have a mate. I am what you land mages would call a maiden.' She did appear young, around twenty-four.

Liam became curious about her body beneath the water. *By the Gods, dude, you have a wife! Get a grip. Then again, it's not like Lana has been faithful.* Liam glanced toward the beach. The people looked like ants from where he sat, so they would not be able to see him talking to Saoirse—not without binoculars, anyway. No one would worry enough to check on him at this stage. He often stayed out for hours at a time. 'Would it be too rude to ask your age, Saoirse?'

'Not at all. I'm twenty-eight. How old are you?'

'You look younger. I guess ocean living does wonders for you. I'm thirty-five.'

She laughed. 'I thought you were younger. I guess we are both bad at picking people's ages.'

'Quite. I wonder what else we have in common.' *Damn! Did I say that aloud?*

She gave him a coy smile. 'From what I've heard, your world is very different to mine. I can't imagine we share too many interests.'

'Oh, I don't know about that. The ocean is like my home away from home. And what about magic? What sort of mana are you attuned to?'

'Elemental and forces mana. I'm a warrior among my people.'

'There you go. I channel the elements too, along with energy. And I am a warlock, a warrior mage.'

Saoirse beamed. 'It would be fun to spar with you sometime.'

Liam laughed, feeling the last of his tension drain away. 'For sure. I'll bring my surfboard next time. That will make it easier.' His stomach rumbled. 'I need to get going, Saoirse.'

'Yes, of course. It was lovely meeting you, Liam.'

'Likewise. When can I see you again? I tend to surf out here around sunrise most mornings.'

'I know. I've watched you before.' Saoirse blushed. 'I'm sure we will meet again soon.' Shooting out of the water, she twirled and flipped like a dolphin doing tricks. She gave him a brief glimpse of beautiful curves, answering his perverse questions. Nothing covered the swell of her firm breasts. Instead of legs, she had a long, glistening tail of turquoise and teal scales leading to a fluke-like fin. Seconds later, she plunged into the depths and disappeared.

With a quickened pulse, Liam made his way back to shore.

After meeting at South Seas Café, Neve walked to school with Caitlin and Fiona. She sipped white chocolate mocha, while the girls reminisced over their weekend. Reaching the gate, they stopped to groom each other for their grand entrance. The girls had ruled supreme over the middle school, but this was the big leagues. There were bound to be new kids who didn't know who-was-who in these parts. First impressions were important.

But as soon as they stepped onto campus, something felt off. Hundreds of people populated the school grounds and none of them were paying the girls any heed.

When they reached the class lists, Fiona stood in shock. 'Why aren't they looking at us?'

'Let's find our homerooms and get our lockers,' insisted Neve. She wanted to find somewhere with more familiar faces.

'Oh rats!' complained Caitlin.

'What?' Neve asked as she leaned over Caitlin's shoulder.

'Fi and I aren't in your class, Neve.' Her finger was pointing to Neve's name under the heading "Room W02: Irene Dempsey."

Scanning the list, Neve found Naomi Rowan—Jasper's sister —was the only friend she would be with. 'Bummer. Where are your guys?'

'We are both in W05 with the new teacher, Mr. Rogers,' replied Fiona. She offered Neve a sympathetic smile. 'At least we are in the same corridor.'

'Yeah. Come on, let's go meet our classmates.' Neve flung her bag over one shoulder and led the way towards the Winters building.

'It's so cool going to a school with buildings named after my friends,' said Fiona as she looked up at the Colonial stone building with Neve's surname signed over the door.

'They named them after our ancestors, not us,' explained Neve. 'Your mum's family name features too, you know?'

'I know. But since I carry my dad's name, I don't have such a strong claim to fame here.'

'I wouldn't say that. The Ryan mages are a big deal in Sydney.' As they approached their lockers, people started to notice them, but not in the way Neve expected. They were gossiping among themselves and sniggering at the girls. *What the hell?*

'Uh, Neve, what's going on?' asked Caitlin.

'I don't know exactly, but it looks like the rumour mill is rife here.' Neve found her locker and dumped her bag in it. She pinned a poster of Dance Heart Cult—her favourite EDM group—inside the door. After retrieving a small pencil case, she slammed the door shut and shoved the lock through it. 'Ignore them, ladies.' As she offered the advice, a guy walked past her and coughed the word 'slut' into his hand. Spinning around to face the offender, she challenged him, 'Excuse me?'

The boy, a boggart named Todd, had attended their middle school for the last three years.

He grinned, revealing a mouth full of sharp teeth. 'No worries, love. You can make it up to me by sucking me off.' Several laughs from the assembled crowd rewarded his foul mouth.

'Ugh, gross! No girl in her right mind would go down there. Get out of my face, Todd.'

He waggled his brows. 'Seek me out when you lose your mind then, love.'

'Oh, thank the Gods, here come our guys!' As Todd walked off, Fiona pointed out the three boys approaching them.

Lorcán Ó Máille, Kane Sheridan, and Rónán Doyle were powerful bloodline mages. Not as formidable as Neve, but her mother was the only other mage she knew who outranked her own gifts with magic. However, these boys were the next generation of Council mages in the making and they knew it. They carried an air commanding admiration and respect. The same was true of Neve's beloved Jasper, but he was two year levels above her, so she'd have to wait until recess to see him. The boys passed Neve's group without a word, giving serious side-eye and chilling her to the bone.

Fiona gasped. 'What is it with the world today? Did we step into some parallel universe where people don't recognise our authority?'

Dread was burrowing its way into Neve's gut, finding its resting place as memories smacked her in the face. 'The enlightened twins.'

'What?' asked Fiona.

'Did you girls see those two enlightened at Jasper's party?' Neve inquired.

'You mean the hot blond guy and his twin sister?'

'Yeah them. Did they approach you at all?'

'No, why?'

'They may be the cause of our troubles.'

Naomi suddenly strode up to Neve. If she could channel the elements, hurricane winds would have whirled around her. 'Is it true? Did you sleep with my brother?'

'What? No! Where did you hear that?' *At least now I know what the gossip relates to.*

'Everyone is saying it. There are witnesses claiming they saw you hook up with him the other night.'

Neve sighed. 'All we did was talk, Naomi. We didn't even get to kiss before those damn enlightened twins interrupted us.'

Naomi's jaw dropped. 'So, you do have designs on my brother? Ick!' Turning on her heels, she stormed off with force to rival her entrance.

The bell rang as Caitlin placed a supportive hand on Neve's shoulder. 'Fill us in at recess, hun.'

Neve nodded and dragged her feet to class.

Alannah collapsed against the kitchen bench and exhaled a long, drawn-out sigh. *Breathe, woman. Neve is finally at school.* She could not remember the last time their morning routine had been such an ordeal. Then again, it was her first day in the senior school and Neve was dressing to impress. As a kid herself, Alannah had hated the idea of school uniforms, but as a parent, she could appreciate their merit. Not that Gaeilge High would ever implement anything so convenient.

Coffee. That's what I need. She switched on the machine and stared into nothingness as it brewed her espresso. *I do hope things start to get easier soon, so I can go back to ignoring mornings altogether.* Taking her drink to the lounge, she curled up on the sofa. She tuned into a news network for the latest on the Melbourne volcano.

The doorbell ringing startled Alannah awake. *Shit! When did I doze off?* It was already after 2PM. She wasted a full day when she should have been working. *Who am I kidding? There's no way I could have focused with everything going on.* The door chimed again. *I hope they aren't a new client.* She had not dressed for a business meeting, instead wearing her faded black short shorts and favourite old t-shirt with the whiskey logo. *Should I pretend I'm not home?* The visitor then resorted to knocking next, and Alannah sighed. Smoothing down her hair with her hands, she stepped up to answer.

Nothing could have prepared her for what, or rather who, waited beyond the threshold. 'Hello Lana.'

Snapping out of her daze, Alannah threw the door shut. But he caught it with his foot and barged into the house. *How did he unlock the security screen?* Someone squealed. For a moment she thought the sound came from Neve's room until she realised it was her own voice. Planting her feet in the middle of the corridor, she blocked Brendan's path. 'Get. Out.'

'It's so good to see you too, *sweetheart.*'

Alannah seethed inside. He knew how much she hated that so-called term of endearment. Of all people, he understood better than anyone the trauma she had overcome: the most horrid man alive had used the word as part of his torture. There was a time when it had even triggered panic attacks. 'What are you doing here, Brendan?'

'I had some business to attend to in town.'

'Good for you. Doesn't explain why you are in my house. I can't imagine it has anything to do with your life of crime and dark magic.'

'A bold assumption. There are plenty of ways I could use you in dark magic.' He leered at her.

Those words almost tripped her up. She hated the way her toes curled, and her core thrummed in response to his veiled threat. *Fuck! Traitorous hormones. I so need to get laid.* Crossing her arms over her chest, she worked hard to remain aloof. *I will not let him think he can get to me again.* 'What do you want?'

'Actually, you were right, this is not a business call. I have a family matter to discuss.'

'Sorry, Liam's not here. You can find him at the police station. Now if you don't mind, I have a life to get back to wasting.' She turned and strode down the hall.

Much to her annoyance, Brendan followed her. 'I wasn't talking about him. I meant *our* family, Lana.'

'You and I are no longer family, Brendan. I don't care what our birth certificates say.'

He scanned the living room with an inquisitive eye. 'I see you've been decorating.'

She shrugged. 'I've had plenty of time and more money than I can count; figured I'd blow it on something I like.'

'Hmph, so this is what two Mage Council salaries can get these days. I prefer to hoard my treasure, like a dragon, you know?'

Feeling her patience slipping, she tapped her feet. 'Are you going to get to a point this side of the Summer Solstice?'

Amusement flickered in his eyes as he glanced at her foot. 'You've got the grumpy-arse mother act down pat there Lana. Which brings me back to the reason for my visit.'

'Thank the Gods,' Alannah muttered.

'Guess what I discovered this weekend last?'

His games were pissing her off, big time. 'Please tell me you have a terminal illness, soon to bless the world with your death.'

'Wow, you have grown bitter over the years.'

'Oh, gee, I wonder why.'

Judging by his wide eyes, her response genuinely surprised him. Then his stone-cold veneer returned. 'Are you suggesting Liam, the shining golden boy, didn't live up to all your expectations? That he hasn't been the perfect husband? I'm shocked, Lana.'

'Fuck off, Brendan. You have no room to criticise Liam. And my relationship with my husband is none of your business.' Tired of standing, she slumped into an armchair. She chose an isolated seat to ensure distance from Brendan.

Rather than make himself at home, he paced the room. He only stopped when Luna walked up to him and started rubbing against his leg.

Turncoat!

Brendan smiled down at the cat, then looked back at Alannah with the same mask of indifference as before. 'You're right, Liam is of little consequence to me these days. *Our* daughter, however, does matter.'

He does know. Alannah had hoped Brendan had been ignorant of Neve's existence; that if he knew, he would have done the right thing. *Speaking of failing to live up to expectations, Brendan!* 'What about her?' she asked through gritted teeth.

'It took a slip of the tongue from Jacob for me to learn of her existence. My friends, my family, and even my current lovers all knew you had a blessed child. Yet none of them thought it worthwhile informing me. Jacob I can forgive; he didn't realise the kid was mine. But you knew, Lana. Why didn't you tell me?'

At first, the revelation of his ignorance floored her. But years of pent up anger began to press against the lid on her emotions like steam in a pressure cooker. 'I didn't see much point when you made it clear you did not want me to contact you.'

'This is different, though. Our child is more important than our… differences.'

Alannah scoffed at his diplomatic choice of words.

'Had I known then, I would have come back for her. Which is why I'm here now. I want to be a part of her life.' Alannah heard what he was not saying: *You weren't worth coming back for, but our baby was.*

Old wounds began to reopen and drain her lifeforce. 'Not going to happen.'

Brendan picked up a framed school photo of Neve. 'Is this her?'

'Yeah.'

'She looks like me.'

Alannah rolled her eyes. ''Cause she looks like me.'

He glared at her. 'Convenient way of hiding the truth. You can't stop me, Lana. Our daughter has a right to know her father.'

'Liam is Neve's legal father, and you can't do shit about it because we conceived her at Beltane.

Council law prohibits you from requesting a paternity test. It's your word against mine.'

'That may be so. But Uncle Brendan is back in town and this time, he is here to stay.'

'Argh, could this day get any worse?' Neve asked Caitlin as they left math together and headed for their lockers at lunch time.

'Tell me about it. I've heard people refer to me as the Ice Queen and Stone Wall, among other less pleasant terms.'

'Hey girls, I have an idea…' Fiona's voice trailed off when she reached Neve. She turned to look at the source of Neve's grief.

Someone had graffitied SLUT in bright red letters on Neve's locker. Her voice dropped to a low, deadly tone as she cast her eyes around, 'Don't these imbeciles know any other words?'

'What about whore?' asked a female voice from a nearby group of onlookers.

Neve stalked towards them.

'Or tramp?' asked one of the other girls before they all erupted in a fit of giggles.

'Do you have any idea who you're messing with?' Neve asked them.

An endarked girl in full goth attire stepped forward. 'Your threats are pathetic, Neve. You no longer scare us. We have friends in high places, and if you touch us, they will kick your arse. You are no longer the greatest power in this town.'

If the endarkened are siding with the enlightened, things just got real bad! Neve returned to her locker, ignoring the slander on its door. Putting her books away, she retrieved some food. While the bullying stung, Jasper's absence was getting to her the most. He had not shown at recess, and Neve began to wonder if she had offended him. Or worse: *did he start the rumours?*

There were no lunch tables free outside, so Caitlin suggested sitting on the lawn.

'Great idea. The weather is so nice today.' They could always rely on Fiona for optimism.

They made their way toward an isolated patch of grass on the oval. Movement in Neve's peripheral vision drew her attention. 'Go on ahead, ladies. I'll catch up.' Once the girls had moved on, she followed the figure skulking off behind the sheds. The flash of dirty blond hair had given Jasper away. Rounding the corner, she lost sight of him. But then she heard a rustling sound from above. Glancing up, she saw a pair of feet dangling over the edge of the sports equipment shed.

Good thing she wore her sunstone ring to school, anticipating a need for magic. The ring provided a source of primordial power, allowing her to levitate.

Jasper greeted her with wide eyes when his face came into view.

Planting her backside on the stable surface of the shed's roof, she gave him a coy smile. 'Hey.' But Neve frowned when she noticed Jasper's black eye, along with other bruises. 'Oh Gods, Jas! What happened?'

'I had a little scuffle at recess,' he explained in a nonchalant tone.

'Is that why you're hiding out up here?'

'I'm not hiding! I got sick of their bullshit.'

Compassion replaced Neve's less pleasant thoughts and feelings. Caught up in her own drama, she had not thought about Jasper's situation. The enlightened twins had taken over his turf and exiled him. 'I'm so sorry, Jas.'

'I don't need your pity, Neve.' His bitterness shocked her.

'Jas, please—'

'Christ, woman! Just leave me alone.'

A sinking feeling took hold of Neve's heart. 'Fine.' She rose and readied herself for the descent but paused. She needed to say her piece first.

'Listen, Jas. I may very well be your only friend through this, and if you keep pushing, you won't even have me.'

'Whatever,' he huffed. 'I don't need anyone.'

With a sigh, Neve returned to ground level and joined the others. Seeing Erik and Elna talking and laughing with Caitlin and Fiona made her hesitate at first.

But Erik's steely gaze searched her out and reeled her in like a defenceless fish on a hook.

What's with this guy?

'What's wrong, Neve? Lovers' spat?' Like his sister, Erik wore expensive, preppy clothes.

'Despite popular belief, Jasper is *not* my lover. What the hell are you doing here?'

'No, I suppose Jasper got what he wanted and discarded you like the rest of his conquests. I was inviting your friends to dine with us at court.' Erik's hand gestured toward a large group of students. They assembled around the central lunch table under the pergola. 'What do you say, girls?'

Fiona glanced at Neve with doe eyes. 'Well? Do you want to join them?'

Elna tittered. 'Sorry, did we forget to mention Neve's not welcome? Not after she declined our invitation on Saturday night.'

Caitlin stood and sidled up to Neve. 'If Neve's not welcome, I'm not going. She is my best friend.'

A warm glow filled Neve's heart at Caitlin's declaration.

'How sweet,' Elna mocked. 'Fiona?'

Fiona's eyes dashed between her friends and the twins. 'I'm sorry, Neve. It would be social suicide to turn down their invitation.' She moved closer to Elna, leaving Neve and Caitlin gobsmacked.

Erik, who had kept his eyes locked on Neve the whole time, smirked. 'Fiona is a smart girl. You'd do well to learn from her example.' He turned and sauntered away with an inhuman degree of grace.

When they were out of earshot, Caitlin huffed. 'Traitorous bitch! I can't believe Fiona!'

'It's okay, Cat. Fi is weak, like the rest of them. Thank you for sticking by me.'

'No worries, hun. I'd do anything for you—I hope you realise.'

Neve smiled at Caitlin. *That's the nicest thing anyone has said to me all day.*

Chapter Four

The front door slammed, and a girl's voice yelled down the hallway. 'Mum, school sucks balls!' The tell-tale clinking, shuffling, and thumping sounds of someone raiding a fridge followed. A teenage girl strode into the living room, guzzling orange juice from the carton. She reminded Brendan of an adolescent Alannah, only less goth and more Mean Girls. But the same 'don't mess with me' spark glimmered in her brilliant green eyes. 'I fucking hate them—' She froze the moment her eyes landed on him.

Alannah cleared her throat. 'Neve, sweetie, this is your uncle, Brendan.'

Neve's eyes flicked between them before settling on Alannah. 'You never told me you had a brother.'

Brendan chuckled. 'I'm actually Liam's brother.'

'Huh. You look more like Mum.' She closed the juice carton and dumped it on the coffee table.

He laughed again. 'Yup. We get that a lot. It's because Liam looks like our mother, while I look more like Dad, who is a Winters.'

Realisation dawned on Neve's face. 'Right. I often forget my parents are cousins. Liam mentioned having a brother living interstate, but never said much about you. How come I'm only meeting you now?'

Brendan looked at Alannah as he replied, 'Well, Neve, I've been asking your mother the same question. You see, I was in town on business and decided to catch up with an old mate. Imagine my surprise when he tells me Alannah has a daughter. Liam and I don't get along too well, hence not staying in touch. But I would have thought news of a baby in the family would warrant some form of correspondence.'

'Well, I think Liam's an arsehole.'

He snickered. 'Something we have in common.'

Neve moved in for a hug. 'It's good to meet you, Uncle Brendan.'

As he held his daughter in his arms, Brendan felt his hardened heart start to soften. 'It sure is, princess.' He glanced at Alannah and spoke in her mind. '*I love this kid.*'

A single tear escaped Alannah's left eye before the infuriating poker face returned.

When Neve drew back from their embrace, she gave him a questioning look. 'Princess?'

He nodded. 'Did you know Neve means snow? You put me in mind of the princess, Snow White.'

She grinned, grabbed his hand and dragged him over to the couch. 'So, Uncle Brendan, what are your attunements and specialisation?'

'Emotions and senses. I'm an enchanter.'

Her eyes widened with delight. 'Can you read minds?'

'Yup. And I can talk to people telepathically.'

'Way cool. Can you teach me how?'

'Depends, what are you attuned to?'

Neve beamed with pride. 'I'm a blessed child, so I'm attuned to the primordial. I can channel whatever mana source I want.'

Brendan looked over at Alannah, who wore the hint of a smile. 'Like your mum, huh?' He returned his focus to Neve. 'I'd love to teach you some enchanter's spells. What magic can you already cast?'

'Mostly conjuration stuff, but I also know how to lob fireballs like Liam. And Grandpa has shown me how to make a few healing potions.'

He laughed. 'Awesome. Make sure you get his hangover cure recipe.'

'Brendan! She's only fifteen,' Alannah rebuked.

Neve giggled and leaned in close to whisper. 'I already copied it when he wasn't looking; but shoosh, don't tell.'

He replied telepathically: *'Don't worry, your secret's safe with me.'* Then he winked.

She looked at him with an expression full of awe.

Alannah broke Neve's trance. 'Tell us about your first day of school for the year.'

The question changed Neve's demeanour. 'Ugh. It was horrid.'

'Why? You used to love school.'

'That was before I met the Alvarsson twins. They think they own the place because they're seelie royalty or some bullshit. I've never had problems with bullies before. Erik and Elna are totes vile.' She held up her fingers to pinch a small amount of air. 'I was this close to burning their perfect golden hair.'

Brendan arched his brow toward Alannah. 'Royalty?'

Alannah frowned. 'The Alvarsson family recently moved to Gaeilge Shores. Estelar is an elvish princess from the Adelaide Hills. She married Alvar Elofsson, a pure mage who migrated from Sweden.'

'That would make the twins enlightened,' Brendan mused to himself.

'And full of themselves,' Neve added.

He smiled at her. 'You know the best way to deal with people like them?'

Neve shook her head.

'You need to fight smarter, not stronger. Learn their secrets and weaknesses, then use the knowledge against them.'

Grinning, Neve nodded with understanding. 'I like it. Thank you.'

'No worries, princess.'

Alannah picked up something from the coffee table with a sigh, drawing Brendan's eye for a moment. He studied her as she started flicking through a magazine. Having kept her figure in perfect form, she did not look a day over twenty-one.

'Tell me, Neve, do you have any little brothers or sisters?'

That got Alannah's attention. She watched him with cold, passive eyes.

Neve snorted. 'No.'

'Curious. Why do you think that is?'

'I know why,' Neve replied. 'Mum and Liam have slept in separate rooms for as long as I can remember. I doubt they've had sex for like fifteen years.'

'*Neve!*' Alannah's pale cheeks turned bright pink.

Brendan chuckled. 'There's something else we have in common, princess. Did you know, when we were younger, I was the only person who could make your mother blush?'

Neve giggled. 'Really?'

He nodded as the front door slammed again and heavy footsteps approached. Stiffening, he braced himself for the reunion.

Liam entered the living room, seething as sparks formed on his fingertips. 'Get. The fuck. Away. From. My daughter.'

A snarl escaped Brendan's lips. 'So good to see you again, *Brother.*'

'Neve, please move away from him.'

With an air of defiance, Neve grabbed Brendan's arm and shook her head. 'Don't you dare hurt Uncle Brendan!'

'*I. Said. Move!*' Liam's tone bubbled over with pure malice.

'*Make me!*' Neve screamed.

Accepting her invitation, Liam rushed forward. He grabbed Brendan by the throat, slamming him up against the back door. The choke hold did not cut off Brendan's air, so he maintained a passive stance and returned his brother's glare.

'*Stop it, Liam!*' Neve continued to cry out.

'Neve, you need to understand Uncle Brendan is a bad man and it's Daddy's job to punish bad people.'

'You're full of shit, Liam.' The volume of her voice had returned to normal, but the tone oozed vitriol. 'Your job is to catch the criminals and let the Council punish them. You have some personal grudge against Uncle Brendan.'

Brendan smirked. 'She's a smart kid. That couldn't possibly come from you.'

Liam's hand applied more pressure. 'Shut the fuck up. Neve, please go to your room. I need to have a private chat with your uncle.'

'Then why does Mum get to stay?'

Brendan glanced at Alannah from the corner of his eye. She still sat in the armchair watching the whole fiasco with an expressionless mask. She locked herself up so tight, he could not even get the slightest read on her.

'Because this involves her too,' Liam replied.

'I call bullshit. You just don't want me to see what you do to him.' She rose from the couch. 'I swear to the Gods, Liam, if you harm Uncle Brendan, I will never talk to you again.' She stormed off, pounding her feet into the stairs and slamming her bedroom door.

'You didn't heed my warning, *Brother*,' Liam spat as his fist collided with Brendan's face.

Alannah sat and watched with detached interest. Brendan pushed Liam back with enough force to bruise, if not crack a rib. The scuffle escalated as the men threw more punches and even kicks. There used to be a time when the sight of them fighting got her all hot under the collar; before Brendan ripped out her heart and tore strips from her soul. He deserved all the pain Liam was inflicting.

It was strange how Brendan remained on the defensive when she knew he could do more damage if he tried. As Liam charged, Brendan flung him back into the bookshelf, sending a bunch of novels flying. When Liam tackled him to the floor, Brendan's knees struck him in the balls. Liam winced, but he did not pull back. He used his position to smack Brendan's head against the hardwood floor.

As soon as Liam pulled a knife on Brendan, Alannah intervened. *'Enough!'*

Liam dropped the knife, but he kept Brendan pinned beneath him.

'Naw, Lana does still care about me,' Brendan jeered in a vicious tone.

'Don't flatter yourself. I don't want your blood on my hands, or my floor. Liam doesn't need a murder charge either.'

'Wow, Lana, you could be an inquisitor with such a lack of empathy.'

Liam grabbed Brendan's chin and slammed his head against the floor again. 'You don't get to talk to her like that.'

She sighed. 'Liam, please.'

'Fine.' He stumbled as he rose.

Alannah flew to help him regain his balance and guided him into the kitchen. After easing him into a chair, she grabbed one of Neve's healing potions from the fridge. 'Here.' She opened the vial and brought it to his mouth.

Brendan stumbled in a moment later. 'Can you spare a drop for an old flame?'

She glared at him. 'Get your own.'

'Don't mind if I do.' Brendan helped himself to one of the tinctures in the fridge. After throwing it back, he relaxed against the breakfast bar. 'Is this Neve's work?'

'Yes,' Alannah replied.

'The kid has a lot of talent.'

Liam groaned. 'Why are you still here? In fact, why are you here at all?'

'I came to meet Neve.'

After attempting to stand and failing, Liam slumped back into his chair. 'Why the sudden interest after sixteen years?'

'Stay there. I'll get you another.' Alannah returned to the fridge.

'Gosh, has it been so long? Doesn't time fly when you're having fun?' Brendan's voice sent a chill through her body colder than the air seeping out of the fridge. 'Tell me, Liam, have you had *fun* playing house with my girls?'

Alannah froze mid stride.

'You lost your claim on Lana when you walked out of her life and shacked up with an endarkened whore,' Liam snapped. 'And Neve's not yours either.'

'See, that's where you're wrong. Tell him, Lana.'

Liam shot her a worried glance.

She bit her lip.

His brow furrowed. 'You conceived her at Beltane. She even has the blessing.'

Brendan gave Liam a smug grin. 'Who do you think spent *all night* with Lana that Beltane?'

Liam challenged her with his eyes. 'Is he telling the truth?'

All she could was nod.

'Fuck!' He attempted to leave in a huff but stumbled and fell back into his chair.

Alannah grabbed the second potion she promised and gave it to him in silence, refusing to meet his gaze. Guilt over all the things she had done and hidden from Liam gnawed at her insides like an ulcer.

As soon as he had recovered enough, Liam left the room without another word.

'Well,' Brendan said, drawing close behind her, 'as far as family reunions go, I'm sure there have been worse, like among the mafia.' Resting his hands on Alannah's shoulders, he pressed into her back.

She stiffened, her upper body turning rigid at his touch. *At least he can't feel the reaction he is getting from my lower half.*

'Christ, Lana! There are suspension bridge cables under less tension than your shoulders. You should think about getting a massage.' His lips pressed against her ear and his voice turned dark and seductive, 'Or you could try getting laid. Sounds like it's been a while.'

Her elbow collided with his gut. She might have done more damage if his abs were not rock hard. At least he winced enough to lose his grip on her, letting her escape his clutches. Swinging to face him, her expression adopted a menacing glare. 'Not as long as you might think.'

Brendan studied her for a moment. 'Hm, if it's true what Neve says about Liam, I'm gonna go out on a limb here and guess you're still fucking my doppelganger. How is Tyler, by the way? I haven't seen the scamp for months now.'

Her mask slipped and her eyes grew wide at Brendan's revelation. *Why would Tyler betray my trust? And why is he still interacting with Brendan, a known criminal and dark mage?* 'Tyler is well. He has been touring the world with Samantha.'

'How lovely for them. Your choice of sexual partner is very informative, Lana. Do you know what it tells me?'

'My sex life is no longer any of your business.'

'It tells me you still want *me*,' he concluded, ignoring her previous retort.

'Get over yourself, Brendan. I don't want you anywhere near me. The sight of you disgusts me.'

'Hmm. I doubt you think so when you feast your eyes upon my magic twin and let him ravish you.' Brendan invaded her personal space again, breathing into her ear. 'What goes through your mind when he ties you to the bed and makes you scream *my* name?'

Alannah felt her cheeks flush. *There is no way Tyler would have told anyone about that, is there?*

Brendan pulled back and laughed. 'Damn I'm good. It was a wild guess—*wild* being the operative word. Good to know I can still make you blush too. I'll be seeing you, Lana.' Turning on his heels, he saw himself out.

Is there no end to Lana's deceit? First her affair, now the truth about Neve being Brendan's. The rage flowing through Liam's body found an outlet when his fist punched a hole in the wall of his bedroom. He collapsed on the floor beneath the site of his destruction. The frail pieces of his marriage crumbled around him along with the plaster. Alannah constantly shutting him out stung far more than his grazed knuckles.

Liam knew deep down in her fortified soul Alannah still loved him, but she was too broken to let people in anymore. It killed him to think he had played some part in it. Abandoning her in gaol and letting Brendan bail her out had opened a rift between them. But he could not shoulder all the blame. Other people had hurt her too. And the biggest offender of all was back in town. *Gods damn you, Brendan!*

His thoughts drifted to Saoirse, wishing he could have seen her that morning. Work had called him in early, forcing him to forgo his morning surf. Her warm smile would have been a welcome relief from his pain. Her soothing voice a tonic for the turmoil twisting him apart. There was no denying the connection he felt with the mermaid. *Entertaining ideas of romance with any woman other than Lana is dangerous.*

It would have been easy to give up on his wife, given how distant she had grown from Liam. But she needed him with everything else going on, even if she would not admit it. He could not bring himself to leave her at Brendan's mercy. Not again. With that in mind, he returned to the living room. The sight and sound of Alannah crying on the couch gutted him and he forgot his anger as he rushed over to her.

As soon as he sat beside her, she climbed into his lap and pressed her head against his chest. 'I'm sorry, Liam,' she mumbled between sobs. Her concern for him, despite her own grief, stupefied him. The emotions and remorse she expressed seemed so alien from who she had become.

There is still hope for us after all. Liam held her in a firm embrace. 'Let it all out for now. We'll talk when you calm down.' Holding Alannah as she wept filled him with fresh wrath toward Brendan. *Death would be too merciful for the bastard, though. He needs to suffer for all he put Lana through. Can I find cause to lock him away? He is a dark mage, so there must be something I can pin on him.* It would not be easy though. Warlock Jaxon Hayes from Sydney did not have a shred of evidence linking Brendan to anything.

When Alannah's sniffles eased and her breathing settled, she looked into Liam's eyes. 'Thank you. I needed that.'

'It's okay, gorgeous.' He tucked strands of hair behind both of her ears. 'I love you, Lana, and I'm not going anywhere. Do you understand?'

A few tears slid down her cheeks and she bit her lip, but she also nodded.

'Good. I'm willing to try anything to fix our marriage, but it's only going to be possible if you want to give it a go too. Do you want to make things work in our relationship?'

She nodded.

'Will you give marriage counselling a try?'

'Yes.' The pitch of her voice rose, and she squeaked a bit when she replied, but the positive intent was clear.

It was music to Liam's ears. He pressed a gentle kiss to her forehead and pulled her back in for a hug. 'I love you with all my heart, Lana.'

Inspired, Neve sat down at her laptop with renewed determination. She refused to let Erik and Elna walk all over her and destroy everything she stood for. The first step, as Uncle Brendan had suggested, was to learn everything there was to know about them. So, she started with social media. There would, of course, be limits to what she could uncover on these platforms. The Council did not allow magic folk to be overt about their powers on public forums. But Neve knew how to read between the lines. Mum had taught her about subtext and double meanings in relation to the magic world.

Most of what she found was useless. There were lots of photos from recent parties. *The enlightened twins are social butterflies — no surprises there.* On the brink of giving up, something caught her attention. Six months ago, Erik and Elna were both all over the same girl. Neve continued her search, and a pattern began to unfold. Whenever the twins cosied up to someone, male and female alike, they were always together. *Curious. Do they share their lovers?*

Then a more insidious thought struck: *Do they touch each other?* Neve scrutinised all the photos of them together but came up blank. *If they do commit incest, they are smart enough to hide it from the cameras.* Still, it was something worth investigating. Such a scandal could ruin their precious reputations. *But how do I find out?* Two options occurred to her and neither of them would be easy. The first involved learning how to read minds. The second required getting intimate with the twins. She shuddered at the thought. *Right, mind reading it is. At least I have someone willing to train me now.*

Neve knew the drill. Whenever a mage wanted to learn a new magic technique, the theory always came first. So, she needed all the books on enchanting from the cellar. Sneaking past the living room proved easier than expected. But upon leaving the doorway, she noticed her mum crying in Liam's arms. The touching sight filled her with hope for their future happiness. She could not remember the last time she'd seen them embracing each other like a real couple. With a smile, she continued on to the cellar.

Neve's phone was ringing when she returned to her room. Dropping the books on her desk, she rushed to grab it. Caller ID showed Caitlin, so Neve answered. 'Hi, hun. What's up?'

'I've been pondering the predicament at school. It's so unfair! Why are they picking on you?'

'Because I didn't bow down to them. Simple.'

'They must feel threatened by you. They are powerful, more so than most bloodline mages, but not as strong as you.'

Neve thought about her first encounter with the Alvarsson twins. Erik had spoken to her with a degree of respect. Her refusal to join them threw a spanner in the works. *I rejected them and they took serious offence.* 'You know, I think you're right. And I intend to show them what happens when they mess with a Winters woman.'

Caitlin laughed. 'I love hearing you talk like that. What's the plan?'

'To start with, we dig up as much dirt on them as possible.'

'Ooh, nice. I was thinking I could peek at Mum's Book of Shadows and learn her spell for computer hacking. Could prove useful in our search.'

'For sure. Accessing your grandfather's files on registered magic people will also help.'

'Indeed,' Caitlin giggled. 'This is a delightfully naughty plan. It makes me feel all hot under the collar.'

'Damn girl! You need to get laid.'

'Well it's not gonna happen anytime soon,' Caitlin replied with a lamenting tone.

'Listen, Cat, Lorcán Ó Máille is not worth crying over. He is pathetic, like the rest of those grovelling bootlickers.'

Caitlin sighed. 'I'm not actually bothered by Lorcán to be honest. We didn't have any chemistry.'

'Really?'

'Where do you think those nicknames for me came from?'

'I figured it was dumb gossip.'

'Nope. Lorcán put the moves on me at the beach party and I refused to put out. He got angry and stormed off in a huff.'

'Oh, shit, Cat! I'm sorry.' Neve felt bad for getting too caught up in her own dramas to notice the pain her best friend was feeling. 'Do you want to come over after dinner to eat ice cream and watch stupid movies?'

'Sounds amazing. See, Neve, you know exactly what a girl needs.'

Chapter Five

Taking her seat at the boardroom table, Alannah glanced at her jittery hand. She wondered if it was her anxiety, *or perhaps the tenth cup of coffee has something to do with it.* Between marital problems, Cole still missing, and Brendan's return, there was no shortage of stress in her own life. Two more volcanoes erupting in Victoria had almost pushed her over the edge of sanity.

At least Brendan hasn't shown his face again since Monday. It was a small comfort considering she knew he was around, and it was only a matter of time before he made his next move. *I bet he's waiting for opportunities to strike when Liam is not home.*

Monique called everyone to attention as High Magus Kieran entered. When everyone settled, she announced the first order of business, 'We have a hearing request from the new mage in town, Sir Alvar Elofsson.'

Kieran sighed. 'Very well, let him in.'

The tall man who entered was the epitome of the Aryan race right down to the blond hair and blue eyes. 'Greetings, Your Honour. I am Magus Alvar Elofsson of the Dalsland province of Sweden and Duke of the Mt. Lofty elves. I come with information pertinent to your cause.'

'Out with it then.' Kieran appeared especially low on patience.

Alannah was glad she did not have any pressing matters to raise.

'First, on behalf of the Seelie Court, I require a seat on the Council.'

A short laugh burst forth from Kieran. 'You have got to be kidding me. One does not simply walk in requesting a seat. I don't know how you did things in Sweden, but there is a full application process here. Besides which, we have no current vacancies to apply for. Now share this *pertinent information* and be on your way.'

Alvar furrowed his brows. 'No seat, no intel.'

'I'm sorry, Mr. Elofsson, but I cannot grant your request.'

'I am Sir Elofsson to you. You are making a big mistake in refusing me. You shall see.'

Kieran rose in a furious cloud of rage and advanced on Alvar. 'I do not take kindly to threats. Get out of my sight before I have my warlocks arrest you.' Once Alvar had left, Kieran slumped into his chair. 'The nerve of that man.'

'From what I've heard, the girls have had issues with Alvar's kids at school,' Alannah explained.

Kieran huffed. 'The man is a pompous fool, so I'm not surprised he fathered spoilt brats. I'm sure the lot of them are harmless enough though. The seelie folk don't usually break the law. Right then, let's get on with the activity reports. Councillor Alannah Winters, please start us off.'

At least Alannah had attained her due position at the table since re-joining the Council. 'There has not been any inappropriate use of Aether, your Honour.'

'Good, next…' The meeting progressed smoothly from then on and wrapped up in record time.

As they were leaving the room, Alannah leaned into Liam's shoulder to whisper, 'I'm guessing you didn't tell Kieran about you-know-who being in town. Did you tell your parents?'

The hint of a growl stirred from his throat. 'No. I'm not telling anyone about any of it.'

Alannah nodded. 'Thanks.'

'For what?'

'Not making things awkward for me.' Once outside, Alannah hugged her in-laws.

'Is everything okay with Neve at school?' Nora asked.

'A few issues with bullies, but she is a tough kid, so I'm sure everything will work out okay,' Alannah assured them.

'Okay. Be sure to let me know if you need my help with anything.'

'Will do. Thanks, Nora.'

They reached the car when Monique ran up to them. 'Excuse me, Liam, but would you mind if I have a private word with Alannah?'

He looked at Alannah with unblinking eyes and arched brows.

'It's okay, babe. Go on ahead. I'll catch a ride with Monique and chat in her car.'

'Okay.' He smiled and kissed the crown of her head before taking off.

'So, I did the investigating you asked me to do,' Monique explained after starting the ignition. 'Most Council mages in Melbourne survived the volcano, but none of them can link it to any illicit magic.'

'Damn. There goes that theory.'

Monique pulled out of the carpark and drove a little way down the street before pulling over.

'Just because the Council have not detected anything doesn't mean dark magic isn't involved. Three volcanoes in five days, all in the one state, is more than coincidence. I'm convinced magic is at work, even if my dad isn't.'

Alannah sighed. 'But without evidence Kieran won't do anything. I need a contact in Victoria who knows what is going on.'

'I may have an answer for you, but you won't like it.'

'What?'

Monique bit her lip and her aura flashed with inner conflict. 'I can't believe I'm suggesting this. There is a dark mage over there who by all reports is more in the loop than most Council mages. A woman known as Lady Jade.'

'Christ! With a name like that, I'm assuming she's Dark Syndicate.'

'An accurate guess. She's not the head honcho there, but she is what they call a spymaster, and she reports to... *him*. Problem is, she won't talk to you without an introduction from another Syndicate member.'

'Thanks for the intel. Jade is a last resort option. I'll start by paying Alvar a visit to see if his request had anything to do with these volcanoes.'

A short time after Mum left for the Council meeting, the doorbell rang. Neve ignored it at first. Years of learning not to answer the door when home alone had instilled her with good habits. Yet when the ringing persisted, she decided to at least see if it was Caitlin or Jasper. Her heart began to race at the thought of the latter.

But Uncle Brendan stood beyond the security screen. 'Evening, princess. Thought you might want to start your enchanter training.'

Neve beamed. 'That would be awesome. My parents aren't here though. They're at a Council meeting.'

'I know. Figured it'd be safer to drop by when Liam isn't here. You may have noticed, he and I don't exactly see eye-to-eye.'

'Oh, right. It's just… I'm not supposed to train without one of them present.'

'It is wise to train with supervision at your age. But you know I'm an experienced mage too, so you'll be safe with me.'

She had a sneaking suspicion letting a rogue mage teach her magic would anger Liam. But Uncle Brendan could not be all bad if Mum had let him into the house and introduced him. 'Yeah, okay.

Come on in.' After opening the door, she led him down the hall. 'I actually started reading some theory books on enchanting.'

'That's good Neve. Shows initiative and a willingness to learn. Your mother should be proud of you. I know I am.'

'Thanks.' She unlocked the ritual cellar with her keys.

Once inside, they got straight down to business. 'Can you cast the circle yourself?' Brendan asked.

'Of course. It was the first thing I learnt following my initiation.'

'Okay then, princess, show me what you got.'

Neve commenced the ritual, calling upon the elements and inviting Brendan into the circle.

'The first thing I want to show you is defensive,' Brendan explained. 'It is a technique I have developed to help mask my aura from the more perceptive eye. I can see you are already skilled with basic aura blocking. Like simple glamour, a skilled magic user can bypass it.'

'Okay. I can see how it would be helpful.' *Especially when it comes to lying to Mum.*

Brendan frowned at her. 'You shouldn't lie to your mother. Save that shit for Liam.'

She laughed despite Brendan reading her mind. 'Okay.'

'Promise me? Because I don't want your Mum kicking my arse for turning you into a deceitful delinquent.'

'I promise.'

'Good. Using this approach bends the forces of light to create an illusion. The problem is anyone well-attuned to senses mana can see past illusions. If you can manipulate the onlooker's sense of sight directly, it becomes much harder to work around. Do you follow?'

'Yes. Makes perfect sense.'

'Good. So, I want you to try manipulating my vision, tricking my eyes into seeing nothing but a white aura.'

Neve began her breathing exercises, using mindfulness to tune into the primordial. Once connected, she needed a visualisation she could link to the five senses. Jasper came to mind. The sight of his toned body wearing a tight shirt and low hanging jeans; the sound of his deep voice; the smell of his spicy cologne; the taste of raspberry soda on her lips as she anticipated their kiss; and the feel of his strong hand cupping her chin. Magical energy surged through her and she channelled it into the task at hand.

When she felt as though she had achieved her goal, she looked at Brendan.

He grinned. 'Perfect. You are very skilled for someone so young. Give me a heads-up next time you intend to fantasise about boys though, so I know to stay out of your mind. I don't need the full cinematic experience of you reliving your hook-ups.'

Neve felt her face turn bright red. She broke the circle and sprang to her feet to hide her embarrassment. 'Sorry, Uncle Brendan. I didn't realise you would see. For the record, there was no kiss. Those damn enlightened twins interrupted us.'

'Just as well. I don't think I could have handled anymore details. There are some things I don't need to know about my d-niece.'

Did he call me Denise or was it a slip of the tongue? She eyed him for a moment.

'How have things been with those bullies at school these last two days?'

Letting her uncle's odd behaviour slide, she focused on the more pressing issue. 'Much the same, although nothing especially bad yet. Mostly name-calling and shunning. It sucks though. I used to be the queen of the school but now I'm like the scum of the Earth, all because I chose to side with Jasper Rowan.'

Brendan stiffened and his calm expression hardened. 'Was he the boy in your visual?'

'Yeah, why?'

'Be careful of him. If he's anything like the Rowan boys of my generation, he is probably trouble.'

Weird. Liam had said something similar, but Neve figured he was being an overprotective git. 'How so?'

'Didn't your mum ever tell you about Clayton Rowan?'

She shook her head. Neve remembered Jasper making mention of the man. 'Jasper mentioned having an Uncle Clayton who was in gaol.'

His visage turned grim. 'Your mum is the reason they locked him away for life.'

'Oh Gods! What did he do to her?'

'In short, to spare you the gory details, he didn't take "No" for an answer.'

Neve felt the blood drain from her face. *First Austin, then Clayton? Sounds like Mum didn't have much luck with guys.* 'Is that why Mum is such an emotional mess and has issues with intimacy?'

Brendan became lost in speculation for a moment. 'You're quite insightful for a fifteen-year-old, Neve. I'm sure the trauma that arsehole put

Lana through hasn't helped her mental health. She didn't strike me as being emotional, though.'

'It's the façade she creates for the rest of the world. But I've seen her get into her moods when she thinks no one is looking. She used to try and deal with it by drinking, but booze made her angry and violent when she wasn't passed out.'

He gaped at Neve, then pulled her into his arms. 'I'm so sorry, princess. I should have been here for you.'

Surprised at first, Neve's body went taut. Then she brought her arms up to circle around her uncle's solid torso and let his warmth seep into her. It was nice to feel loved and protected, something lacking in her life of late.

Brendan eased back out of the embrace. 'I should probably go before Liam gets home. Next time we'll work towards the extension of the aura shielding spell. It's a bit more complicated, so you should start reading up on mental manipulation in the meantime.'

Neve's jaw hit the floor. 'Mind control? That's like hardcore enchanting. I'm not sure I'm ready for something so… intense.'

Brendan grinned. 'Maybe not, but it won't hurt to start training towards it. Mind reading is part of the training path.' He winked, then turned and left the cellar.

Brendan screwed his nose up at the familiar stench greeting him as he returned to his motel room. Years of filth and grime had embedded themselves into the wood panels and upholstery. He could only begin to imagine the debauchery the walls had witnessed. Not that he lacked the imagination to think of everything. The mere thought of doing so turned his stomach. Even as a sadist, he had his limits.

A quick spell dulled his sense of smell. He collapsed on the bed and loaded up the local real estate listings on his laptop. *Nothing in the rentals.* Brendan sighed, then clicked over to the houses for sale. Training Neve had confirmed his need to re-establish a home in Gaeilge Shores. *So, why not look at buying? It's not like I lack the funds.*

Finances are the least of your problems, Brendan, a niggling voice in the back of his mind reminded him. Pausing his search, he glanced at his phone and considered making the call. His heart still ached from their betrayal, but he needed Caleb and Bridey more than ever. Spending more time with Neve would mean more time around Alannah. There was no avoiding her bitter hatred and the constant reminder of everything he had lost.

Can I convince Caleb and Bridey to move here? Is it even a good idea? Too many conflicting thoughts and feelings swirled around in Brendan's head. He took a few deep breaths. There was one variable he could control: his living arrangements. *Anything has got to be better than this dive.* The first result looked exactly like his dream home: 'This picturesque country home offers serenity and seclusion with the benefits of modern living.' *Thank the Gods.*

Flicking a message to the property agent, he arranged an inspection. He set the computer aside and let his thoughts wonder. Neve had shed some interesting light on Alannah's state of mind. *Is it possible my Lana is still in there somewhere?* He became consumed with ideas for breaking down her barriers until she begged him to take her back. It was enough to make his dick hard. The plan was dangerous. Getting close would endanger their lives, especially if he proved his doppelganger theory; not to mention incurring the wrath of a jealous lover. Bridey could do a lot of damage to his citadel of crime, an organisation he needed to gather intel. Those resources were bringing him closer to the truth Tara had spoken of.

His thoughts slipped into a loop of inner turmoil, typical when given leeway. But leashing his thoughts had become more difficult thanks to Alannah's proximity. He needed to adopt a cautious approach when speaking to Alannah. It would not surprise him if the Council kept close tabs on her and he did not need those jerks breathing down his neck.

Grr… Argh! He lay back on the bed and tried some more mindfulness. He drifted into sleep, but his subconscious did not let Alannah go…

He had her completely at his mercy. The warm glow of five candles surrounded the ritual circle. Light decorated the floor, illuminating her bold curves and pale skin. Skin that is mine to mark. *Sucking in a sharp breath, Brendan took a moment to admire the sight of her. He had bound her wrists and ankles to the polished ebony cross, displaying her back. Alannah's body was bare except for the black leather collar around her neck. He stepped up to her and ran a gentle hand along the exposed side of her face. 'What's the safe word, gorgeous?'*

'Richard, Sir.'

'Good girl.' Inhaling her musky aroma stirred his desires. He placed his hands on her shoulder blades. Caressing her back formed pretty, little pebbles on her soft skin. When he increased the pressure of his massage,

she began to moan. Such a delightful noise. *But it was not the sound he most wanted to draw from her throat. With her skin warmed up, he picked up the cat-o'-nine-tails and struck her back, releasing the most sensual of screams. Four more lashes brought her close to the edge. Brendan's dick turned hard as a rock. But it was not time to take her. Not yet. With the other four senses evoked, he needed to taste her first.*

Dipping to one knee, Brendan brought his lips to her core. He groaned as the flavour of strawberries mingled with sweet musk on his tongue. When he brought her crashing over the edge, he could no longer contain himself. Dropping his black leather pants to the floor, he unleashed the demon of lust possessing him.

Brendan awoke to the rush of power surging through him. He had soaked the bedsheets with sweat and the release of his arousal. Not surprising, considering the subject of his dreams. But spotting the mana rings on his fingers did startle him. He never wore those to bed. *Shit! Not good. Mistakes like this could be deadly. I need to get my head back in the game.*

For the second time that week, Liam headed out for a morning surf. He would have gone on Tuesday, but he wanted to be there to help Alannah with the morning routine. After the tender moment they had shared on Monday night, he thought family life would improve. Unfortunately, things had gone back to normal. When she was not snapping at him, Alannah was frostier than a midwinter morning in the valley. So, he chose to avoid her morning grumps for the rest of the week.

The swell was excellent on Friday morning. He did not need to improve conditions with magic. This surprised him, considering the onshore winds. Loving the glassy conditions, he rode the waves between first light and the end of sunrise. Once he had caught enough, he took a moment to drift on his board.

A feminine giggle broke his reverie. 'Did you enjoy my waves?'

When he opened his eyes, Liam looked straight into Saoirse's smiling face and felt joy touch his heart. 'That was your magic?'

'Yes.'

'They were incredible. Better than anything I've ever managed,' he admitted.

Her eyes widened with pride. 'Really?'

'Absolutely. I missed you yesterday.'

Her brow furrowed as sorrow replaced happiness. 'I'm sorry. I needed to tend to my father. He took a turn for the worse.'

'Hey, there is no need to apologise. Your family should come first. I'm sorry to hear he is not doing well.'

'Thanks. So, um…' Her eyes lowered as her cheeks turned pink.

Liam's body charged with electricity at the sight. 'Yes?'

'Did you want to, um… spar?'

A small laugh slipped out when she voiced such an innocent request. 'I would love to.' Then it occurred to him her culture was different to his. *Did mermen and mermaids usually spar together? If so, were there sexual connotations when they did?* Liam decided to ignore those possibilities and stick to what he knew. They were having some harmless fun.

'Prepare yourself then.'

Liam adjusted his weight on the surfboard and put up some basic shields. 'Okay, I'm ready.'

She drew a large wave out of the sea and hurled it at him. There was considerable force behind it, but he was able to keep his balance.

He grinned. 'I hope you're not going easy on me, Saoirse.' He blasted her with a kinetic shockwave.

But Saoirse was quick. Leaping into the air, she let the blast make a large splash spraying foam all over Liam. She squealed with delight as she dove back into the water. Manipulating the air currents, she sent a small, powerful whirlwind in his direction.

In the time it took to ready her spell, Liam prepared to send it straight back at her. This time, she ducked beneath the surface to avoid the small storm. 'You are a skilled mage, Liam.'

He chuckled. 'High praise, I'm sure.'

An impish gleam shone in her aquamarine eyes. 'But you are too cocky.' Crooking her finger, she ripped Liam's surfboard from beneath him, plunging him into the depths.

He avoided swallowing a lungful of water, and it did not take him long to push back up to the surface. Laughing, he shook his head as he swam towards her to retrieve his board.

Her own sounds of mirth warmed him to his very soul. 'I call that a victory,' she declared.

Grabbing his surfboard, he leaned into it, remaining at eye level with Saoirse. 'Indeed. I concede defeat this time, but I am wise to your tricks, so I'll do better in future. I had fun, thank you.'

She moved close enough to touch the opposite side of the board. 'You are welcome, but I should be thanking you. I do not get many opportunities to play like this.'

He frowned at the thought. 'It saddens me to hear that, Saoirse. A young, beautiful woman such as you should be enjoying the prime of her life.'

Saoirse gasped, colour filling her cheeks. 'You think I'm beautiful?'

'Of course. I doubt there is a man alive who would disagree with me.'

The air between them supercharged with tension as their eyes searched each other. But Liam's thoughts turned to Alannah and the promise they had made each other. Clearing his throat, he looked away a moment. When he glanced back, Saoirse had backed off, allowing him to breathe with more ease. 'I should get to work. Same time tomorrow?'

She forced a smile, and it killed Liam to think he had offended her. 'I will come unless circumstances prevent me.'

'No worries. Thanks again.'

She nodded, then dived into the depths without another word.

Damnit! I've upset her. Does she want more than my friendship? The possibility excited him. There was no denying the attraction he felt to Saoirse, but exploring their attraction posed a risk to his marriage. His relationship with Alannah did not need any more complications. Torn between desire and duty, Liam paddled back to shore.

Chapter Six

Neve felt like she existed in an alternate reality: one where the weekend excited her because it meant seeing fewer people, not more. Unfortunately, this *was* her reality. *TGIF!*

'What do you want to do this weekend?' Caitlin asked as they walked to school together.

Taking a sip of her white chocolate mocha, Neve decided it was much too sweet for the bitter edge on her thoughts. *I should switch to coffee.* 'Homework, and maybe some gymnastics practice.'

'Do you want to come over to my house? We could study and practise together.'

'Yeah, I guess.'

'Neve?' A deep, masculine voice asked from behind.

Both girls turned to glare at Jasper, but it was Caitlin who challenged him, 'What the hell do you want?'

'A word with Neve.' Jasper's gaze lowered in sheepish submission. He squirmed with hands in his pockets as he scuffed his foot against the pavement. His whole demeanour was foreign compared with the confident flirt she knew.

When she nodded, Caitlin huffed. 'Fine. I'll see you in first period.' She picked up her walking pace, leaving Neve alone with Jasper.

Neve narrowed her eyes and stared at him in silence.

'I'm sorry for pushing you away. Like really, really sorry.' His head lifted on the last sorry. 'I'd like to be friends, and I hope you can forgive me for being such a...'

'Moody moron?' Neve offered.

'Yeah that.'

'Or how about selfish prick?'

He threw his hands up, and a grin snuck onto his face. 'Okay, no need to get carried away. Forgive me? Please?'

Neve's heart melted for his warm, red-brown eyes pleading with her. 'Fine. But you're gonna have to apologise to Caitlin too.'

Confusion furrowed his brow. 'What did I do to Caitlin?'

'You hurt me, and she can be very protective of me.'

Jasper nodded his understanding. 'I'll smooth things over with her. It must be nice to have a loyal friend who sticks up for you.'

It pained her to think of everything Jasper had lost. 'I can be a loyal friend to you. I'm already on your side against the Alvarsson twins.'

The sweetest smile brightened his expression as they resumed walking. 'Yeah, you are a good friend. Thank you, Neve. I'm sorry for being a dick. I'm not accustomed to having someone to talk to when the going gets tough. The guys I used hang with weren't close friends, so if things got heavy, I got through on my own.'

It was one of the saddest things she had ever heard. He could not even turn to his parents for such matters. Not that Neve could either, but she did have Caitlin. 'Must've been hard for you. But hey, anytime you need someone to talk to, about anything, I'm here for you.'

'Thanks. It means more than you'd know.'

Mm, music to my ears. Knowing she meant something to Jasper renewed a hope she had almost lost. When they reached the school, Jasper continued with her as far as the Year Ten area, surprising Neve. 'Are you walking me to my locker now?'

'Is that okay?'

Neve blushed, thinking it was the sort of thing boyfriends did. 'I guess.'

When they neared her locker, a snide male voice echoed through the hall, 'Oh look, Jasper's going back for seconds. Neve must be amazing in bed.'

They both tensed at the hurtful words.

A few sniggers sounded, then another guy responded, 'Or he's getting desperate since no one else will touch him.'

'I reckon it could be both,' said James, one of the ogres. He approached Neve with drool dripping from his disgusting mouth as he leered at her body. 'I'd totally tap that.'

Caitlin strode up the corridor and confronted James, poking his chest. 'Don't. Fucking. Touch. Her.'

A bellowing laugh roared from James. 'Oh, this is precious, seein' you sticking up for the big bad Neve Winters. Anyone would think you wanna piece o' that fine arse too.'

Caitlin paled but held firm.

'Well damn, check it Lorcán. No wonder the bitch went all frigid on ya. She's a lesbo.'

Lorcán strode up to James, with Kane and Rónán following close behind like trained lapdogs. He grabbed the massive ogre by the collar of his flannelette shirt. 'Did I ask for your imbecilic opinion?' he spat. 'In case I've lost you on this one, the answer is "no". Next time I want footy tips or help lifting a keg, I'll consider calling you. Until then, keep your gargantuan nose out of my business.'

Neve barely registered Lorcán's tirade. She focused on the glistening tears threatening to flow from Caitlin's eyes. 'Hey, hun, don't worry about it. They're only words. Meaningless names and titles.'

Before Caitlin could respond, Mr. Rogers bellowed down the corridor, 'Break it up, boys.' Then the first bell sounded. 'Show's over, everyone. Get to homeroom.'

Caitlin spun without a word and dashed to her classroom.

'Hey, Neve, are you okay?' Jasper asked.

She turned to see his furrowed brow. 'Yeah, I'm fine. Worried about Caitlin though.'

'Look, I wanted to—'

'Have you forgotten where your class is, Jasper?' asked Mr. Rogers. 'I would have thought sharing a name with the building housing it would make it easier for you.'

Jasper frowned. 'I didn't forget, I was—'

'I don't care if you were about to unravel the mysteries of string theory, Mr. Rowan. You belong

111

elsewhere, and Neve has her own class to get to. Begone.' Mr. Rogers flicked his wrist in a dismissive wave.

With a sigh, Jasper turned away from Neve and left.

More of the Newer Volcanic Province was waking up from its slumber. It was occurring in a direct line towards South Australia. *How could Kieran not recognise the signs?* Alannah decided she needed to act, and soon. A quick call to Monique got her the address she required, so she jumped in her upgraded Tesla. It lacked the custom plates of her old model, but she had wanted to cut all ties to the Syndicate when Brendan had taken over.

The sky was dark, the atmosphere bleak as Alannah wound her way along the country road. Under different circumstances, she would have welcomed an overcast day. She preferred wintry weather to summer sun any day. But the ashy haze covering half of Australia was something else. The need to wear a face mask outside was strange. Not even the Covid-19 pandemic had been of much concern to Alannah. But there was a big difference between human infections and volcanic ash. Pure mages were immune to the former, but the latter was toxic to most living things. *If it's like this out here, I hate to think how bad conditions are in Melbourne.*

When she reached her destination, Alannah wondered if she had the right address. The property she had driven onto was full of thick scrub. There is nothing but trees for miles. *Where is their house?* Eventually the glimmer of glamour caught her eye. Piercing the veil, she gasped at the structures built amongst the canopy. It put her in mind of Tolkien's Lothlorien but on a much smaller scale.   The way elves and seelie fae worked with nature was remarkable. They did not bulldoze a forest to make space and use the dead remains to build something. Instead, they employed its features to enhance their accommodation.

After ascending the spiralling ramp, Alannah searched for a doorbell. What she found was a traditional brass ringer that made a warm chime when struck. *Can they even hear it?* Movement beyond the locked door soon answered her question.

Alvar himself greeted her with a glowering look of disdain.

'Do you know who I am, Sir Elofsson?'

The Swedish mage gave her a once over. 'One of the Council's pets, I presume? You have the aura of a bloodline mage and I recognise your face from the meeting.'

'It is true I have a seat on the Council, but—'

'I have no further desire to associate with your sort.' He went to close the door in her face.

But Alannah struck her hand out and used magic to stop it. 'Please. Hear me out.'

'Why should I? The Council were not willing to listen to me.'

'I'm not here on Council business. In fact, I rarely agree with those chauvinists.'

Suspicion clawed at the corners of Alvar's eyes. 'Why then are you here?'

'I wanted to ask you about the volcanoes. I have a theory and—'

'Sounds very much like Council business. Goodbye Lady…?'

'Winters. Alannah Winters. I assure you the Council knows nothing of my investigation. The High Magus does not even believe magic is behind the volcanoes.'

'The High Magus is a fool, Lady Winters.'

A nervous laugh slipped out. 'I tend to agree. So, you agree there is a magical cause for the volcanoes?'

'I will not discuss this or any other matter with you. Now if you don't mind, I was in the middle of something.' Alvar turned.

'If you know what's behind this devastation, you should disclose the knowledge. Withholding this information is grounds for treason under Council law.'

He spun to face her, lethal rage burning in his eyes. 'Do not threaten me, Lady Winters. Your pathetic Council does not scare me, and the lot of you would do well to remember your place in this world. You have become too caught up in the ways of the human world, losing sight of the bigger picture, and you will all be sorry.'

'You sound like a fascist.'

He scoffed. 'Your Council has more in common with fascism, I am a realist.'

'If you don't care for the Council, why did you want a seat?'

'For the Council's benefit, not mine. Think of it as a test. One the lot of you failed. Now get off my land before I throw you off.'

'What test?'

Energy sparked between Alvar's fingers.

Not wanting any real conflict, Alannah raised her hands in surrender, then turned and left. Frustration rippled through her nervous system on the drive home. *Alvar knows something. Why won't he tell me? Is he protecting someone? If so, who? Why?*

The rumours spread rife by recess. Everyone Neve passed in the hall was talking about Caitlin's lesbian crush on Neve. It was absurd. She beelined for Caitlin's locker, understanding her friend's need for comfort. She was not a moment too soon, judging by the way Caitlin hung her head in shame. 'It's okay, hun.' Neve pulled Caitlin into her arms, prompting several wolf whistles from bystanders. 'Let's get out of here.'

Sniffling, Caitlin nodded as she wiped her eyes with the back of her wrist.

Neve grabbed her hand and dragged her from the building toward their spot on the oval.

'You shouldn't touch me,' Caitlin warned, trying to free her hand from Neve's grasp. 'They will start a fresh round of gossip about you.'

Her jaw clenched at the thought of leaving Caitlin to suffer because of the pettiness of others. 'I don't care what people say, Cat.'

Jasper was waiting for them on the oval, prompting a snarl from Caitlin. 'What does he want now?'

'Your forgiveness, since I already gave him mine,' Neve explained.

'You're too merciful for your own good sometimes.'

'Hey ladies.' Jasper wore the same sheepish smile from earlier. 'Uh, Caitlin, I wanted to apologise for my behaviour. I'd like to be friends with both of you. Do you think you could find it in your heart to forgive me?'

'Wow, Jasper, did you practise those lines?' Caitlin asked.

'A little, why?'

'Because they sound more rehearsed than heartfelt.'

'Well I mean them. I needed to practise them because I was nervous.'

'Ha! The great Jasper Rowan too nervous to talk to a girl. Never thought I'd see the day.'

He sighed. 'I'm trying here, Caitlin. Please.'

'Let me be clear,' Caitlin explained, 'I have my doubts about you, Jasper. You are going to have to work hard to gain my trust. I will tolerate your presence because Neve wants you around. But I'm keeping a close eye on you.'

Jasper gulped. 'Understood.'

Is he seriously afraid of Caitlin?

'Good.'

117

Once they sat on the lawn, Neve's phone chimed with an email alert. When she opened it, she cursed. James had sent the photo to the class group mailing list with the caption LESBIAN LOVERS.

'What is it?' Caitlin asked.

'Nothing.'

'Neve, please show me.'

Conceding, she handed the offensive slander to Caitlin, who swore at the photo. It showed them holding hands: nothing new for Neve and her friends.

'Can I see?' Jasper asked. He took the phone Caitlin handed him and frowned. 'For fuck's sake. People are idiots. Who cares if you girls are hot for each other?' A lewd grin formed on his expression. 'Okay, scrap that. I'd care, but in a good way.' He waggled his brows.

Neve rolled her eyes.

'Ugh, you're disgusting,' replied Caitlin.

He waggled his brows. 'Beside the point. Turning people's sexual preference into the topic of scandals irks me. No one batted an eye when Debby came out.'

'It's because the issue concerns their latest scapegoats,' suggested Neve. 'Plus, relationships in general are a hot topic in this school. I mean, look at the way they were going on about us.'

'True. Still, if either of you want me to beat the shit out of James for spreading this around, I'd be more than happy to oblige.'

'Thanks, but we can handle the hick,' replied Neve.

Caitlin snapped a carrot stick in her mouth as she glared at Jasper. 'For the record, acting all macho and offering to pulverise people is not the way to win me over.'

'Yikes! Tough crowd.' Jasper leaned back with his elbows resting on the grass. His attention shifted from Caitlin to Neve, locking her eyes with his. There was heat in his gaze promising predatory intent.

All the air evacuated Neve's lungs. *Just as I'd started to give up on the possibility of him chasing me.*

'If you really want to assist us, Jasper,' Caitlin's voice broke the tension between them, 'you can help us get dirt on the Alvarsson twins.'

Jasper's grin could have eclipsed the sun. 'Oh, if you have a plan to take those jerks down, I am so in.'

As Saturday kissed the sun goodbye, Alannah was an emotional wreck. Another volcano prompted more questions than she had answers. And knowing Brendan lurked somewhere close by, she itched for a release. Toying with the thought of her two biggest vices, she opted for the less destructive one and gave Tyler a call.

'Hey beautiful, how are you?' His deep, rich voice was intoxicating, sending sparks rushing through her veins.

'I'm a mess.'

'Hm, sounds like you need to get your sexy arse over to Sydney so I can spank it raw.'

Alannah's pulse picked up with anticipation. 'Does that mean you're home?'

'Yep. Got in today actually. The volcanoes going off around the world put an end to the rest of our holiday plans.'

'Damn. Wait—did you say volcanoes have been erupting all around the world?'

'Uh yeah. It's been all over the news. Haven't you heard?'

'I heard about the ones in Victoria. It's part of the reason for my shitty mental state. But I didn't know about the rest of the world.'

'It's pretty nasty business. Sam and I had to catch a cruise back 'cause they grounded every airline in the world. At least it was a nice ship.'

'Shit! Things are worse than I thought.' She no longer doubted magic was causing the volcanic activity. *But what sort of magic? Do the Council know? Are they pleading ignorance while investigating on the sly?*

'Hey, you know the deal. No more doom and gloom before you get over here and let me have my way with you at least once.'

'Are you sure it's okay? You must feel exhausted from your trip.'

'Do you think I'd offer if it weren't okay? Besides, I've missed you and I need to get my Lana fix stat.'

'I'll be there shortly.' After signing off, she threw a change of clothes, a few sets of lingerie, and her basic toiletries into a tote bag. Striding down the hall, she knocked on Neve's door.

Electronic music blasted Alannah's ears as Neve opened it.

Thank the Gods for soundproofing wards.

'What?' Neve demanded.

'I need to head out for the night. Your father is still at the Sailing Club. Can I drop you off at Caitlin's?'

'Fine. Whatever.'

As they made their way across town, Alannah lamented the sweet daughter she had once known. *Is it my fault she acts like this? Or is it the hormones?* She tried to think back to what her own early puberty interactions with Aileen had been like. But she could only summon good memories. 'Are you okay, hun?' she asked as they pulled up outside Steve and Monique's house.

'Yeah, I'm fine.' Neve glanced at her to show a passive mask, then left the car. She was learning to hide her emotions, and Alannah did not know if she should be proud or worried.

After parking the car at her safehouse in the middle of nowhere, she magiported to Sydney. As always, Tyler had checked in to the hotel first. She greeted the desk clerk, obtaining the room number and key card. As soon as she opened the door, Alannah gasped at the sight of the man rising to greet her.

Tyler wasted no time preparing for her. He had changed into black leather pants and dispensed with any form of shirt. Sixteen years ago, Tyler had tried to infiltrate a dark mage cult. The mission had involved disguising himself as Brendan. Ever since then he had continued styling his hair and stubble exactly like Brendan. He even added the eyebrow ring. She wondered if he kept the resemblance for her benefit, or if Tyler had other reasons.

His eyes devoured her from beneath a lidded gaze. 'Hello, gorgeous.' He spoke with a deep and gravelly voice full of want. 'Gods, I've missed you.'

She rushed into his arms. Their lips collided with the heat of a thousand volcanoes, their passion unfettered and furious. A moan slipped from her mouth as Tyler's hard, unrelenting body pressed into her.

Large, soft lips tickled the tender spot on her neck, then his heady voice filled her ears, 'Strip for me, beautiful.'

'Yes, Sir.' Her response had become second nature in the bedroom setting. Lowering her gaze, Alannah took her time removing each item of clothing. Sexual tension filled the air between them. The pressure in her core had been building during Tyler's absence, reaching new heights. Judging by Tyler's heavy breathing, she figured he felt the same. Once naked, she dropped to her knees to assume her submissive pose.

'Sorry, Lana, but the full flogging will have to wait. I'm aching too much to be inside you.'

The confession made her smile. 'Understood, Sir.'

'Hands and knees on the bed.' Tyler's words had become the sweetest of all in the English language.

Assuming the pose, Alannah presented her backside. Anticipation flooded her with carnal need. When the mattress sank under Tyler's added weight, she began to quiver with excitement.

'Fuck! It's been too long, beautiful. I wish I could have taken you with us.' It was not the first time Tyler had expressed such a desire. He had not exactly hidden his feelings from her.

A pang of guilt shot through her. Tyler's hands began to rub her backside, drawing her mind back to the moment, to the sensation. He knew exactly how to touch her. *Smack!* Alannah groaned from the jolt of pleasure-pain brought on by the stinging bite of his hand. As soon as his fingers found her delicate folds, she lost herself in pure ecstasy.

…

Tyler must have sensed when Alannah came crashing back to reality. He rolled on to his side and threw a comforting arm across her. 'Talk to me, beautiful.'

'Brendan returned to Gaeilge Shores and paid me a visit.'

Shock possessed every part of Tyler's expression. 'Shit!' After a pregnant pause, Tyler took a deep breath. 'Not that I'm complaining, but if the real deal is back in town, why are you coming to me?'

Alannah winced. 'Tyler, you mean more than that to me. You're not just a Brendan substitute.'

'The old flames didn't rekindle, did they?'

Damn him for deflecting me. 'No. Far from it. The air between us was like an arctic frost. The interaction brought back a lot of unwanted emotions.'

'I bet.'

'Tyler?'

'Yessum?' he replied as he tucked a strand of hair behind her ear.

'Brendan knew about us. Did you tell him?'

After heaving a heavy sigh, Tyler's shoulders slumped. 'I'm sorry, Lana. I kind of let it slip the first time I met him… after my fists became acquainted with his face.'

A slight grin curved her lips. 'You punched him for me?' *Is it wrong to feel joy from the thought of Tyler hitting Brendan?*

'Fucken oath I did. No one hurts one of my girls and gets away with it.' It was a heart-warming gesture, albeit somewhat caveman in nature.

But there was another thought weighing on her mind. 'Brendan also mentioned you still see each other these days. Are you like mates now, or something?'

'Hardly,' Tyler scoffed. 'Sometimes we call on each other for work, but that's it.'

Alannah gaped at him. 'You work with him? He's a damned crime lord. Not to mention the whole dark mage thing.'

'There are times when law enforcement need help from criminal underworld.'

'So what, he's like a C.I.?'

Tyler nodded. 'Yes. But this stays between us. If Brendan's associates knew he snitched on them, he'd be in a world of pain. While I can imagine the thought pleases you, I suspect his death would hurt you more than his betrayal.'

Damn it, but Tyler is right. Knowing Brendan used his connections to help the good guys went some way to easing her poor opinion of him.

Chapter Seven

'Why don't we start with the reason you sought counselling?' Rose plastered a fake smile on her face as she looked between Liam and Alannah.

Liam remained sceptical of the nymph counsellor even though Bianca had recommended her. 'It was my idea, and I thought it might help to bridge the gap between us. Lana and I... well we haven't been intimate for fifteen years. At first, I thought she had shut me out like she did with everyone else, except for her *therapist*. But... she recently confessed to having an affair.'

'Thank you, Liam. I understand it can be hard to talk about painful things like this. You are doing well.' Rose turned to Alannah. 'Liam mentioned your therapy sessions. I don't mean to replace your therapist—'

Alannah snorted.

Wincing, Liam clarified, 'Her, uh, *therapist* was who she had the affair with.'

'I see…' Rose bit into her pen. 'Well, these sessions will not take the place of any personal psychology or psychiatry. However, it would be helpful to gain some insight into why you feel the need to shut people out, Alannah.'

'I don't intentionally shut most people out,' Alannah explained. 'I guess it's a side effect of turning off my emotions.'

'And why do you turn off your emotions, Alannah?'

'Because they fucking hurt.'

Leaning forward in her chair, Rose adopted an expression of professional concern. 'Why do they hurt?'

Alannah's eyes were brimming with tears. 'Because he ripped my soul to pieces and left me.'

'Who left you?'

'Brendan, Liam's brother.'

With a hand gesture, Rose prompted Alannah to continue.

'He was my… soulmate. We were still in the honeymoon phase, when he severed the link and left. Took off with some endarkened bitch and moved to Sydney. At first, I had no idea where he was, or what he had done. We thought someone might have kidnapped or killed him and I was beside myself. Then he rang Liam…'

When Alannah did not continue, Liam broke the silence. 'Brendan rang me, telling me how he'd run off with another woman. He asked me to pass on a message to Lana, to let her know he had found "a real woman" or some bullshit.'

'After the initial shock,' Alannah continued, 'I rebounded with another guy before eventually returning to Liam. We'—she waved in the air between herself and Liam—'already had history, having been in a relationship for years. But when I was in prison and needing him more than ever, Liam *dumped* me.' The acrid tone in her voice pained Liam.

'Do you still carry resentment?' Rose asked.

'A little. I forgave him a couple weeks after, but I never forgot how it felt and I guess I let the bitterness fester over the years.'

Liam reached for her hand. 'I'm so damn sorry, Lana.'

She sighed. 'The breakup was inevitable. Things with Brendan had been brewing for years.' Alannah began to sob. 'He was... my best friend... my perfect match... and he promised never... to leave me.'

Rose handed her a tissue box. 'Liam, why did you break off your previous relationship with Alannah?'

'I was angry at the time because I thought Lana was a traitor. But the biggest reason was because I knew she was in love with Brendan. I never approved of my brother, and it killed me to see Lana fall for him. Figuring he would end up hurting her, I tried to keep him away from her for years. But in a moment of weakness, I slipped up and let her go. Brendan swooped in and grabbed her before I realised my mistake. A few weeks after we'd split, Lana made the ultimate commitment to Brendan.'

Stunned for a moment, Rose's mouth was agape as she stared at Alannah. 'You were only with Brendan for a few weeks before forming the soul link?'

'I know it seems rushed. I guess it was, but we didn't know what we were doing. Brendan already felt his side of the empathic link, and he asked if I wanted to share it. We didn't know about soulmates at the time.'

Rose nodded her understanding. 'Alannah, did you love Liam when you returned to him?'

'Yeah. We went through an ordeal together and my feelings for him resurfaced. Afterwards, it felt natural to resume our relationship,' replied Alannah.

'I never stopped loving Lana,' Liam explained. 'I was not going to give up on her again.'

'How was your relationship at this stage?' Rose asked.

'Good,' replied Liam.

Rose looked at Alannah.

'It was okay, I guess. I was still grieving Brendan, but Liam was sweet and understanding.'

'When did things change?'

Alannah glanced at Liam, then turned her gaze downward. 'When I gave birth to my daughter.'

'Postnatal depression?' asked Rose.

'That was the diagnosis,' replied Alannah.

The sudden realisation hit Liam then.

'In truth, it was because my daughter, Neve, was Brendan's child. She was a constant reminder of the man who'd torn out my heart and ripped open my soul.'

'Did you know about this, Liam?'

He shook his head. 'I only learnt the truth a week ago. I never questioned Lana because she conceived Neve at Beltane. She started seeing her therapist around this time for the post-natal depression. Was this when the affair started, Lana?' Liam tried to curb the accusatory tone in his voice but found it difficult.

'No.' Alannah bit her lip, and her eye contact wavered. 'The affair started in Sydney, and my therapist was never a qualified professional.'

After a moment of confusion, Alannah's cryptic words fell into place. 'Shit! Tyler?'

The last of Alannah's fighting spirit faded from her eyes as she looked at him and nodded.

The fairgrounds of Gaeilge Shores thrived with the festival spirit. For the human populace, the night marked the opening of the harvest festival. To the magic community, it was Lammas: a night of sending prayers to the Gods for a blessed harvest. Thanks to the Council's protective wards, Neve walked among the festivities. She inhaled the scent of fried food and cut grass rather than volcanic ash. Laughing and squealing filled the air, much of which came from sideshow alley.

'Wanna go for a ride?' Jasper asked, waggling his brows as they reached the Ferris wheel.

Neve grinned at him. 'Sounds like fun.'

'Ugh,' Caitlin interjected. 'The pair of you are disgusting.'

Jasper approached the ticket booth. 'Will you join us, Cat?'

'I may as well. Someone needs to chaperone you two.'

He glanced at Neve. 'Hmm, should I rescind the invitation?'

'Don't even think about it, Jas,' Neve responded. 'We are not leaving my best friend down here on her own.'

After grabbing three ride passes, Jasper's gaze turned to one full of pure lust. 'Down for a threesome, huh? Sounds kinky, and I love it.'

Neve laughed as they climbed into their capsule.

Jasper pulled her into the seat next to him, leaving Caitlin to sit across from them.

She was glaring at him.

'Shit! That was super insensitive of me, Caitlin. I'm sorry.'

'It's okay, Jasper. The thought of you without clothes repulses me.'

He chuckled as the ride began to move, while Neve read between the lines of Caitlin's retort.

Could the rumours be true? As they reached the top, the view captivated Neve.

Jasper pressed his lips to her ear. 'Romantic, huh? Makes me want to come back up here alone with you.'

Warm tingles travelled from where his breath tickled her neck, all the way down her body. 'I'd like that,' Neve replied in a whisper.

'Anything you kids want to share with the class?' Caitlin asked with a pointed look at Jasper.

'Not especially. But next time I want someone to cockblock me, I'll be sure to call on you, Miss Maher,' Jasper replied in good humour.

Caitlin rolled her eyes and turned her attention to the sight of the twinkling lights below them.

Seizing the opportunity, Jasper slung an arm over Neve's shoulders. He gave her the most wonderful smile and spoke in her ear, 'I know this is not my usual style, but I've never met anyone who makes me feel the way you do, Neve. I don't just want in your pants; I want in your heart.'

A gasp slipped from Neve's throat. 'W-what are you saying, Jas?'

'I want to go out with you. Will you be my girlfriend, Neve?'

Gobsmacked, Neve felt her eyes popping from their sockets.

'Christ, Jasper! What did you say to the poor girl?' Caitlin asked, breaking Neve's stunned silence.

Ignoring Caitlin, Jasper's expression darkened as he waited for Neve's reply.

Eventually Neve smiled and nodded. 'Yes, Jas. I'd love nothing more.'

Jasper's lip curled into a victorious grin.

'What's goin' on, guys?' Caitlin's nervous voice asked.

The ride jerked to a stop, and a pimply-faced boy ushered the three of them out before she could reply. As soon as they were standing on solid ground, Jasper snatched up Neve's hand. 'This beautiful lady has agreed to be my girlfriend.'

Caitlin spluttered. 'Ah, excuse me. For a moment there, I thought I heard Jasper talk about having a girlfriend.'

'Because you heard right,' replied Neve. 'Why is it so hard for you to accept?'

'I guess I'm sceptical. I've never known a player to change his spots.' Caitlin scowled at Jasper. She turned and started walking away. 'I'm getting ice cream now.'

Neve offered Jasper an apologetic look. 'I'm sorry—'

'Hey, you don't need to apologise, especially not for Caitlin. I understand her need to protect you. I don't have the best rep, after all. Come on.' He tugged on her hand, following Caitlin.

As they finished their frozen treats, two sets of eyes found Neve's. Their chilling glares rivalled the iced confection. The Alvarsson twins ignored the sycophants surrounding them; their attention focused on Neve.

'Well if it isn't the loser squad.' Elna's voice could have cut glass. 'Tell me Neve, are you sleeping with both of your friends? Or are you still choosing between them?'

Erik snorted. 'Please, Elna, if Jasper had slept with Neve, he wouldn't still be hanging around her like a bad smell.'

Jasper gritted his teeth. 'Fuck off, Tinkerbell. My personal life is none of your business. Neither is the nature of my relationship with Neve.'

Keeping his gaze fixed on Neve, the hatred in Erik's eyes intensified. There was another emotion too, one she could not put her finger on. 'Is that so? What do you think, Neve? Should the nature of your relationship with Jasper be of any concern to me?'

Neve could sense Jasper watching her warily, but she could not tear her eyes away from

Erik. She needed to know what else the arsehole was feeling. *What I would give for a glimpse of Erik's outer aura. He must be using the spell Uncle Brendan taught me.*

The hint of a smirk touched Erik's lips before he masked his visage completely.

'No. None of my relationships are any of your business,' Neve finally replied.

Erik's voice sounded in Neve's mind, a wicked gleam shining in his eyes. *'If I had more patience tonight, I'd argue the semantics of your statement. But I do not, so I will make do with advising you are wrong, Neve. Some of your relationships are of great interest to me. I will* make *it my business to learn everything about them. One wrong move, and I will ruin you and your boy.'*

Neve huffed. 'How could you ruin us anymore than you already have?'

A malicious laugh burst from Erik's mouth. 'You haven't seen anything, yet.' His eyes darkened as his voice filled her head again. *'You would do well to heed my warning, sweetheart.'* The twins turned and strode away with their groupies trailing behind.

'What the hell was all that about?' Caitlin asked.

'Neve?' Jasper's voice filled with concern, as Neve continued watching Erik disappear into the crowd.

Snapping out of it, Neve turned to her friends. 'I think I know a way to get the intel we want.' She paused for a moment and looked into Jasper's eyes. 'But you're not going to like it.'

'Hey, I'm down with any plan that gets results. Those enlightened bastards are going down.'

'Even if the plan involves hiding our relationship?'

Jasper paled as the pieces came together. 'You mean to befriend them?'

Neve squeezed his hand. 'Exactly.'

Surrounded by such a lively crowd, Alannah felt quite out of place at the Lammas festival. Things had been tense with Liam since their counselling session two nights ago, leaving her in a funk. Rose had explained it would take time to get results from their sessions. *But do they normally make people feel worse?* Liam had not spoken a word to Alannah since learning the truth about Tyler.

'How did the first counselling session go?' Cara asked as they joined the line for coffee and donuts.

'Pfft. Terrible. I made Liam hate me.'

'How so?'

Alannah heaved a sigh. 'Because I confessed *who* I was having the affair with.'

Cara looked confused. 'Wait, I thought you told him already.'

'No. I'd simply told him I was sleeping with my "therapist." I don't know what bothers him more: the fact Tyler is one of Liam's friends or knowing how much I still crave Brendan.'

With wide eyes, Cara blinked three times. '*You what?*'

Alannah bit her lip. 'Why do you think I kept going back to Tyler?'

'I figured Jerkface was your initial excuse. Surely you've got something special goin' with Tyler himself after sixteen years.'

'We do. He is one of my best friends and the sex is amazing, but I'm not in love with him. Not like…' Alannah stopped herself from admitting the most painful truth of all.

'Christ, woman!' Cara stepped up to the coffee cart and placed her order, adding Alannah's request while she was at it.

Reaching into her bag, Alannah retrieved her wallet. 'Here, let me cover my—'

Cara raised a hand in protest. 'This is my treat. You've got enough on your plate right now.'

Alannah paused before putting her purse away.

'I don't know if I should mention this, but...' Cara paused for effect, sipping her coffee.

'But what?'

'I heard *he* is in town.'

Glancing down at her cappuccino, Alannah dragged her bamboo spoon through the foam. 'I know. He dropped by the other day.'

'Shit! Why didn't you tell me Dickhead rocked up at your door?'

'Because I've had a hard time processing it all. There's more, Cars.'

'Oh Gods. Should I sit down for this?'

A short laugh slipped from Alannah's throat. 'Probably best.' They found a bench seat. 'The reason Brendan showed up was not for me, but for Neve, *his* daughter.'

Abject horror marred Cara's face and she turned white as a ghost. 'How?'

'Well, Cara, when a mummy and a daddy—'

'Ha-de-ha. How did either of you know? Neve is a blessed child.'

'*He* was my only partner at Beltane that year. When Jacob mentioned Neve's age and her means of conception, it wasn't hard for Brendan to figure it out.'

Cara shook her head. 'And you've known all this time?'

Alannah dropped her gaze and nodded. When she looked up, a figure in the distance caught her attention.

'I know it's not customary to discuss the fathering of a blessed child, but I still can't believe you kept this from me. Gods, no wonder…' Cara's voice faded into the background.

With her attention fixed on the arrogant bastard, Alannah began advancing toward him.

'*Alannah?*' Cara asked, raising her voice.

'Sorry, Cars. Give me a sec,' she replied without taking her eyes of her target. Picking up her pace, she chased after him. '*Alvar!*'

He turned to face her with a grimace. 'What is it, Lady Winters?'

'I wanted to apologise for offending you the other day.'

Alvar grunted. 'You reek of insincerity.'

'I am quite sincere, I assure you. Please, Sir Elofsson, I beg you to help me out here. Is there anything I can do for the information? Money, favours? Anything?'

A slight smile tugged at one side of his lips. 'How about grovelling on your knees?'

Damn, this man is irritating! Alannah knelt before him and adopted a pleading expression.

His mouth grew into a full, devious grin. 'If I had known it was this easy to get a Winter's woman on her knees...'

She gritted her teeth. 'Please, Sir Elofsson, this is not my usual style.' *Outside of the bedroom,* she added silently. 'I am desperate to learn more about these volcanoes.'

'I'm sorry, but as amused as I am by your beseeching, I refuse to talk to any Council members. Don't take it personally.'

'But I told you, this isn't Council business.' Alannah was feeling desperate. 'Please give me something, anything.'

Alvar sighed. 'Your allegiance to the Council prevents me from talking about this matter. I'm not ignorant of their methods for extracting intel from their own members.'

Memories of Richard's abuse filled her mind, sending a shiver down her spine. 'They could interrogate *you* if they even cared to know.'

'They can try,' Alvar replied with a smirk.

'Please tell me, are you making them erupt?'

'No, this is not my doing.'

Finally, the begging is paying off. If she had not spent years learning to submit to Tyler, this whole ordeal would have been impossible. She felt humiliated as it was, and the public venue did little to ease her shame. 'Then who is doing it?'

Alvar turned on his heels. 'Goodbye, Lady Winters.'

'Please! For the sake of all those innocent lives!'

'What innocent lives?' Alvar scoffed as he glanced back over his shoulder. 'And what does it matter? You can't stop them.'

Standing, Alannah watched on in frustration as her best lead walked away.

With a jolt, Brendan awoke from his restless sleep. Alannah had haunted all his dreams and nightmares. Turning his head to glance at the red LED display on the bedside, he cursed. *It's only 4AM. I couldn't even manage two hours. I should handle my business with Jacob now.* Sitting up, he reached for his phone and dialled the number for his local spymaster.

'Yo! Sup?' Jacob's bright, bubbly voice asked.

STARLA

'Oh good, you're still awake.'

A soft chuckle came through the line. 'Of course I am. The pre-dawn hours are when I do my best work. I just got back from the latest job.'

'Good. I want to talk to you about it. Meet me at the motel.'

'Be right there.'

When Jacob arrived, Brendan scanned their surrounds. Heightening his senses, he ensured no one had seen his visitor arrive. Confident the coast was clear, he closed and locked the door. 'Wanna drink?'

'Is the High Magus a dick?' Jacob's light, humorous tone brought a much-needed smile to Brendan's weary features.

After pouring them each a double shot of whiskey, Brendan slumped onto his bed. He offered the only chair to Jacob.

Ignoring the invitation, Jacob chose to sit beside Brendan. A flirtatious gleam twinkled in his eyes and heat radiated from his stocky body. Jacob referred to himself as pansexual—open to anything so long as it involved sex.

'Forget it, Red. I'm not in the mood.'

Jacob's full lips protruded into a pout. 'I could make you forget about her for a few hours.'

144

Brendan growled. 'No one can make me forget about Lana.'

'Not even Caleb?' Jacob asked, knowing how spectacular Caleb was in the sack.

Memories of all the amazing times spent with his two endarkened lovers filled his mind. A pang of homesickness and heartache stabbed at him. But he recalled the bitter betrayal over Neve and felt himself spiralling. 'Not even Caleb. Ironically, I doubt Lana could make me forget Caleb either. They are both so entrenched under my skin. Now can we get on with business? What did you learn?'

Jacob eyed him as though dealing with a wild animal that could lash out at any moment. Given Brendan's current state of mind, Jacob would not be far off the mark. 'I got a lead on the Rhapsody imitation. Looks like it might be seelie work.'

'Are you fucken serious?' Brendan asked with wide eyes.

'Yep. The shit they are putting on the market is potent, but its side effects are giving our stuff a bad rep.'

'So, they want to sabotage us. What sort of side effects are we talking?'

Casting his eyes down into his glass, Jacob drew his bottom lip between his teeth.

'Tell me, Red.'

'The worst cases wind up… dead.'

'Fuck! What else?'

'Some are reporting impotence after they come down. Others are more agitated and aggressive.'

After throwing back the rest of his drink, Brendan rose and fixed himself another. 'This is bad. Can you trace the source?'

'Probably, but it could take weeks.'

Brendan shot Jacob a stern look. 'I want you on this full time. Find those bastards and end this. We should halt production and put warnings out in the meantime.'

'Do you know how much that would cut into our bottom line?'

'I've seen the numbers; you don't need to remind me. But these jerks could do a lot more damage to our profits if we don't act now. Let me deal with our stuff while you hunt down theirs.'

Standing, Jacob finished his drink and placed the glass on the desk. 'Looks like I'm in for a road trip.'

'Indeed. Just… be careful. I may not show it much these days, but your friendship means a great deal to me.'

Jacob nodded and embraced him.

When Jacob didn't pull away at the appropriate time, Brendan cleared his throat.

'Sorry man, but I gotta make the most of this. I don't get to see you enough and Gods know when I'll be back.'

With a sigh, Brendan indulged his best mate. Then he watched as Jacob drove away. *I hope I didn't sign your death warrant.*

The door slammed behind him when he stepped back inside. Cringing, Brendan prayed he hadn't drawn unwanted attention from his neighbours. *I need to do something about my frustrations.* The whiskey bottles caught his attention. Seeing no other option, he settled on numbing his emotions. He was on his second bottle before the world faded around him.

…

Bile rising in his throat pulled Brendan out of his stupor. Rushing to the bathroom, he made it in the nick of time. When his guts had emptied, he downed a shot of the good green stuff. It was the only thing he could thank his father for. *Hell, it's been a while since I got black-out drunk.* Observing the

147

time, he smiled. *Did the trick though*. It was a little after midday and he felt better for the induced sleep.

But as soon as he hit the shower, his thoughts returned to Alannah. *Damn it! Resistance is futile!* That was when the epiphany struck. *I will win her back; consequences be fucking damned!* Once he had finished dressing, a new sense of determination took hold. Before leaving the motel, he made a point of running through the essential checklist: *keys, wallet, phone, mana rings*.

Much to Brendan's relief, the drive to Alannah's house was brief. After sneaking around the rear of the property, he got to work on picking the lock and disarming the wards. He stalked his way through her home, scanning for bugs and making note of every device he detected. Alannah's off-key humming travelled through the door of her sewing room, bringing a smile to his face. He felt compelled to enter, halting with his hand on the doorknob. *Not yet, you moron!* He still needed to finish checking the other rooms.

The first of the bedrooms he entered was Liam's. It reeked of the man's overpriced cologne and had all the style of an 80s pop music video. Knowing he would not bother spending time in there, Brendan moved on.

Neve's room came next, and he took his time, not only to be thorough in his search, but to snoop a little. Typical teen girl paraphernalia filled her space. Everything from posters of Hollywood heartthrobs to stuffed animals. Clothes and books had been strewn across the floor. Her diary caught his attention. He hated the idea of being *that* sort of dad. *I'm only doing this to get to know my daughter better*. Flicking through, something in bold letters turned his stomach: I LOVE JASPER ROWAN! *Does your mother know about this, princess?* He doubted it.

Finally, he found Alannah's room. Her familiar musky scent filled his nostrils, sending a rush of desire through his body. He would have given anything to wrap himself in her bed covers. Pushing the thought aside, he focused on his task. Intoxicated by her essence, Brendan could not help opening her lingerie drawer. He slipped a pair of black lace panties into his pocket.

'What *the hell* do you think you are doing?'

With a seductive grin plastered on his visage, Brendan turned to face her. 'Hello, Lana.'

Chapter Eight

'Erik?' Neve called out as she glimpsed him walking across the schoolyard at lunchtime. 'Can I talk to you for a sec?'

The twins turned and glowered.

'You dare approach us?' Elna snapped.

'Let's hear what Miss Winters has to say,' responded Erik in an icy voice.

Crossing her arms, Elna huffed. The simple gesture revealed more about their relationship dynamic than she realised.

'I'm sorry for dismissing you before. I come seeking forgiveness and admission to your court.'

'Yeah right! You had your chance—' Elna began.

But Erik cut her off with a dismissive wave as his eyes connected with Neve's. The hypnotic green gaze glowed, pulling her in, and she felt her breath hitch. His expression transformed into a wicked, yet seductive grin. 'I might be willing to accept you. But I'll need a show of good faith first.'

Neve felt every muscle in her body tense. 'Of course. What do I need to do?'

'I want you to bring Jasper to my party this weekend.'

She swallowed hard against the lump in her throat. 'W-what do you plan to do to him?'

Sadistic malice flashed in his eyes. 'It's a surprise. Make sure he shows up and go along with whatever I ask of you on the night and we will pardon you.'

'How do I convince him to come? He'll be suspicious of your motives for inviting him.'

Erik shrugged. 'That's for you to work out. Seduce him with the *false* promise of taking your virginity for all I care.'

A titter burst forth from Elna's lips. 'Oh, and if we do let you into our court, you can't spend time with Jasper anymore.'

Neve nodded. 'I figured as much. What about Caitlin?'

'Our only quarrel with Caitlin is her association with you. If you join us, we will welcome her,' Erik explained. 'Oh and the party is lakeside, so wear your bathers.'

'Okay. Thank you.' Joining her friends on the lawn, she ignored the student body. They huddled together, whispering and snickering.

'Well?' Jasper asked as she settled down beside him.

'They will let me in on two conditions.'

'Hmph. Figures they'd expect something,' Caitlin remarked. 'What do they want?'

Neve looked into Jasper's eyes, feeling emotion swelling in her own. 'I'm sorry, Jas.'

He brushed the pad of his thumb across her cheek. 'Hey, I knew I was signing up for bad shit when I agreed to this plan. Tell me.'

'Once I'm in, we can't let people see us together.'

Jasper's expression saddened. 'We knew it would be likely. What's the other condition?'

'They have something nasty planned for you at their party this weekend. I don't know what, but I have to make sure you go.'

He cursed under his breath. 'Hey, it can't be much worse than everything they've already done. If this helps our plan, I'm there.'

Neve forced a smile. 'Thank you. I hate that we can't date in the open.'

'I know, baby. Silver lining, there's the fun of sneaking around and the threat of getting caught. Keeps things interesting.' He winked.

Giggling, she slapped his chest half-heartedly. But when her hand collided with solid muscle, Neve gasped, and they became locked in a heated stare.

'Puh-lease people. No PDAs at school,' Caitlin complained.

'Seriously dude? We weren't doing anything,' replied Jasper.

'Not yet, but I could see it coming. Besides, I doubt Neve wants her first kiss to be at school. Try somewhere more romantic, or at least private.'

'Caitlin!' Neve shrieked, horrified she'd let the truth slip.

Jasper leaned in, breathing against Neve's neck as he whispered, 'You've never kissed anyone?'

Sucking on her bottom lip, Neve shook her head.

'Mm, I look forward to being your first, in so many ways.'

Eep! Neve felt her face overheating as a fluttering sensation rose from her chest.

'Are you free on Sunday?' he inquired.

'Yes.' Her voice didn't rise above a whisper.

'Naomi has plans, so I have the house to myself. You wanna come over?'

Neve's whole demeanour lit up brighter than any sun. 'I would love to.'

'Awesome. It's a date then,' Jasper beamed.

Alannah's eyes darted between her open drawer and the bulge in Brendan's pocket. When her gaze met his, she glared.

'This is not what it looks like,' he proclaimed.

'Oh? So, you didn't steal my underwear?' She employed a harsh, accusatory tone.

'Oops, I guess I'm busted.' Brendan's eyes sparkled as he gave her his lop-sided grin.

Refusing to lose herself in the sexy-as-sin expression, she glanced down and retrieved her phone. 'Give me one reason I shouldn't call Liam now and have your arse hauled off to the Council's prison.'

Brendan tensed. 'Hmm, read any good books lately?'

'The fuck? What's that…' Her jaw dropped. He must have been referring to the various magical tomes and translation notes that had started showing up about fifteen years ago. Jacob had delivered the first by hand, explaining that it came from her great aunt. 'Those—'

Rushing forward, he clamped a hand over her mouth. 'Shoosh,' Brendan hissed.

Her eyes rounded not only from the surprise of Brendan manhandling her, but due to *his* proximity. The unwelcome response in her core intensified when his lips pressed against her ear.

'I've been scanning the place for bugs. Turns out someone wired most of your house. I haven't finished in here, so I don't know if it is safe to talk yet.'

Well, shit! She should have figured the Council would do something like this. *Does Liam know?*

Brendan stepped back, and a gust of air whooshed from Alannah's lungs. Returning to the dresser, he picked up his phone and waved it around as he explored her room. When he crouched beside the bed, he dragged a familiar black tub from beneath it. The box, along with its sordid contents, had once been theirs. Looking up at her, he smirked, and Alannah's cheeks flushed with heat.

Once he completed his sweep, he drew close to her and whispered, 'This room is clear, but best we keep our voices down since there are some in the hall.'

'Okay. Are any other rooms safe?'

'Nope. This is the only one.'

Mystified, her brow furrowed. 'Why not in here?'

He shrugged. 'Maybe they don't want to hear those amazing noises you make when you climax.' His eyes darkened with lust as he added, 'Their loss.'

'Brendan!' Alannah felt herself scowling even as her blood heated. Recalling the hidden microphones, she lowered her volume. 'I only used this room for storage before moving out of the master bedroom. Should I remove any of the devices?'

'No. It will arouse too much suspicion.'

'Then what should I do?'

'Carry on as normal and keep secretive discussions to this room or outside the house.'

She studied him, noticing the dark circles surrounding his eyes for the first time. *Looks like he is struggling with sleep as much as I am. Could it be due to his guilty conscience? Does he even know what remorse feels like anymore?* 'I assume that includes all our conversations, what with you being a dark mage these days.'

Brendan stepped closer and lowered his voice further. 'It is vital we conceal *all* our conversations, Lana. For your sake as much as my own.'

Makes sense. The Council frowned upon her interactions with the last Dark Syndicate Boss. Why would Brendan be any different? 'Those tomes Jacob gave me came from you?'

'Yup.'

'Why did you lie about them coming from Dana Winters?'

'First and foremost, to protect you. But also, to make sure you read the damn things. If you knew they'd come from me, would you have opened them or discarded them outright?

She hated to concede his point. 'Most likely the latter. But why did you send them to me?'

'Tara had intended for you to continue your training. I was in the best position to obtain information for you.'

Alannah gasped when realisation smacked her in the face. 'You've been carrying on her work all this time! Is this why you became the Syndicate's Boss?'

He nodded.

'Was there a reason for this visit and all the bug scanning? Don't tell me you're moonlighting as a panty thief these days?'

The impish gleam returned to his eyes. 'Are you wondering what I'll do with them? I bet the thought alone gets your juices flowing.'

More than I care to admit. 'In your dreams. Give them back,' she demanded with an outstretched hand.

Drawing close, he brought his chest in contact with hers. Brendan brushed his mouth against the sensitive spot beneath her ear. The tender touch sent tingles shooting all over her skin. 'I won't stop you recovering them from my person.'

She sucked in a breath. Big mistake. She inhaled his aroma: musky cologne mingled with a natural body odour that was all male and far too hot for television. The hint of a moan escaped her lips before she could stop it.

A victorious smile stretched Brendan's mouth wide as he stepped away. 'Then again, I think I'll keep them.'

Is this some new variation of sleazy chicken? Play until I go weak at the knees, then back off. Sadistic bastard! Alannah cleared her throat. 'So, um, the point of your visit?'

'The bug scan was the main reason. I wanted to prepare for future conversations, to know where they can take place.' His lips curled into a wicked grin. 'How convenient, *your* bedroom is the best place for us.'

Alannah shot him with dagger stares. 'What makes you think I'll let you back in here ever again?'

He wore a smug expression. 'Not like I waited for an invitation this time.'

'Good point,' she mumbled. 'I could upgrade the wards to keep you out.'

'I suppose you could, but then you'd miss out on all my valuable intel.'

She let out a frustrated sigh. 'Why are you helping me, Brendan? What do you get out of it?'

'I want to uncover the truth Tara referred to, and I know we need to work as a team to do so.'

That's it then. I'm only a means to an end for him. 'I think I preferred working together when you were a silent partner,' *because then you couldn't mess with my head and heart.*

'Too bad. Things are different now, so you'll have to deal with it.'

'What's different?'

'I learnt the truth about Neve… among other things.'

Caitlin placed the plate of healthy snacks beside her bed, eliciting a groan from Neve.

'I keep forgetting your house is a junk food free zone these days. Would it kill your mum to stock the odd chip packet?'

'Hey, don't knock the carrot sticks and hummus!' Crossing her legs, Caitlin sat atop her bedspread and leaned back into the headboard. It was good to finally have her girl alone for a few hours.

'I've been thinking,' Neve declared.

'Uh oh!'

Neve promptly stuck her tongue out before continuing, 'What are we gonna do about Fiona when the Alvarsson twins welcome us into their "court"?'

With careful consideration, Caitlin replied, 'I don't think we can trust her. We should be friendly to avoid suspicion, but let's not get too close.'

'I agree.' Neve lay down beside her with a sigh.

The sight of her best friend sprawled out across Caitlin's double bed stirred a range of emotions. Grabbing a carrot stick, she crunched into it for a distraction.

'I'm way excited, and nervous about Sunday.'

Caitlin contorted her face as confusion set in. 'Sunday?'

'My date with Jasper. The one *at his house*.'

Shit! I must have zoned out when they made those plans. 'Well, being alone with Jasper would be terrifying.'

'Cat! I'm serious. I'm anticipating my first kiss. What if I suck at it?'

'Doubtful.'

'But I don't know what I'm doing. A guy of his... calibre will notice my inexperience.'

Caitlin snorted. 'Let him take the lead. I'm sure he's used to it.'

Neve sprang upright. 'Hey! I have an idea. What if I practise with you?'

The blood drained from Caitlin's face and she mouthed an enormous 'No.'

'Look, no one has to know, and it wouldn't mean anything.'

Her head began to shake of its own accord. 'That's the problem,' she muttered. *Fuck! Did I say that out loud?*

'What do you mean?' Neve asked with a blank look. It didn't take long for comprehension to transform her visage. Knitted brows shot up and she clapped a hand over her gaping gob. 'Oh Gods, Cat! The rumours...'

Standing, Caitlin began to pace the room. 'I'm sorry, hun. It's just...'

'Just what?' Neve asked with a trembling voice.

'It's hard not to love you. You're sweet, smart, and… hot as hell.' Her cheeks flushed as the admission poured forth.

Neve froze.

'I'm sorry. I don't want this to ruin our friendship. I understand if you're not into me.' Her heartrate skipped out of control. Taking a deep breath, she tried to will the stupid organ into submission before it broke for real.

'Is… is this why you dislike Jas?' Neve squeaked.

'Gods no! I don't trust him. I'd be fine if you were dating *almost* anyone else in our school. I care about you, Neve, and I want to see you happy.'

'It's okay. I… I'll try not to freak out on you. Might take some getting used to though. I'm sorry, Cat, I can't—'

Caitlin threw her hands up. 'Hey, it's cool. You're as straight as my ruler and I'm not going to pretend otherwise. It's why a practice kiss is bad idea.'

'Of course. I… I'm sorry I suggested it.' Neve looked down, interlocking her delicate fingers and rubbing them together. 'Why don't you trust

Jasper? Is it his rep or is there more?' she asked as her gaze lifted.

Returning to her seat on the bed, Caitlin thought about how to approach the topic. She did not want to betray her mother's trust, but felt the circumstances were excusable. 'It's because of his family.'

Neve frowned. 'You mean Jasper's uncle? My uncle Brendan mentioned Clayton and what he did to Mum. But one bad egg doesn't mean Jasper will turn out rotten.'

Caitlin stared at her in shock.

'What?'

'You've met Brendan Winters?'

'Uh, yeah. He's back in town. Why?'

'Shit! Don't you know what he is? Who he is?'

'No,' Neve admitted hesitantly.

It never ceased to amaze Caitlin how much Neve's parents kept her in the dark about their family's past. 'Hun, Brendan is a dark mage and the head of some big criminal organisation.'

Every drop of colour faded from her porcelain complexion. 'So that's why Liam reacted so violently to Brendan's return.'

'Part of the reason, yes. Then there's the history your mum and Brendan share.'

'What history?' she asked with wide, blinking eyes.

'They were lovers once. Soulmates even. Until Brendan ran off to Sydney with another woman, breaking your mum's heart.'

'By the Gods! Why am I always the last to learn this shit?'

Caitlin offered a sympathetic look. 'I'm sorry.'

'It's not your fault. I wish Mum would open up more about—oh hell! When was she with Brendan?'

'I'm not sure exactly. Why do you ask?'

Neve gnawed at her bottom lip. 'I was wondering if… maybe…'

'Yes?' Caitlin prompted.

'Is there a chance Brendan's my father?'

'Neve, you know you're a Beltane baby. You even have the blessing.'

'So? Something about Brendan feels… familiar. I don't know how to explain it, but there's still a chance he hooked up with Mum at Beltane right?'

'I suppose,' Caitlin ventured, unsure about continuing with Neve's heretical line of inquiry. 'But—'

'He doesn't seem all bad to me, Cat. Brendan was more fatherly with me in the short time I've known him than Liam has ever been.'

'You walk a dangerous path even questioning your bio dad's identity. Not to mention the consequences of connecting with a Syndicate Boss. What about the way he broke your mum's heart?'

Neve exhaled all her frustration in one loud huff as she fell back into a prone position.

At least she still feels comfortable lying on my bed.

'Look, I know it must suck not knowing the identity of your real dad, but Liam still loves you as his own.'

'Can we get back to the issue with Jasper?' Neve's tone turned irritable.

'Fine. I don't know much about Clayton, other than the fact he went to prison on sexual assault charges. But he isn't the Rowan family member I was referring to.'

Neve shot her a surprised look.

'Chester, Jasper's dad, did something to my mum when they were younger.'

She sat bolt upright. 'Shit! I... I had no idea.'

'I know. Mum hasn't told anyone other than me and Dad.'

'Could this town be anymore twisted?' Neve asked as she slumped against the bed.

Conditions were choppy as Liam paddled out past the break. Not ideal for surfing, but he enjoyed manipulating the elements to suit his needs. It also meant there were no grommets around. After taking a moment to centre himself, he bent the oncoming wave into the perfect barrel. He charged the crest, feeling the need to vent his frustrations. At least the ocean would not complain about his mood.

The more he dwelt on Alannah's affair with Tyler, the more his heart sank. *They share a connection I will never have, not with Lana.* He did not even care to admit the underlying reasons for her choice of lover. Putting those ugly thoughts aside, Liam focused on surfing.

Having worked off enough steam, he took a moment to rest on the board.

'You had some impressive moves today.' Saoirse's soft voice drifted across the breeze, bringing him out of his meditation.

Turning, he smiled at her. 'Thanks. How are you, Saoirse?'

'I am well, thank you. And yourself?'

His expression soured. 'I've been better.'

'Oh?' Her own smile slipped away. 'What's wrong?'

'It's… personal stuff. I'd rather not talk about it, okay?' He needed more time to process his emotions and did not think it was fair to burden her with them.

She nodded. 'I've been meaning to ask: what do you know about these volcanoes?'

Relieved by the change of subject, Liam relaxed. 'Not much. The leaders of the Mage's Council haven't said anything about them. Why?'

'The Mer Council fear something magical is causing it all. So many of them going off at once, can't be a coincidence.'

Liam did not realise the issue had become so widespread. 'How did you know about them?'

'There are a lot of volcanoes in the ocean. According to global reports, an alarming number of volcanic tsunamis have occurred lately.'

'I see.' *Why didn't Kieran mention this?* Liam wondered if the Arch Mage had concerns. 'Have the eruptions hurt any of your friends or family?'

'No. Nothing has happened in our area. But I'm worried it is only a matter of time. Do you think you could ask your superiors if they know anything? I recommend an alliance with the Mer Council.'

It would not be the first time the mages of the land and sea worked together. But it had been centuries, and Liam was curious to know what the current leaders would think of the idea. 'I can try.'

The sweetest smile lit up her features. 'You are so kind.'

He could not hold back the short laugh. 'You are too generous with your words. I haven't done anything yet.'

Saoirse swam closer, their faces only a hair's breadth apart. 'I know you are a good man. I can feel it in my gills and see it in your eyes. Your intentions are noble, and I respect that.'

Again, he laughed as he brought a hand up to touch the side of her face. 'You are a precious pearl, but what do you know of my intentions?'

Their gazes locked together, and something transpired between them. The blue tones of Saoirse's aqua eyes darkened as her lids lowered. Out of water, the valve controlling the use of her lungs opened, letting in short, shallow breaths. She leaned into his hand. 'Liam?' Her gentle, dreamy tone snapped him out of it.

He jerked back, breaking contact with her. 'Shit! I'm sorry, Saoirse. I must have come across like a total sleaze then.' *What the hell was I thinking?* *Saoirse may be stunning, but we live in separate worlds and… I have a wife. Albeit a disloyal, deceitful, and distant wife. But I still love Lana. Leaving her now after everything Brendan did would destroy her.*

'There you go proving my point,' Saoirse claimed. 'Most men don't apologise for seducing a woman.'

How did a mermaid become so wise to the world above sea level? 'I guess not, but we ought to apologise when leading you on.'

'Are you saying you don't want me?'

Fuck! Why did she have to be so damn candid all the time? 'N-no. It's… we can't, Saoirse. Now is not a good time for me. I'm sorry. I never should have touched you.'

Her cute little heart-shaped mouth pouted, and it made him want to kiss the disappointment out of her.

'Can we still be friends?' he asked.

'Of course. Next time, could we have another sparring match?' Her eyes filled with a glimmer of hope.

'I'd like that.'

Flicking her tail, Saoirse splashed water in Liam's face. The tension eased between them as they both laughed. 'See you then.' She pulled off an aerial backflip and disappeared.

Liam sighed. *What am I going to do about my broken and twisted love life?*

Chapter Nine

A bonfire in the middle of a forest was not exactly what Neve expected to attend during fire ban season. Then again, there were plenty of magicals around with elemental attunement. No one would let the blaze get too large. She walked in blind, without a plan. She had stressed about Jasper and Caitlin rather than prepare for the trials ahead. Her friends flanked her, Jasper to her right and Caitlin on her left.

Everyone they passed stopped to stare at them before whispering with their neighbour. Several spectators even snickered or giggled. It was anything but a warm welcome. *Christ! What have I signed on for?* She tried to dry her sweaty palms against her legs but the thin chiffon of her red party dress proved useless.

The twins were sitting a short distance from the fire. They lounged in wooden chairs resembling thrones. When Elna spotted them, she turned and said something in Erik's ear.

Erik smirked. 'So good of you to join us, Jasper.'

The crowd around them erupted with laughter.

'What the hell do you want with me?' Jasper demanded.

Erik feigned offence with a hand to the heart. 'Is that any way to thank us for our hospitality? We invited you here out of the goodness of our hearts because it is time to put our differences aside. Please, stay and enjoy yourself.'

Jasper cast a dubious eye in Neve's direction before returning his attention to their hosts. 'Fine. I'll bite. Show me where the booze is at.'

Pointing towards the tubs of drinks, Erick smiled with devious delight. 'Please join me, Neve.' He gestured toward the vacant camp chair between the twins.

A few gasps wafted across the night air.

Tiptoeing forward, Neve kept scanning her surrounds for traps or surprise attacks. When none came, she took the final step and lowered herself into the green canvas seat.

'Please make yourself comfortable too, Caitlin,' Erik implored.

Neve watched as Caitlin settled into a vacant chair on the outskirts of the throng. *Does he plan to divide and conquer?*

A boy approached, presenting her with a beverage tray. He was shirtless, although he wore a black necktie to match his black pants.

She wanted to turn him away, but Erik narrowed his eyes. 'Please, I insist.'

Yielding to the pressure, she took what looked like a glass of cola and hoped no one had spiked it with any drugs. 'Thank you.' One sip told her it was anything but straight cola. She spluttered, trying to swallow the strong taste of alcohol. 'What is this?'

'Bourbon and cola, Miss,' the 'waiter' replied.

'Is it not to your taste?' Erik asked.

'No, it's fine. I didn't expect the bourbon.' Neve downed another mouthful. Armed with the benefit of hindsight, she braced herself for the alcohol burn. It was easier to digest this time. The bourbon went some way to soothing her nerves when Erik and Elna engaged her in small talk.

'What sort of music do you like, Neve?' Erik's deep, green eyes watched her with genuine interest.

'Most forms of EDM, especially trance. I'm keen to learn club and hip-hop dancing someday.'

He arched an eyebrow. 'You like to dance?'

Neve nodded. 'I did jazz ballet when I was a kid, and it was heaps of fun.'

'I'll have to keep that in mind. My own taste in music is more obscure, likely due to my grandmother's influence. Ever heard of trip hop?'

She shook her head. 'Is it a subgenre of hip-hop?'

Erik laughed. 'Yes and no. Honestly, I think it sounds more like jazz fusion with elements of hip-hop sounds. It was a popular genre in the 1990s and I'd love to see a revival.'

'Sounds interesting. Can you recommend any groups?'

'Portishead is a personal favourite. Check them out sometime.'

'Will do.'

As the night wore on, most of the party had moved into the lake. 'Time for a swim,' Erik declared as he rose from his seat.

Elna prompted Neve to stand with her, and they both followed Erik to the water. Throwing her dress aside, Neve drew several sets of eyes as she revealed her red bikini. Confident in her figure, she had expected the attention. But Erik's brief, heated stare caught her off-guard. Acting nonchalant, he tried to pretend he had not checked her out. She knew he had though. Prickles of awareness touched her skin whenever his eyes fell upon her.

Neve swam out until the depths covered her chest. Erik waded through the water, standing right in front of her. She could feel Elna closing in behind her and her heart raced as the pair of them caged her in. *Surely, they won't try to drown me in front of all these people, will they?*

'I'm beginning to see how you got your reputation, despite your virginal status,' Erik remarked after another glance toward her cleavage.

'Not fair. Those rumours were *your* fault, and you know it.'

'Is that so?'

She glared at him. 'What makes you so sure I'm a virgin, anyway?'

Mischief sparkled in his eyes. 'Please, Neve. I'm a fae enchanter. Looking at someone's aura tells me if they are sexually active.'

Fascinated, Neve put her personal feelings aside for a moment. 'Really? I'm still learning to read auras myself. How do you distinguish?'

'People with an active sex life will always have a faint ring of bright red between their inner and outer aura. The more action they get, the more pronounced the ring.'

'Wow. Way cool.'

Erik grinned as the heat of Elna's body pushed into Neve's back.

'It's time to act now, Neve,' Erik stated.

She tensed. 'W-what do I need to do?'

'Don't look now, but we have an audience. Let's give them a good show.'

Neve wasn't sure she liked where this was going. 'What do you mean?'

'I mean no pulling away or acting repulsed when I kiss you. I want you to pretend you are enjoying yourself.'

Oh shit! Neve did not need to look to know Jasper was watching. It was the whole point of having him there. *Erik intends to make Jasper jealous. To take everything of his, including his girl.* She had to admit it was impressive as far as evil, sadistic schemes went. What the twins had not banked on was her pact with Jasper. They promised each other, no matter what happened, it was all pretend. Still, it sucked to be offering up her first kiss to a boy she hated rather than one she loved.

'Are you ready?' he asked.

'Yeah,' she muttered breathlessly.

His hand caressed her cheek as he placed his lips against hers, gentle at first. But he demanded more the moment his body sandwiched her against Elna. The contact lit a fire inside, and she moaned into his mouth. Erik took it as an invitation to slip his tongue between her teeth, exploring the taste of her. Neve became acutely aware of the tang of his own citrus flavours tingling her tastebuds. Her mind was racing. She couldn't focus on any specific detail for long. When Elna began dropping soft, feathery kisses along her neck, she bucked against Erik's hard body.

Not only did their mouths push her pleasure points, but the twins surrounded Neve with soft, platinum hair as their hands roamed across her body. She lost track of who was touching her where. Without thinking, Neve reached her arms up behind Erik's neck and deepened their kiss.

'Mm, you even convinced me,' Erik mused as he pulled back with a smirk. 'Good work, Neve.' Flinging an arm across her shoulder, he turned them to face their spectators.

Neve's knees wobbled as a medley of emotions messed with her faculties. But Jasper's eyes wrenched her back into the cold, harsh reality of her situation. He was trembling and his eyes swelled with the threat of tears. *Oh Gods, Jas!*

'By Royal decree,' Erik announced in a booming voice, 'Neve Winters is now a member of the noble ranks. I grant her all the privileges and protection befitting her station. Elna and I also claim Neve for ourselves. This means no one shall touch her intimately in *any* way without seeking our express permission.'

What the—? This was not part of the deal. Neve watched with horror as Jasper turned away from the scene. Lobbing his beer bottle in the fire, he stumbled away.

Council meetings were the last thing Alannah felt up to after her rendezvous in Sydney. 'It's too damn early,' she grumbled as Liam stood at the foot of her bed with his arms crossed.

'I can't believe I'm having more difficulty rousing a grown-arse woman than my teenage daughter. Neve's already out of bed despite being tired from staying up all night doing Gods know what. What's your excuse?' Liam demanded.

Morning grumps got the better of her. 'I spent the *whole* night fucking Tyler.'

Liam's nostrils flared. 'You're done pretending now, huh?'

'You asked.'

'Can we save this discussion for tomorrow's counselling session? The emergency summons is important. It relates to the volcanoes.'

Alannah lurched up in bed. 'Why didn't you start with that?'

His shoulders deflated with a sigh. 'You are a member of the Council; I shouldn't need to give you reasons to attend meetings.'

'So sorry I don't share your love of bureaucratic bullshit. Give me a few minutes to shower and dress.'

'Fine!' He snapped, slamming the door on his way out.

Hoping for answers, Alannah moved through her morning routine in a hurried blur. 'Has Kieran finally pulled his head out of his arse?' she asked, slumping into the passenger seat of Liam's SUV.

'There are too many concerned parties for him to ignore the possibility of dark magic at play.'

'About time.' They continued the rest of the drive in uncomfortable silence.

With the frivolous formalities out the way, High Magus Kieran turned to Liam. 'Warlock Winters, please tell us what you know.'

Alannah's eyes popped out of their sockets when she turned her attention toward Liam.

'Thank you, Your Honour,' Liam began. 'A mermage recently approached me with news of the ocean's volcanoes. They are erupting all around the world and she believes her people are at risk. The mermages believe magic is behind this volcanic activity. They would like to form a coalition with us to combat the threat.'

Alannah held Liam's gaze as he finished his explanation. *Is he having an affair with a mermaid?* She knew she had no grounds to complain, but the likelihood of losing him outright increased tenfold if he were. Her heart began palpitating at the prospect.

'Lady Alannah, you raised similar concerns when the first volcano erupted in Melbourne. What gave you cause for alarm?' Kieran asked.

You mean aside from realising I might lose my husband? 'Call it a woman's intuition, I suppose. Why else would a dormant volcano defy all scientific theories? It went off five-thousand years early. The way the rest of them have been waking up in a direct line toward our state also supports my theory.'

'You haven't had any contact from the dark magic underbelly?'

Fuck! Does he know Brendan is in town? That we have spoken? 'No one has approached me about this matter, no.'

'Not what I asked, Lady Winters.'

'Yes, my brother paid us a visit,' Liam interjected. While most of the assembly gasped, Nora's reaction was the most pronounced.

'What was the purpose of his call?' Kieran asked.

'Family issues,' Alannah replied. 'Nothing to do with volcanoes or dark magic.'

'That may be so, but both of you should have reported to me. Keep me abreast of all communication with Brendan Winters, solicited, or otherwise.'

'Yes, Your Honour. It was remiss of me to keep you out of the loop. I apologise.' Liam's grovelling tone could have curdled cream.

Kieran looked at Alannah.

'Yes, Your Honour,' she mumbled.

'Right, back to the matter at hand. I want you all to investigate these volcanoes using everything at your disposal. Report back to me as soon as you learn anything useful.' He dismissed them, but called out as Alannah approached the door, 'Lady Winters? A word please.'

She exchanged a concerned look with Liam. 'I'll wait in the hall,' he assured her.

When the door clicked shut, Alannah turned to face Kieran with trepidation. 'What is it, Your Honour?'

'What family issue brought Brendan back to town after all this time?'

'I'm sorry, but it's a personal matter, Your Honour.'

Kieran's brow furrowed. 'Being a Council member makes all your family and personal matters my business.'

Alannah recalled the bugs in her house and shivered. 'He wanted to meet Neve. He recently learnt of her existence.'

'Why would he have interest in your daughter?'

She squirmed under his scrutiny, not wanting to admit the truth of Neve's parentage. 'Brendan thought he might be Neve's father, because of the timing of her conception.'

'But she is a blessed child, yes?'

'Yes, Your Honour.'

'Which means he has no right to question her fathering.'

'Indeed.' She gave him a fierce look, demanding him to drop the subject.

'But he knows something that justifies his suspicions, correct?'

'With all due respect, Your Honour, why are we still discussing such heresy?'

'I cannot turn a blind eye to the implications of a dark mage fathering someone with Neve's... gifts.'

Her blood boiled with red-hot rage. 'Are you suggesting he tainted my daughter?'

'No, not at all. But she is young and may be susceptible to Brendan's influence, especially if she learns the truth. Did you know he has been training her?'

'*What?*'

'I'll take that as a no. I don't like telling parents how to do their jobs. But when it comes to magic and its potential misuse, I have every right to step in. You need to keep a closer eye on Neve.'

'Thank you for your concerns, Your Honour. I will deal with her. Is that all?'

'Yes.'

Alannah stormed out of the boardroom, marching straight passed Liam.

'What's wrong, Lana? What did Kieran want?' Liam hurried to keep up with her.

'He knows.'

'Knows what?'

She waited until they sat in the car. 'The identity of Neve's bio dad.'

Liam's jaw dropped. 'Oh. Shit.'

At least I know who wired the house.

Anxiety reigned supreme in Neve's trembling body as she stood on the threshold of Jasper's house. *Is our date even on still? Only one way to find out.* She rang the bell with a hesitant hand.

He took his time answering and when he did, the dark circles around Jasper's eyes clenched at her heart. 'Oh hey. I didn't think you were still coming.' Moving aside, he gestured for her to enter.

At least he isn't turning me away. Stepping passed him, Neve took in his dishevelled appearance. Grey wrinkled t-shirt, black track pants. and tousled hair. *Yet he still manages to look hot as hell.* 'Why would you think that? We promised each other, Jas.'

'Sorry, I guess I found your acting too believable. Gods, it looked like he took you straight to second base.'

'Jasper, please. It was just a kiss and it meant nothing.' She drew close enough to touch his face gingerly. She was not lying, even if Erik did blow her mind with the most erotic kiss of all time.

He snatched her hand by the wrist, squeezing it in his large hands. 'Your first kiss should've been with *me*.'

Neve's eyes began to water. 'I know. I'm sorry, but I—'

He shoved her against the wall and claimed her lips with such violence it felt like a clash of wills. It was a far cry from what she expected of her first kiss with him. Yet there was something about the urgency of it, the rawness. Neve swooned as she returned the kiss. 'Did he fuck you?' Jasper rasped in her ear.

'What? No! Jas—'

'So, you're still a virgin?'

She wanted to be mad at him for asking, but she could not. Not with everything the Alvarsson twins had done to him, to them. Her expression softened as she nodded. The moment her feet left the ground, Neve shrieked. 'What are you doing?'

'Taking you to my room.'

'I can walk on my own.'

'I know.' He met her eyes with an impish grin. When they reached their destination, he kicked the door shut behind them and lay her across his bed. Pinning her down on the queen-sized mattress, he kissed her again. Jasper filled her senses with the welcome taste and fragrance of coffee. After tickling her neck with his breath, Jasper's gruff voice sounded in her ear, 'Have you ever orgasmed, Neve?'

Her heart skipped a beat as she sucked in a breath. 'N-no.'

'Splendid. It's one first I can take before *he* does.'

Neve gasped. 'Jas! I'd never go there with Erik.'

'I bet you thought the same about kissing him too. I'm not gonna take my chances.' His hands moved to her thighs where he slowly lifted the hem of her dress.

Her eyes grew wider. 'I-I'm not ready for sex, Jas.'

The house could have burned down from the heat in his eyes. 'Don't worry, baby. I'm not gonna take things that far… yet. You'll have to beg me for it when the time is right. I want to make you feel good… with these.' He wiggled his fingers in her face.

A lump formed in her throat as she tried to swallow. 'O-okay.'

The sexiest smile took over Jasper's features. After removing her panties, he straddled her legs and stared at her bare flesh.

Neve's cheeks flushed with embarrassment. 'Jas?'

'Wax or shave?'

'What?' she croaked out her response.

The soft tips of his fingers brushed across her mound, covering her body in goosebumps. 'How do you get this so smooth? Waxing or shaving?'

'Neither.'

Jasper's faced paled. 'Oh hell, Neve, I—'

The cause of his concern dawned on her, so she cut him off before he continued getting the wrong idea. 'I use magic. Don't worry, I've started puberty.'

His eyes bugged out. 'Damn, girl! Most chicks don't start this sort of grooming until they are much older. And I've never heard of them using magic in a non-glamour way. This is... hardcore.'

A nervous laugh slipped out. 'I don't like having hair there. It's messy.'

'I can't say I disagree with you.' His mouth curved into a lop-sided grin. 'Now I'm dying to go down on you.'

Her body jerked under his touch. 'Jesus, Jas, you're killing me here.'

'In a good or bad way?' He waggled his brows, prompting Neve to snort. 'Again, I promise I'm not going all the way today, not unless you want me to.'

Releasing her breath, Neve smiled. 'Thank you.'

'Don't thank me yet, sweetheart. I haven't even started.' Without further ado, his fingers slid lower. Prying apart her folds, he stroked against her opening.

Closing her eyes, Neve lost herself in the sensations Jasper ignited within her core. He started slow, one finger at first. The teasing exasperated her. Before long, she was grinding against his hand, wanting more friction.

Jasper groaned and plunged two more fingers deep inside her. 'By the Gods, you are beautiful, Neve!'

The combination of his hand action and the words spoken by his deep, masculine voice sent her over the edge. She cried out something unintelligible as the pressure in her core (and head) exploded. It took a few minutes for the fuzzy, coloured spots to vanish from her vision and a few more to find her words. 'Fucking hell!'

His weight shifted above her. Jasper's brown eyes shone with pride... among other emotions as he smiled above her. 'I'll take that as a compliment.' He followed up with more kisses, sending her into oblivion for the rest of the afternoon.

Liam watched as Rose crossed her legs and opened her notepad. She offered one of her fake smiles. 'How have things been since our last session?'

He gave some thought to how much their relationship had declined in such a short period. 'Worse than ever.'

'I second that,' Alannah agreed.

At least we can reach consensus on something.

'How so? What has transpired between you?'

'More arguments,' explained Alannah. 'And things feel more tense.'

'Why do you think that is?'

'*She won't stop fucking Tyler!*' Liam blurted out with all the venom he had been suppressing.

Rose's eyes widened with alarm at his outburst. 'It is good to get your feelings out in the open, Liam. But remember these sessions are a safe place for *both* of you. Rather than pointing the finger, try explaining how you feel about what happened.'

'Fine, you want to know how I feel, Lana?'

With her gaze downcast, Alannah fidgeted with her fingers. She peeked up at him and nodded.

'After a fifteen-and-a-half-year drought, I find out you've been having an affair. Learning you were cheating on me because I'm lousy in bed was bad enough. Then I find out you're sleeping with

Tyler. Not only is he my friend, but he is also a dead ringer for my brother. And you're *still* seeing him. Knowing all this makes me feel betrayed, furious, frustrated, devastated, and... worthless.'

Alannah's eyes were brimming with tears. 'I-I'm sorry.'

Rose handed Alannah a tissue box. 'Before we proceed with these sessions, we need to explore Alannah's feelings more. Are you in love with Tyler?'

The seconds Alannah took to blow her nose and wipe her eyes were excruciating. 'No. He is a great friend and I love him, but I'm not *in* love with him.'

'Thank you, Alannah. Why have been seeking sexual gratification outside of your marriage?'

'At first it was because Tyler is the spitting image of Brendan. I was struggling to let go.' She paused to clear her nose again. 'But if that was all there was to it, I would have remained intimate with Liam. It has more to do with our incompatibility in the bedroom.'

'Go on,' Rose encouraged her.

'Liam is too straight-edged, too... gentle with me.'

'You like rough sex?' Rose inquired.

Alannah snorted. 'To put it mildly.' She turned to face Liam. 'I've tried to tell you before, but I don't think you ever understood what I meant. I'm a complete masochist. I don't just enjoy pain; I *need* it to achieve full satisfaction. I also prefer to forgo all control during sex.'

He shook his head in disbelief. 'Are you saying you let Tyler hurt you?'

'Yeah, that's exactly what I'm saying.'

Memories of something Richard Lane once said, during their kidnapping, returned to Liam. 'Is this a side of yourself you discovered with Brendan?'

'Yes and no. I explored it much more with Brendan, but I was already aware of my kink to some extent long before we ever hooked up. It probably started with Cole, or…'

'What?'

'Maybe it did start with Brendan… when we were kids, and he was always the rogue.'

Shit! How had I been so naïve and stupid? A horrid realisation set in. 'Is this my fault? Did you develop this fetish because I always cast Brendan in that role?'

Alannah shrugged. 'Hard to say. All I know is the way he caught me and pinned me down was thrilling, and this played into my fantasies when I hit puberty.'

Liam clenched his teeth. Hearing Alannah talk about her feelings for Brendan stung like barbs of wire. 'Am I a lost cause? Because I'm not kinky enough for you?'

'I don't know.' Alannah chewed on her bottom lip.

His heart sank deeper into despair.

'I hope not,' she added. 'Because I am still in love with you.'

Liam shot her a look of surprise. 'Really?'

Alannah nodded. 'Really.'

'A promising sign,' Rose suggested. 'It sounds like you both want to make things work. Try heating things up in the bedroom.'

He could feel the glimmer of hope he clutched at slipping from his grip. *How the hell do I spice things up enough for Lana when the thought of hitting a woman repulses me so much.*

Chapter Ten

Luna greeted them with a demanding *meeeooow*. The moment Alannah put her foot through the front door, the cat pounced on it and clawed at her leg. 'Hey kitty, you must be starving by now.' Monday night counselling sessions ran late, well past dinner time. They had stuffed their faces with drive-through burgers on the way home.

'Why hasn't Neve's lazy arse fed her yet?' Liam grumbled behind her. After kicking off his boots, he shuffled down the hall after Alannah.

'Good question.' She spooned a serving of stinky fish into Luna's bowl and dropped it on the kitchen floor.

'Neve!' hollered Liam. No response. 'The brat sound-proofed her room again. Why did you have to teach her that warding spell?' Liam asked.

'Would you rather listen to her hideous techno music blasting at all hours?' Alannah jogged upstairs to Neve's bedroom. No sign of her. *Shit!*

'*Neve*?' she cried out. Flying down the stairs, she tried to outrun her racing heart. 'She's not upstairs!'

'I'm sure she's okay.' Liam assured her. 'She's probably at Caitlin's and forgot to message us.'

'She never forgets! Jesus, Liam, how can you be so calm about this?'

'Because you need me to be. I'll ring Steve, see if Neve is there, or if he knows where she is.'

Alannah nodded, thankful for Liam's cool head in a crisis. *Must be from his training as a cop.* Perching on the edge of the couch arm, she gnawed away at the inside of her lip. She had recently developed the habit to cope with her elevated stress levels. *Better than drowning myself in a bottle of Jameson's, right?*

'Hey man … Neve's not home. Is she at your place? … I see … Much appreciated, thanks.' Liam held the phone away from his ear as he addressed Alannah, 'She's not there, but Steve is checking if Caitlin knows anything.' Sitting on the couch beside her, he pulled her into his arms.

She fell into his lap, letting him hold her.

'Yeah man, I'm here … Who? Are you fucking serious? … Sorry, I didn't mean to snap at *you* … thanks for your help.' Liam signed off and the throbbing vein in his temple appeared ready to burst. 'According to Caitlin, Neve is at her *boyfriend's* house.'

'What boyfriend?'

'Those were my thoughts exactly. My warnings were not enough. She is with Jasper Rowan.'

Bile shot up Alannah's oesophagus, and she swallowed hard to suppress it. She had heard about Jasper's man-whoring ways. Signs suggested he would follow in his uncle's footsteps.

'Do you want me to retrieve her?' Liam's stern voice betrayed the rage brewing inside him.

Alannah sighed. 'I don't think it will help the situation. She's being rebellious. If you drag her out of there kicking and screaming, she will run back to him. It's about time I had a heart-to-heart with her.'

The front door slammed, and Neve appeared a moment later.

Feeling like a weight had lifted from her chest, Alannah breathed easier. 'Hi sweetie. Is everything okay?'

Neve beamed. 'Never been better.' Pausing, she took in the sight of Alannah sitting in Liam's lap. 'Looks like the marriage counselling is working out. I should leave you two lovebirds alone.'

Alannah felt Liam's muscles tense.

In her attempt to make a quick escape, Neve turned toward the stairs.

'Neve, honey. I was hoping we could have a chat.'

She froze. 'Is this about my lack of message?' Turning back, she wore a coy smile. 'I'm sorry. I didn't think I would be out so long.'

'You thought you could sneak around behind our backs while we were out?' Liam demanded with an accusing tone.

'Liam, please, let me handle this,' Alannah pleaded. 'Neve, it shouldn't matter how long you are taking, or where you are. It is important to let us know in case something happens. But that's not what I wanted to talk about.'

'Oh?'

'I'm gonna excuse myself from this one.' Liam patted Alannah's thigh as he rose.

She let him leave the room and summoned Neve to join her on the sofa.

'This isn't "the sex talk" is it? Because I don't think I need any more of those.'

Alannah sighed. 'There is a lot more to sex than the mechanics of round peg in round hole and the use of protection. Think of this as more of a relationship talk.'

Neve rolled her eyes and collapsed beside Alannah. 'Go on.'

'I was younger than you when I lost my virginity,' Alannah explained. She supressed a smile at the way Neve's mouth gaped open. 'Eleven to be exact. I barely knew the guy. While it didn't bother me then, in hindsight I regret not waiting for a more meaningful first time. I'm not talking hearts and flowers. I've never been much of a romantic, but it would have been nice to give my virginity to a boy who respected me. I gave it away free and easy back then because I did not value myself enough.'

Neve gasped.

'I don't know if my hedonistic nature was the problem, but there were some men who took advantage of me. The first perpetrator was a vampire who wanted to turn me.' She closed her eyes and took a deep breath.

'Yeah, I heard about Austin,' Neve whispered.

Snapping her eyes open, Alannah stared at Neve intensely. 'Who told you?'

'Caitlin.'

'Figures. Monique must have told her. The thing is, Austin claimed to love me, and I have no doubt he had told the truth. He just had a funny way of showing it. I suffered far worse at the hands of other men whose intentions were anything but pure. One such offender was Clayton Rowan, Jasper's uncle. He was a respected warlock for the Council, and we used to be friends. I knew he was a womaniser, but it wasn't until my short stay in prison that I got a taste of it. I never led him on or showed interest in him, but it didn't matter. He saw what he wanted and took it without asking. He raped me, Neve.' The tears brimming beneath the surface stung.

With wide eyes, Neve hugged Alannah. 'I-I'm sorry Mum. It must have been horrible. But Jasper is not like his uncle. He is sweet and kind. And—'

Alannah jerked back, shaking her head. 'You don't need to defend Jasper. I'm not going to tell you who you should and shouldn't sleep with, Neve. That would be far too hypocritical of me given what I got up to in my teenage years. I hope you will take something away from the harsh lessons I have learned. Give more thought to the people you open your heart and body to.'

'Okay Mum. Thanks for the chat.' Neve rose and took two steps before turning back. 'Caitlin also mentioned what Uncle Brendan did to you.'

Every muscle in Alannah's body stiffened.

'I'm guessing it's a story for another day, but when you feel ready, I'd like to hear it.'

'Thanks, hun. Goodnight.'

'Night, Mum.'

After a few deep breaths, Alannah ventured upstairs, pausing when she reached Liam's door.

'Come in,' Liam called out from his bed. He put the latest edition of the *White Waves* magazine on the nightstand.

Alannah appeared in the doorway. 'Hey.' Long black hair framed her face in a tangled mess thanks to her daughter-induced panic attack. But she still looked gorgeous.

'Hey. How did things go with Neve?'

'Okay.' She tiptoed forward, treating their marital bed like foreign territory she feared invading.

Liam patted the space beside him, hoping to relieve her anxieties. He had never shut her out of their room or bed—that was all on her. 'What's the deal with her and Jasper?'

A heavy sigh slipped from her plump lips as she settled on the edge of the mattress. 'I'm not sure. She was quick to defend his merits, even after

I shocked her with the story of Clayton. But she appeared to take note of my implied warning.'

'I hope so.'

She glanced at his magazine and laughed. 'Your idea of water sports is much different to mine.' Her fidgeting hand toyed with the quilt, drawing his eye. Before he realised what he was doing, Liam's fingers crawled over to join it. Alannah sucked in a sharp breath at the initial contact, and they met each other's gaze. Her eyes widened with surprise, but she did not pull her hand away. Alannah's lids lowered, and her pupils dilated.

The air thickened around them, and Liam parted his lips to make breathing easier. His mouth movement captured Alannah's attention. Having her eyes fixed on him... stirred Liam's emotions... and desires. His left hand shot up to grab the back of her neck, wrenching her against him, and he stole a kiss from her. She remained rigid at first, and Liam worried he was pushing her too far, too fast. But she groaned a second later and yielded.

Christ! I've missed this so damn much! Her mouth still tasted like musk sticks. The strawberry fragrance emanating from her hair filled his nose, urging him on. As his arousal intensified, doubts crept in. *Am I even turning her on?* With the way she was straddling him, Liam knew Alannah could feel how much he wanted her.

Grinding her hips against him, Alannah moaned, vanquishing his prior misgivings. With her dress hitched up to her waist, only two layers of fabric stood between them and sex: satin and lace. The true barriers to entry were not tangible though.

Her mouth moved to his ear. 'Fuck me, Liam. Fuck me hard.'

'Mm, Gods, you have no idea how much I've wanted to hear you say that. I want you so much right now, but I'm afraid to disappoint you again. I don't think I can do the… stuff you like.'

Alannah's eyes looked deep into his own. 'What if we start with something easy?'

'Like what?'

'Pin my arms down and have your way with me.'

Is it wrong to feel so excited by her proposal? 'I should be able to manage that.' Tugging her dress over her head gave him an idea. He tucked the material behind her neck. Using the garment to help pin her arms in place, he pushed her back against the bed. Alannah moaned, and Liam could smell the way her core flooded with carnal need. Slipping a hand inside her black lace panties confirmed his assumption. He ripped the soaking wet lingerie down her legs.

Making use of her natural lubricant, he thrust all four fingers of his right hand inside. A guttural noise emerged from the depths of her diaphragm. Using his thumb, he applied pressure to her clit.

'*Fuck!*' she hissed.

Fearing he had hurt her, he instinctively eased back.

'Don't you dare stop!'

Oh hell. I'd almost forgotten how hot she was when she got horny like this. 'Is this okay?'

'Absolutely. I can take a lot more, baby. If by some chance you exceed my threshold, I'll be sure to let you know. Now stop asking and start taking.'

He took his time teasing her, making her squirm beneath him before tearing an orgasm from her with his hand. The next time she came was courtesy of his mouth. Liam was dragging the foreplay out as much as possible. He told himself it was to maximise her pleasure, but it was partly due to the niggling nerves messing with his mind.

During her third climax, she was bucking against him, grazing herself on his teeth. He knew he could not put things off any longer. Fumbling with his boxer shorts like a damn virgin, he mumbled a curse. 'Shit.' He took a deep breath to settle his nerves. Plunging deep inside his wife, he fucked her for the first time in over fifteen years.

When the haze wore off, Liam heard music blaring through the walls from the neighbouring room.

Alannah snorted. 'Oops. We should have put up a soundproofing ward.'

Scooping her into his arms, he spooned her warm, quivering body. 'She could have put up her own. Besides, our daughter's sensitivities were the last thing on my mind.' He emphasised his point with a nip of the skin beneath her ear.

'Mm.' Minutes later, Alannah's breathing softened, and she slipped off to sleep within Liam's embrace.

A horse-drawn carriage was waiting for her when Neve stepped outside the next morning. Even before spotting Erik, she knew it would be him. Seelie fae were not fond of cars because of their environmental impact. Yet she had not been expecting a royal freaking coach! After jogging down the front steps and along the path, she greeted him with a shy smile. 'Um, hi.'

'Morning, Neve. Given you are now mine, I thought it best we ride to school together.'

The shock of his words made her jump back. 'Firstly, what? Secondly… what?'

A sly grin crept across his lips.

Lips that taste and feel amazing. Neve startled herself, wondering where those unwanted thoughts came from.

'I missed you yesterday. Apologies for my absence, but there were… family matters to attend to. It was remiss of me not to assure you I had not forgotten our deal.'

Neve could only blink.

Erik drew closer, tucking a strand of hair behind her ear as his eyes sought hers. 'Nor have I forgotten our kiss.'

'Th-that meant nothing. It was a show to hurt Jasper.'

'Stop fooling yourself, Neve. You and I both know you weren't faking the extent of pleasure you exuded. You may not have displayed your aura, but I could *feel* the connection.'

Shit! No wonder the scene upset Jasper so much. 'So what? I got a little caught up in the moment. It still meant nothing.'

He circled Neve, pausing with his mouth inches away from the back of her neck. Erik's breath tickled her protruding vertebrae. Shivers travelled down her spine and tendrils of goosebumps shot across her skin. 'Why do you continue to resist me?' he inquired with a menacing tone.

'What do you want from me, Erik?'

'I thought I made my intentions clear when I claimed you. Now come on, I don't like being late.' He moved to the door of the carriage and gestured for her to enter.

Averse to appearing ignorant, Neve resolved to investigate fae claims through other channels. Climbing inside, she found Elna staring out the window with a look of impatient boredom.

'About time,' she huffed.

'Try to play nice, Elna,' Erik jeered.

Squashed between their imposing forms, Neve struggled to breathe. The movement of their vehicle jolted her brain back into place. 'Wait! What about Caitlin?'

Erik turned toward her, placing a hand on her thigh. 'What about her?'

Jesus! The warmth and pressure of his hand feels too damn good. 'I had plans to meet her at the café and walk with her. It's our morning routine.'

'I'm sure she is capable of purchasing coffee and finding the schoolyard without you holding her hand,' Erik replied callously. 'Send her a text to let her know your plans have changed.'

Prickling heat enveloped Neve as her blood boiled with rage. 'I never agreed to turn my back on Caitlin. You said she was welcome, and I'm not prepared to abandon my best friend.'

Elna snickered. 'This one's feisty. I can respect a woman with guts to stand up to you, Brother.' Leaning in toward her, Elna began playing with Neve's long, black locks. 'I could like her after all.'

Erik sighed. 'Fine. If it means so much to you, we will pick up Caitlin on the way.'

'Thank you.' Neve began to wonder what she had gotten herself into. *How much intimate contact will they expect from me? Should I let them use my body for the sake of my plan? What price am I willing to pay in my attempt to ruin them?*

Caitlin had never been one to stay quiet. Yet the sight of Neve arriving at their meeting spot in a horse-drawn carriage struck her dumb.

'He insisted on taking me to school,' Neve whispered by way of explanation when she hugged Caitlin.

Neve returned to her position between the Alvarsson twins and Caitlin sat opposite.

'What do you think of the music I sent you?' Erik asked once they were moving again.

'I haven't heard it yet.'

'And why not?' he demanded.

Neve scowled at him. 'Oh, I'm sorry, I didn't realise it was compulsory listening.'

Titters burst from Elna's lips, and she became even more touchy-feely with Neve.

The chill of Erik's reciprocated glare approached absolute zero. 'As an honoured subject of mine, you ought to see the merit in showing interest in the things that please me.'

Biting her lip, Neve cast her eyes in Caitlin's direction. She chided herself for being so pig-headed about something so insignificant. *It will not do to anger him so much if I want to get close enough to learn their dirty little secrets.* 'I'll check it out tonight.'

He graced her with a smile. 'Thank you, Neve. It's all I ask.'

Yeah right.

Elna's hands travelled all over Neve's body. The intimate contact drew Caitlin's attention, who glanced at Neve with sad eyes. Then she jerked her gaze to the view out the window.

Oh crap! Now Caitlin's jealous of the twins too. It was not like Neve wanted Elna to touch her. Pushing Elna away would endanger the progress of her scheme, however; the same went for Erik. At least she kept telling herself as much.

The tragic news came by way of phone call from Emma Tuesday morning: *'Cole is dead.'*

Alannah did her best to console Emma, the very picture of a grieving widow. Once the conversation ended, she snuggled with Luna on the couch. She shed her own tears of grief for the loss of a good friend. Sandpaper kisses tickled her wet cheek and she smiled at her kitty cat. 'Thank you, sweet girl.' Sorrow turned to simmering rage as she thought about the nature of Cole's death. She grew more desperate for answers. *It's time for my last resort.* Grabbing the fresh burner phone, she sent a text to Brendan: I NEED INFORMATION. PLEASE MEET ME AT MY HOUSE — EBONY.

His reply came seconds later: OK, BUT SO WE'RE CLEAR, I'M NOT RETURNING YOUR PANTIES.

The groan slipping from her throat consisted of nine parts cringe and one part… arousal. *Get a grip woman! Don't forget how the arsehole broke your heart.* She pushed aside images of Brendan jerking off while holding her black lace G-string. Instead, she focused on memories of the amazing night she had spent with her *husband*.

Not even bothering to knock, Brendan snuck in through the back door. He wore one of his sexy-as-fuck business suits. A startled gasp slipped from Alannah. After shushing her with a hand signal, he pointed to various points around the room to remind her of the bugs.

Nodding her understanding, Alannah made them both a coffee and offered him a chair in her dining area. Grabbing the shopping list notepad and pen, she paused when an idea occurred to her. Picking up the television remote, she switched on a free-to-air news channel. *Should cloak any noise or suspicious lack thereof.* Once seated, she scrawled a note in messy cursive: *I NEED TO MEET YOU AT A SECURE LOCATION. DO YOU KNOW ANYWHERE SAFE?*

Brendan grabbed the pen and waggled his brows as he slipped his reply across to her. WHAT'S WRONG WITH YOUR BEDROOM? His neat handwriting surprised her.

After an eye roll, she wrote: *NEED SOMEWHERE ALLOWING FOR MORE TIME AND NOISE.*

His brows skyrocketed, then his eyes lowered in a lustful gaze before he responded. HAVE YOU FINALLY COME TO YOUR SENSES, LANA?

'What? Oh.' She scribbled her response on the page. *I'M NOT TALKING ABOUT SEX. I NEED TO DISCUSS SYNDICATE STUFF AND LIAM COULD WALK IN ANY MINUTE.*

He eyed her a moment before replying, FOLLOW ME. Brendan strode upstairs and into Alannah's bedroom. He eased the door shut behind her and cast a soundproofing ward with the click of a finger. She stared in awe at his efficiency. Drawing close to her, he spoke in a hushed voice. 'What's going on, Lana? Looks to me like you've been crying and now you're asking *me* of all people for information.'

'Why are we still whispering?'

'Extra precaution in case my wards don't hold. Now answer my question.'

Heat radiated from Brendan's well-built body, and their proximity distracted her. *His physique is better than Liam's these days.*

Brendan caught her perving on his bulging biceps and gave her a wicked, lop-sided grin.

Turning away, Alannah attempted to hide the colour in her cheeks. 'I want to know who or what is setting off the volcanoes. There must be a magical cause, I'm sure of it. I know you have dark magic contacts in Melbourne, so...'

'Did Kieran put you up to this?' he spat.

She looked deep into his eyes to convey the sincerity of her words. 'No. My interest in this matter is... personal.' More tears trickled down her face.

His stern mask softened as realisation dawned on Brendan's visage. He leaned in to wipe away her tears.

The kind gesture only served to deepen her anguish and with a huge sob, she shoved him. '*What the hell?*' she hissed.

Ignoring her protests, Brendan snatched her into his arms. He held her tight against his solid chest. 'What happened, Lana?'

She choked out her reply between sniffles, 'The volcano... it... it got Cole... he... he's dead.'

'Bloody hell, Lana. I'm sorry.'

Alannah wanted to push him away, to stop his ludicrous antics. But she found too much comfort in his arms. 'Can you hook me up with one of your contacts in Melbourne? At a safe place?'

He nodded. 'I will sort something out and let you know.'

Brushing her mouth against his ear, she whispered, 'Thanks.'

Grabbing her wrist, he sent a jolt of heat straight through the skin and into her veins. 'There are better ways to thank me, Lana,' he rasped, 'and most of them involve your lips somewhere on my body.'

Alannah's heart began to race. She could not hide the evidence either. Not while Brendan pressed her pulse point with his thumb.

Brendan's gaze grew hotter than hellfire as he backed her against the wall. One hand gripped the hem of her dress and the other pinned her wrist above her head. He pressed his weight against her and clamped his teeth down on her earlobe.

'Ah-un-gn,' she mumbled, too engrossed in the sensations he evoked to use her words.

'Admit it, Lana: You still want me!'

Her breathing laboured. *Need. Space.* So, she did the one thing she knew how in her situation: a solid, bony knee straight to his nuts.

Brendan stumbled back and doubled over in pain. 'The fuck?'

With much needed distance between them, she reassembled her emotional fortress. 'Stop being a dick, Brendan.'

'Not until you stop being a bitch.' Glowering, he marched out of her room.

Chapter Eleven

A light tapping at her door roused Alannah from the fugue she had slipped into. Looking up, she met Liam's concerned eyes as he popped his head through the narrow opening of the door.

'Hey. I heard about Cole. Figured you'd need some comforting.'

'How…'

'Cara told me.' Liam pushed the door open wider, admitting the cat. Luna dashed through the opening and leaped onto Alannah's lap.

Amidst the Brendan-induced turmoil, Alannah forgot she had messaged her best friend. She needed Cara to chair the women's lobby group meeting that night because Alannah felt unfit for the job. 'Please, come in.'

He beelined for the spot beside her on the bed and pulled her into his arms. Remaining silent, Liam allowed her to weep against his chest. He was oblivious to the fact she was grieving the loss of not one, but two ex-boyfriends. 'Cole was a good man.

A little odd, but he had a good heart. How is Emma coping?'

After wiping her nose, Alannah looked up into his loving eyes. 'She's not coping at all. Losing Cole devastated the poor girl.'

'I can imagine. The thought of losing you, Lana, in such a... permanent way. Fuck. I don't think I could deal with it.'

Her eyes widened. 'Even after everything I've put you through over the years?'

Liam nodded, tucking strands of hair behind her ears. 'I'm not gonna lie. The way you shut me out all these years was unbearably painful. Then you told me about Tyler... but I always had hope you'd come back to me. And now look at us. Last night was amazing. I meant it when I said I will never leave you again. Whatever happens between us, I am committed to working through it *together*.'

A hideous gurgling noise slipped from Alannah's throat. 'You are too damn good for me.'

'I've always thought the reverse. It's why I feared living up to your expectations after... you know who. Turns out I wasn't half wrong when it came to sex,' he choked out.

'Shit! Liam, I'm so fucking sorry for telling you in such a spiteful way. I wish I had been more open and honest with you in the beginning.'

He shook his head. 'In hindsight, I understand you were trying your best to communicate your needs. I knew what you wanted back then, I just… couldn't. I'm still not sure I can.'

'What you did last night was incredible, Liam. With time we could make it work.'

His hand stopped mid-stroke at the top of her ear. 'Really?'

Biting her bottom lip, Alannah nodded. 'I know you have a dominant streak in you. I've seen it in the way you conduct Council business as well as your police work. I caught a glimpse of it in bed last night. I may be the matriarch of the family now and your equal on the Council. But the bedroom is the one place I like to give up all power and control. I don't expect you to go full sadist on me.' Pausing, she gave him a playful grin. 'Not yet anyway. Do you think you could try to be more… forceful and assertive with me when intimate?'

Exhaling in a sharp breath, his hand trembled as it slid down her back. 'I'm afraid of hurting you, Lana. After what happened with Clayton and Richard—'

She silenced him by placing her fingers on his lips. 'You are nothing like those vile men. Having your way with me will not evoke traumatic memories. I'm not made of glass. But if it worries you, we can use a safe word. If I ever call out the name Richard, it's your cue to stop.'

'Okay. I'll try, but only when you come to me in our room. I want to continue respecting this as your space.'

A pang of rejection cut at her. 'You want to continue sleeping in separate beds?'

'Gods no! I want you to sleep with me all night, every night. But you can always escape here when you need to. This room has been your haven for years and I'll understand if there are nights you need to be alone.'

His sweet, considerate words floored Alannah. *Such a contrast to what Brendan has turned into.* 'Thank you,' she whispered.

Holding her closer, Liam breathed in her scent and froze. 'Fuck!' Jerking back, he stared at her with his mouth agape. 'Why the hell do you smell like Brendan?'

Panic seized her heart, and she blinked a couple of times to clear her thoughts.

Enough time lapsed for Liam to assume the worst. He jumped up and paced the room, combing fingers through his hair. The sudden movement startled Luna, and she scampered to her hiding place beneath the bed.

'It's not what you think, Liam. Nothing happened, okay?'

'If nothing happened, why do you reek of him? Christ! I can't believe I didn't notice earlier. I guess I got too wrapped up in feeling sorry for you—'

'Liam, please,' she screamed. 'He hugged me. That was all. Brendan saw me crying over Cole and… took advantage of my grief to hold me.'

You could have lit a blaze to engulf the entire nation with Liam's volatile eyes. He became livid. 'Are you saying he touched you without invitation or consent?'

'Not express permission, no. But he didn't touch me anywhere… inappropriate.'

He ceased pacing and clenched his hands into fists. 'I'm gonna fucking kill that man.'

'Liam! Please let it go.'

With two long strides, he stood in front of her, staring down into her eyes with a menacing glare. 'Are you defending the arsehole now?'

'No! But I need him—'

Liam's nostrils flared in unison with his eye sockets.

She lowered her voice. 'I need Brendan to help me track down intel on the volcanoes. Kieran asked us to use everything at our disposal, so I'm using my one contact with the dark magic world.'

'He's not your *only* contact, Lana. What about Jacob? As much as I detest the boggart, I'd rather you spend time with him than Brendan.'

'Jacob is out of town on some family business. I don't know when he'll be back.'

'Please Lana, call it what it is. For Jacob, family business is code for dodgy shit. Those unseelies are all a bunch of crooks.'

Alannah wanted to argue and defend Jacob's honour, but she knew it was a moot point. He probably was doing something illegal. 'Quite beside the point. Jacob is out of town, and I can't reach him. So, I asked Brendan for help. It's not like I'm the only Council member who seeks intel from the criminal underworld. But please don't tell Kieran.'

'Fine,' he hissed through gritted teeth. 'But if I catch Brendan touching you in any way, I will smash his head in. I've already been too soft on him considering how much he hurt you.'

She sighed. 'Liam, you need to be more careful with Brendan. He was holding back the last time you wailed on him. But he's not a pushover anymore. If you attack him again, he could retaliate with lethal force.'

Liam scoffed. 'I'd like to see him try. I'm a full-fledged warlock these days, with much more power than in our earlier years.'

'And he is more powerful too. Plus, he has his third attunement.'

'What attunement?'

'I thought you knew. All dark mage initiates connect to the stygian element. He's been channelling nether for years now.'

'Jesus! I had no idea. Can he block my magic like Richard did?'

'Yeah, he can. It's why you need to be careful.'

He collapsed next to her, defeat evident in his eyes. 'How the hell am I supposed to protect my girls from such a dangerous man?'

Climbing into his lap, Alannah wrapped her arms around him like a spider monkey. 'Are you forgetting I can look after myself? If it comes to it, I can use my link to the primordial. But I doubt Brendan will attack me, or Neve.'

Liam growled. 'You're right. But he doesn't need to inflict physical harm to hurt you. He can do enough damage by messing with your head and heart. It scares me to think how much he could get under your skin while you work with him.'

She held him tight, wishing she could reassure him. But he was right, and Brendan had already started burrowing.

As the first rays of daylight filtered through the ocean's surface, Saoirse caught sight of Liam. She knew pursuing anything with the man was pointless. Yet she could not fight the invisible tether pulling her toward him. For an attraction to be so strong, it must be mutual. *So why does he push me away?* Her father's words filled her mind, reminding her of all the things she could never have:

> *You are a warrior, Saoirse. It is a privilege to have such power, but it is also a heavy burden to carry. You will forever remain duty-bound to our clan, and a warrior can never be a lover.*

His voice echoed in her soul. With a flutter of her gills, she surged upwards, determined to have a little fun in the name of training. She watched, letting Liam's manoeuvres enthral her. He rode an enormous wave he had summoned with his elemental attunement. His sculpted face glistened from hundreds of tiny droplets of water. Liam's thick, brown hair was wet and tousled, gleaming in the light of dawn and showing hints of sun-kissed gold. Saoirse's eyes trailed down the length of his torso. The navy-blue wetsuit he wore was a perfect fit, highlighting every impressive muscle.

Blinking, she broke from her trance as a daring thought came to her. She channelled physical forces and flipped Liam's board. This sent him crashing into the deep blue sea.

Liam startled at first but recovered in time to close his lungs off from the drowning tide clawing at him. With strong arms and legs, he pushed past the current and broke through the surface in no time.

Pulling up alongside him, Saoirse could not hold back the giggles.

He spun around to face her, his mouth agape. 'You did that?'

'Uh huh.' More laughter burst from her.

A stunning smile crossed his face, and ripples of mirth resonated across his own vocal cords. 'I didn't realise we were duelling.' Something wicked flickered in his eyes. 'You know this means war, right?' One side of his mouth curled into a sly grin.

'Oh, I know.' She returned his devious expression. 'You'll have to catch me first.' Ducking into the water, she propelled herself up into the sky before diving into the depths. Saoirse continued her tricks, but she failed to account for Liam's tenacity, not to mention his magic proficiency. On her third dive, a pair of powerful arms grabbed her. Twisting within his grip only served to bring her face-to-face with him.

'Caught you.' The look of victory he wore suggested a fierce competitive side. But his expression transformed when the proximity of their bodies registered. Liam's eyelids stooped and his gaze lowered to her lips.

Saoirse gasped, feeling like a fish out of water. Being a warrior meant the mermen of her clan avoided her. No one had ever touched her in an intimate way. Yet her heart knew exactly what it wanted, as did her body. Pressing herself against him, she leaned in to claim his luscious lips. Electricity sparked between them as her mouth brushed against his.

Liam jerked back. 'Shit! I'm sorry Saoirse. I don't know what came over me.'

'Why are you apologising? I want this too.'

He sighed. 'That's the problem. I know how you feel and I'm leading you on. I should go.' With a quick tug of kinetic energy, he pulled the wayward surfboard back into his arms and climbed onto it.

A lump formed in Saoirse's throat as a riptide of emotion tore through her. 'Why Liam? Tell me why you deny us?'

Pain furrowed his brows when he turned back to face her. 'I'm married, Saoirse. I have a wife back home who needs me.'

Her jaw hit the ocean floor. Reality nipped at her like pincers. Unable to voice the litany of words passing across the tip of her tongue, she turned and swam away from him. *He is married. Liam has a mate.*

'*Saoirse, wait!*' Liam's voice trailed behind her, carried along the soft summer breeze.

Why didn't he tell me about his wife before?

'*Please, Saoirse!*'

A warrior can never be a lover. The mages on land must have different rules. Serves me right for trying to defy the ways of my own people. She dipped below the surface, making her way back to the veiled city she called home. Saoirse wanted to despise Liam for his dishonourable actions. Yet the intensity of her affections would not allow such wretched feelings to take root; although, it was more likely her own nature preventing her. There was not a hateful bone in her body. Still, it would take time to recover from such a blow to her delicate heart.

The current shifted as she neared her home, putting Saoirse on high alert. Her instincts told her something was wrong.

Esme, her aunt, swam out to greet her with ashen cheeks. 'Come quick, child. It's your father.'

As soon as the school bell rang in the start of lunch, Erik sprung to his feet. He was eager to see his snow queen again. *Snow queen? Where did that nickname come from?* It fitted her though, considering the meaning of Neve. Combine it with her beautiful white skin and ice-cold heart. Determination drove him to melt her heart; or failing that, shatter it into a million icicles. Either way, she would be his.

Other students rushed to clear a path for him as he glided through the corridor with his head held high. He spotted Elna approaching from the other end of the hall. When their eyes met, she beamed with adoration. His heart swelled at the warmth emanating from his doting sister. Erik was about to return the smile when a familiar scent caught him off guard. *Did my queen come to meet me?*

Following the fragrance led him to a classroom with a closed door. He reached for the door handle, but logic kicked in before he lost his chance to eavesdrop. Using magic, he enhanced his hearing and listened.

Neve's commanding voice broke the silence. 'Are you crazy, Jas?'

Erik's shoulders stiffened. *Jas? As in Jasper?*

The devil himself chuckled. 'Yes, Neve. I'm fucking insane. I can't stay away from you.'

The bastard! If he so much as touches my queen…

'Jasper, please. You need to try harder. Erik will kill you if he catches you… doing things to me.'

Damn straight!

'It's a risk I'm willing to take.' A chair screeched across the polished floor.

The sound of furniture moving followed a playful squeal.

The fuck? Erik turned the handle, opening the door in a slow, deliberate fashion. He only needed a slight gap to peer through. And when he did, *by the Gods!* His blood heated with rage.

Jasper held Neve, propping her up on a desk as he stepped between her legs.

The sight of another guy's hands on *his girl* sent shivers down Erik's spine. Thistles of envy prickled all over his skin. *Why isn't Neve resisting his advances?* He pushed the door open further, catching Jasper's attention.

Shock morphed into bitter contempt as Jasper pressed his body closer to Neve's. Both of his arms wrapped around her.

'Jas?' Neve queried in a soft whisper. Her back was to the door, so she remained unaware of Erik's presence.

'Get. Your. Hands. Off her.' Erik seethed as he approached them.

Neve let out a startled whimper and attempted to free herself from Jasper's clutches.

Jasper scowled, tightening his grip on Neve. 'Or what? I'm a bloodline mage. Your seelie rules don't apply to me.'

'Please, Jasper.' Neve pleaded with him as she pushed against his muscular chest. He did not budge an inch. She was either a pathetic weakling or her attempts were half-hearted.

Erik thought back to Saturday night when his own fingertips had skimmed much of her body. There had been definite muscle tone in her arms. *Didn't she also mention something about being a gymnast?* He narrowed his eyes on Jasper. 'Even your precious Council honour our most sacred laws. If you don't get your filthy paws off her this instant, you will find yourself in a world of pain.'

'Nothing but empty threats,' Jasper scoffed.

'Have you already forgotten what exile feels like?'

'Strangely, it was a hell of lot better because at least I was free to be with Neve.'

Gasping, Neve turned her gaze back to Jasper.

Is she so damn naïve to the extent of Jasper's feelings? Hmm. A devious plan formed in his mind. 'Suit yourselves.' Erik left the room, pausing at the door. 'Don't say I didn't warn you though.'

One, two, three...

'Erik, wait!' Neve called after him.

He grinned to himself as he continued walking away.

Brisk footfalls followed. 'Erik?'

Her grovelling, a pleasant melody to his ears. He continued to ignore her, to make her squirm.

Elna looked up at him when he stepped up to their lunch table. Then her attention diverted, and her gaze darted between him and Neve. 'What's going on?'

'Erik, please listen to me,' Neve continued begging.

Once he took his seat, he clicked his fingers at her. She drew closer and he indicated his desire by pointing to the ground in front of him.

She stared at him blankly. 'What?'

'I am in no mood to listen to your excuses. Shut your mouth and kneel at my feet.'

'You can't be serious!'

He glared at her. 'Oh, I'm deadly serious. Would you rather face the same fate I have in store for Jasper?'

With tears brimming in her eyes, she shook her head.

'Good. On your knees, *now.*'

Neve lowered herself before him, filling his mind with several improper thoughts.

Elna's snicker broke him free of his mental porn reel. He glanced at the crowd gathering around them before focusing on Elna. 'I found Jasper attempting to take something of ours.' He inclined his head toward Neve by way of explanation.

'Is that so?' Elna shot dagger stares into Neve's back. 'What does Miss Winters have to say for herself?'

'Nothing yet. I won't hear another word from her lips until I have had time to cool down.'

'Is it wise, My Lord? You are giving the devious little whore more time to concoct her lies.'

'That may be so. But I need to be in a rational headspace when I hear what she has to say.' A mischievous half-smile tugged at his lips as he looked at Neve, her eyes full of remorse. 'In the meantime, I'm going to enjoy punishing her.'

Neve answered the door to Brendan when he arrived late in the afternoon. He smiled at his daughter. *My child. Christ! That's gonna take some getting used to.* 'Hi princess, mind if I come in?'

She shrugged and opened the door before turning on her heels and walking off in a huff.

'What? No hug for your uncle tonight?'

'I don't hug arseholes,' she replied. When Neve reached the stairs, she took them two at a time to make a quick getaway.

Damn! Has Liam been filling her head with rubbish? No, she wouldn't listen to him. Did Lana open up? The moment he entered the living area, Brendan froze.

Given what he knew of their declining relationship, he had not expected to see them kissing. But that is exactly what he found. It was like something teleported him back in time by sixteen years. Alannah was even straddling Liam's lap in the same way she had on the dreaded day. Only this time Brendan did not run. He stood there in shock, watching like a creeper. *And those noises of hers.* He remembered what it was like to make her moan in the same way.

The heat kicked up a notch when Alannah began to grind against Liam.

Surely, they won't start fucking on the couch where Neve could walk in on them at any moment? The smell of her arousal flooded his senses, somewhat debunking his theory. Seeing Liam as the source of her stimulation slapped him in the face, waking him from his trance. He cleared his throat.

Alannah shot him a look of confusion transforming into anger. 'What the hell?'

'Neve let me in. Good thing she ran straight upstairs, else she might have seen the pair of you dry-humping on the sofa like horny teenagers. Don't you guys have a bedroom?'

Alannah turned back to Liam. 'Give me a sec, babe.' She pecked him on the lips and rose, revealing a small wet patch on her dress.

With his eyes pinned on her pelvis, Brendan snorted. 'I take that back. Your make out session was anything but dry.'

'You're disgusting, Brendan.' She led him into her workroom and shut the door.

'I'm disgusting? Please, your display made me throw up in my mouth.'

'I'm not going to apologise for kissing my husband.'

'No. I can't imagine you've ever been sorry about it,' he muttered.

Her eyes narrowed on him. 'What's that supposed to mean?'

'Nothing. Forget it.'

'What are you doing here, anyway?'

'Oh, you know, the usual. Catch up with Neve. Annoy you.' He grabbed a pen and paper and wrote her a quick message, I SECURED A SAFEHOUSE. LOT 20 HIGHWATER ROAD.

'Well, consider me annoyed.' She grabbed the note and shoved it in her pocket as she stormed out of the room and approached the stairs. '*Neve! Get down here!*'

Heavy footfalls stomped along the upper level and thundered down the stairs. It was hard to imagine so much noise coming from such a small girl. Neve was a force to be reckoned with, like her mother. '*What?*'

'Your uncle is here to see you.'

'Yeah, well I don't want to see him.' She turned and sped away.

'She called me an arsehole before,' Brendan explained. 'Am I right in guessing you finally told her our history?'

'Actually, you have Monique and her daughter to thank.'

'Jesus! Someone helped Monique breed? Who's the unlucky bugger to father her child?'

'Monique's not so bad these days. She married your cousin Steve. I guess that makes her daughter, Caitlin, your first cousin once removed. Oh, and Caitlin is Neve's best friend.'

Brendan's head was spinning with all the information coming at him in rapid fire. *So much for Jacob keeping me in the loop.* 'Can I go talk to her?'

'Will my lack of permission stop you? I know you already went behind my back to train her.'

'How?'

'I have my ways.' She tapped her ear and swept her arm around the room, indicating whoever bugged her house must have told her.

Damnit! I should have thought of scanning the place earlier. 'Well, given I have a right to see her, you can't stop me talking to her.'

Alannah threw her hands up in the air. 'Whatever.' She showed her crossed fingers as she continued. 'You can talk, but I don't want you training her.' Dropping her hand by her side, she glowered at him. 'If anything you do brings her to harm, you will face my wrath. Trust me when I say my current abilities put both Liam and Tyler's warlock powers to shame.'

'Thanks for the show of faith, Lana. You ought to know there is no way in hell I would endanger Neve's life.' He made his way upstairs, tapping on Neve's door.

'What?'

'Neve, please talk to me,' he pleaded.

'Go away!'

'Can you at least explain why you think I'm an arsehole?'

The door creaked open a tiny slither. 'Are you for real? After everything you did to Mum, you want me to justify my reasons for hating you?' Her words were like a hot poker straight through his heart.

'What have you heard, Neve?'

She opened the door to let him enter her room. 'I know you made her your soulmate before breaking her heart and running off with another woman.'

He exhaled sharply, slumping into her desk chair. Hearing other people bring up his past with Alannah was never easy. 'Has it ever occurred to you I had reasons for my actions? Non-arsehole reasons.'

'What possible justification is there?'

Brendan shook his head. 'My past relationship with your mother isn't any of your business, Neve.'

'Like hell it isn't. You broke her, Brendan. More so than any of those other creeps who abused her. You're the reason she became a negligent alcoholic.' She collapsed on her bed with tears flowing down her cheeks.

He stared at her in shock. 'You don't believe that, do you?'

Biting her lower lip, she nodded between sobs.

'Shit! Neve, I'm sorry for what transpired between me and Lana. I sure as hell hope it was not the reason for her… alcohol problem. I guess it's easier for everyone to cast me as the villain.' With a sigh he rose and headed for the door.

'Wait. I'm sorry, Uncle Brendan.'

Brendan offered her a fake smile, unable to conjure enough joy for a real one. Neve's outburst made him question everything.

'There is something I'd like to run by you… if you still want to talk.'

Returning to the chair, he gestured for her to continue.

'What does it mean for seelie royalty to claim someone?'

His eyes bugged out at her question. 'Does this have something to do with those enlightened twins at your school?'

She nodded.

'An enlightened claim is akin to a betrothal. The claimed must be a virgin and remain so until the fae matrimonial rites. No one can touch the claimed intimately without the permission of the claimant.'

Neve gulped. 'W-what happens to someone who touches the claimed without permission?'

'Depends what they do. There are varying degrees of punishment for the level of intimacy. If someone takes the virginity of the claimed, their life is forfeit, and the claim is void.'

Neve's jaw dropped. 'E-even if they are a pure mage?'

'Christ, Neve. What have you gotten yourself into?'

Chapter Twelve

The sun cast its first rays upon the gentle ripples of the sea as Liam swam out toward the rocky reef. He did not know why, but he felt compelled to investigate the area. It had been nigh on two months since his last visit. The area was unsuitable for surfing. The girls loved it though. Both Neve and Caitlin often used the large boulders to sunbake in peace. So, whenever they asked him, Liam would take them out in the boat.

He was alone that Thursday morning. *So why am I here?* After passing the first stone goliath, a flicker of teal and aqua caught his attention. Someone was sitting on one of the distant rocks. Liam glanced around to look for boats, but there were none. Worried some poor fisherman had shipwrecked himself, he pushed on ahead. When he reached the figure, his heart sank. *Not a fisherman.*

Saoirse sprawled out face down across the rock.

It was hard to hear much above the ferocious beating of his heart, or the crashing of waves against the reef. *Oh Gods, please no.* With slow, deliberate strokes, he moved around to the side her head was resting on. He could finally make out the gentle rise and fall of her chest, letting a breath of relief into his own lungs. 'Saoirse?'

Her head shot up to look at him. 'Liam? W-what are you doing here?'

'Surfing.' He took in the sight of her bloodshot eyes and tear-stained cheeks and felt his heart break all over again.

'You never surf near the reef.'

'Okay, so I took a detour. I- I don't know why I came out here today.' Drawing closer, he wiped at one of her tears with his thumb. 'What's wrong?'

She recoiled at his touch. 'Please don't.'

A pang of guilt pierced his chest. 'Saoirse, why are you crying? Is this because of me?'

Saoirse shook her head, grief tricking from her eyes.

'Then what? Are you...' Liam paused as a horrid thought struck. 'Is it your father?'

Her weeping intensified.

'Oh Gods! I'm so sorry.' Liam's arm hovered above her back with hesitation, but he withdrew it.

He was not the person she needed. Knowing a degree of the pain she felt and being unable to touch her stung like a bitch. 'I want to hug you, Saoirse, to comfort you, but I don't want to make you feel worse. I-I should go.' Reluctantly, he pushed off from the rock and swam towards his usual spot.

Saoirse dived into the water a few inches in front of him, splashing water in his face and startling him. Upon re-emerging, she threw her arms around him, pressing her naked flesh against his chest. 'P-please don't go.'

He wrapped his arms around her, holding her tight and letting her mourn in silence.

'He-he's dead. Gone f-forever,' she sobbed sometime later.

Liam stroked her long hair to soothe her. 'What was he like, your father?'

Still maintaining her grip on Liam, her head reclined on his shoulder. 'My father was a good man. Strict, but he was caring, and he had a great sense of humour.' She sniffed.

'I wish I could have met him. At least he is no longer suffering.'

She nodded, curling up in his embrace to cry more. At least fifteen minutes had passed when Saoirse's head rose, her red-rimmed eyes full of sorrow. 'Thank you, Liam. I should get back to my family now.'

'Of course. My condolences to you all.' He watched with a solemn heart as she swam away. *What is her home like?* Water droplets sprayed everywhere as he shook those dangerous thoughts from his mind. *Lana needs me* became his mantra for the rest of the day.

For the third morning in a row there was a horse-drawn carriage waiting for Neve when she stepped outside her house. The sight still startled her. It would take some getting used to. As would the twins claiming her. Finally knowing what it meant, the mere thought sent shivers down her spine. *I never asked for any of this.*

Erik was waiting beside the carriage door, glaring at her.

Neve strode up to him with a defiant look, crossing her arms across her chest when she stood before him. 'I didn't think you would bother picking me up this morning.'

Somehow his icy stare dropped several degrees. 'Displeasing me such as you have will not free you of my company. You are still mine.'

She gulped. 'How were you able to claim me? I never consented to any of this.'

He sneered at her. 'Oh, but you did.'

'When?'

'During our kiss. Now get in, you know how I despise being late.'

Shaking her head in bewilderment, Neve climbed inside. An arctic chill greeted her when Elna's eyes met hers. Neve turned her attention to the front of the vehicle. 'I still don't recall agreeing to anything as long-term as your claim,' she explained as Erik sat beside her.

'Not verbally, no. But your soul acquiesced.'

'My soul. Right, of course,' Neve scoffed. 'How the hell would you know what my soul wants when I don't?'

Erik let out an exaggerated sigh. 'I'm an enchanter, Neve.'

Like that's any sort of explanation. 'What if I don't want your claim anymore?'

Both twins gasped, as though Neve had said the most horrendous thing.

Leaning in close, Erik placed a firm hand on her thigh. 'The only way you can break our claim on you is by losing your virginity. Good luck finding anyone willing to risk themselves over your temper tantrum, sweetheart.'

'Jasper would.'

Erik growled. 'Jasper is an idiot. Being a pure mage does not excuse him from seelie law. I doubt he will want to try me again after I dish out his current punishment.'

'You can't punish him for hugging me.'

Malicious laughter burst forth from Erik. His eyes narrowed on her. 'Do you think I'm an idiot, Neve?'

'But—'

'Save your breath. I won't hear your excuses until recess.'

Their ride came to an end, putting their conversation on hold as Erik helped Neve down the steps. Caitlin had refused further lifts to school— not surprising after their awkward time on Tuesday morning. Neve missed having someone in her corner when dealing with the Alvarsson twins.

The first two periods of the day passed without incident. Neve was a nervous wreck by recess. Doubt and disbelief plagued her mind, leaving little room for thoughts of schoolwork. *What exactly does Erik know about my relationship with Jasper?* Seeing the large group assembled around Erik fed her anxiety. She took hesitant steps toward him.

Erik's glacial green eyes searched her out. 'And speaking of the devil.' He gestured for her to join him.

The crowd parted as she approached, closing in behind her. It felt like the whole school came to bear witness to her explanation. When Erik pulled her into his lap, she noticed Jasper standing within the inner ring of people. Two orcs were restraining him. *Not good.*

'As you all know,' Erik announced, 'Elna and I staked our claim on Neve Winters at our party on Saturday night. Since then, I have seen a change in her aura. Someone has been pleasuring her, yet we have not granted anyone such permission. All evidence points to Jasper Rowan. Neve, do you deny Jasper is responsible?'

Hearing her personal life aired in front of the whole school, Neve's face blazed with humiliation. 'It was not Jasper.'

The assembled group murmured among themselves.

'Quiet!' Erik ordered. 'If not Jasper, then who has been touching you, Neve?'

'Me,' she whispered. Her lie would suffice if her aura was all he had to go on.

Blinking, he stared at her. 'I'm sorry, I didn't hear you. Please speak up and tell me who has been making you orgasm.'

Several titters sounded around her, intensifying the burn in her cheeks.

She raised her voice enough for Erik and Elna alone to hear, 'It was me. I have been…' —she gulped—'touching myself.'

Erik arched a brow. 'Is that so?'

The mob pushed in closer to hear them.

'Are you telling me you have been masturbating?' Erik projected his voice well enough for all to hear.

More laughs and muttering.

'I require a demonstration, Neve.'

The blood drained from her face, returning her cheeks to their usual pallor. *Surely not here—*

'At my place tonight.'

This time, Jasper paled.

She did not blame him. First base was one thing, but this was more action than she had bargained for. *Please don't give the game away, Jas.* Her eyes pleaded with him for a brief second.

'If you prove you are capable of such a feat,' Erik continued, 'I will pardon Jasper of all charges.'

Exhaling through gritted teeth, Neve nodded. *Sparing Jasper from Erik's cruel and unusual torture will make it all worthwhile. Now to work out where I can get a vibrator on such short notice.*

Gripping her thigh, Erik pressed his mouth to her ear. 'Don't worry babe, your hands won't be doing all the work tonight.'

An odd tingle shot through her bloodstream. 'Is that a threat or a promise?' she asked bitterly. At least she tried to sound hateful, but it came out more like a plea.

His frosty stare melted, giving way to sweltering lust. 'I was going for a promise. Although now I get the impression you might enjoy the threat.' He bit her earlobe, sending more signals straight to her core.

Gods! How does he turn me on when I despise him?

The winding, gravel driveway stretched on for at least a kilometre. Alannah parked her Tesla in front of a modern homestead. The house sat nestled among several varieties of native trees and shrubs. The property put her in mind of Cailleach Estate. The building itself bared no resemblance, however. It was large but sprawled over a single floor with a light grey façade. Stepping up to the door, she paused to gather her thoughts before ringing the doorbell.

'Hey Lana.' Brendan wore an expressionless mask when he greeted her. 'Come in.' He led her through the front lounge room into an open plan kitchen and living area. 'I gotta say, I didn't think you would be the first guest I invited into my new home.'

Leaning against the kitchen bench, Alannah took in the view. Light filtered in through floor-to-ceiling windows. It danced along the white marbled floor and granite benchtops. The space was bright and roomy, and she had to admit the house was stylish, even if it was not to her tastes.

'You seem impressed,' Brendan remarked.

'A little. What's the rent like on this place?'

'I dunno, but it cost a small fortune to buy.'

Alannah gaped at him with wide eyes. 'You purchased this house?'

'Yup. I decided to stick around to see Neve more.'

Tears threatened to show in her eyes, so she doubled her concealment efforts. 'How did you get through the settlement process so quick?'

'Oh, you know me. I can be rather persuasive when I want to.'

She frowned. 'You mean shonky.'

'Pfft. Details. Point is, I have a safehouse no one can trace back to me, unless you go blabbing to the Council.'

Alannah glared at him. 'You ought to know I wouldn't.'

'There was a time when I would have taken your word for it, but it turns out I didn't know you as well as I'd thought.'

'I could say the same for you.'

Brendan shrugged as he pulled his phone out and waved it around her.

'What are you doing?'

'Scanning for bugs.'

'Are you going to pat me down for weapons too?' she scoffed.

He gave her a lewd grin. 'Only if you want me to.'

Drawing her lip between her teeth, she clamped down on certain… urges. 'Don't flatter yourself, Brendan.'

Stepping back, Brendan returned the phone to his pocket. 'You're clean, of devices anyway. I can't say the same for your filthy mind.'

Alannah's cheeks flushed. She chided herself for lowering the walls enough for Brendan's keen senses to see over. 'Do you have the intel I need, or what?'

'I can do you one better. I've organised a vid call with my spymaster in Melbourne.'

Resisting the impulse to fall on old habits, Alannah nodded instead of hugging him. 'Thank you.'

They sat in front of his laptop at a solid wood dining table big enough for twelve place settings. 'I'm setting up a secure network,' Brendan explained as he typed away in some high-tech interface that looked foreign to her.

Glancing around, Alannah recognised the plant pot sitting in the kitchen windowsill. She had gifted him the blue-grey granite container when he first moved out of the family home. The plant was unlikely to be the same, but it was still lemon balm. A wave of nostalgia overcame her, and she needed to blink a few times to swallow the lump in her throat.

'Jade, can you see me okay?' Brendan's voice drew her attention back to the moment.

'Clear as day, Lord Jet.' A deep, husky voice came through the computer speakers.

'I would like you to meet an… associate of mine. Jade, this is Lady Ebony.' Brendan gestured for Alannah to move closer.

She shimmied in next to him, leaning forward to avoid contact with his shoulders. 'Hello, Lady Jade.'

The green-haired woman gasped at the sight of Alannah. 'Apologies My Lady, but you look so much like Lord Jet.'

Alannah held back the eye roll. 'Indeed. And before you ask, no, we are not siblings.'

'Of course. I'm sorry. What can I do for you, Lady Ebony?'

'What can you tell us about the volcanoes? I need to know what dark magic faction is behind these eruptions and why.'

'These volcanoes are definitely not the result of dark magic,' replied Jade.

'Are you sure?'

'Yes. There is no way a dark mage plot like this would escape my attention. The magic underworld here are as spooked as the Council. But there is one community who don't seem bothered.'

Alannah exchanged a look with Brendan then returned her attention to Jade. 'Who?'

'The Seelie Court. A nobleman requested a seat on the Council immediately before the tremors started. An enlightened fellow claiming he had information pertinent to their cause. When they refused to grant him a seat, he told them they would be sorry. No one has seen him since the first eruption.'

'Curious. Thank you, Lady Jade.'

'Not a problem. Let me know if there's anything else I can do.'

'Actually, there is,' Brendan interjected. 'I want you to track down this elusive seelie noble and get some answers out of him. By any means possible.'

A wicked gleam flickered in Jade's eyes. 'Certainly, My Lord.'

Alannah began to pace the room as Brendan shut down his laptop.

'You're making me nervous here, Lana. What's wrong?'

When her gaze returned to Brendan, he had perched his backside on the breakfast bar. She drank in the sight of him and the way the black designer suit hugged his broad chest and muscular legs. The lack of tie lent a casual air to his appearance. He had even opened the top few buttons of his grey shirt. Alannah's eyes rose to meet Brendan's, and he gave her a knowing look. Turning to hide the colour in her cheeks, she sat in one of the blue suede armchairs. 'Do you recall Neve mentioning the Alvarsson twins?'

His brows furrowed. 'The school bullies. I remember.'

'Their father approached Kieran with the exact same request for a Council seat.'

Fear widened his eyes; the first real emotion he had shown her all day. 'Shit! Where is our nearest volcano?'

'As far as I know, Mount Burr or possibly Mount Muirhead in the southeast. There are several volcanoes down there. If they all go off, the lava flow won't travel this far, but a hell of a lot more ash will fill our sky and clog our lungs. The Council can only do so much to ward and clean the atmosphere.'

'I don't get it, Lana. The Seelie Court are all about preserving the environment. Why would they unleash such devastation on the world? This can't be good for all the wild critters.'

Logic and reason evaded Alannah's thoughts as her mind tried to piece the puzzle together. 'I don't know, Brendan. The only thing I'm sure of now is Alvar lying to me about his involvement. He denied responsibility, and I believed him. I may not be as skilled at reading people as you, but I was quite confident in my assessment at the time.'

Brendan gave her a smug grin. 'Flattery will get you everywhere, Lana.'

This time there was no stopping the eye roll.

After a short laugh, Brendan's expression turned serious again. 'Alvar might not be directly responsible, but his fae brethren must be. This calls for some good old-fashioned interrogation.'

'True. And I reckon I have enough incentive to get Kieran to act.'

His eyes narrowed. 'I thought you said the Council weren't investigating this.'

'They weren't, until recently. Don't worry, I won't reveal any of my sources.'

'Even so, I thought *we* were going to investigate this together. Screw the damn Council.'

'Firstly, there is no "we;" and secondly, this issue is far greater than you and me. It is going to take the Council's global resources to deal with.'

Brendan jumped off the kitchen counter and scowled. 'The Syndicate is also global and better equipped than the Council.'

Alannah rose to face him off. 'For once, could you try operating *within* the law? Let the Council handle this first. If that doesn't work, we can do things your way.'

'Fine, whatever. Let me know when I can be of use to you again.' Brendan stormed off into one of the back rooms, slamming a door behind him.

After letting out a heavy sigh, Alannah showed herself out of Brendan's house and made her way home.

Chapter Thirteen

Erik and Elna were waiting with heated gazes outside the school gates. They stood beside their horse-drawn carriage. Neve took nervous steps toward them, sucking in a deep breath as she crossed the school's threshold. Jasper watched through the fence, his expression a tumultuous tempest of emotion. She bit down on her lower lip. It was hard enough for Neve to distance herself from Jasper. She imagined it would be more difficult for him seeing her with Erik. *With any luck, I'll get my intel tonight.*

Tugging Neve close, Erik pecked her on the lips before ushering her inside the carriage.

She figured it was for show because he never greeted her with kisses outside her house in the mornings. Not for the first time, Neve wondered what Erik had against Jasper. *Why use me to make him suffer?*

Erik instructed the driver to take them straight home.

'Wait,' Neve interrupted. 'I need to get something from my house first.'

Two sets of suspicious eyes met with hers. 'What, pray tell, could you need?' Erik asked.

Neve blushed. 'My um… I uh… don't use my hands alone.'

He gave her a sly grin. 'If you use sex toys, Neve, you should at least be able to refer to them by name. What do you need?'

Her cheeks would have matched the bright pink streaks in Erik's hair. 'My v-vibrator.'

Elna snickered. 'I can't wait to see this.'

The summer heat stifled Neve, especially with the twins sitting either side of her.

Leaning forward, Erik called out with new directions for the driver. When he sat back, he focused all his attention to Neve's sweltering body. 'I can't wait either.' His fingers trailed upward along her inner thigh. 'I want to see the look on your pretty little face when you come. I want to hear the noises you make. But do you know what I'm most looking forward to about tonight, Neve?'

Shaking her head, she let out a small squeak when his fingertips brushed along the edge of her panties.

'Tasting you.'

Her eyes flicked wide open as she gasped. Breathing became next to impossible and her heart was slamming into her ribs. Jasper had not yet gone so far with her. The twins were about to take another first from him.

'Mm, I bet you taste sweet,' Elna mused as her own hands explored Neve's body.

It was a relief to alight on solid ground when they reached Neve's home. She sucked in a lung-full of air before stepping through the gate, halting when Erik followed her. 'You can't come inside. My father would freak. He doesn't let me bring boys home.'

Erik beamed. 'Sensible man. It could work in my favour with Jasper sniffing around. Elna? Would you escort Neve inside and ensure she finds what she needs?'

Neve's pulse picked up the pace.

Stepping up beside her, Elna linked arms with Neve. 'Of course.'

Once inside, she beelined for the living area, hoping to find her mother. The humming of the sewing machine's motor told Neve Alannah was in her workroom. After knocking twice, she opened the door. 'Hi Mum.'

Alannah looked up and smiled. 'Hey sweetie.' She glanced at the arm wrapped around Neve's. 'Who's your friend?'

'This is Elna. She's helping me with my… biology homework.' She hoped her mum did not detect the moment of hesitation in the explanation.

'Hi Elna.'

'Hello, Lady Winters.' Elna curtsied. It was a small gesture, but so strange given the informal situation.

Luna looked up from her seat on the windowsill and meowed at Elna.

Gazing at the white cat, Elna smiled. A silent exchange passed between them after which Luna rose and rubbed against Elna's legs.

Damn faerie gets on better with Mum's cat than I do.

Alannah inspected Elna. 'Are you Lord Elofsson's daughter?'

'Yes, I am, My Lady.'

The confirmation made Alannah stiffen. 'Elna, would you mind giving me a moment alone with my daughter?'

'Not at all, My Lady.' She curtsied again before exiting the room.

With a quick hand wave, Alannah erected a sound ward, and beckoned Neve closer. 'I thought you said the Alvarsson twins were giving you a hard time at school.'

'They were, at first. But we are friends now.'

Mum's brow furrowed. 'I'm not sure I like you being friends with them, Neve.'

'What? Why?'

'I can't say too much yet, but I have reason to believe the Council may soon outlaw the Seelie Court.'

Neve's jaw dropped. 'Is this about the volcanoes?'

Mum sighed. 'I shouldn't be telling you this much, hun. Promise to be careful?'

She nodded adamantly. 'So uh, did you get the thing I messaged you about?'

With an eye roll, Mum reached under her desk and retrieved a black paper bag. 'Yeah, I even charged it like you wanted. I still can't believe you asked *me* for this. I'm not condoning such behaviour, but there are ways and means to get these things yourself.'

'I'm sorry, but it was urgent.'

'Does this have anything to do with your "biology" project?' Mum employed air quotes, implying Neve was up to no good.

Figures, considering her own sordid history. Neve offered a coy smile. 'Maybe.'

'Christ, Neve. Your father's going to kill me after he's done burying your corpse.' She held the bag out.

Neve took it and peaked inside. In addition to her request, there was a box of condoms. She frowned at the post-it-note attached to them: DON'T GET PREGNANT. Holding it up, she scowled. 'Mum!'

'What? I'm not ready to be a grandmother.'

'Yeah, well there's no way it's gonna happen anytime soon. Erik warned all the other boys at school to stay away from me, and he doesn't believe in sex before marriage.'

Mum's eyebrows rose sky high. 'Are you — you know what? I don't think I want to know anymore. Be careful and don't trust the seelie.'

After unboxing the rabbit, she dropped it in her backpack, along with the other goodies. She led Elna upstairs to her bedroom.

'What did your mum want?' Elna inquired.

Neve grabbed the box of condoms out and threw them at Elna. 'The sex talk.' She used Elna's distraction to sneak the vibrator into her underwear drawer.

Elna laughed before her expression turned doubtful. 'Why would she buy these for you? Does this have anything to do with Jasper?'

Shit! 'Of course not.' Neve sighed with relief as an excuse came to mind. 'Mum knows I'm seeing Erik, but not about the claiming.'

'I thought you said your parents would freak if you had a boyfriend?'

'My father would if he knew. Mum's cool though.'

'So, where is this sex toy of yours? I'm keen to get on with… things.'

'In here.' Neve opened the drawer and showed Elna the purple rabbit.

'Cute. Now let's go.'

Erik was pacing when they reconvened. 'What took so long?'

Elna tittered. 'Neve's mum thinks you're going to get her baby girl pregnant, so she insisted on the sex talk.'

His eyes widened as they shifted to Neve. 'Is that so?'

'Yeah. She doesn't know about you claiming me. As far as she's aware, we're just dating.'

'Why haven't you told your parents? It would go some way to ease your father's fears.'

Neve was not so sure after what Mum had told her about the Seelie Court. 'I will. The timing isn't great at the moment.'

Erik huffed. 'Fine. Let's go.'

A ball of nervous energy, Alannah took her seat at the Council's table.

'I want to hear what each of you have uncovered on this volcanic activity,' Kieran demanded in a stern tone. 'We'll start as usual with Councillor Alannah Winters in the seat of Aether.'

'Thank you, Your Honour. There has not been any misuse of Aether. I do have some disturbing news to share regarding the volcanoes.'

Liam shot her a wide-eyed look. Unfortunately, she had not had time to debrief him before the Council meeting, but such was their life.

'I have word from a source in Melbourne who convinced me this is the work of the Seelie Court.'

A chorus of gasps and murmurs travelled around the room.

Kieran raised a hand to silence them all. 'Quite the accusation. What grounds do you have to make this claim?'

'A seelie noble approached the Melbourne Council with the same request as Alvar. No one has seen or heard from this guy since the Melbourne volcano erupted. Also, the seelie are the only magic community over there who are not freaking out.'

'I see. Are *you* certain dark magic is not responsible?'

Alannah read between the lines and considered her reply. 'Not one hundred percent, no. While my contact in Melbourne is reliable, I cannot vouch for the legitimacy of her own sources. That said, this is a strong lead worth investigating.'

'I agree,' replied Kieran. 'It is too much of a coincidence. I will put surveillance on Alvar. Councillor Maher in the Seat of Senses and Warlock Winters, I'd like you to work together to coordinate this. Feel free to use any registered Magus in the district.'

'Yes, Your Honour,' replied Liam and his uncle.

Kieran returned his attention to Alannah. 'Is there anything else, Councillor Winters?'

'No, Your Honour.'

The meeting continued without any further news on the volcanoes.

An uncomfortable silence descended upon Alannah and Liam as they drove home. Flicking on the light, Liam threw his keys on the shelf in the entryway and frowned. 'Neve's not home.'

'She's at a friend's house.'

'What sort of friend?'

Alannah sighed. 'A girlfriend.'

He nodded and strode down the hall.

Alannah headed into the kitchen and fed the cat. Grabbing some curry leftovers from the freezer, she set the microwave to defrost and put some rice on. Her eyes blurred as she watched the food spinning around.

'I need to know who your source is.' Liam's voice startled her out of her trance.

'Liam, I can't tell you.'

'If I'm going to be investigating Alvar and the Seelie Court, I need more context to your intel. Does she have anything to do with B—'

She flew at him, clamping a hand over his mouth.

His eyes bulged at her.

'Not here,' she whispered. Grabbing his hand, she led him up to her room, shut the door and threw up a sound ward. 'Kieran has bugged the house. This is the only safe space for confidential discussions.'

The surprise registering in Liam's visage assured her he had had nothing to do with the privacy invasion.

'The Council cannot know I'm working with Brendan.'

'So, he *is* your source?'

Alannah shook her head. 'Not exactly. He put me in contact with his spymaster in Melbourne. She doesn't know I work for the Council, so she was forthcoming with the information I needed. I sensed Kieran's suspicions when he asked about the likelihood of dark magic. That's why I couldn't tell him I am positive it has nothing to do with the volcanoes. If it had, the spymaster would have told me.'

'Christ, Lana. I can't believe you're getting wrapped up in this shit again. How did Brendan put you in contact with this spymaster?'

'Secure video conference at his uh… new house.'

'*You went to Brendan's house?*' Liam screeched.

'Shush, please, Liam. It was all business.'

Liam huffed. 'It's never *just* business with Brendan.'

'I promise nothing else happened.'

'Why are you protecting him from the Council? What does it matter if Kieran knows you are getting intel from Brendan?'

'This isn't about protecting Brendan.'

He narrowed his eyes on her. 'Then what is this about?'

'Secrets. Epically-sized secrets of the Tara Winters variety.'

Neve's journey to Erik and Elna's house was arduous. The air between them had shifted, and Erik kept tapping his foot while staring out the window. *He is such a moody bastard. Good thing he isn't my real boyfriend.*

Jerking his head back to face her, Erik gaped at her. 'What do you mean I'm not your real boyfriend? Who *is* your real boyfriend, hm?'

Cursing herself for letting her mental shield slip, Neve steadied her breathing. She assumed a neutral expression. 'I don't have a *real* boyfriend, Erik. You scared all my prospects away with this farce we have going. How long do you intend to keep this up for? I'm pretty sure Jasper is plenty jealous already.'

Frosty eyes glowered at her. 'Is that what you think this is? Nothing but a show to hurt your precious Jasper?'

Neve returned to the death stare. 'Yes. Isn't it what you're doing?'

A humourless laugh slipped from his mouth. 'Hardly. Jasper was nothing more than an annoying bug to squash when we first came to this school. The only reason I developed a vendetta against him was because he had something I wanted. Or rather, someone.'

She gaped at him.

'Oh, don't looked so shocked, Neve. I know you felt something in our first kiss. Hence my claim on you.'

'You mean you've claimed me for real?'

'Yes, of course it's real. I would never mess around with such sacred laws.' The vehicle came to a stop as they reached their destination. Erik's eyes gleamed with wicked delight. 'And now I'm going to prove how much I want you.' He glanced across to Elna. 'We both are.'

Neve felt like a fly caught in a spider's web. Believing herself to be clever and playing them at their own game, she had flown right into their trap. *No use struggling to free myself. I may as well see this through and hope I can at least save Jasper.*

She followed them inside, gawking in awe at the natural beauty surrounding her. The massive log-cabin structure spread though the canopy of about twenty trees.

Erik abruptly dragged her inside a bedroom and Elna shut the door behind them. A massive bed with a magenta quilt took pride of place in the centre of the room. The only other furniture being a dresser, couch, and walk-in wardrobe. There were no personal touches about the place.

'Is this a guest room?' Neve asked.

He pulled her close to him, letting her bag drop with a thud to the timber floor. 'No. This is our room.' When she blinked in confusion, he looked over her shoulder at Elna. 'Mine and Elna's room.'

Elna pressed into Neve's back. 'Erik and I share *everything*.'

Bingo! Neve had little time to think about her small win before Erik devoured her lips in an all-consuming kiss. Where Jasper's kisses were deep and passionate, Erik's were wild and full of possessive need. Neve's hormones took over and she yielded to him despite herself. He spun her around to face Elna, removing Neve's top in the process.

'Ever kissed a girl, Neve?' Elna's eyes flickered with the flames of desire.

'No.'

Elna cocked her head to one side. 'Not even your lesbian friend?'

She winced, recalling Caitlin's confession. 'No.'

'I'll be the first. Lucky me.' A huge grin lit up Elna's face as she moved in to claim Neve's lips.

Too shocked to move at first, Neve paused before sinking into the moment. Elna's soft lips and tongue against her own, two sets of hands gliding across her skin. Erik's deft fingers stripped away her clothes while Elna continued to kiss her. Before she knew what she was doing, Neve extended her arms around Elna's waist. Returning the kiss with equal fervour, she savoured the sweet taste of honeydew melons on Elna's lips.

'Easy there, Elna. We don't want to bring Neve too close to the edge before her demonstration.' Erik spoke in a gruff voice as he pulled Neve back and released her bra.

Gasping, Neve realised she was completely naked.

Erik stepped in front of her to take in the view. 'Gorgeous,' he whispered.

'Beautiful,' Elna agreed.

'Show us how you pleasure yourself, sweetheart,' Erik demanded in husky tone.

Neve's heart was racing as she grabbed the vibrator and cleaned it. The twins each sat on opposite sides of the bed and Erik patted a spot toward the middle to show where he wanted her.

Taking a deep breath, she settled into a comfortable position and turned on the toy. *Here goes nothing.*

Closing her eyes, she held it against her delicate folds. She almost bucked off the bed from the initial intensity of the sensation. *Christ it tickles!* Assuming Erik would try to read her mind in the process, she decided to keep it clear. It would have been easier to get off to thoughts of Jasper but doing so would be asking for trouble. She did not expect images of Erik and Elna to invade her subconscious. Nor did she expect those visualisations to bring her over the edge with the help of one little rabbit.

When the fog began to clear from her orgasm, Neve switched off the vibrator. She lifted her hands, intending to end the show.

But a firm hand stopped her, and Erik rasped in her ear, 'Incredible. Here, let me help this time.' He took over controlling the rabbit with one hand. The other gripped the fingers of her right hand, guiding them to the sensitive spot above her opening. A guttural sound burst from Neve when he pushed her own finger down on the little jewel of pleasure.

Elna's velvet fingertips crept across the surface of her breasts. Her touch sent sparks of arousal shooting through every nerve ending. The twins worked in synch to unravel Neve. In a matter of minutes, they reduced her to a quivering mess of emotions and sensations.

Brendan was halfway through his eighth glass of whiskey when the doorbell rang. Given the seclusion, his visitor was unlikely to be some random Bible basher. Very few people knew where he lived. Glancing at the clock told him it was late. *Could it be Lana? Her Council meeting would be over by now.* Hope fuelled his legs as he sprang from the couch and stumbled toward the front door, crashing into the wall a few times on his way.

He flung the door open to reveal two disgruntled endarkened.

Bridey stood with her arms crossed over her chest. Caleb was slouching against one of the wide beams supporting the veranda.

If he were not so drunk, Brendan might have acted more surprised. Instead, he nodded to them with a simple 'Hey.'

'That's it?' Bridey demanded. 'We travel over a thousand kays to see you after being apart for weeks and all you give us is a hey? What's going on, Brendan?'

'Why don't *you* (hiccup) tell me?' Glancing over Bridey's shoulder, he noticed his black Jag in the driveway. 'You (hiccup) drove my car?'

'He's drunk,' Caleb stated.

'Somebody give this man a (hiccup) trophy for his keen observation.'

Bridey pushed past Brendan. Her heels clicked against the tiles as she marched into his house.

'Make yourself at home (hiccup), why don't ya?' Brendan sneered.

Caleb shoulder checked Brendan as he entered. 'Don't mind if I do.'

Heaving out an exaggerated sigh, Brendan followed his *guests* to the main living area. 'How did you find me anyway?'

'I had someone watching you,' Bridey confessed.

Brendan's jaw hit the floor. 'You were spying on me?' *A sobering thought.*

'Don't be ridiculous, Brendan. I had one of our associates looking out for you. You can't fault me for wanting to make sure you were safe, given how much the Council despises you here.'

'Fair point.' He collapsed back into his armchair, watching as Bridey and Caleb sat beside each other on the couch. Neither of them wore their collars. Brendan's heart formed a lump in his throat.

His relationship with Bridey was... complicated in every sense of the word. It started out as a one-night stand. Then it turned into a business partnership when Brendan first went rogue. From there it progressed to sexual slavery when he sold her his soul to escape the pain of Alannah's betrayal. During his period of servitude, a strange bond developed between him and Bridey—some would have called it Stockholm Syndrome. Whatever you want to call it, lust and hate transformed into a deep, passionate love. Months later, they reversed their roles of Dom and sub.

Things were much simpler with Caleb. They had been good mates through high school. During this time, Brendan was oblivious to the huge crush Caleb had on him. Their friendship soured briefly when Brendan hooked up with Bridey—due to the twisted feelings Caleb felt for his sister. But all the bitterness and jealousy left Caleb when Bridey ordered the guys to fuck it out of their systems. The intense chemistry between them surprised Brendan. He had always thought of himself as straight. Sex with Caleb helped Brendan discover his own bisexual persuasion.

Brendan had the honour of collaring them five and a half years later. The three of them were inseparable until his most recent trip to Gaeilge Shores. Discovering Neve had left him questioning everything.

'I'd like to know why you didn't tell us about this place,' Bridey fumed. 'And more importantly, why did you buy this house at all?'

'Turns out I have a daughter in town.' He paused to read their expressions. Bridey was a blank page, well-rehearsed in hiding her emotions. Caleb bit his lip and wiped sweaty palms on his pants. 'Of course, you both knew about Neve, didn't you?'

Bridey shrugged. 'So what? You put that part of your life behind you. After the way Alannah broke your heart, we figured news of the kid would open old wounds.'

Leaping from his seat, Brendan towered over Bridey and Caleb in a fit of rage. '*You had no fucking right to hide my child from me!*'

Caleb's eyes watered, and he lowered his gaze. 'I'm sorry, Sir. I thought I was saving you from further heartache.'

Brendan's heart melted for Caleb and his obvious remorse. He turned his attention to Bridey, who still wore a neutral expression.

'What? You expect me to cower before you like my spineless brother? Not bloody likely! You could have called to tell us what was going on. Were you even planning on coming home?'

'I am home,' Brendan spat.

Pain and rejection shone loud and clear in Caleb's eyes as he shot Brendan a look.

Bridey rose to face him head on, challenge burning in her eye. 'So that's it then? You're giving up on us because of some brat you conceived at the Beltane rites? Legally, she's not even yours, Brendan!'

'*You think I don't know that?*' Brendan bellowed. Turning, he threw his whiskey glass against the wall. It smashed, spraying shards of glass across the room. 'I'm a fucking mess, Bry.' Collapsing against her, he let all the pain, anger, and frustration wash out of him in hideous sobs.

After a moment, Bridey embraced him, soothing him as she whispered sweet nothings in his ear. 'Caleb,' she called in a commanding tone.

'Yes, Madame?'

'Pick up the broken glass, would you?'

'Of course, Madame.'

As Caleb disappeared into the laundry, Bridey pulled Brendan down onto the sofa with her.

'Don't be too hard on him. He was following my orders.'

'Figures,' Brendan scoffed. 'Tomorrow we are gonna have a serious chat, Bry.'

She nodded.

'But tonight, I need you to help me forget all the pain.'

Smiling, Bridey kissed him. 'Anything for you, Sir.'

Chapter Fourteen

Neve woke to unfamiliar surrounds with a start. Soft light trickled in through the leaves providing natural blinds outside the window. When she rolled over, Erik's smiling face reminded her why she was not in her own bed. The warmth in his features was another foreign sight. She much preferred it to his usual harsh, cruel manner.

'Morning, beautiful. Sleep well?'

'Like a log.' Her parched throat made her voice sound gruff.

Trailing fingers along her side, Erik chuckled. 'Sexiest log I've ever seen.'

She felt her cheeks flush. 'What time is it?'

'Sunrise.'

'If I were to look at a clock, what would it say?'

His eyes gleamed with mischief. 'If the clock could talk, I hope it would tell you to kiss me.' Placing a hand on her face, he moved in close.

Neve shook her head. 'I have morning breath.'

'Does it look like I care?' Pushing her onto her back, he pinned her down and kissed her.

One pair of cotton boxers, the only barrier between them, did little to hide the extent of Erik's arousal. He was grinding against her most sensitive parts, driving Neve wild. She bucked against him with wanton abandon. *Gods, I'm so weak-willed.*

'Christ, Neve, you're killing me here.'

She blinked.

'You don't think I want this as much as you? I can't wait to seal the deal.'

'Seal the deal?'

Entwining her fingers with his own, Erik held her hands against the pillow above her head. 'Consummate the matrimonial rites.'

She opened her eyes wide, gulping hard against the lump in her throat. 'Do you seriously intend to wait until marriage before having sex for the first time?'

Erik laughed. 'I'm not a virgin, Neve. Only the one I claim needs to maintain their virtue until our wedding night.'

Sitting up, Neve pushed Erik back as the mood for intimacy fled. 'How barbaric! Not even bloodline mages subscribe to such sexist bullshit, and we still live in a patriarchy.'

He groaned. 'You misunderstand me, Neve. This isn't about gender. I could have claimed a male mate and he would need to remain a virgin. Female seelie also make claims. It is a sacred rite. Our claim should be an honour.'

Neve gaped at him. 'You think I should be happy about remaining chaste for the next three or more years. Meanwhile, you get to sleep around until you see fit to marry me?'

Erik grabbed her shoulders. 'Elna and I have no interest in stepping outside the bounds of our relationship with you.'

She squeaked with surprise. 'Really?'

Nodding, he pulled her into his lap. 'I also intend to give you as much pleasure as possible without breaking your precious hymen.'

'Why?'

His brow furrowed. 'Why what?'

'Why claim me? How do you know you'll still want me after three years? Why not wait until you're older to claim me?' She shot the questions in rapid fire, trying to wrap her head around an Erik Alvarsson-shaped puzzle.

'It is hard to explain why I chose you, except to say I recognised a kindred spirit when I first glimpsed your soul. As to the timing, I can only claim a virgin. Seeing how Jasper had his eye on you, I knew I needed to act quick.'

Neve fell quiet for a moment. It was a lot to process. 'Say, for argument's sake, the woman you claim loses her virginity. What then?'

He frowned. 'For one thing, I'd kill the bastard who took your virginity. If that happened, I would lose my claim on you.'

'So, you wouldn't be able to marry me at all?'

'Not under seelie law.'

'How necessary is marriage?'

Erik sighed. 'For me, essential. I have a kingdom to inherit, so I need a partner who will give us an heir.'

'How would it work if you claimed a guy?'

'Gods, sweetheart, what's with all the damn questions?' His tone became short.

'I'm trying to understand your situation,' she mumbled.

'If I had claimed a guy, Elna would have carried the legacy.'

Her mind raced with too many thoughts. *Does this mean I'll need to become a seelie queen? What about my position in mage society? As the first Winters woman of my generation, I have my own family legacy.* She struggled to breathe as panic set in.

'Neve, please try to relax.' His hand was rubbing her back.

'What's wrong with her?' Elna asked, stepping through their ensuite door in nothing but a towel.

'She's having a freak out,' Erik explained.

'Why?'

'We were talking about the future; I overwhelmed her.'

Neve took some deep breaths and tried to quiet her nerves.

Elna shrugged. 'She'll have to come to terms with it all eventually. She needs time for her simple mage brain to process everything.'

'Do you have to be so snarky all the time?' Erik turned to Neve. 'Would you like a shower?'

All she could do was nod.

He helped her to the bathroom, pausing when they reached the door. 'Do you want me to join you?'

Unable to stand on her own, she nodded again.

He sat her on the edge of the bath. After turning on the water, Erik dropped his underpants, and the reality of her situation sank in.

Duh! Of course he needs to get naked to shower, but ho-ly shit! She could not take her eyes off Erik's erection, wondering how she would ever fit such a monstrosity inside her. Neve half expected Erik to make a smart-arse comment about her staring. Instead, he helped her into the shower, holding her close.

With the hot water cascading down around her, the muscles in Neve's body began to relax. Erik pushed a strand of her hair away from her face and cupped her cheek in his hand. 'Are you feeling better?' His concern touched her heart, sending jitters down her back and between her legs.

'Yes.'

A grin lit up his face and he kissed her ardently, making her swoon against him. 'We can still have lots of fun exploring each other's bodies.' Erik's hand guided hers down his body, enclosing it around his shaft. Her eyes grew wide. 'Is this your first time touching a guy this way?'

'Yes,' she murmured, blushing.

'After everything we did to you last night, it amazes me how shy you can be about touching me. Go on, have a play.' He grinned, releasing his hold of her hand, and grabbing her hips.

She brushed her fingers along his skin, eliciting shivers throughout his body. 'Is this okay?'

'Gods, yes. But don't be afraid to grip me firmly.'

Following his suggestion, she watched in wonder as Erik closed his eyes and tilted his head back. Long blond hair fell around his broad shoulders, and the pink streaks glowed brighter, adopting more of a reddish hue. Seeing the effect she had on him empowered her.

Dropping to her knees prompted Erik's eyes to shoot open. They flickered before growing heavy and darkening. Taking him into her mouth was a thrilling challenge. Neve had no idea what she was doing, but Erik did not complain when her tongue circled around him. He tasted salty. As soon as she picked up the pace, he let out a guttural roar, grasped her hair and thrust himself into her throat. She gagged, but it did not matter. Neve revelled in the way Erik unravelled.

When he came apart in her mouth, a realisation shook the foundations of her soul: she was falling for Erik.

Staring through the eye of the needle, Alannah held her hand steady. She brought the black thread closer to its target. The door clicked shut behind her, causing her to flinch. She snapped the delicate needle, stabbing herself with it. 'Jesus fuck!' She spun around to face her intruder.

Brendan smirked, pressing a finger to his lips to remind her the Council was listening.

Shoving past him with a scowl, she climbed the stairs to her room. Once they were both inside, she shut the door and threw up a sound proofing ward. 'Try knocking next time,' Alannah grumbled, her eyes on the stinging puncture wound in her thumb.

'You know I can't knock without alerting them to my presence. Here, give me a look.' He moved in close and grabbed her hand. She failed to pull away quickly enough. 'Hm, I'm no expert, but I think you'll live. Does it hurt?'

'I stabbed myself with a sharp needle. What do you reckon?'

He cocked a brow. 'I should kiss it better.'

She tugged her hand free. 'That won't be—'

Brendan took it back, plunging it into his mouth and sucking hard.

Her eyes widened a moment before their lids grew heavy and she moaned involuntarily. 'What do you want, Brendan?'

Mischief sparkled in his gaze as he looked at her, thumb still in his mouth.

Damn those eyes. 'Why are you here now?'

Keeping his eyes fixed on hers, Brendan dragged his tongue across the surface of her thumb. 'I came for an update. I assume you told the Council what you learned from Jade?' He continued holding her hand and Alannah lost the will to fight for it back.

'I told them at last night's meeting. Kieran is putting surveillance on Alvar.'

'About time he took the issue seriously.' He started to say something, but hesitated. The hint of an unfamiliar emotion lingered in his eyes while he brushed his thumb along the side of her hand.

'What?'

With a sigh, he dropped her hand, glancing at the ceiling as if it held the answers he sought. 'I don't know how to broach this topic... I'm not exactly used to the whole parenting gig.'

The implication of Neve being in trouble made her heart race. 'What have you done?'

He huffed. 'I let her confide in me. I don't want to break her trust, but I'm worried about the kid.'

Seeing Brendan express parental concern fractured part of Alannah's defences. 'Does this have anything to do with the Alvarsson twins?'

'Yup. So, you know what she's up to?'

'Not exactly. She told me she befriended them and she's dating the boy. It's about all I know.'

'Thing is, she's not actually dating him. Her relationship with the twins is a ruse to get close and discover a way to take them down.'

'Hmph. Sounds familiar. Hearing she's not friends with them fills me with relief.'

'Yeah, that's the thing. Her idea of getting close is rather sexual in nature, and I doubt it's going down well with her real boyfriend.'

Alannah felt the blood draining from her face. 'Real boyfriend? Don't tell me you mean Jasper?'

'Sorry Lana, but Neve claims to be in love with Jasper.'

'Damnit! I warned her about him.'

'You haven't even heard the worst of it yet. The Alvarsson twins bear a serious grudge against Jasper, so to make him jealous they laid claim on Neve.'

'*The fuck?* There is no way the Seelie Court are going to claim my baby girl.' Alannah felt herself sinking. When her arse did not hit the floor, she realised Brendan had caught her.

He lifted her over to the bed and sat beside her. 'I take it you're familiar with seelie law and their archaic marital practices?'

'I've read about the seelie extensively. They may be on the right side of the law, but they seem far worse than the unseelie.'

'There's something we can agree on. Although, it sounds like they have been breaking the law.'

'Yeah,' Alannah mused. 'Do you think the Alvarssons would lose their claim on Neve if the Council outlawed their court?'

'It wouldn't happen automatically, but you could appeal to the Magus courts to annul the union. Council law still prevails for bloodline mages.'

'Here's hoping.'

'Hey,' Brendan stroked her back, sending waves of calming magic into her frazzled nerves. 'Even if Kieran can't prove they are behind the volcano issue, I may have something else to pin them on.'

'Oh?'

'Jacob has been investigating a lead. Looks like the seelie have been selling their own form of Rhapsody—one far more dangerous than mine.'

'For real?'

'Yup. I'm not a hundred percent sure they are behind it, but Jacob should have proof soon.'

'That's strangely reassuring. Thank you, Brendan.' Without thinking, she rested her head against his shoulder.

He snaked an arm around her waist and pressed his chin to the crown of her head. 'You're welcome, Lana.'

She could have sworn he sniffed her hair. For a few precious minutes she basked in the comfort he offered her. She almost forgot the way he had broken her heart and shattered her soul. It was a miracle she was able to keep her walls up. She hated to think what Brendan would do if he caught a glimpse of her true feelings.

'I should go. I need to get back to work.' When he rose, she missed the warmth of his body.

'Me too.' Alannah glanced at her injured thumb: the bleeding had ceased, the pain eased to a dull throb. 'For the record, you did the right thing telling me about Neve. Our loyalties are to her health and safety above her privacy.'

'I figured.' He smiled.

'What?'

'Nothing. I'll catch you later, Lana.' He made a quick escape, leaving her to ponder what was going on in his depraved mind.

The front door slammed downstairs, and Jasper braced himself. Slumping onto Neve's bed, he ceased wearing out the carpet with his pacing. Watching Neve with Erik at school had torn him up inside like some barbaric form of torture. The way he doted on her, the way he looked at her with those hungry eyes.

Neve jumped at the sight of him in her room. 'How did you get in here?'

He pointed to her window. 'You left it open. Your folks should put up better wards if they want to stop boys breaking into your room.' There was no hiding the bitter resentment in his tone.

She crossed the room and sat beside him. 'Only pure mages can cross the threshold without alerting my parents.'

It's something at least. Erik won't be able to sneak into her bed. 'Tell me what happened last night. I need to know.'

When she drew her bottom lip between her teeth, Jasper feared the worst. Neve studied him. 'Are you sure? Knowing the gory details will hurt you more and it won't change what happened.'

'If I don't know I'll go crazy imagining the possibilities. Did Erik touch you?'

Neve nodded.

Cursing under his breath, Jasper resumed his trek back and forth across the floor. 'How far did things go?'

'As far as they can without actual sex.'

His eyes grew as large as golf balls. 'Jesus, woman!' He needed a few deep breaths before he could continue. 'Did you get the intel you wanted to ruin them?'

'Not yet, but I'm close.'

Jasper leaped at her, pushing her back into the mattress, he pinned her in place with his powerful limbs. 'How much closer can you get? Do you have to sleep with the guy before you learn his secrets?' Lifting her skirt and sliding her panties aside, he shoved a finger inside. 'I should fuck you here and now before I miss my chance at taking your virginity.'

Her pretty, little cheeks flushed red. '*Jas!* Please don't do this.'

'Would you rather give yourself to the haughty faerie than to me?' he hissed while thrusting into her again.

Neve bit back the moan trying to escape her delicate throat. 'No! I'm not going to have sex with him at all! If you take my virginity now, you're as good as dead. The seelie take their sacred laws seriously.'

'How can I be sure Erik won't take what's mine?'

She frowned at him. 'Why are you being such an arsehole?'

A short, humourless laugh tumbled out. 'Are you kidding me? Do you expect me to behave like a cheerful puppy while my nemesis screws around with the girl I love?'

Neve's jaw gaped open. 'Do you mean it?'

'Mean what?'

'That you love me?'

Jasper sucked in a breath, not realising he'd let it slip. His features softened as he withdrew his hand from Neve's moist centre. 'Yeah, I mean it. I intended to tell you under better circumstances though.'

A slight smile tugged at her lips. 'Tell me again.'

This time he would do it properly. He hovered above her face, their noses touching. 'I love you, Neve.'

Neve's smile widened. She pulled his mouth down to hers, initiating a gentle kiss. It soon transformed into something more urgent and sensual. She pulled back to whisper, 'I love you too, Jasper.' Those sweet words soothed his aching heart.

With a groan, he returned his attention to her legs, or rather the treasures between them. Her skirt was a mess from the way he'd manhandled her before. The sight gave rise to a pang of guilt. 'I'm sorry, baby. I hope I didn't hurt you.'

Her eyes glistened from unshed tears. 'No. I'm okay.'

Jasper removed her clothes with care. Pausing, he admired the view of her soft, milky skin before kissing every inch of her. Jerking bolt upright, he wore a victorious grin as he wiped his lips on the hem of his t-shirt. 'I should go before I do something dangerous.' He waggled his brows.

Neve rewarded him with the sexiest little giggle. 'If you keep that up Liam will kill you before Erik even gets a chance.'

Hearing Erik's name soured his mood, and he sighed. 'I'm worried, Neve. I feel like I'm losing you to *him*.'

Sitting up, Neve leaned in and combed her fingers through his hair. 'If anyone takes my virginity before marriage, including Erik, he loses his claim on me. I know he intends to drag this thing out for as long as possible.'

'So, what's the plan?'

'Last night, I learned the twins share the same bed. Elna even confessed to sharing *everything* with Erik. I'm almost certain this includes acts of incest, but I need evidence.'

He screwed his nose up. 'Ick. I knew there was something off about them. How do you intend to get evidence?'

'I need a hidden camera I can plant in their room. My uncle agreed to get me one, and I should have it soon. From there it is a matter of waiting until they... you know.'

Jasper grinned. 'You'll be a great spy for the Council one day.'

Neve laughed. 'Hardly.'

'I'm serious. Don't sell yourself short, babe.' Huddling close, he whispered in her ear, 'You'd make a sexy femme fatale.' He pressed a kiss to her neck, eliciting a wave of shivers from her bare body.

An abrupt knock on the door sent Jasper jumping out of his skin and flying across the room. Perched on the windowsill, he blew her a kiss. Then he climbed down the convenient gum tree.

Friday night was not an ideal time for Brendan to meet his spymaster for a business meeting in the pub. But he could not wait to hear what Jacob had to say and he needed space from Bridey. At least their table hid them in the alcove to the rear of the place, and the ambient noise masked their conversation.

Jacob rose to greet him.

'Hey Red, sorry I'm late. I got held up at home.'

Confusion furrowed his brow. 'Held up how?'

'I guess you haven't heard yet. Violet and Sterling decided to crash my private party.'

'Yikes. I bet they were pissed.'

'To put it mildly.' He sat down, pouring himself a beer from the jug on the table. 'What have you got for me?'

'Not much, I'm afraid. Those damn seelie are good at covering their tracks. Every trail I followed led to a dead end.'

'Damnit!' Brendan hissed. 'Hm, I wonder....'

'What is it, Sir?'

'Kieran is putting surveillance on the local seelie nobles. I doubt those stuffy Councilmen would recognise any mention of the drugs. Can you hack into their wire taps? If you catch wind of something, send the Council an anonymous tip. They'll swarm in and eradicate our problem for us.'

'Secretly helping our friends, who are actually our enemies, do their jobs properly by putting a tap on another tap, so they can take care of our... other enemies? Pure genius, Sir.'

Brendan smirked. 'So, can you do it?'

'Breaching the Council's infrastructure won't be easy, but it's not impossible.'

'Good. Hack into this camera feed while you're at it.' He handed Jacob a note with an IP address on it. 'It is Neve's laptop. She has her own little espionage project going on with Alvar's kids. Promise me you won't look at any video footage of Neve.'

'You have my word, Sir. I wouldn't dream of it. The girl is like a niece to me.'

'Thank you. Also, get Stirling to monitor the comms with you. Take shifts so we have ears on them twenty-four-seven.'

'Yes Sir, although do you think you could assign a third helper?' he pleaded with pouting lips.

Brendan laughed as comprehension struck. 'Fine. Violet can help too. Should give me some peace at home.'

Jacob leaned back into his seat, sipping his ale. 'I sense trouble in paradise.'

'No more than usual. We resolved the stuff about Neve and buying the house. It's just…' Tilting back his head and closing his eyes, Brendan sucked in a deep breath. Thoughts of his encounter with Alannah filled his mind. 'I'm torn.'

'How so?'

'Lana is still holding back on me, but every time I see her, I get glimpses of desire. I'm not talking simple lust, either.'

'Oh boy. You know that way lies madness, right?'

'You don't need to remind me,' Brendan scoffed and skulled the rest of his beer. 'Still, if I could break through her emotional barricade, I might have a chance.'

'A chance at what? I hate to be the voice of reason here, but you were the one who told me it was too dangerous to be with her.'

'Obviously, I'd have to be careful. Keep it secret and whatnot. I haven't forgotten the risks.'

Jacob shook his head. 'I hope you know what you're doing here. If you screw this up, I stand to lose two of my closest friends. And say you win her over again, what of Violet and Sterling?'

'See, that's where I'm torn. I'm in love with them all. I know Violet despises Lana and I'm pretty sure the feeling is mutual, so I doubt we'd make one big happy family.'

'Truth. Sterling wouldn't mind, though. I don't know about now, but he used to have a massive hard-on for Alannah.'

'Yeah, he told me. Problem is Sterling and Violet are a package deal.'

'You are their Dom; you could order them to accept Alannah and vice versa.'

He went to argue against the absurdity of Jacob's suggestion but paused to consider it. 'You make a good point. The approach worked for Violet when Stirling and I were at each other's throats.' The thought of making Lana and Bridey fuck each other was appealing in more than an ironic sense. 'Hot damn.'

Jacob chuckled. 'Easy tiger. You haven't even won Alannah over yet. And you're forgetting the other big hurdle in your plan: she is still married to your meathead brother.'

'Trust me, there's no forgetting *him*. Thing is, I don't need Liam to exit the picture. It's not like I subscribe to monogamy anymore.'

'But would Alannah break her marriage vows for you?'

Brendan grinned. 'Why not? She did for my magic twin. She's been fucking Tyler for the last sixteen years.'

'No way!' Jacob bellowed, slamming his palms on the table, and knocking over his glass; the dregs spilling out. Cries of 'Taxi!' echoed through the pub as he snatched a pile of paper napkins to mop up the mess.

Sitting back and casually enjoying the last of the beer in the jug, Brendan watched on with amusement. Once Jacob settled back into his chair with a new round of drinks, Brendan grinned. 'Now do you see why I'm feeling hopeful?'

'Yeah, but you still have your work cut out for you. Alannah's as cold as a midwinter's morning in Antarctica.'

'Yet she is still hotter than the fires of Beltane. I know she has changed; I just have to work the right angle. And after today, I think I know what that is.'

Chapter Fifteen

'I don't have anything!' Neve complained. 'What are you supposed to wear to a Valentine's-themed party hosted by the Seelie Court when you're the guest of honour?'

Caitlin laughed. 'Beats me. I'm sure you have something. Give me a look.'

Neve stepped aside to let Caitlin look through her wardrobe. 'I should stay home. It'd be much safer for all concerned.'

'Don't be silly. This is your perfect opportunity to plant a camera. You did get it, right?'

'Yeah. It's right here.' Neve walked across to her dressing table. She picked up the tiny device Uncle Brendan had left in her room the day before. He had also left detailed instructions for use, so she was able to pair it with her computer. 'It's set to send an audio-visual feed to my laptop.'

'Oh wow! This is gorgeous. It's the perfect colour for Valentine's, or so I'm told.' Caitlin held out a red knee-length cocktail dress with a designer label.

Neve frowned. 'I dunno. It was my great-grandmother's.'

Caitlin's eyes bugged out. 'For real? I didn't think they had fashion like this back then.'

'It's not *that* old. Eighteen years tops.'

'How... Oh, *that* great-grandmother. Yikes. Why do you have one of *her* dresses?'

She shrugged. 'Mum didn't want to throw it out and she thought I'd like it when I'm older.'

'Weird.' Caitlin giggled. 'You know it could be absurdly inappropriate to wear the dress of a dead cursed woman to this Valentine's do.'

Grinning, Neve grabbed the dress and hung it on her door. 'I like your thinking. I'll try it on.'

'What's the deal with Erik hosting a Valentine's party anyway? The magic world doesn't care for the grossly misappropriated occasion. It's not even the right date for it.' Caitlin turned away as soon as Neve started changing her undergarments.

'He said something about catering to his human followers. I guess the hype at school on Tuesday rubbed off on him.' She had gone lingerie shopping especially for this night. Anticipating the private afterparty, she'd bought a sexy black lace set. Tara's dress fit perfectly. 'Can you give me a hand with the zip?'

Caitlin gasped the moment she cast her eyes upon Neve. 'So. F-ing. Hot!' She moved behind Neve to pull up the zipper.

Looking at herself in the mirror, Neve had to agree with Caitlin's assessment. 'I dunno, this might attract too much attention.'

'Pfft, you already have everyone's attention. May as well look stylish while you're at it.'

'Okay, fine. I'll wear it,' Neve conceded. 'Now help me out of it for now.' Once she was back in her shorts and singlet top, she slumped onto the bed. 'I never should have gotten myself into this mess.'

'What mess? What are you talking about, hun?'

'Do you understand what a seelie claim means?'

Caitlin shook her head.

'It's a betrothal. In three years, they will expect me to marry them.'

With wide eyes, Caitlin stared aghast. 'What the? I thought they were messing around to give Jasper the shits.'

'I thought so too. Turns out Erik is dead serious about his claim on me, which makes it legally binding.'

'Does he even love you though? And don't your feelings count for anything?'

Neve shrugged. 'I don't honestly know how either of the twins feel about me. I mean there is obvious attraction, and they want my body. What they did to me on Thursday night proved as much.'

'Oh Gods! What did they do?'

Her cheeks flushed as memories flooded her mind. 'Everything up to and including third base.'

'Isn't that like sexual assault?'

'It would have been if I didn't want it.'

Caitlin fell silent as she stared at her a moment.

Neve fidgeted under Caitlin's scrutiny.

'Are you saying you're okay with this? With the Alvarsson twins using your body?'

'I'm not sure if they are using me, or if they genuinely like me. But, yeah, I've been consenting and enjoying what they do to me... hence the mess I'm in.' Tears began to trickle from her eyes. 'I'm developing... feelings for Erik.' She sobbed. 'I know it's all sorts of wrong, and...'—another sob—'I still love Jasper. I don't know what to do.' Neve collapsed against Caitlin, who pulled her into a comforting embrace.

'Oh, hun. I'm so sorry.' Caitlin offered soothing words. Her gentle stroking lulled Neve into a serene state of being.

'What should I do, Cat?'

'Is there a way to break their claim on you?'

'Only by losing my virginity; but if I do, I put some poor guy's life at risk.'

'What do you mean?'

'According to seelie law, Erik and Elna have the legal right to execute anyone who takes my virginity.'

Sheer horror filled Caitlin's eyes as her face paled. 'That's barbaric!'

'You're telling me. Their whole system is.'

'Wait. What if Erik takes your virginity? What happens then?'

'They lose their claim on me. Erik assured me he won't let things get that far. It's the only way I've been able to placate Jasper after Thursday night.'

'I hate to say this, hun, but seducing Erik may be your only way out of this deal. Get *him* to take your v-card.'

Neve gaped at Caitlin in disbelief. 'I can't believe you would suggest something so... sordid! For one thing, it would destroy Jasper and everything we have, and I'm not even sure I'd be able to pull it off.'

'If you explain the situation to Jasper, he might understand. Better than never having a chance with you. As for seducing Erik, there are… potions you could use.'

'Christ! You're talking about date-rape, Cat. I'm not okay with that.'

'An arsehole like Erik would have it coming though. Alternatively, use your feminine wiles. I'm sure you'll find a way.'

'I dunno. Having sex with Erik would make things more complicated.'

'What other choice is there?'

Neve sighed. 'I could elope with Jasper.'

'Oh hell. Do you really want to spend the rest of your life on the run? Always looking over your shoulder? Wondering if an assassin will take out the man you love today or tomorrow?'

A nervous chuckle slipped from Neve's lips. 'You've been watching too much Jason Bourne lately. You're right though, damnit! I'm screwed, except not in the fun way.'

'What else can you do? Break it off with Jasper and go all in with Erik and Elna?'

Liam sighed as he clicked SUBMIT on his latest warrant application. He preferred the Council's approach to law enforcement to the human way. Compared with his fellow police, he considered himself a patient man. Even so, the hoops he needed to climb through frustrated him. Most cases were time sensitive. The local drug dealers would clean up before he would get a chance to search their property.

'Sergeant Winters?'

He glanced across his desk at the latest rookie on front desk duty. 'Yes, Constable?'

'The mayor is here to see you. He said it was about your latest field assignment. I put him in the first interview room.'

'Thank you.' Liam made his way across the station with urgent steps and a racing heart. Upon opening the door, he found High Magus Kieran pacing the room. 'Your Honour?'

'Let's dispense with the formalities for now, Winters. Please sit.'

Taking the chair across from Kieran, he poured them both a glass of water and waited in silence.

'I need results, now. I can't wait for something to come of Maher's surveillance.'

'Why the sudden urgency?'

'There was a tremor in the southeast. The seismologists suggested Mount Schank is about to erupt. The magic community down there are up in arms about it, and the pressure is on me to give them answers.'

'Shit! Not good. What do you need from me?'

'I want you to put the pressure on Alvar, make him talk.'

'With all due respect, Your Honour, I'm a warlock, not an inquisitor. If Alannah couldn't get the truth out of him with all her powers, how do you expect me to achieve anything?'

'Her approach was wrong. What Alvar needs is a show of force. I've seen how you handle yourself on the field: you can be intimidating, and you have the guts to take this guy down.'

Liam shook his head. 'I'm used to dealing with lowly street scum. Alvar won't fear my empty threats.'

'Then make the threats real. Your attunement to the elements ought to do the job.'

Blood drained from Liam's face as he stared aghast at Kieran. 'You're suggesting torture. I'm not cut out for that sort of thing.'

Kieran narrowed his eyes. 'Would you rather see toxic plumes of ash decimate your home?'

'No, Your Honour.'

'Right, I'm glad we understand each other. Best get on it quick. Those volcanoes could go off any day now.' Kieran swallowed his glass of water in one gulp and rose. 'I'll show myself out.'

Slumping forward, Liam burrowed his head in his arms. He understood Kieran's desperation. *But torture?* Violence and bloodshed were nothing new to Liam, he was a battle-hardened warrior. But when he fought, it was with honour and a sense of justice. He was not a sadist. There was not a cruel bone in his body. *Ironically, my brother is better suited to Kieran's latest assignment.* Liam considered calling on Brendan. *Lana will know how to contact him.* Yet the idea of admitting cowardice to his archrival was absurd, so he dismissed it.

A strange, intrusive thought came to him out of nowhere: *I could use this to become the man Lana needs.*

Alannah startled. She almost dropped her towel when she stepped from the ensuite into her bedroom. Brendan had snuck in again and was sitting on her bed. 'You need to stop doing this. Send a warning text to my burner phone next time.'

He gave her a cocky grin. 'But this approach is more fun, especially when you greet me attired such as you are.'

With an eye roll, she marched across the room to her wardrobe. 'I don't have any more updates for you. Sorry to disappoint.'

Brendan laughed. 'I'm far from disappointed. Besides, I'm the one with news this time.'

With clothes in hand, Alannah gestured for Brendan to turn around.

'Why? It's not like I haven't seen it all before.'

'Don't make me kick your arse.'

His smirk widened. 'Still not much incentive.'

Scowling, she stormed toward him.

'Okay, fine.' He turned to face the window. It wasn't the opposite direction, but at least he wasn't watching her outright.

'For the record, my body has changed a lot since you last saw it,' Alannah explained while hooking her bra in place.

'Right,' Brendan scoffed. 'That's why you still look amazing in the same old clothes from high school.'

She felt her cheeks blush at his compliment. *Stupid feelings!* 'I'm not talking about my figure overall. I look different when naked. Childbirth takes its toll on a woman's body.'

He shifted on the bed, gawking at her before she had a chance to finish dressing.

'Brendan!'

'You still look good to me.'

Frowning, she threw her t-shirt on. 'You can't see the stretch marks from there.'

'Come closer, then.'

'*No!*'

Leaping from his seat, Brendan tugged at her t-shirt, pulling her up to the bed where he perched on the edge. She bit her lip as he trailed a finger along the marks on her thighs, sucked in a breath as he lifted her top to inspect her belly. 'They're just scars, Lana. Everyone carries them, although sometimes on the inside. Don't feel ashamed of them. If anything, you should feel proud. They signify the life you carried inside you, the beautiful child you raised.'

A single tear escaped Alannah's eye before she realised her guard was slipping. Taking a deep breath, she clamped down on her emotions.

Brendan flicked at the diamond in her belly button. 'You still have this.'

'It's not the same ring. I took the old one out during the pregnancy and got the piercing redone when Neve turned one.' Needing to put some distance between them, she stepped back and put her skirt on.

'Do you think…'

Alannah stood before him again, feeling more comfortable with all her clothes on. 'Do I think what?'

'Could you show me some baby photos of Neve?'

Damn him! She felt more of her defences crumbling away. 'I suppose so. But first, what news did you have for me?'

'I heard there was a tremor in the southeast, near Mount Schank. They reckon it could blow any day now.'

'Shit! We need answers ASAP.'

'My offer still stands. I could get the Syndicate to investigate the Seelie Court.'

'What's in it for you? There's always a cost with dark mages.'

'I don't expect anything from you, Lana. I'm as concerned as you are.'

She studied him, looking for signs of deception, but saw none. 'Okay. I'd appreciate anything you can do to help.'

Beaming, Brendan rose and hugged her. 'That's the spirit. Promise I won't disappoint.'

'Don't make me regret asking a bunch of crooks for help.'

He stood back and saluted her, an impish gleam in his eye. 'Thief's honour.'

Alannah laughed and Brendan joined her. 'Okay, wait here. I'll get the photo albums.'

She returned, carrying three albums. Brendan had made himself comfortable on the bed, leaving a narrow space either side. 'Shove over,' she demanded, climbing in beside him. He shuffled over a couple of inches, meeting Alannah's glare with a smirk. She suffered the contact her leg made with Brendan's. *It's not so bad.* But that was the problem. She enjoyed his touch too much.

The first photo book was a complete record of Neve's first year. Brendan took his time perusing each page. 'I love the way you decorated the pages,' he admitted.

'Thanks. It's called scrapbooking.'

Reaching the last page of the baby book, he slid a finger across the plastic sheet protector. 'She was such a sweet, little thing. And we made her.'

Alannah could not talk, not without giving away how she was choking up.

He closed the baby album. 'Are there more?'

'Yes,' she squeaked.

Tugging her face toward him, Brendan gazed upon her and wiped away one of her tears. 'Hey, are you okay?'

After taking a deep breath, she nodded. 'Yeah. Looking at these photos brings out my sentimental side. Here.' She handed him Neve's toddler album.

A broad smile grew on Brendan's face as he turned the pages. 'You can see her personality coming out in these photos.'

Alannah laughed. 'Yeah. She was such a brat back then. Stubborn and insolent.'

'Gee, I wonder where she got that from,' Brendan jested.

She slapped him without thinking.

'What? It's the truth.'

'I guess she got a double whammy because her bio dad was just as bad. Still is as far as I'm concerned.'

Brendan turned on the smouldering eyes when he faced her. 'Is that so, Lana?'

He kept her eyes locked on his, reeling her in. Yet he did not use magical compulsion. Alannah could still exercise her own will. Blinking, she broke his hold on her and turned her attention back to the photos of Neve. 'These go all the way through to her kindy years. The third book is Neve at primary school.'

'Right. Thanks for showing me all these. It's not the same as being there, but it helps.'

She almost retorted: *Whose fault is that!* But a pang of guilt made her bite back the remark with a sigh instead. Brendan did not know about her until recently. Things might have been different if she had told him.

A knock sounded at the door. A second later the subject of their conversation stood in the doorway. Neve eyed them. 'Sorry Mum, I didn't realise you had company.'

'It's okay, hun. Come in.' As Neve closed the door, Alannah recast the soundproofing ward. 'I was showing your uncle Brendan some photos of you.'

Neve drew up beside Alannah to see the primary school photos. 'Oh gawd, I look like such a dork there.'

'Nonsense. You've always been a beauty,' Alannah countered.

She scrunched up her nose. 'You're biased, Mum, so your opinion doesn't count.'

Brendan laughed. 'For the record, I agree with your mum.'

'You're still family, so your opinion doesn't count.'

'Hm. What would your two boyfriends have to say on the matter?' Brendan teased.

Neve's jaw dropped. 'I don't know what you're talking about.'

Alannah placed a hand on her arm. 'Neve, sweetie, I know all about what you're doing. And I know about Jasper.'

She glowered at Brendan. 'You told her?'

'Don't blame this on your uncle,' Alannah interceded, 'I forced it out of him.'

'And I worried about you,' Brendan added.

'I thought I could trust you, but you're just like my father!'

Brendan gasped. 'You take that back!'

'Neve, calm down, please,' Alannah pleaded. 'Neither of us are trying to discipline you here. Your predicament is punishment enough. I want to know how I can help.'

'Unless you can find a way to break Erik and Elna's claim on me, there's not much you can do.'

Brendan put the album aside and sat up straight. 'Actually, we are both working on possible solutions.'

Neve's eyes lit up. 'Really?'

'Yes,' Alannah replied. 'Try to keep Jasper out of trouble in the meantime.'

'You're the best!' Neve jumped onto the bed and hugged them both, corking Brendan's thigh with her knee in the process.

'Ooof!'

'Oops, sorry.' Neve gave him a coy smile.

He mussed up her hair. 'I'll live.'

'Was there anything else?' Alannah asked. 'I assume you had something to say or ask me when you first entered the room.'

'Oh right. I was planning to lie about going over to Caitlin's tonight. But since you know about my plan, I guess you may as well know the truth. I'm going to a party at Erik and Elna's house tonight. It's my best chance to plant the hidden camera in their room. I'll slip away for a bathroom break when they get distracted. I've already sussed out the perfect spot for it.'

'I can't believe I'm letting you do this, but okay. Your surveillance may end up proving useful in more ways than you realise. But hun, *please* be careful.'

'I will. Thanks Mum.' Neve pecked her on the cheek before bouncing out of the room.

Alannah sighed as the door closed. 'Welcome to parenting.' Turning to look at Brendan, she noticed he wore a massive grin. 'What's with the dumbass smile?'

'She said I was like her father.'

'You know it was an insult, right? She was comparing you to Liam.'

'I know, but she still came close to calling me Father. I could get used to it.'

'Brendan—'

He clapped a hand over her mouth. 'Shoosh. I know what you're going to say. Please don't spoil this moment for me.'

She gave him a small nod before taking stock of their positions.

Brendan removed his hand, but remained in place, staring down at her.

Clearing her throat, Alannah glanced to where his legs straddled her. When she met his eyes again, he leaned in with obvious intent. She halted his progress with two hands on his rock-hard chest. 'Don't push your luck, Brendan.'

He jumped to his feet. 'Shit! Sorry, I guess I misread your signals.' After trudging across the room to her window, Brendan spun around growling. 'You know what? I'm not sorry, Lana. Encrypted military comms are easier to read than the mixed messages you keep giving off. Do all those feelings confuse you, or do you enjoy messing with my head?' Not sticking around for an answer, he made a quick exit through her window.

The nerve! To accuse me of messing with his head after the way he keeps toying with my emotions! Tears threatened to break through her emotional dam, while her core throbbed with a need only one man could satisfy. Rolling onto her side with a huff, she hid under her quilt, and tried to push all thoughts of Brendan aside.

The sound of the television was the only sign of life greeting Liam when he got home that afternoon. Not even the smell of cooking titillated his taste buds. 'Lana?' He strode down the hall and found her staring at the evening news in a near-catatonic state. He knelt in front of her. 'Are you okay, babe.'

She blinked. 'Huh?'

'You were zoning out. I asked if you are okay.'

'Sorry, I guess I got lost in my thoughts.'

When Liam placed a hand on her thigh, she flinched, sparking another warning signal. He perched beside her. 'Did something happen today?'

'Our first volcano.' She spoke with a distracted tone while staring into the distance.

His heart rate picked up. 'What?'

Alannah finally focused her attention on him. 'There was a tremor near one of our volcanoes in the southeast. I've been watching the news because it's only a matter of time.'

'Oh yeah, that. Kieran spoke to me about it today. The magical folk down there are crying out for action, so he wants me to step things up with our investigation.'

'I'm glad.' She smiled. 'You're a good man, Liam.'

He huffed. 'You might not think so after I do what Kieran asked of me.'

'So long as you don't go breaking any hearts.'

'No, just flesh and bones.' As the implication of her words struck him, Liam cursed. He wanted to ask her about Brendan, but recollection of the bugs stopped him. Putting an arm around her instead, he tried to pull her against him, but she remained stiff as a board. 'You're freaking me out here, Lana.'

Looking up to his face, she revealed the shimmer of unshed tears. 'Sorry.'

He tucked some loose strands of hair behind her ear, again making her recoil. 'I don't think you're the one who should be sorry. I know you're hurting, but please don't shut me out. Not after all we've been through. We have come so far.'

'I don't know if I have the strength anymore.'

Confusion furrowed his brow. 'Strength for what?'

Her head dropped against his shoulder, and her voice dropped to a whisper. 'The more I open up and let you in, the harder it is to keep him out.'

Liam tensed. 'Did he—'

She shook her head. 'Seeing him again has brought up lots of repressed feelings I worked hard to bury. My feelings for him are tangled with my very essence. It's why I closed myself off. I'm sorry, Liam.'

He felt as though she was dragging his nerves over a cheese grater. 'Lana—'

'I'm still in love with him.'

Closing his eyes, he sucked in a deep breath to calm himself. 'I know, I've always known it. I guess I was kidding myself to think I could compete with him.'

Alannah reached out and took his hand, clutching it in her lap. 'Does everything have to be a competition with the two of you?'

Swallowing hard against his Adam's apple, Liam nodded. 'Kinda yeah, when it comes to you it does.'

Her hand reached up to cup his face. 'I love both of you.'

'But you can only have one of us.'

'It might have been an impossible choice.'

'What are you saying, Lana?'

'He made the choice for me when he left, and you stood by me.'

Liam rose along with his temper. 'Am I the fucking consolation prize?'

Alannah stared at him in wide-eyed terror. 'Gods, no!'

'Really? Because it's how I've felt for the last sixteen years. We wouldn't be here having this argument if he'd never left. You never would have married me if he'd stuck around.'

'But he did leave.'

'And now he's back. What happens when he makes his move?' Liam shot his hand out to silence her interruption. 'Don't tell me he won't try anything, because you'll only be fooling yourself.'

'What do you want me to say?'

'The truth. Always the truth.'

'I already told you how I feel. I don't know any more.'

'I guess this leaves us in a holding pattern for now. I need some air.' He made for the front door.

'What about dinner?' Alannah called out.

'I'll get something at the pub.' He could use a drink anyway. The sound of her breaking down in a sobbing fit stopped him at the door. If not for his foul mood, he would have stayed to comfort her, but he was no good to her in his condition.

After the short drive to the pub, Liam's stomach had twisted in knots. It was no use. Food and drink were unlikely to stay down. Glancing in his rear-view mirror confirmed he had the gear for an evening surf. He cranked the ignition and high-tailed it down to the beach.

After hanging the last of the party decorations, Elna turned to find Erik watching her. His neutral expression gave nothing away. Yet the way his eyes followed her had Elna wondering about the dark places his mind went. She hopped down from the step ladder. 'Penny for your thoughts?'

'Nice try, sweet pea. You know it's a one-way street with me.'

She pouted. 'Not fair. My mind is an open book to you, and you won't even give me a hint of your wicked musings.'

Closing the distance between them, his lips curled into a crooked smile. 'All in good time, sugarplum.' He tapped her nose.

Her attempt to bite his finger failed, prompting a snicker from him.

Towering over her, Erik's eyes darkened. 'Besides, if you didn't want me to know all your dirty little secrets, you would have blocked me out with your mind shield.'

She crossed her arms in a show of defiance. 'Perhaps I will from now on.'

Erik gave her a smug grin. 'A bit late, sweetheart, but go ahead and try.'

With a huff, Elna turned on her heels, strode across the living room, and sat in her armchair.

'What has you in such a wretched mood?'

'Why not save your breath and read my mind?'

He perched himself on the edge of the sofa. 'Because I want you to tell me.'

'It's the Winters girl. I know you think she's the one, but I don't trust her.'

'Are you sure this isn't the green-eyed monster rearing its ugly head?'

She glared at him. 'I might be jealous but at least I'm not blind. With all your skills as an enchanter, how can you not sense she is trouble?'

'Oh, but I do. It's part of what draws me to her.'

'You are a love-struck fool.'

He scowled at her. 'Do not insult me so. I am aware of the risks. Fear not, my little blossom, I will not endanger you.'

'It is not me I worry about.'

His tone softened. 'I love how much you care for your cruel-hearted brother. For what it's worth, my charms have been working. I know for a fact Neve is falling hard. She will profess her undying love in no time, you'll see.'

'Maybe so, but I still think we should do something about her feelings for Jasper.'

'Hm… very well. If it will ease your mind.' He grew silent for a few minutes and Elna could almost see the gears turning as he concocted his scheme.

Elna fidgeted with the hem of her short summer dress. It pleased her no end when she caught Erik's eyes on her legs.

'Quit it, Elna.'

Adopting a coy smile, she fluttered her lashes. 'Sorry, am I distracting you?'

'You know you are. The sight of your legs would drive most people to distraction. Now stop drawing attention to them and let me think.'

Sighing with satisfaction, she straightened her dress and kept her hands busy by scrolling through her social media feed.

'I have an idea,' he announced at last. 'Did Jasper reply to our invitation?'

She brought up the event page. 'Yes, he has marked himself as going.'

'Good. I want you to make sure there is an unseelie dealer present tonight.'

'Okay. Should I switch the supply?'

'Not this time. For my plan to work, it needs to be the genuine article.'

The pieces fit together in Elna's brain, and she giggled with delight. 'You are such a devious devil sometimes.'

Erik grinned. 'You mean all the time.'

Chapter Sixteen

The sun was dipping below the horizon by the time Liam's temper had settled. He dropped onto his board to soak up the last of its rays while focusing on some breathing exercises.

'That was quite a display of raw fury.' Saoirse's smiling face greeted him as it peaked over through the ocean's tumultuous surface.

He sighed. 'Hi Saoirse. How are you?'

'I'm okay, all things considered. The funeral rites finished, and I finally feel a sense of freedom setting in.'

'Good to hear. I suppose you will want to travel the seas of the world now.'

'Eventually, but not yet. I am still a warrior with obligations.'

Shutting his mind off to the fears and doubts nagging him, Liam forced a smile. 'I know exactly what you mean.'

'You appear troubled, Liam. Would you like to talk about it?'

He shrugged. 'I'm not sure if I should.'

'It might help ease your worries.'

Liam considered how to approach the topic. 'There are two issues giving me grief. The first has me torn between my sense of duty and my... moral code, I guess you could say. My superior has tasked me with a secret mission. It involves forcing information out of someone by any means necessary. That includes torture.'

She nodded her understanding. 'You have a good heart, Liam. I can see why this would unhinge you. Do you have good reason to suspect this man is guilty of something?'

'Yes and no. I'm quite certain he is withholding critical information. I don't believe he committed the crime in question. He doesn't deserve to suffer unspeakable pain.'

'Then don't do it. Find another way.'

Liam huffed. 'If only it were so simple. Hundreds—possibly thousands—of innocent lives are on the line pending this information.'

Her eyes widened. 'This about the volcanoes, isn't it?'

'Yeah.'

She fell silent for a moment, lost in thought. Her eyes lit up when she spoke again. 'What if you look at this like a battle? A few innocent lives lost or hurt for the greater good. What is one man's pain if you can save thousands?'

'You sound like the High Magus. I get your point, Saoirse, but it doesn't make my job any easier.'

Her countenance slumped. 'I guess not.' She studied his face a moment. 'What was the other issue?'

'Gods, where do I even start?'

'How about the beginning?' she suggested with a coy expression.

'How long do you have? This might take a while.'

'For you, Liam, I have all night.' Her eyelashes fluttered. 'But we should move to the reef first; that way you can sit on something more stable than your surfboard.'

'Good point.'

They swam together, Liam using his board. Once they settled on the rocks, he began his long narrative:

> *I've been in love with Alannah Winters since before I understood the full meaning of the word. We lived and played together as children until her father took a job interstate when I was nine. But not even the distance*

between us was enough to quell my feelings for her. I stayed in contact with her as much as I could. Hearing about her first boyfriend was heartbreaking. I tried to move on with my life, even started dating a local mage, all to no avail. I could not shake the connection I had with Lana.

Imagine my relief when I learned she was finally returning home. Unfortunately, I wasn't the only one looking forward to Lana's homecoming...

Saoirse listened to his convoluted history with Alannah and Brendan.

He teared up when he got to the part where Alannah had been on trial, and again when he thought he had lost her to Brendan. Their recent ordeals gave him the most difficulty. His voice choked up numerous times.

'Hm,' she mused with a furrowed brow, after a long pause when he finished.

'What?'

'I have a theory, but you won't like it.'

'It can't be worse than all the depressing thoughts I've had on the matter. Tell me.'

'The wisewoman of my clan believes it is possible to love more than one person in our lives. But we only have one soulmate, one person who connects with us on a deep, spiritual level. After hearing your story, I am inclined to agree with her. Alannah might love you, but her soul belongs with your brother.'

Liam sucked in a sharp breath through gritted teeth. 'You're right, that is a hard pill to swallow. Especially since I know it's true.'

The party was already in full swing when Neve arrived with Caitlin. Lanterns lit the path up to the house twinkling with fairy lights inside and out. The interior was aglow with shades of pink and red. Light danced among the glittering streamers hanging up all about the place. Trip-hop music completed the sensual ambience.

'Wow. This place is incredible,' Caitlin admitted.

'Yeah. More so tonight than usual, although it was pretty before the decorations.' As soon as they stepped into the living room, Neve locked her gaze with Erik.

His eyes popped, and he beamed at the sight of her. 'Ladies and gentlemen, please bow before your future queen, the Lady Neve Winters.'

The crowd hushed, making a path for her and dropping to their knees.

'This is so strange,' Caitlin whispered in her ear, clinging to Neve's arm as they approached Erik and Elna.

'You're telling me.'

The Alvarsson twins sat upon makeshift wooden thrones covered in red hearts. There was a third, empty throne between them. As soon as Neve reached the twins, they both rose to greet her with a hug and chaste kiss on each of her cheeks.

Erik held Neve by the arms as he looked her up and down. 'You look exquisite tonight, my dear.'

'Thanks.' She thought he looked stunning in his tailored black suit. Even Elna looked hot in her long, sleek dress of pink silk, matching Erik's shirt. 'You both look gorgeous.'

Grinning, he exchanged a look with Elna before instructing her to sit beside him. 'On second thoughts, you are much too far away. Come here, sweetheart.' Erik gestured for her to sit in his lap. His arousal pressed against her backside.

Heat flushed Neve's cheeks and coursed through her bloodstream when his lips brushed her ears. 'I'm going to have a hard time behaving in a respectable manner tonight.'

No kidding. Caitlin's suggestion could work, after all. Seduction would be Neve's backup plan if she didn't get the intel she needed. She ground herself against him, leaning back to whisper, 'I hope we don't have to behave *all* night. I'm keen to escape to your room as soon as possible.'

'Mm, I like your thinking, but there are a few formalities to get through first.'

Neve puckered her lips in a pout, making Erik laugh.

He tapped her nose. 'I appreciate your appetite for pleasure. But it is important to remember our positions of power come with responsibilities. Our subjects have certain expectations.'

With a sigh, she relaxed against him, content to tease him as much as possible in the meantime. 'I hate waiting so many years before tying the knot. In times gone by, we could have married and screwed each other's brains out by now.'

'Indeed.' Erik's hands settled lightly around her throat. 'Although I doubt you would have liked the way men treated women back then.'

After an hour of small talk with various guests, Neve observed Jasper entering the room. It took every ounce of willpower to avoid reacting to his presence. He glanced about, adopting a casual attitude for appearances' sake. Their eyes met, but he averted his gaze before either of them could betray their feelings.

She felt Erik chuckle. 'He may fool others, but I can tell he still wants you.'

'Why would he still want me?'

'Have you looked in the mirror lately, beautiful? You're the prettiest girl in school.'

Her heart skipped a beat.

'Quite besides which, you are also the one who got away. Guys like Jasper get a real bee in their bonnet about that sort of thing. Do you have any regrets about leaving him for me and my sister?'

'No. I am extremely happy with both of you.'

'I am pleased to hear it because I have a surprise for you.'

She looked at him.

He smiled. 'You will need to return to your own seat for this.' As soon as Neve obliged, Erik rose. 'Ladies and Gentlemen, I have an announcement to make.'

The room grew silent.

'With a joyous heart I announce the forthcoming betrothal of Neve Winters and myself.'

Gasps and murmurs filled the room, but they did not compare to the look of abject horror on Jasper's pale face.

Erik dropped to one knee before her. Capturing her undivided attention, he produced a white gold claddagh ring. Jade formed the heart centrepiece. 'Neve, this ring represents my promise to remain faithful to you. I will love and cherish you until the day I can solidify my vows in marriage. By accepting it, you promise to honour the sanctity of my claim on you.'

Neve's heart escaped her chest and made its home in her throat. Overcome by emotion, she lost the ability to talk, so she took the ring and placed it on her finger.

He swept her up in his arms and kissed her deeply, prompting a cheer from their audience. 'Dance with me.' Erik tugged her hand, leading her onto the dancefloor in the lower room.

As they passed through the swarm of people, Neve noticed Jasper disappear into the crowd. A pang of remorse churned her stomach. *This is going to take some explaining. I hope he believes me because at this point, I'm doubting myself.*

In desperate need of a tension release, Brendan stormed into Caleb's room, only to find it empty. *Damnit! He must be with Bridey.* If so, Brendan knew he would have to share, but he was not in the mood for a threesome.

Bridey had locked the door to her room. *What the hell? She never locks me out of their fun.* Brendan pressed his ear to the door to listen but could not hear a peep. With his ring of blue lace agate, he channelled senses mana. He heightened his hearing, but still got nothing. *Did she erect a sound ward?* Using his nether attunement, he detected and broke through the barrier.

Bridey's voice came through loud and clear. 'Mm, it's been too long since I've marked you. I'm quite pleased with the pattern of welts I've left on your back.'

Brendan smiled, knowing how much Caleb loved a good flogging.

'Indeed, Madame. But I'm guessing you didn't put those wards up to block out my screams. Did you also want to discuss business?' Levi's voice replied.

The smile slipped from Brendan face as alarm bells rang. Bridey had set Levi free, along with the rest of her slaves, years ago. *Why is she still meeting with him?*

'An astute observation, my love. Did you know Brendan is in contact with Alannah again?'

Shit!

'I thought you and Caleb had wrapped him around your little fingers?'

Bridey sighed. 'We did, but someone spilled the beans about his kid. I'm guessing it was the damned boggart Brendan came here to do business with.'

Why is Bridey discussing this with Levi?

'He wouldn't have called on Alannah if it weren't for discovering his daughter. He has a soft spot for this child,' explained Bridey.

'Christ! He could be getting close to Alannah again. Do you know if they are on good terms?'

'I'm not sure, but we need to act fast if we are going to stop their alliance. I still don't know how much Tara told Alannah before she died, but I'd put money on Brendan discovering part of the truth.'

'Hey, Winters, what are you doing?' Caleb's voice called out from behind.

Bottling his panic, Brendan turned and grinned as he released the door handle. 'I was looking for you actually.'

'Oh? What can I do for you, Sir?'

'You can get that sexy arse of yours into my bedroom and assume the position, pronto.'

Running his tongue along the piercings in his lower lip, Caleb grinned. 'Yes, Sir.'

While Bridey had not yet resumed her submissive role, Caleb was wearing his collar again. Good thing too, because Brendan could not fathom holding back. He took out all his frustration on Caleb's body, after which he made love to the man like his life depended on it.

A dark part of Brendan's subconscious did not want him to sleep. Even with his sex-addled brain, the dreams returned: visions and voices of revenge against Liam filled his mind. The methods were always different yet they all gave him the same perverse sense of satisfaction. Watching the life slip away from his victim always thrilled him.

Climbing out of bed, he took care to avoid disturbing Caleb's sleeping form. After the door closed behind him, he let out a deep breath before heading towards the kitchen. Stopping at the linen press, he grabbed a towel to wipe his sweaty brow. Without the air conditioning on, the house sweltered, so he decided on a cold drink.

'Couldn't sleep either, huh?' Bridey's voice startled the ice right out of his hands. Cubes of frozen water ricocheted across the kitchen tiles.

He spun around to face her. 'Christ, Bry! Are you trying to give me a heart attack?'

'Not my intention. You seem awfully jumpy.'

Picking up the plastic tray, he dropped the surviving ice cubes in a whiskey tumbler. 'The dreams are back.' *I need a double shot—screw that, make it a triple shot.* Drink in hand, he rounded the breakfast bar.

Bridey's eyes lit up at the sight of him. 'I see you've already taken to walking around this house naked.'

Brendan shrugged. 'It's my house. I don't need to worry about offending any of *your* guests.'

'Indeed. About that, I was thinking of setting up a new base of operations nearby, for business purposes. Although, it could also serve as my home too.'

It felt as though a vacuum had sucked all the air from his lungs. 'What are you saying, Bry?'

'Correct me if I'm wrong, but I don't think you want to live under the same roof as me.'

'Consider yourself corrected. I know things are currently confusing, but I still love the heck out of you and Caleb. I don't want you going anywhere.'

Her eyes brimmed with tears. 'Really?'

He sat on the couch and pulled her into his lap. 'Yes. But this is my house, Bry, so I agree you should set up your consultation parlour elsewhere. I'll need to set up a new office too.'

'So, you're not dumping us for your cousin?' Her question reminded him of the suspicious conversation he had overheard earlier.

His hackles perked up. 'Is that what this is about? Look, I'm staying here for my daughter, not because of Lana. The only reason I don't want to conduct business here is because I'd like this to be a safe place for Neve to visit.'

'Okay, I understand. Thank you, handsome.' Bridey rose and retrieved something from her room. She handed him the violet collar embellished with silver thorns. 'Will you do the honours, Sir?'

Feeling the genuine call of nature, Neve excused herself from the festivities. After using the nearest bathroom, she snuck upstairs. Finding their room unlocked eased her anxieties a tad. She did not expect to find Jasper sitting on their bed, however. 'Oh Gods, Jas, what are you doing here? This is Erik and Elna's room. You could get in serious trouble for being in here.'

He looked up at her with solemn eyes before glancing around. 'This space is so bland I figured it was a guest room.'

'You need to leave, *now*.'

Ignoring her, he trailed a hand along the pink bedspread. 'This is where it happened, huh?'

'Where what happened?'

His eyes pierced her with fierce intensity. 'Where Erik stole my girl.'

'Jasper, please, you know—'

'Why didn't you tell me you were getting engaged to the guy?'

She sighed. 'It's a betrothal, not an engagement; although I haven't seen a written contract yet. This is all part of their claim on me. For the record, I don't intend to go through with it. Now, can you please get out of here before they catch you? I need to plant this camera and get back to the party before they grow suspicious.'

Neve headed over to the ensuite door. Retrieving the small screwdriver from her purse, she removed one of the screws from the door's handle.

'I'm surprised you're still going through with this plan,' Jasper remarked with a bitter tone.

'Why would you think that?' she asked while replacing the screw with a high-tech replica. The head of the new screw contained a minuscule camera and microphone. The tail was the transmitter.

'Have you forgotten how I can read emotions, Neve? You let your shield down during Erik's announcement. I saw how much you wanted him.'

'That wasn't what it looked like. I was faking it all.' With the camera in place, she turned to face him. Panic struck her when she saw him gazing upon a clear vial of liquid. 'Oh hell, Jas! Whatever you're thinking or feeling over this, it's not worth dying for!' She rushed forward to grab the vial from his hands.

'Relax, babe. This isn't poison.' He produced a second one from his pocket. 'It is a feel-good potion. I bought these from a guy downstairs thinking we could take them together sometime.'

Neve's brow furrowed as she studied the potion. 'How do you know this stuff is safe?'

'I got a good read on the guy who sold 'em. I'm confident they are the genuine article. Anyway, I had planned to wait until our date tomorrow, but I want to take them now.'

'I don't know, Jas. What exactly is this stuff?' Alarm bells started going off in her head. The potion vials looked sinister and the hairs on the back of her neck were prickling.

'Ever heard of Rhapsody?'

Shit, no wonder I don't like the look of it! 'Isn't it an illegal drug?'

'Yeah, but it's only illegal because the unseelie make it. It's safe.'

'Why can't this wait until tomorrow? I should get back—'

Jasper seized her by the waist and pulled her into his lap. 'For one thing, I could use the pick-me-up after that display of yours. I also need the reassurance I haven't lost you to him. Take it with me and show me your true feelings.'

Her eyes began to water. 'Are you saying you don't believe me when I tell you how much I love you?'

'You've become such a good actor lately, it is hard to discern the truth from your lies. I need proof, Neve. Solid proof right now that you love me. Without it, I'm walking out of here and our relationship is over.'

The tears began to trickle down her cheeks. Looking into his eyes, she saw the reflection of her own anguish. Jasper was hurting because of her. 'Okay. If this is what it takes to prove how much I love you, I'll do it.'

With a sigh of relief, he opened his vial and waited for her to do likewise. Together, they threw the foul-tasting liquid down their throats like bitter medicine. 'The guys said this stuff is fast-acting, so we shouldn't have to wait long.' Drawing her closer, he whispered, 'Thank you, gorgeous.' Jasper's mouth claimed hers in a fervent kiss. Before long they were rolling around on the bed in a frenzy of passion.

By the Gods, whatever else this potion is, it sure is a-mazing! Neve giggled as fingers brushed against soft flesh. 'Tickles.'

'Hm, how about this? Does this tickle?'

Gasping, she closed her eyes as pleasure shot through her body. 'No, *that* feels awesome.'

'Do you want more?'

'Yes, please.'

Her world exploded in ecstasy. Every feeling heightened. The colours were all so rich and bright. The eyes looking down at her shone like jaspers, and she giggled. 'Your eyes look like your name.'

He grinned. 'Gods, I love you, Neve.'

'I love you, Jasper.'

'Let me show you how much I love you.' He was kissing her all over.

She giggled. 'How do you plan to show me?'

His beaming face hovered above her again. 'By making love to you.'

'Making love? That's such an odd expression? How do you *make* love?'

Jasper laughed. 'You are so damn cute. Would you like me to show you?'

'Yes.' She nodded for emphasis.

His fingers were moving inside her again, bringing her close to the edge. 'Like this, only better.'

Neve heard herself moaning. The sound was distant compared with Jasper's heavy breathing. 'More.'

He sat up and she found herself missing the warmth of his body. Thankfully, he returned soon enough. Fireworks were going off inside her brain while her body erupted like a volcano.

Minutes, or hours later, Neve became aware of Erik's cold green eyes. They didn't try to stop her. They didn't leave. They watched her.

Chapter Seventeen

Alannah looked up from her pity party where melancholic dread was the guest of honour. Her mood was so dark, even Luna had avoided her since breakfast.

Cara offered her a sympathetic smile when she stepped through the bedroom door. 'The guys are out looking for Liam. You wanna tell me what's going on?'

Waking at dawn, she had discovered Liam had never come home during the night. She freaked. In all their years of quarrelling, it was unheard of for him to stay out the *whole* night. Not wanting to alarm her father-in-law or the Council, she decided to call on her friends for help. 'We had a fight.'

'About Tyler?'

She shook her head and took a deep breath. 'About Brendan.'

Cara stiffened. 'Shit. What did the arsehole do?'

'He has been putting the moves on me and I'm hell confused.'

'Did Liam catch him touching you? Is that why he took off?'

Alannah sighed. 'No. He doesn't even know what Brendan is up to, although he figures it will happen eventually. The argument with Liam was over my feelings for Brendan and how they make him feel inferior.'

'Christ, that man's a tool!'

'Which one?'

Mischief gleamed in Cara's eyes. 'Both of them, although I was referring to Liam. I never could understand the extent of the petty jealousy those guys feel for each other.'

'I know, right! Their rivalry is almost mythic. Such a shame they'll never agree to share me. I get Liam's stance on the matter, but Brendan's? The man lives and breathes polyamory, but he still can't bear the thought of me with Liam.'

Tittering, Cara grinned. 'Hottest threesome ever.'

She whacked Cara across the arm. 'You're not helping.'

Cara frowned. 'Sorry. My mind has taken up permanent residence in the gutter. I blame Ben.'

Alannah arched her brow. 'You hooked up with Ben?'

Lowering her sheepish gaze, Cara nodded. 'Please don't tell anyone. This thing is new and uncertain. Plus, Ben's pack are putting pressure on him to mate with his own kind.'

'Your secret is safe with me.'

Cara sat on the bed beside Alannah. 'So, what's the deal with Brendan?'

Her shoulders heaved in an exaggerated shrug. 'Fucked if I know. He has been running hot and cold, confusing me no end. I don't know if he's playing sick, sadistic games with me or if he wants me back. What I do know is how he is succeeding in breaking down my defences and it scares the hell out of me.'

'What are you scared of?'

'Giving in to him.'

Cara fell silent a moment. 'I'm a little puzzled, so bear with me. Brendan, the man you love more than anything in the universe, has been hitting on you? Why are you afraid of giving in to what you want?'

'You're kidding me, right? Have you forgotten who Brendan is? What he does for a living? You dumped Jacob's arse over less significant crimes. Not to mention all the pain Brendan put me through.'

It was Cara's turn to exhale her exasperation. 'Do you want me to be honest with you, or are you looking for a cheerleader?'

Alannah slumped against her bed head. 'Go on, hit me with it.'

'The only time Brendan committed a crime, the Council stripped those charges from his record. There is no evidence to suggest he is guilty of dark magics, even if he happens to be the head of the Syndicate.'

'Pfft, he might not get his own hands dirty, but he has control over those who do.'

'Let me finish, would ya? As I was saying, there is no evidence. The Brendan I knew didn't have the heart to order people to do evil shit. Not the sort of things the Council are pinning on his organisation. I'm suggesting you give Brendan the benefit of the doubt and find out for yourself.'

'How?'

'Ask him to drop his aura shield and use your magic to read him.'

'Easier said than done, but I guess it's worth a shot. What if I don't like what I see?'

'Then you need to ask yourself if you are willing to forgive him. Do your feelings for him run deep enough to work through the baggage?'

Alannah's phone lit up with an incoming call from Connor and she answered on the first ring. 'Hey.'

'We found him.' Connor's tone sounded ominous.

'And? Where is he? Is he okay?'

'I'm sorry, babe. Liam's not in a good way. I found him passed out and hypothermic on a rock in the middle of the reef. This is beyond my healing skills, so we took him straight to Ross.'

'Gods! Does he have any other injuries?'

'Not that we can see.'

'Okay, thanks Connor. I'll be right over.' Tears were stinging her eyes when she signed off. 'Did you hear?' she asked Cara.

Cara nodded. 'Want me to come with?'

'Yeah.' Alannah took stock of her emotional state and realised she was shaking. 'I need you to drive.' When they both rose, her legs gave way, leaving Cara to catch her. 'This is all my fault. If anything's happened to Liam—'

'Stop, hun! You are not responsible for Liam's actions. Now is not the time to become riddled with guilt.' She eased herself under

Alannah's arm, supporting her like a crutch. 'Let's go see him, okay?'

Alannah consented with tears of trepidation cascading down her cheeks.

It was gratifying to wake to the sight of Neve's satisfied grin, to hear her soft snore. Warmth seeped through every part of Jasper until his brain switched on and panic set in. Sunlight was peeking through the slit in the magenta velvet window coverings. The curtains reminded him which bed he lay in. He had been lucky to survive the night after the stunt he pulled. *I need to get out of here before the faerie bastard catches me.*

He shook Neve. 'Hey, gorgeous, we need to go.'

She mumbled something incoherent and rolled over.

Damnit! After shaking her a few more times, Jasper sighed. The thought of leaving her naked in Erik's bed chilled him to the bone. Time, however, was not on his side. After dressing in haste, he tried the window, lifting it with ease. The trees supporting the building were a convenient escape route. His feet hit the leaf-littered ground in short order.

When it became clear he was near the rear of the house, Jasper cursed under his breath. Scanning the area, he looked for possible exits along the back fence, but saw none. He crept around the side of the house, cringing every time a branch snapped beneath his feet. He got as far as the thicket in the front yard when a firm hand clamped down on his shoulder.

'Leaving so soon?'

Sweat poured from his forehead and a thumping noise pulsed in his ears. Jasper spun around to face the blond man towering above him. 'Uh, hi Erik. I kind of passed out at the party, sorry.'

Sculpted brows rose to meet Erik's hairline. 'You think a simple apology will excuse you after what you did?' With a vice grip, he tugged Jasper by the throat, pulling him onto the porch and shoving him into a chair. 'By rights, your life is mine.'

His mouth gaped open.

'Oh yes, I know exactly what you did. Drugging my girl and taking advantage of her. Shameful.'

'It wasn't like that,' Jasper hissed.

'No? How do you explain the two empty Rhapsody vials beside my bed? The very bed I saw you fucking her in?'

It was becoming impossible to swallow past the lump forming in his throat. 'I needed to know how she felt about me. I never planned to—'

'Enough! I do not care for your pathetic excuses. You took what was mine, and now you must pay.'

He rose to meet Erik head on. 'Go on then.' Jasper had expected a flashback reel of his life to play in fast-forward, or even rewind. Yet, in the face of death, the only thing in his mind's eye was a vision of the woman he loved. *At least we had one moment of pure happiness together before the end.*

Erik snickered. 'You are a fatalistic fool. Death seems too merciful for the likes of you. I have something else in mind.'

It felt as though millions of tiny pin pricks pierced his skin. 'L-like what?'

'If I don't tell the Seelie Court what you have done, they will spare your life. I'm willing to keep my mouth shut on one condition.'

Breath returned to his lungs at the prospect of a long life. 'Name it.'

'You will break off your clandestine relationship with Neve.'

He nodded, already thinking of ways to continue seeing her surreptitiously. 'Fine.'

'I expect a public display of heartache and humiliation that makes her run into my arms for comfort. Anything less and both of your necks will end up on the executioner's block.'

Sharp, stabbing pains emanated from Jasper's tightening chest. 'What?!'

'You heard me. Neve's betrayal warrants the same punishment owed to a scumbag like you. I'm willing to overlook both of your indiscretions if you cut all ties with her.'

'Why spare us?'

'Are you telling me you can't work it out? Not even with your attunement?'

Shit! 'You love her too.'

Erik's lips curled into a lopsided grin. 'What the Court doesn't know won't hurt them.'

The implications terrified Jasper. *The thought of living without her is bad enough. But to see Neve happy with Erik….* Biting back on such dreadful thoughts, he swallowed the metallic taste of his own blood. His teeth had broken through the skin of his bottom lip. *Neve's life is on the line. I need to focus on keeping her safe.*

Confusion set in the moment Liam opened his eyes. 'Lana?'

She was sitting in a chair beside his old bed, hunched over and sobbing. Her gaze snapped to him at the sound of his voice. 'Oh, thank the Gods you're okay.' Alannah leaped forward, wrapping her arms around him.

He stiffened. 'What happened?'

'You almost froze to death. They found you out on the reef. What were you doing out there?'

Memories flooded his mind, and he winced.

'Shit! Are you in pain? Did I hurt you?'

Yeah, but not physically. Liam shook his head. 'I'm okay. I was surfing then...' Saoirse's sweet smile came to mind. 'I grew tired and took a rest on the rocks.'

Alannah's eyes bugged out. 'You fell asleep in the middle of the ocean?'

'Yeah.'

'That's so dangerous! Why were you surfing in the middle of the night?'

'I needed to blow off steam.'

She choked on a sob, tears streaming down her face. 'You almost died, Liam! You almost fucking died, and it would have been my fault. I'm so sorry.'

Relaxing slightly, he put his arms around her. He pulled her tight against his pounding chest. 'Shh. I'm okay. We're okay.' He prayed the lie sounded convincing to at least one of them. 'Is Mum around? I'd love some of her sandwiches.'

'Of course. I'll get her.' After pressing a chaste kiss on his lips, Alannah rose and left the room.

Liam took a moment to focus on his breathing. He had some tough choices to make, but in the interim, there was one clear path to take. Jumping out of bed, he grabbed some old clothes from the wardrobe. He was lucky to find something to still fit over his first stage dad bod.

Mum entered a few minutes later. She carried a platter of sandwiches quartered in perfect triangles. 'What are you doing out of bed? You should be resting!'

'I'm fine, Mum.' He glanced over her shoulder to see worry in Alannah's eyes. 'Really, I am.' He took a handful of the meat and cheese-filled parcels. 'Thanks for the grub. I gotta run.'

Two sets of eyes widened, and Alannah stepped forward. 'What's going on? Is this about our… fight?' Her voice wavered as she spoke.

'No. I have an urgent Council job to get to. I'll see you at home tonight.' He pressed a quick kiss to her forehead and ducked past them both, calling over his shoulder, 'Send my regards to Dad.'

Once outside, he spotted his SUV in the carport. *Someone must have moved it from the beach.* The door was unlocked, and the key sat in the ignition. After shovelling the food into his mouth, he took off toward the address Kieran had given him.

Alvar's home was a decent drive out of town and concealed among the scrub. It was just as well Liam had his glamour-piercing glasses on, else he might have missed the building itself. Dressed all in black with a ski mask to hide his identity, Liam kept to the shadows when he approached. He found a dense patch of forest with a view of the front door where he lay in wait.

When Neve emerged from the house, his breathing spiked. *What the hell?* Alvar's son followed her, stopping on the porch to pull her into his arms and kiss her. A furious fire coursed through his blood. *You stupid, stupid girl. Of all the boys to get mixed up with!* Curbing his desire to throttle the fae creep, Liam watched them leave in a horse-drawn carriage.

A few hours lapsed before Alvar stepped outside.

He is alone, thank the Gods. Channelling energy, Liam threw a lasso around the man and reeled him in.

Alvar's eyes bulged, and a startled cry slipped from his throat.

With a deft grapple, Liam pushed Alvar prone, face-down in the dirt. He pressed his weight into the man's back and a dagger to his throat.

'I wondered when Lord Jet would see fit to send one of his minions after me,' Alvar scoffed.

Hm, he thinks I'm part of the Syndicate. This could work in my favour. 'Tell me what you know.'

'I'd rather die than spill our secrets to the enemy.'

'Sounds like an admission of guilt to me.'

'You want to talk about guilt? You and your kind are the ones polluting the world with dark magic. You're as bad as the humans and the power-hungry Council protecting them.'

'Is that why the Seelie Court are making the volcanoes erupt? You think some mass-destruction will cull our numbers?'

Alvar burst into laughter until he began choking on inhaled dirt. When the fit subsided, he turned his head and spat. 'The Unseelie Court have become too modern. Have you all forgotten the Covenant?'

'The Covenant?'

'Each of the magic races swore to protect the Earth. In turn, the mages held them accountable. But who watches the watchmen?'

Liam froze as bits of ancient lore trickled into his mind: recollections of old books read to him long ago. 'The primordials,' he whispered.

'Ha! You did study your history books. They are returning, and there is nothing you can do to stop them.'

'I thought human armies drove them out of our world in the Middle Ages.'

'No. They never left. They were biding their time until the herald summoned them forth. They slumbered in the primordial depths, or volcanoes as the humans call them. They are waking up as we speak.'

'So, the eruptions are what? A side-effect of them rolling over in bed?'

'Essentially, yes.'

'What happens when they finish waking up?'

'Along with the entire human race, everyone guilty of breaking the Covenant will burn.'

Liam slammed Alvar's face into the ground and took off at lightning speed toward his car. Once inside, he floored it back to town. *Shit, shit, shit!* This news was worse than anything he could have imagined. He stopped in a no-standing zone. *No time to care.* Once inside the Council chambers, he flew passed the reception desk.

'Excuse me sir, you need to—'

He skidded to a stop and spun around. 'Tell the mayor Liam Winters is here to see him.' Turning back toward the stairs, he bolted, not wanting to wait for the lift.

High Magus Kieran gasped at the sight of Liam panting in his doorway. 'You have news, Warlock Winters?'

Taking a moment to catch his breath, Liam nodded. He shut the door and slumped in one of the visitor's chairs. 'The Seelie Court are not responsible for the volcanoes.'

Kieran frowned. 'Do you know who is?'

'Yeah and it looks bad for all mage-kind. We've failed, Your Honour. We broke the Covenant, and we're all going to die.'

'What on Earth are you talking about?'

'The dragons are returning!'

The moment she had the house to herself, Alannah grabbed her burner phone. She sent Brendan a message: I'M ON MY WAY OVER WITH AN URGENT

UPDATE. The news Liam had shared with her the day before could not wait any longer.

His reply came swiftly: NO! MY SAFEHOUSE HAS BEEN COMPROMISED. I'LL COME TO YOU. A few seconds later her phone buzzed again. I'LL BRING BREAKFAST.

Is that some Syndicate code I don't understand? Alannah collapsed onto the couch and thought back to her conversation with Liam. *Is there anything the Council or Syndicate can do to prevent the end of the world? Is this the big secret Tara was referring to? Is it my job to save the innocent?* Her mind swam with all the possibilities.

Movement in the corner of her eye drew Alannah's attention to the back door.

Brendan waved at her through the glass, his hands laden with food bags and coffee cups. As soon as she opened the door, he held out one paper bag with a note written on it: CAST A TEMPORARY SPELL TO DISABLE THE BUGS.

Why hadn't I thought of that before? She took the food offering and sat at the dining table. Closing her eyes, she concentrated on channelling matter. From there, she zeroed in on the listening devices and visualised each of them switching off. She opened her eyes and let out a deep breath. 'Done.'

'Good. I don't suggest using this trick for too long or too often. Could make them suspicious. Here.' Brendan handed her a latte in a South Seas Café keep cup.

Brendan had remembered her favourite coffee shop *and* her order. Another crack formed in her walls. 'Thanks.' After setting the table, she retrieved a bacon and egg roll from her bag and placed it on a plate.

Brendan swallowed two large bites of his meal before broaching the topic. 'What's this urgent news you have for me?'

Alannah eyed her food. The fluttering in the pit of her stomach had gone some way to stifling her appetite. 'Liam found out who is erupting the volcanoes.'

Sipping on his coffee, he looked at her. 'Spit it out already. The suspense is killing me here, Lana.'

'You might find this hard to believe: the dragons never died out or left. They were sleeping… in the volcanoes.'

Brendan's eyes widened.

'Now they are waking up with a serious grudge against us.'

'What do they have against us?'

'Not *us* specifically, but all mage-kind. And humans too. Something about us destroying the natural environment rather than protecting it.'

'Christ, Lana. This is huge! Are you saying every one of those volcanoes houses an individual slumbering dragon?'

She shrugged. 'Your guess is as good as mine. I'm a little iffy on the details.'

'Sounds like an awful lot of fire-breathing destruction.'

'Yeah. Nothing short of a global army could stop them. Even if the Arch Mage can mobilise all the Council's forces, we don't stand a chance. Not without an alliance of some sort.'

'Sounds pretty damn bleak to me.'

They fell into a sombre silence while Brendan finished eating.

Alannah felt a need to shift the topic from such doom and gloom. 'How was your place compromised?'

He glanced at her with shifty eyes.

She used her attunement to the stygian element to bypass any aura blocks he was throwing up.

Brendan sighed with resignation. 'Bridey and Caleb came to town recently. They are staying at my house.'

Incredulous, she stared at him with wide eyes. 'Bridey is here? In town?'

He shrugged. 'I can't speak for her current whereabouts, although my new house is not technically in town so—'

'Brendan! I thought we were working together. How did you fail to mention a major detail like the reappearance of that bitch in my town? Are you...'—she gulped—'still in a relationship with Bridey?'

His eyebrows rose. 'Jealous much? I gotta say, muddy green doesn't suit you.'

'Deflecting much?'

Brendan snorted. 'Yup, that's still a thing I do and so is Bridey.'

The weight of his words crushed Alannah's heart. *He is still with* her.

'I'm sorry, Lana. I was hoping to spare you from all this business.'

'What business? What exactly *do you* do within the Syndicate?'

'I spend most of my time gathering intel and mystic lore.' With a sigh, he leaned back into his chair. 'I also oversee potion trafficking and artefact acquisitions to maintain my street cred. I leave most of the nasty stuff to our great aunt.'

Her jaw dropped. 'You're working with Dana Winters?'

He nodded.

'And you don't practise dark magic yourself?'

'No. I learned how to create a false aura to trick Syndicate members into thinking I've gone completely dark.'

The tension eased in Alannah's muscles. 'Can I see your real aura?'

Brendan smirked. 'Only if I can see yours.'

'Okay, fine. On the count of three. One. Two. Three.' She dropped the last of her emotional barriers, letting him truly see what she was feeling. When Alannah's eyes focused on Brendan's aura, her pulse kicked off at a gallop. Dark, murky clouds within the bright yellow centre were clearing before her eyes. His outer aura shone bright pink and red. The colours of love and lust. Alannah noticed how Brendan was looking at her with ravenous eyes. 'What?'

He blinked a moment, then a neutral mask returned to his face. 'Sorry. I forgot myself for a moment there.'

'Why were you looking at me like that?'

Arching his brow, he adopted a smooth playboy tone. 'Like what, Lana?'

Desire simmered in her core as her eyes narrowed on him. 'Like you were about to eat… me.'

Brendan sucked in an audible breath, then grinned lewdly. 'If memory serves correctly, you make for quite the delectable dish, so I wouldn't say no if you're offering.'

Blushing, Alannah gave him an eye roll. 'Give it a rest, Brendan. I'm done playing your games.'

He rounded the table in two powerful strides, pulling her out of the chair into a firm embrace. 'I'm not playing, Lana. I'm sure my aura's about as bright red as yours right now.' He spoke with a gruff voice as he backed her into the table. With one swift movement, he propped her backside on the ledge. His right hand hooked her left leg around his waist. Their lips almost touched as his thumb stroked small circles along her thigh.

Gee-zus! Her body screamed at her to give in to him, aching for the sort of pleasure only Brendan could give her. But her mind kicked her in the arse as she remembered how he had left her. 'Why are you trying to get back in my pants when your *real woman* is at home?'

There was the hint of pain in Brendan's visage, but it vanished as his signature bedroom eyes pinned her gaze. 'Do you want the full list of reasons, or an abridged version?'

Hyper-aware of Brendan's thumb reaching the edge of her lace panties, Alannah gulped. She was not about to let him get the better of her. 'I want the full list.'

The biggest smile she had ever seen took over Brendan's face. 'One: "home" is a subjective term.' He pushed her back onto the table. 'Two: she won't care if I sleep around because we're in an open relationship.' After hitching her dress up, the sound of fabric tearing echoed through the room.

A cool breeze brushed against Alannah's most intimate parts. She realised her panties had vanished.

'Three: I wasn't lying about how good you tasted.' Brendan knelt on the floor and pulled her to the edge of the table.

A trembling mess, she did not know how much more her nerves could take, but her legs parted of their own accord.

'Four: this delicious pussy still has a magnetic pull on me.' His tongue flicked at her sensitive spot.

The moan she let out was involuntary. Alannah felt common sense retreating into the deepest, darkest depths of her mind.

'Five: the fact is, every part of your gorgeous body is like a siren calling to me. Damn me all over again if I don't want you to blow me far off course.'

Two fingers penetrated her sanity, bringing forth a guttural sound.

'Six: you are more real to me than any other woman.' With his last confession, Brendan devoured her.

Chapter Eighteen

Neve strode right up to Jasper—who stood at his locker—not even caring if she made a scene in front of Erik or his 'subjects.' She did not take kindly to him ignoring her, not after what happened on Saturday night; yet Jasper had ghosted her for the entirety of Sunday. Every text, every call went unanswered. He didn't even respond to her banging down his front door. His sister Naomi must have thought she was crazy. 'What the hell, Jas?' she hissed in a hushed voice.

He glanced at her with a look of bitter contempt before returning his attention to the books in his locker. 'What do you want?'

Ice-cold prickles covered every inch of Neve's flesh, and her heart began playing a dubstep beat. 'What's going on, Jas? Why didn't you talk to me yesterday?'

Slamming his locker shut made her jump. His rich brown eyes glared at her. 'Nothing's going on, Neve. That's the point. You and I are through. Over. Capiche?'

Her mouth gaped open, and words failed her for a fleeting second. Tears trickled from her eyes. 'Why? I thought I proved myself to you.'

'How do I put this? I got what I wanted from you—now it's time to move on to my next conquest.'

Neve could not believe what she was hearing. 'Y-you can't mean it Jas! You told me you were in love with me, and I believed you… I felt it.'

Jasper scoffed. 'You are a naïve fool, sweetheart. Why don't you run along to your beloved faerie prince?'

She shook her head. 'You're the one I love, not—'

Drawing closer, Jasper got right in her face. 'Quit the fucking lies. I saw your true feelings on Saturday night, for both of us.'

'So that's it? You're too jealous of how I feel about him to give us a chance?'

He let out a derisive laugh. 'I don't give a shit how you feel about the tosser. I told you already: I'm done with you. The challenge is over. I hope you live a long happy life together and have lots of pretty faerie babies.' Jasper turned and strode away, slipping into a classroom before Neve could catch up.

Neve only noticed the crowd assembled to watch the show when she ceased her pursuit. A tall, blond boy waited in the centre of it all. She shuddered as all the ramifications sank into her mind like lead balloons.

Erik stepped up to her, his face an expressionless mask. 'I did warn you about him.'

Furious heat washed away the icicles on her skin as she stood there staring aghast at him. 'You know what? Fuck you, Erik. Fuck you and your damn family.' Neve sprinted from the building, from the school, running until she reached her front gate. She paused under the shade of the front porch to wipe her brow and catch her breath before heading inside.

The front door slammed shut and her mother's cursing travelled down the hall to greet Neve's ears. *It's no wonder Grandpa blames Mum for my own foul mouth.* Neve ambled into the living area and froze when two sets of startled eyes met hers. The hairs on the back of her neck instantly stood on end as she glanced between her mum and uncle. 'What's going on?'

Mum blushed as Uncle Brendan licked his lips.

Neve's attention shifted to a scrap of black fabric on the floor. When she realised it was the remains of Alannah's underwear, the penny dropped. She shot her mother an accusing look. 'On second thoughts, I don't think I want to know. I'll be in my room.' Turning her back on the awkwardness, she made her way to the stairs.

'Why are you home already?' Mum called after her. 'Are you feeling sick, honey?'

'You might say I'm sick of boys.'

Brendan snorted. 'Wise kid.'

Something in his tone drove away the embarrassment she had felt. She marched back into the dining room and stared at him. 'Are you my real father? Why have you been showing all this sudden interest in me?'

He gulped. Audibly.

'Yes, Brendan is your bio dad,' Mum replied.

'Why didn't you tell me? There I was thinking you were interested in spending time with *me*. Wanting to make up for lost time. But now I can see you only wanted to get back in Mum's pants. How long until you leave us this time?' Storming off, she muttered, 'Fucking men!'

Brendan whistled. 'Angsty.' It was the last thing she heard before climbing the stairs.

He better not try to talk me down.

As soon as Neve collapsed on her bed, Mum rushed in. 'I'm sorry, sweetie. I swore Brendan to secrecy. That's why he didn't tell you... he is your dad. I didn't tell you because—'

'It's okay Mum. I get it, he's a jerk, like all men.'

'Why do I sense you are projecting your own issues onto my situation? What happened at school?'

Neve's eyes brimmed with tears again, and she swallowed against the painful lump in her throat. 'I thought he loved me, like I loved him.' It was no use holding the sobs back any longer.

Pulling Neve into her arms, Mum stroked her head. 'I know baby. Breakups are hard. I wish I could say they get easier, but they never do.'

After wiping her nose on her sleeve, Neve sat up. 'This was no ordinary breakup Mum. I trusted him enough to...' The words failed her.

Mum's eyes widened. 'Did the Alvarsson boy harm you? I swear to the Gods—'

'No Mum. Not Erik. Although he can go die in a fire too. I'm talking about Jasper.'

Her mother's eyes became searing globes of fire. 'What. Did. He. Do?'

Neve muttered a curse under hear breath. 'It was all consensual, Mum. I wanted it at the time because I thought he loved me. Turns out I was another notch on his bedpost. Although…' she sobbed. 'It was technically Erik's bed.' The memory of Erik's cold green eyes watching her came to mind. She huffed. 'Jasper deserves whatever punishment Erik dishes out. He dumped me in front of the whole school and…' — another sob — 'he said such hateful things.'

Mum's jaw dropped. 'Are you saying you had sex with Jasper Rowan?'

She blinked sheepishly and nodded.

'And Erik knows?'

Again, Neve nodded.

'I know it seems hard for you to see the bright side now, but this does free you of Erik and Elna's claim. I just don't understand why Jasper would risk his life for a conquest. Clayton still wears the arsehole crown, but Jasper takes the stupid cake in the Rowan family.'

Hope surfaced in Neve's sea of misery, and her pulse quickened. 'You make a good point Mum. Why would Jasper risk his life for one night in the sack? What if *this* is Erik's punishment? I need a way to safely contact Jasper without Erik knowing.'

Alannah did not expect to see Brendan still sitting in her house. 'Oh hey. I thought you would have left by now.'

He had made himself comfortable on the couch. 'Are you for real? I'm not the sort to eat and run, Lana.'

'Hmph. No, you give it a few weeks.'

Brendan sighed. 'I also happen to care about our daughter. She was seriously distressed, and I want to know why.'

She sat next to him. 'Boy troubles.'

'No shit, Sherblock.'

Alannah snorted at their old joke. 'Jasper used professions of love to convince her to have sex with him on the weekend. He got what he wanted, so he dumped her today.'

'Slimy, little weasel. Wait… why would he do it, given the risks?'

'My thoughts exactly. I wish I'd kept those musings to myself though. They renewed Neve's heart with hope, and it will hurt much more when he breaks it again.'

'Of the two of you, I'm having a hard time working out who's more jaded.'

'Don't get me started on all the reasons why that's my honour.' She glared at him. 'I'm looking at one right now. Good thing Neve walked in when she did. She saved me from making the second-biggest mistake in my life.'

Brendan sprang to his feet. 'Christ, Lana! What's your damage?'

She stood to challenge him head-on. 'You are. What you did to me was far more damaging than anything Austin or Clayton did. You broke me, Brendan—and it feels like you're doing it all over again.'

The colour drained from his face. 'I had no idea you were hurting so much.'

'How could you? You'—she stabbed his chest with her index finger—'ran off to Sydney where you were too busy fucking Bitchface, a woman who you are still with. Do you think you can win me back while *she* is in your life? Or is this all some sick, sadistic joke to you? To see how much further you can injure my soul?'

'I'm not playing games, Lana. For the record, I tried to get back to you. But I was Bridey's sex slave. I couldn't leave.'

Alannah huffed. 'Some ordeal *that* must have been. Sounds like your dream job.'

He growled in her face. 'Don't make light of it. I'm deadly serious about the slavery thing. I was at her beck-and-fucking call. And she had ways of keeping me in line, preventing me from leaving the house without her.'

Falling back into the sofa, Alannah's eyes doubled in size as she stared in disbelief.

After returning to his seat beside her, Brendan continued, 'The message I asked Liam to pass on to you was my cry for help. I needed to code it so Bridey wouldn't understand because she sat beside me when I rang him. I guess it was too cryptic for you, although I'd had hopes you'd understood when I first saw you at the nightclub with Tyler.'

She recalled feeling like someone was watching her that night. 'You were there? Why couldn't I see you?'

He shrugged. 'Bridey used some powerful glamour to hide me. Tyler's good looks must've distracted you. You never noticed the shimmer, so you didn't pierce the veil. I almost approached you, but Bridey caught me and dragged me out of the place.'

'Wowsers. I had no idea. For the record, I thought there was more to your message at first. I figured "whiling away the hours" referred to the song we danced to on our first date. That told me the evil intent part. I knew without a doubt you were quoting Bridey with the whole "real woman" bullshit. When I rang Caleb to check if Bridey had enchanted you, he told me you went to her willingly…. So, anyway, I assume she's lengthened your tether or something? How are you back in town and able to visit me?'

'Fucking hell, Caleb,' Brendan muttered. He took a deep breath and looked straight into Alannah's eyes. 'No, I'm not her slave anymore. Our roles have somewhat reversed, and she is one of my subs.'

Alannah struggled to process his words. 'How?'

'It's a long, twisted story. Gist of it is, I fell in love.'

Her mouth opened, but no words came out, and she closed it. This process repeated a few times. 'You fell in love with the woman who captured you and made you her slave?'

'Eventually, yeah. But she wasn't the reason I stuck around when I got my first taste of freedom. Bridey wasn't the only Hawthorn I fell in love with, nor was she the first.'

'Are you telling me Bridey has a sister, or a cousin I don't know about?'

'No, Lana. I'm talking about Caleb.'

'You were in a sexual relationship with Caleb?'

'I still am.'

Whistling through her teeth, Alannah took a moment to let the news sink in. All manner of thoughts flowed through her mind, some of them downright dirty. 'I knew Caleb was bi in high school, but I had no idea you were.'

'Neither did I until Bridey made him fuck me.'

Alannah did not know what shocked her more: the thought of Bridey forcing the guys to hook-up or how the mental image turned her on so much.

Placing his arm along her backrest, Brendan leaned in closer. 'Wait. You knew Caleb was bi back then? How did I miss the memo?'

'I dunno. You're the enchanter. I'm surprised you didn't see the way he lusted after some of the guys in our group, especially Locky. I suspect they had a thing.'

'They did. He told me about it. Caleb also confessed to having a crush on you.'

That was news. Her core began to tingle as naughty ideas filled her head.

'You're thinking about a threesome with me and him, aren't you Lana?' Brendan's gruff voice broke her trance while his hand slid up her leg.

'No,' she lied. There was no hiding the fire in her cheeks, let alone the obvious tells she likely displayed in her aura.

He laughed. 'I could make it happen. Caleb would be all for it.'

'What about Bridey?' Alannah snarled, pushing his hand away. 'I'm sorry, Brendan, but I'm not okay with her being in the picture. If you want anything further from me, you'll have to ditch her.'

'An ultimatum huh? Hardly seems fair when you won't choose between me and Liam. Oh, wait—you made your choice when you married *him*. It's one of the reasons I kept my distance for so long.'

Moisture pooled in Alannah's eyes. 'I only married him so *your* child would grow up with a father figure. He was loving and supportive, but he wasn't you, Brendan.'

'Shit!' Brendan hunched over and cradled his head in his hands. 'Why did you kiss him?'

'What are you talking about?'

'The night we announced our soul link to the fam. You ran off after him when he threw his tantrum. Then you jumped into his lap and kissed him.'

Alannah was gasping for air, unable to pull enough oxygen into her lungs. 'I didn't jump into his lap—'

'*Bullshit, Lana!* Don't fucking lie to me. I saw you.'

'You must need your eyes checked then, because Liam pulled me into his lap and kissed me. Not the other way round. I pushed away from him, not wanting to reciprocate. I chewed him out for it, too.'

Brendan's eyes ballooned. 'Jesus, fuck! I didn't stick around to see the rest. I was too exasperated.' He rose and paced the room. 'Liam's a dead man!'

'Brendan, please calm down. It was one lousy kiss. I'm sorry you had to see it, but—'

When he spun round to look at her, Brendan's face had turned red, his fists clenched. 'That one lousy kiss is the reason I left, Lana. Wanna guess what happened next?'

She swallowed back the bile rising in her throat. 'What?'

'I sold my soul to a devil named Bridey.'

Alannah blinked with a blank expression plastered on her face.

'To make the pain go away, I asked her to break our soul link.' Tears began to stream down

Brendan's face. 'I wasn't thinking straight, Lana. When she named her price, I blindly agreed.'

'Oh Gods! It's how you became her slave?'

'Yup. I thought you had chosen Liam over me, so I gave up. It's the biggest mistake I've ever made, but now I know the trigger was all Liam, not you…' He returned to wearing out the rug. 'Shit! I need to cool off.' Brendan strode across to the back door. 'I'll be in touch.' He rushed out the back door.

Liam slumped over the Council's boardroom table, struggling to keep his eyes open. Sleep had eluded him since his discovery. Rather than lie awake for hours to no avail, he had decided to learn as much as he could about the new threat. *Dragons.* Mundane police work was piling up on his desk, but it would hardly matter if they were all dead. *Because of dragons.* Even his relationship dramas felt inconsequential at this point. *Fucking Dragons!*

'I hope I'm not keeping you awake, son?' Kieran's stern voice inquired.

He jerked to his feet. 'Sorry, Your Honour.'

After a dismissive wave, Kieran gestured for Liam to sit down. 'At ease, warlock. We have much to discuss. I've called you in because I know you have been doing extensive research and I need your help planning our next move.'

'Certainly. I'll do anything I can to help.'

Smiling, Kieran nodded as he reached for the conference room phone.

The recipient of his call picked up on the second ring. 'Greetings, Your Honour. I have the full task force assembled here, and you are on speaker.'

'Thank you, Warlock Grant. I am also on speaker, and I have Warlock Winters with me. Please give me your status report.'

'A few more rumblings, but the craters remain cold.'

'Good. I'm hoping you can approach the Mount Schank dragon before it sets the volcano off.'

Liam's eyes bugged out. The suggestion was suicide.

'How do you propose such a feat, Your Honour?' queried Grant.

'I have arranged for an excavation crew to accompany you. They will unplug the main vent and dig an access tunnel connecting to it. You will use this to delve into the depths of the magma chamber.'

'Excuse me, Your Honour?' Liam interjected.

'What is it, Warlock Winters?'

'Will the crew have the means to deal with the toxic vapours arising through the vents?'

'Of course. We will provide self-contained breathing apparatus, along with hazard suits. Warlock Grant, will you and your men be capable of manipulating the lava flow, should it come to it?'

'Yes, Your Honour. I have three other warlocks on the team, so elemental manipulation shan't be a problem. It is the dragon who worries me.'

Kieran fixed his expectant gaze on Liam. 'Warlock Winters, I understand you have been reading up on these primordial beasts. What can you tell us?'

'They are intelligent and attuned to all forms of mana via the primordial. Thanks to centuries of practice, they are more adept at magic than any mage. I am unsure about their dimensions since accounts vary so much. It is likely they come in various shapes and sizes, so you should prepare for anything. They could be as small as their ten-foot-tall wyvern offspring. Or they could be hulks towering over six-storey buildings.' He paused to sip on some water.

'What about communication?' Grant asked. 'I doubt they speak English.'

'I'm not sure what languages they know. They are capable of long-distance telepathic speech and mind reading. This is how they have been able to contact each other across the globe.'

'Perhaps we could use this to our advantage.' Kieran suggested. 'If you can request parlay with the dragon via telepathy you might not need to enter the volcano. I'd like to reach a peaceful resolution if possible. Failing that, kill the beast. What are its weaknesses, Warlock Winters?'

'Folklore tells of knights slaying them by piercing their abdomen. I'm thinking you'll want a variety of weapons, from swords and pikes to bows and crossbows. Imbue them with as many powers as possible, to be safe. Warlocks might also have some luck with ice shard spells, given the dragon's affinity for fire and magma. Avoid straight water though, because you might cop some nasty steam burns. All my sources agree they breathe fire.'

Grant whistled through his teeth. 'I sure hope we can call a truce. I don't fancy fighting one of these monsters.'

Kieran sighed. 'If you can't come to some sort of agreement, you'll be facing more than one of them, I'm afraid.'

'Understood, Your Honour.' Grant and his team signed off.

Liam eyed Kieran askance.

'What? Speak your mind, Warlock Winters,' Kieran demanded.

'I don't mean to question your approach, but I don't believe those men stand a chance against the dragon.'

'I fear you are right, but those men are our only hope at this stage.'

'Should we start forming a contingency plan, Your Honour?'

'It would be wise. If Grant and his men fail, we are looking at a full-fledged war, and we will need a much bigger arsenal. It is time for all the dwarves in the state to fire up their forges and the conjurers to do what they do best. Tell your wife to start with your own weapons.'

A man on a mission, Liam beelined for home. The house was unusually quiet. No hum from the sound of the sewing machine. Not even the din of Alannah's music filtered through from her workroom. He peeked inside and found the room empty. *Strange.* His heart began to pound in time with his hastened steps, stopping when he found her in the living room.

Alannah sat curled up on the couch, clutching a plush cushion to her chest. Her clothes appeared dishevelled, and her blood-shot eyes stared at a blank patch of wall.

Rushing forward, he dropped to his knees in front of her. 'Shit! Are you okay, Lana? Are you hurt?'

Her gaze shifted to him. 'Oh, hey. You're home early. Must be the day for it.'

Liam scrunched up his face. 'What are you talking about?'

'Don't you mean who? Neve came home early too.'

His pulse hit double time. 'Is Neve okay? What happened?'

'One of her boyfriends dumped her. She's in her room, grieving over lost love.'

Relaxing his shoulders muscles, he released a heavy breath. 'Is that what you've been doing too? Grieving lost love, I mean.'

Her puffy eyes narrowed in him. She brushed a finger beneath his eyes. 'Why haven't you been sleeping?'

Gaping at her, Liam shook his head. 'Why do you think?'

'Is this about my feelings for Brendan?'

Rising as his blood began to boil, Liam raked his fingers through his hair. '*Gods, Lana!* Not everything is about you! How can this damn obsession for my jerk of a brother occupy so much of your mind? There are much bigger problems to worry about!'

Alannah stared gobsmacked.

'Dragons, Lana. We are on the brink of a war unlike any this world has ever known. I need your head in the game. Without your help, none of us stand a chance.'

She gulped. 'Yes, of course. I'm sorry. What can I do to help?'

'Kieran is about to send out conscription alerts. You will need to imbue a bunch of weapons and armour. In the meantime, I need you to start with our own collection.'

'I've already blessed all those.'

'Blessings alone won't suffice. I'm talking matter enhancements, along with elemental, energy, and physical damage on the weapons. The armour will also need spell absorption, negation, and elemental immunity.'

Her eyes grew wider with each spell effect he listed to the point where they were popping out of their sockets. 'It's a lot of work.'

'Get Neve to help. It's about time she learned some practical skills.'

She jumped up, letting the cushion fall to the floor. 'Are you sure? We haven't even told her about the dragons yet. I thought Kieran wanted this kept under wraps for now. Besides, she's not in the best headspace.' The words were charging from her mouth in rapid succession.

'Neither are you. But this is important work. Who knows, maybe you will both find welcome relief from your depressing thoughts. But yeah, you'll need to swear her to secrecy.'

Alannah sighed. 'Okay. I'm on it.' Pushing past him, she made her way upstairs.

It was all Liam's fault. Brendan could not shake the mantra replaying in his mind. Everything he had lost with Alannah: her love, their soul link, years of waking up beside her. *Raising our daughter together.* All those precious moments that could have been theirs, could have been his. Liam had stripped them from the realm of possibility. *It was all Liam's fault.*

Even after downing a bottle of whiskey, Brendan could hear his inner demon crying for release. It yearned to sink its talons into the flesh of the man who had taken everything from him. *It was all Liam's fault. Fuck it!*

The house was quiet, with Bridey and Caleb both asleep. He grabbed his keys and took the Jag.

The drive into town was short and before he knew it, Brendan was parking outside Alannah and Liam's house. *Shit! What am I doing here? It's the middle of the night, they are probably all asleep.*

'*That'll make it easier. Catch him unawares,*' suggested Brendan's darker aspect.

Locking the car, he crept around the side of the house where the light in the study drew him like a moth. Climbing onto the window casing proved easy and he peered inside. Liam sat at his desk, reading. *Not asleep then.* Brendan dropped to the ground, cursing when a twig snapped underfoot.

'What was that?' Liam asked from within the safety of his home. A moment later, the laundry door opened, and Liam appeared, wielding a torch.

Brendan stepped out from the shadows and scowled at Liam. 'You couldn't leave well enough alone, could you?'

'Brendan? What are you doing here?' Liam's brow furrowed. 'You better not be here to hurt Lana.'

Brendan scoffed. 'Lana is the least of your concerns right now, *Brother.*' Leaping forward, he tackled Liam to the ground, grabbing the torch and sending it flying well out of reach. Liam's knee drew up, aiming for Brendan's stomach. Brendan anticipated the move by tuning into Liam's surface thoughts. 'You've forgotten how to fight a skilled enchanter.'

'Like hell I have.' Liam's hands clamped around Brendan's arms and searing heat transferred through his grip.

Grinning with his teeth bared, Brendan stifled Liam's attempt by channelling nether. 'Oh no you don't!'

'What do you want, Brendan?'

He let out a snarky laugh. 'What do I want? How about the life you stole from me? I never would have left town if it weren't for you. I would not have been Bridey's slave. Lana would still be mine, and I could have seen my daughter growing up. Fuck you, Liam! I am going to make you pay for what you did.'

The fire Liam could not release from his hands gleamed in his intense stare. 'What I did? You're the one who broke Lana. You destroyed her.'

Brendan shook his head. 'No! You don't get it, do you? You're not listening! If you'd kept your hands and lips to yourself that night, my own heart and soul would still be intact, and so would Lana's. *It's all your fault!*' His hands slid around Liam's throat.

Tap, tap, tap.

As Brendan increased the pressure, Liam's eyes began to bulge, his face turning a sickly shade of blue.

Tap, tap, tap.

Is that the sound of my brother's heart?

Liam tried to push Brendan's hands away, but he lacked the strength. Brendan overpowered him, so Liam's arms flailed about in attempts to hit Brendan, to deter him.

Tap, tap, tap.

Are you scared Brother? You should be.

When Liam's eyes closed, his limbs fell limp and his windpipe crunched under the crushing weight.

Tap, tap, tap. Tap, tap, tap.

Stop fighting it, Brother.

It was satisfying to watch the life drain away from Liam's body.

Tap, tap, tap, tap, tap, tap, tap, tap.

Brendan sat bolt upright.

Tap, tap, tap, tap, tap, tap, tap, tap.

What's with the incessant knocking? He wiped the sleep from his eyes and gave them a few seconds to focus on his surrounds. *What the hell?*

Chapter Nineteen

After dinner, Liam headed out in his kayak. *I must tell the merfolk about the dragons.* He was also hoping for more intel, having read every book he could get his hands on. It was not like High Magus Kieran had expected him to research the dragons. Liam's role in the mage army—equivalent to a human Lieutenant Colonel—called for such due diligence.

A strong swell was developing. Under normal circumstances, he would have relished the opportunity to conquer the waves. With a heavy sigh, he continued to paddle out to his usual spot. Saoirse was not yet visible, so he flashed the light of his torch.

The shining beacon drew her attention, and she appeared before him with a furrowed brow. 'Are you okay, Liam?'

'Not really, to be honest.'

Saoirse gasped and pulled herself up into his boat. 'Are you hurt? Give me a look.'

Shaking his head, half a smile tugged at his lips. 'No, nothing like that. I have lots on my mind.'

Her muscles relaxed as she eased back into the fore of the cockpit, her tail flopping over the edge. 'Did you learn what you needed to from the man you needed to… torture?'

'Yes, although the torture wasn't necessary in the end. He thought I was someone else and let the truth slip. Things don't look good for us, Saoirse.'

'Us?'

'Mage kind. Humans too. In fact, most magical people are in for a rough time of it. I'm not sure how this affects merfolk, but I figure you ought to know.'

'What should we know about?'

'The dragons. They never left. They have been hibernating in the depths of the volcanoes, and now they are waking up.'

Saoirse gasped. 'I had no idea. But why do you say this is bad for all mages? The dragons were more concerned with dark mages in the past.'

'You know about the ways of dragons?'

'Only a little, from the lore my grandmother read to me as a child.'

Liam's heart and mind buzzed with a flicker of burning hope. 'I need to know everything you and your people can tell me about them. It looks like they intend to wage war against us. Something about destroying the planet and breaking the Covenant.'

Her mouth formed the sweetest little O, and those lips captivated him. Her cheeks flared with heat. 'W-what do you want to know about them?'

He blinked and refocused on her eyes as they mirrored the turbulence of the sea. 'Everything. To defeat an enemy, it helps to understand who they are. What motivates them, their physical and psychological weaknesses, their history, and so forth.'

Casting her eyes downward, she twirled her long locks between her delicate fingers. The gesture drew Liam's attention to an alluring distraction.

As her eyes met his, she caught the direction of his momentary gaze and blushed again. 'W-why do you keep staring at me like that?'

Pursing his lips, Liam whistled as he exhaled. 'Sorry. I know I shouldn't. It's just… where I come from… I'm not used to conversing with half naked women outside of my bedroom.'

'Oh.' Those heart-shaped lips pressed into another cute shape. 'I have read about the modesty of land dwellers. The concept of nudity is quite foreign to my people because we do not dress. What you see is what you get with us.'

His eyes bugged out as realisation hit. 'Wait, so you're like completely naked right now?' Despite his better judgement, curiosity got the better of him and he scanned her lower body.

'I suppose I am.' Her cheeks reddened. 'Merfolk bodies are neater than yours. We have less need to cover ourselves when everything below the waist is tucked away.'

Liam considered himself a master of the elements. But there was no dousing the fire raging between his legs. Not with *his* mana attunements anyway. *'Dragons!'* he sputtered. 'Tell me about dragons, please.'

'Right. So, I guess the first thing that comes to mind is how dragons were the first intelligent life indigenous to Earth. The dinosaurs inspired the Gods of Wisdom, who created dragons from the primordial. This was their first attempt at making life. They thought their attempts were successful. Later, they realised the dragons could not breed like other forms of life evolving around them. It had not occurred to the Gods to incorporate the means of reproduction into their creation. As I'm sure you know, Nature Gods took a great interest in the ways of natural life and in doing so, they attempted to replicate the process by mating with each other, giving birth to the elves. Seeing this, the Gods of

Wisdom mated with their dragons by magical means. But they produced a smaller, less powerful reptilian race: the Wyvern.'

Nodding every so often, Liam continued to listen, even though she had not yet told him anything new; although she had confirmed dragons were bigger than wyverns.

'That was their big lesson. The Gods realised they could not craft true life like a sculpture, nor could they make it perfect. Life flourished on Earth and people evolved. The Gods recognised the threat humanity would pose upon the rest of nature. They turned to the magic folk, asking them to protect the natural world, thus giving rise to the Covenant. The dragons only ever attacked people who had committed crimes against nature. But humans were ignorant and stubborn: they fought back. Over time, the dragons grew weary of the battles. Many of them ceded defeat, while the rest disappeared.'

'And now we know where they went,' Liam huffed.

'They also stepped in to punish your kind when they turned dark.'

'The dragons will get extremely angry when they see the state of the world today. I guess it's why Alvar warned me. Along with the unseelie, mages will be on the shit list. He was right about how modern we have become. We love human technology. Oh hell! We're fucking doomed. What about your people? Are they at risk?'

Saoirse shook her head. 'We have kept our vows to the Covenant to the best of our abilities. We do not reap more than we sow. Our healers are always saving injured marine life. We even send sirens out to sabotage fishermen who take more than the ecosystem can handle.'

Releasing a deep breath, Liam relaxed a little. 'I am glad you are safe.'

She smiled. 'Thank you for caring. I know your priorities are to protect your own people. If things become too bleak, I'd be happy to offer you and your family shelter in my home.'

Liam let out a short laugh. 'Thank you, Saoirse, but I don't see how it would be possible. Our bodies aren't equipped for living underwater.'

'Not currently. But there are spells to fix that. It's happened before: mages and even humans becoming merfolk.'

His jaw hit the deck. 'Seriously?'

'Yes. My great-great grandfather was a land mage who chose to become a mermage when he fell in love.'

Why had the possibility never occurred to me? All the barriers standing between him and Saoirse evaporated. Liam's eyes travelled down her body, and blood rushed from his brain, travelling south. Leaning forward, he cupped her face with his palm. Her eyes widened, but she did not push him away or ask him to stop, not even when he closed the distance and kissed her.

Saoirse's soft, salacious lips yielded, deepening the kiss. She moved into his lap, exciting him further. Liam's hands glided from her face, around her sleek shoulders and down her back. They landed on her backside. Her warm, fleshy, firm buttocks. *Pure perfection.* Her scaly fish tail started lower at the back than in the front because of her... mammalian parts.

The boat rocked with their unbridled passion. Liam broke the kiss within a split second of capsizing. He regained control of the vessel as well as the water surrounding them. When his breathing settled, the reality of his actions slapped him hard across the face. Bile rose from his stomach. The organ was too busy doing somersaults to concern itself with its contents. His mind was racing, but two thoughts shone brighter than the rest: *Lana needs me; the Council needs me.*

When Saoirse leaned in to claim another kiss, Liam put a hand up to stop her. 'I'm sorry. I shouldn't have done that. I need to go.'

Unshed tears glistened in her eyes. 'Of course. I'm sorry.' Leaping out of the boat, she plunged into the depths of the ocean without another word.

It felt as though someone was playing tug-of-war with his heart. Thoughts of remorse for both Saoirse and Alannah riddled his mind. A mental debate over whom he should be with raged on for the better part of the night. Choosing duty above all else, he paddled back to shore.

Turning the corner onto his home street, the house came into view. Something else caught his attention, boiling his blood: the black Jag parked outside.

Tap, tap, tap, tap, tap, tap, tap, tap.

Brendan lowered his car window. Fog was still clearing from his head as he puzzled over how he wound up sleeping in his car. The last thing he remembered was drifting off in his bed with two sets of warm arms surrounding him. *Then the dream.*

'What the fuck are you doing here?' Liam demanded. 'Are you stalking Lana? How often have you been sleeping outside my house like some creeper?'

Did I drive here in my sleep? Brendan crinkled his nose. 'I'm not stalking anyone. I-I honestly don't know what I'm doing here.'

Frowning, Liam huffed. 'Right. Seems pretty obvious to me. Stay the fuck away from my wife! She has enough to worry about without your damn mind games.'

Remnants of his dream filtered through. The rage that had brought it on returned and Brendan's pulse spiked. He snarled at Liam. 'You and I both know she was never *yours*. Now Lana and I understand what went down that night, it's only a matter of time before she comes to her senses.'

Liam's eyes narrowed. 'What the hell are you talking about? What night?'

'The night I lost her. The night your filthy lips kissed *my* woman! Now get the fuck out of my sight.' He hit the close button on the window, forcing Liam to step back to avoid a broken nose. Brendan needed to get the hell out of Dodge before his dream became reality. After firing up the engine, he gunned it, not even worried he was speeding away from a cop. *Just try to give me a ticket, jackass!*

Bridey was waiting for Brendan when he entered his living room. 'Where were you?' she asked with a sharp, accusatory tone.

Fire still coursed through his blood as he marched toward her. 'You dare question your Master?'

Glowering, she rose to face him. 'I'm not Caleb! You know this shit only works on me in the bedroom. I want to know why you snuck off in the middle of the night. Was it to see *her*?'

'Jesus, Bridey! What do have against Lana? You're happy for me to fuck anyone else, but as soon as Lana is back on the scene you turn into a jealous housewife. What gives?'

She replied through gritted teeth, 'I don't trust her, not after the way she hurt you.' Bridey grabbed his hands in her own. 'You need to be careful of Alannah. Don't forget she is still part of the Council. I wouldn't put it past her to turn you over to them.'

He shook his head. 'You don't know her like I do, although I'm tempted to arrange a little meeting. Sort of like how you brought Caleb and me together.'

'Not bloody likely. You need to stay away from her. Please.'

Looking down at their hands, Brendan stroked her soft silvery skin with his thumbs. 'Lana is not our enemy, Bry. She could even be a powerful ally. As for the way she hurt me, it was a fucked-up

misunderstanding. Lana never stopped loving me—
'

Jerking back, Bridey dropped his hands.
'Stop! I've heard enough. If you must know—I
detest the woman. I will not share your bed with
her, nor will I allow Caleb to do so. You need to
make a choice, handsome: my brother and I, or
Alannah. Before you jump to your decision, think
about your position in the Syndicate. I will not
follow a Boss who aligns himself to the Council. I
can't imagine many will.'

'You insolent bitch! I cannot believe you
would threaten mutiny because of something so
petty.'

Slap! Her hand struck him hard across the
face, and he caught it with fast reflexes. Her eyes
burned with intense focus. 'How dare you talk to
me like that!'

Crushing her wrist in a vice grip until she
yelped, Brendan smirked. 'How dare you raise a
hand against your Master. I will not switch roles
with you again, sweetheart. Save your sadism for
Caleb… or Levi.'

Bridey gasped. 'You know?' She tried to
wriggle free of his hold, to no avail.

'Not much goes on under this roof without
my knowing. How about you tell me why you *really*

want me to stay away from Lana?' Her lips pursed together to emphasise her stubborn refusal to speak. 'Fine. If this is how you want to do things….' Grabbing her, he hoisted her over his shoulder and carried her downstairs. The space had once been a wine cellar. Brendan had repurposed the cold, concrete room into a dual-purpose dungeon. Bypassing the play equipment, he bound Bridey in the cold iron manacles against the wall. 'Tell me.'

She sniggered. 'Do you think you can interrogate me with torture? This shit is foreplay for us, handsome.'

He gave her a sly, lopsided grin. 'For me, maybe. I happen to know your limits.' Grabbing his lighter, he sparked it to life in front of her eyes.

'Fire doesn't scare me,' she scoffed.

'This is no ordinary fire, Bry. It's hellfire. Hot enough to burn through to your damned soul.' He waved the flickering crimson flame lightly across the surface of her hand. Bridey's guttural scream echoed through the room. 'Hm, I like the acoustics in here. What do you think?'

She snarled at him.

'Do you need another demonstration?' He brought the lighter close to her other hand.

'*Wait!*'

Dropping the lighter, he gave her a smug grin. 'That was easier than I anticipated.'

'I thought you loved me, Brendan. Why are you doing this?'

He sighed and picked up the lighter. 'I did love you, Bry, but I have no room in my heart for traitors.'

Tears pooled in her eyes. 'I am only trying to protect you! Please, Brendan.'

'Please what? I'm still waiting for answers.'

'Then listen,' she whispered. Bridey fell silent and blinked several times.

It took a moment for Brendan to realise she was referring to her mind. Cold iron cuffs blocked her access to mana, so she was unable to project her thoughts. It was up to him to read her.

The moment he tapped into her mind, Bridey's surface thoughts assaulted him. *You need to stop this line of questioning. You are going to get us all killed. Don't even try telepathy.*

Staggering back, Brendan clenched his fists and threw his head back. *Fuuuck!* He took a few deep breaths to ground himself. 'I'm listening. Tell me.'

'I love you, Brendan. I don't want you to get hurt and seeing Alannah is a guaranteed path to heartache.'

'Fine.' Turning, he made his way to the door and paused without looking back. 'I'll be back shortly. When I return, I intend to take my frustrations out on your body. If you act like a good little subbie, I might even fuck you.' He heard her moan before he closed the door.

Once upstairs, he grabbed his bug scanner. He did not have the time or patience for a full sweep. It could wait. He only needed to confirm his understanding of Bridey's hint. Even so, it took almost thirty minutes to locate the first device. *Shit! Of course, an expert planted the bugs. Explains why my routine scans did not pick up on them.*

Slumping into his armchair, Brendan sank into the gravity of the situation. *Who is Bridey working for? And why?*

With the apocalypse on the horizon, Neve wanted to resolve things with Jasper. She did not fancy the idea of hiding in a bunker by herself when the war began. Her mum was a conjurer, which meant she would likely join the frontline alongside Liam. The High Magus had even summoned her grandparents to provide support. There was a chance she could stay with her bio dad, but things were still too up in the air between him and Mum. If she had to choose one person to lock herself away with for weeks, or months, Jasper was the clear winner.

This was her reasoning when she rocked up to school the following day. She was at her locker when a familiar cold chill wafted through the hall and settled upon her skin. She had managed to avoid him thus far by leaving early and walking to school.

'Why didn't you ride with us this morning?' Erik's frosty voice asked.

Slamming the door shut, she spun round to face the Alvarsson twins. 'Why are you still bothering? You lost your claim on me.' She tried to push past them, but Erik grabbed her arm.

'Our claim remains, as far as the Seelie Court are aware. I haven't told them what happened.'

Neve's eyes bulged wide. 'Why?'

'Because Elna and I still want you.'

She sucked in a breath through clenched teeth. 'But I love Jasper.'

The neutral expression on Erik's face slipped, giving way to a grimace. 'Jasper is an arsehole who doesn't deserve your love. Besides, didn't he dump you yesterday?'

'Yes, but I get the distinct impression someone forced him to do it. And by *someone*, I mean you.' Shrugging out of his grip, Neve marched away. She wanted to find Jasper, but she needed to wait for a time when Erik was not around. Pulling the truth from Jasper would be fruitless otherwise.

Glancing up from her locker, Caitlin forced a smile. 'Hey. How are you feeling today?'

'Pissed off.'

Caitlin let a short laugh slip. 'That's my girl. Jasper's a dick and you can do way better.'

Neve shook her head. 'I'm not mad at Jas. I reckon Erik blackmailed him or something. Erik is the reason I'm seeing red today.'

'Oh wow. What makes you think so?'

'Call it a hunch. Besides, why would Jasper risk his life to take my virginity if he didn't have feelings for me? It doesn't make sense.'

Caitlin fell silent and chewed at her bottom lip.

'What?'

She released her lip with a sigh. 'You're assuming Jasper even took the threat seriously. He can be rather pig-headed.'

Doubts began to creep into Neve's mind. *What if I misread the whole situation? No. Not possible. Jasper loves me... doesn't he?*

'Are you going to confront him about it?' Caitlin asked.

Before she was able to reply, a couple of boys wearing football jerseys appeared in front of Neve. Leering at her, the taller guy crowded her personal space. 'Hey sugar, if you aren't busy tonight, I thought you might like to hook-up with me and Dustin. What do ya say?'

She gulped. 'Um, how about no thanks?'

Dustin snorted. 'It's okay babe, you don't need to play hard-to-get with us. Unlike Jasper, we don't have any one night only rules. We'll show you a good time whenever you want.'

Caitlin stepped forward. 'She already said "no," jerkface.'

Dustin looked Caitlin up and down. 'You're the lesbo friend, aren't you? Don't worry. We're totally down with you joining in, right Jayden?'

'Hells yeah. I love a bit of girl-on-girl action.' Jayden laughed at the gaping expressions Neve and Caitlin gave him. Backing away, he winked at Neve. 'Think about it, and send me a message if you change your mind.'

When Jayden and Dustin rounded a corner, Neve remembered to breathe. 'So creepy.'

'I know, right?'

A chorus of pings echoed through the corridor, followed shortly by giggles. Neve scanned the crowd, wondering what the joke was. Most of the people around her glued their eyes to their phones. Slowly but surely those faces rose to meet Neve's, whose unsettled stomach began to churn.

'Why—' Her own phone vibrating cut off her whispered query.

The message came from Jasper: PAYBACK IS A BITCH. A weblink followed.

As soon as she opened the video, all the blood drained from Neve's face. Two writhing bodies filled her screen, both moaning and groaning. She hit pause, unable to watch anymore, and focused on the caption: *'My latest virgin conquest. Such a tight pussy and so worth the challenge. Five stars.'* When she looked up, the room was spinning. The floor gave way beneath her as the black spots in her vision grew bigger.

'Neve!' Caitlin's screech was the last thing Neve heard before darkness overwhelmed her.

Warlock Patrick Grant tapped his foot against the limestone step. He watched as the excavation crew finished the dig. Sweat was dripping down his body and pooling in his boots, having nowhere else to go thanks to the hazmat suit.

'Hey man, are you ready?' asked Danny with a voice muffled by a full-face mask.

'I was ready two hours ago.'

Danny slapped him on the back. 'Let's do this!'

'Don't you—'

Jogging off toward the tunnel, Danny thrust his sword in the air, shouting, 'Lee-roy-*Jenkins*!!'

Patrick face palmed and shook his head, although he could not hold back the chuckle. 'Asshat!' He led the rest of the team to the entrance, where Danny stood waiting; a shit-eating grin on his face. 'I swear to the Gods you'll be the death of us one day.'

Danny shrugged. 'Carpe diem!' A blessed warlock with an ego the size of Jupiter, he was the cockiest bastard in town. The way women flocked to him, stroking his ego, did not help matters either.

Turning to Hamish, the team's enchanter, Patrick gave the signal. He took point with his crossbow loaded and ready for action. Hamish stuck close behind him, reaching out for the dragon's mind as they entered the volcano. The air grew colder the deeper they went, much to Patrick's surprise. It gave him hope the magma chamber was nigh on empty.

'Are we sure this is the right mountain?' Danny called out from the rear flank.

The ground shook beneath their feet, knocking a few men off-balance.

'Does that answer your question?' Patrick retorted.

'Shh!' Hamish hissed.

They all froze and watched him with wisps of bated breath. By the dim luminescence of a mage-light spell, Patrick saw Hamish's eyes cloud over. It looked like an acute case of cataracts. 'What the hell? Hamish? Are you okay?'

Nothing.

Patrick shook Hamish, gently at first, then with more force. '*Hamish?*'

Nothing.

Suddenly, Hamish pushed past Patrick and marched ahead.

'Fuck!' Patrick ran after him. He tried to hold Hamish back, but there was no stopping the man. Another tremor rocked the cavern and Patrick stumbled against the wall. After righting himself, he gestured for the rest of the team to follow. An eerie silence surrounded the group as they edged forward. All Patrick heard was the rapid thumping of his pulse and the shuffling of his feet against the dirt.

Something touched his shoulder and Patrick jumped. 'Shit!'

Danny gave him a sheepish look. 'Sorry man. Didn't mean to startle you. I wanted to ask: what's the deal with zombie Hamish?'

'I dunno. I'm guessing the dragon has used telepathy to enthral him.'

'Hm. So what's the plan now?'

'Follow Hamish and hope they have reached a peaceful resolution by the time we get there. Failing that, we go with plan B.'

Danny nodded, giving Plan B a theatrical flourish. 'Right.'

Trudging on hours later, there was still no change in Hamish. The excavated tunnel had joined a natural cavern network by this stage. Patrick was growing tired, in need of a rest stop. But he was not about to give up on Hamish, who had been like a brother to Patrick since they were five.

Another few hours, and the air was heating up. 'We must be getting close now,' Patrick mused. Walking around a bend, they all gasped at the large open chamber. A warm, red radiance permeated the darkness. Glancing over the edge of a chasm,

Patrick could see a lake of molten lava. He whistled through his teeth.

Danny sidled up and expressed his awe in much the same way. 'So, where's this dragon?'

The ground shook and Patrick pulled Danny back with him to avoid plummeting to their deaths. He hunkered down, grabbing onto a rock as the tremor continued.

'Oh fuck!' Danny bellowed.

Patrick peeked over the rock, and his jaw immediately dropped. His peepers widened as they came face to face with the amber glow of another set of eyes.

Steam billowed from two enormous nostrils. Anyone could have mistaken them for passageways in the limestone warrens, at least until they entered the fleshy cavities. A rich, baritone voice spoke in Patrick's mind. *'Are you looking for me?'*

Swallowing against the golf ball-sized lump in his throat, Patrick felt a slight trickle down his leg. 'Y-yes we h-have come t-to request p-parlay.'

Raucous laughter filled the chamber. *'Is that why you approach me with so many weapons? Do not take me for a fool. I have been inside your friend's mind; I know all about your plan.'*

'Then you ought to know peace is our primary objective.'

'*If your kind wanted peace, you would not have sided with humans.*' The goliath rose within the cavern, giving them a dazzling display of his golden scales.

'We have not allied ourselves with them per se. Integration in their society was necessary for survival. They were hunting us too.'

The dragon cocked a brow. '*If you speak the truth, you will have no qualms with their complete and utter destruction. Step aside or die defending them.*'

'What you are planning will result in the death of countless innocent lives! All the magical races live among the humans. Please reconsider your approach.'

'*The magical races must return to their own domains if they wish to survive my brothers' onslaught.*'

Danny crawled over to Patrick and whispered, 'Can you buy us time to evacuate the magicals?'

'*The wheels are in motion, Warlock, and you cannot stop them. If you intend to save lives, tell your Council to move quick.*'

Patrick shared a look with Danny, gesturing for the younger warlock to get right on it. After a moment of hesitation, Danny fled the cavern, leaving Patrick to carry out Kieran's orders. He had been waiting for an opportune moment. As soon as

411

the dragon's belly was in range, Patrick aimed his crossbow and took the shot.

Flinging his head back, the dragon roared, fire spewing from his mouth in the process. A moment later, the chamber flooded with lava.

Chapter Twenty

Neve woke in a state of hazy confusion, and it took her several minutes to recognise her surroundings. She was alone in the big old bed with its magenta quilt, and déjà vu began to set in. *Were the last few days a dream? Or nightmare, rather?*

The toilet flushed in the adjacent bathroom and Elna stepped through the door a moment later. 'Oh good, you're awake. How is your head feeling? Do you need any painkillers?'

Rubbing at the dull throb in her temples, Neve nodded. 'I could use something.'

Elna handed her a potion vial. 'This is my own recipe.'

Glancing at the blue substance, Neve arched a brow. 'What is it?'

'A simple herbal concoction to speed up the healing process. It's safe.'

Neve cocked her brow even higher, giving Elna a sidelong glance.

'Don't worry, I have zero desire to poison you, despite all the trouble you have caused,' Elna assured her.

'I'm a little wary of potion vials after…' Neve's voice trailed off.

Elna snorted. 'I would be too if my boyfriend gave me a date-rape drug and recorded the results for public viewing.'

Bile surged up from Neve's stomach, and she rushed to the bathroom to let it out. *I guess it was all real then.* The way Elna held Neve's hair back was at odds with the cold, calculating girl she knew.

'You must have a mild concussion,' Elna observed.

'What happened to me? How did I end up here?'

After helping Neve stand, Elna guided her across to the sink and cleaned her up. 'You fainted at school, likely in response to Jasper's horrid stunt. Erik ran to catch you, but he didn't make it in time. You hit the floor hard. We brought you back here so I could keep an eye on you while he took care of things.'

'What do you mean, "he took care of things?"' Neve took the tincture Elna had offered, wincing as the bitter taste assaulted her tongue.

Tucking Neve back into bed, Elna snuggled in next to her. 'Erik removed the video from the internet. Then he traced all the downloads, ensuring anyone possessing copies deleted them.'

Neve's muscles relaxed, and she breathed a sigh of relief. 'Thank the Gods. I still can't believe Jasper would do such a thing.'

A door slammed somewhere in the lower levels of the house, and Erik appeared moments later. Neve gasped at his bruised and battered face. He sported a black eye and blood-encrusted nose.

'W-what happened?' Neve asked.

'I taught the bastard a lesson.'

Elna inspected his injuries and sucked a breath through her teeth. 'Looks like Jasper was the one teaching you a lesson.' She reached into the dresser drawer and retrieved another vial of blue goo. 'Here.'

Erik huffed. 'Jasper got far worse than he gave, trust me. Getting his arse suspended made this all worthwhile.' He wrapped his hands around Elna's and smiled down at her. 'Thank you.' Uncapping the vial, he drank the potion before disappearing into the ensuite to wash up. When Erik returned, he climbed into bed next to Neve and cupped her face in his palm. 'Are you okay?'

Tears welled in her eyes from the onslaught of mixed emotions. 'Not really.'

He cursed under his breath. 'Did Elna give you a dose of healing tonic?'

She nodded. 'Physically, I'm fine. But I'm still reeling from what happened with the… sex tape. Thank you for acting so quickly to get it removed.' Neve straightened. 'Wait, how did you manage that? Did you post the video as part of some sort of frame job?'

Erik scowled at her. 'You have the nerve to accuse me of such a vile act when Elna and I have done nothing but help and comfort you? Besides, releasing evidence of you losing your virginity does not help our cause. If the Seelie Court catch word of this, we lose our claim on you.'

'For all I know, this could be part of some elaborate revenge scheme to get back at me for sleeping with Jasper.'

'Fuck's sake, Neve!' Erik straddled her, pinning her arms to the headboard. 'What will it take to prove myself to you?'

With her heart galloping, Neve sucked in a sharp breath. 'Proof. That's exactly what I need. Prove Jasper's guilty of this. How did he even get the video footage? We were both high as a kite at the time.'

'Why don't you check your hidden camera feed and find out for yourself?' Erik hissed.

Neve gaped at him. 'How do you know about that?'

'My father is the definition of paranoid. He is always scanning this house for bugs. Given the time and location, it wasn't hard to figure out who'd put it there.' Erik's grip tightened around her wrists. Tickling her neck with his breath, he pressed his lips to her ear. 'Why don't you tell me why you were spying on us, sweetheart?'

'I...'

'Go on.' His gruff voice sent tingles down her spine.

The tingles turned to a throbbing in Neve's core, and she squirmed. 'I wanted to see if you were having sex.'

Erik's eyes bugged out. 'You were the one screwing around behind *my* back. I'm not the disloyal one here.'

With her gaze downcast, Neve bit her bottom lip. 'I wasn't questioning your loyalty.'

'They why did you do it?' he demanded.

'I-I was curious about... the two of you.'

Elna laughed. 'She wants to know if we fuck each other.'

Neve shot Elna a look. 'You did say you share *everything*.'

Grinning, Erik was having a hard time containing his own laughter. 'You could have just asked us.'

She furrowed her brow, feeling as though she was the butt of some private joke only the twins understood. 'Fine. Then tell me the truth. Do you… (gulp)… fuck each other?'

The front door slammed, and another needle snapped when Alannah startled. 'For the love of the Gods. I'm never gonna finish sewing this dress.'

Liam appeared a moment later wearing his police uniform. 'Come on. The High Magus has summoned us to a meeting.' His fingers tapping against his legs indicated he was entering crisis management mode.

With a sigh, she threw the makings of her latest design aside and followed him outside. 'Do you know what he wants?'

'Not exactly. Could be an update on the recent expedition at Mount Schank.' He opened the passenger door of his SUV for Alannah. Rounding the vehicle, he jumped in and took off for the Council Chambers.

The message came through to her phone a moment later: ALL WARLOCKS, CONJURERS, AND ELEMENTAL SHAMANS MUST REPORT FOR IMMEDIATE DUTY AT YOUR NEAREST COUNCIL OFFICE. Frowning, Alannah returned the phone to her handbag. 'Looks like this war is about to start.'

Liam remained silent for the rest of the drive. His muddy blue outer aura confirmed her suspicions. He was afraid—not for his own safety, because his soul radiated courage now more than ever; no, Liam feared for his loved ones and the innocent lives all mages swore to protect.

Kieran was waiting for them in the boardroom. He dismissed their formal greetings with a wave of his hand. 'Please. In the absence of others, I don't expect either of you to stand on ceremony with me.'

'Has there been word from Warlock Grant?' Liam asked.

With a furrowed brow, Kieran shook his head. 'Not directly but reports from some of my other Councillors down there imply things did not go well. There have been a few minor tremors, and the tunnel they dug out collapsed. None of the team members returned.'

Liam cursed under his breath. 'So, what now?'

'Now we prepare for war. I need you, Warlock Winters, to head up a team. You will evacuate the bloodline mages from the Limestone Coast district. Bring them to the Fleurieu Peninsula, and we will put them up in safe houses. Once they settle, report back to me so you can lead the army to war.'

'Yes, Your Honour.'

Kieran turned to Alannah. 'Lady Winters, I want you to start imbuing these crates of armour.' He gestured toward the metal boxes stacked in five piles at the end of the table. 'Take them to Cailleach Estate and work in the ritual space there. That house is much safer for you and Neve. The Winters clan have warded the property well, and it will hold up better than most when the dragons attack. If the fires do get through the protections, seek refuge in the stone cellar.'

Opening one of the aluminium cases, she stroked a lightweight armoured vest. It was warm to touch, and Alannah's fingertips tingled as she became aware of the magic within the garment. 'Someone has already blessed these, Your Honour.'

'I know, but they need more than blessings. I want the works: full elemental resistance, glamour cloaks, spell absorption, spell reflection, and…' —he lowered his voice—'spell negation.'

Alannah gasped. 'That would require—'

'I know what it entails. This is why I'm asking *you* to do this. You have unique qualifications, Lady Winters. I'm willing to do whatever it takes to keep my men alive, even if we have to break a few rules. Don't let the troops know what you did to their armour.'

She nodded her understanding. Kieran accepting the absurdity of the Council's laws about the use of nether pleased her. There was nothing evil in channelling the stygian element. As with all mana sources, the way a mage used it determined the effect it would have on one's soul. 'Are there any weapons for me to work on?'

'No. I'll be sending those to my other conjurers. I want you to focus on armour. This is only the first shipment. I'll send plenty more to keep you busy during the coming months.'

Her mouth gaped open. 'You mean to keep me shut away during the war? I'm a trained soldier too, don't forget.'

Liam stepped forward. 'Lana, please—'

Snarling, she shot him an angry scowl. 'Stay out of this, Liam.' She returned her attention to Kieran, blood boiling in her cheeks. 'I've seen more battle action than most of your warlocks, and you know I can hold my own. Don't lock me away like some helpless housewife.'

Kieran squared up in front of her, adopting a glare as hard as diamonds. 'I cannot risk you, Lady Winters. You must not go anywhere near the frontline.'

With hands on her hips, she straightened to gain as much height as possible. 'Why not? My fighting skills are as good as Liam's.'

'I'm not doubting your skills, Alannah. This is about your safety.'

'I'm not stupid, Your Honour. I know this is dangerous, but I still fail to see how you are better off without me on the field.'

'*Because if you die*, Neve loses her mother. And… the Council loses its second-most powerful mage in the world!'

Alannah gaped. She had never received such high praise from Kieran.

'You are the future of mage-kind, Alannah. When my time in this seat comes to an end, I want you to take my place. You have enough support to secure the seat. From there it is only a matter of time before you ascend the ranks. You could become the first female Arch Mage. Don't waste this opportunity by running into war and getting yourself killed.'

Still speechless, she closed the crate, letting it slam shut and echo through the room. After a pregnant pause, Alannah's posture relaxed. 'Thank you, Your Honour.'

Liam grabbed a few of the cases. 'I'll start loading these into the car.'

She nodded and took one in each hand before following him.

When they returned to the boardroom to collect more crates, the ground began to shake. Several of the cases flew across the room as Alannah met Kieran's wide eyes.

'Get under the table!' Liam cried, pushing Alannah down in the process.

She collapsed under the weight of Liam's solid body as he barrelled into her. She crawled from beneath her muscular shield of a husband into the cover of the solid oak table. Liam crouched in front of Alannah, with Kieran flanking her while they waited for the tremor to subside. *'What's going on?'* she called out to Kieran.

After watching his phone for a minute, Kieran swore. *'The volcanoes are erupting.'*

'Which volcano?'

'Probably all of them!'

'Shit! What about the dragons? Have they appeared?'

'No reports yet,' Kieran replied. The earth settled, and they all released audible breaths. 'The dragons could get here any day now. It's time to pull the kids out of school,' he announced. 'Alannah, take Neve with you and keep her safe.'

Waiting for their response, Neve forgot to breathe.

'No,' Erik replied, his hands still clasped around her wrists. 'We have a great many kinks, but incest isn't one of them.' By letting his emotional guard down, Erik allowed Neve to see his aura. He was not lying.

'Before you put your shield back up, tell me: did either you or Elna record and release the sex tape?' Neve asked.

'No. We are not responsible for the video in any way.' As far as Neve could tell, Erik was being honest.

The moment she began to relax, the windows rattled, putting her back on high alert. 'What was that?'

'A minor earth tremor from the volcanoes,' explained Erik. 'Don't worry, we are safe here.'

Narrowing her eyes, she glared at him. 'How can you be sure?'

Releasing her left arm, Erik brought his right hand up to her face, tucking a strand of hair behind her ear. 'Because the dragons are not interested harming the seelie fae. We are not guilty of breaking the Covenant.'

Neve's jaw hit the floor. 'How did you know about the dragons? It's classified information. I shouldn't even—' It dawned on her. 'Did you read my mind?'

Erik laughed. 'Well yes, but it's not how I knew. The Seelie Court have always known the dragons would return. We have had plenty of time to prepare. Our magics are strong enough to withstand any fallout from the dragon attacks.'

Bile brewed in her belly. 'Why didn't you warn us?'

'It wasn't my place. My father would have told your High Magus if your Council had passed the test. But they failed like all the other Councils. There is little I can do for most of your mage friends, but I can protect you, Neve. Stay here with us, and we will keep you safe.'

'But what about my family?' As if on cue, Neve's phone rang a second later. Erik sat back, letting her retrieve the phone from her backpack.

Glancing at the display, she saw her mother calling, so she answered, 'Hi Mum.'

'*Where the fuck are you?* I'm at your school right now, and I've just learned you left campus to play hooky with those enlightened twins. What the hell, Neve?'

'Mum, please calm down.'

'Not until I know you are safe!'

'I *am* safe. There was an incident at school this morning, and I fainted. Erik and Elna took me home to look after me.'

Alannah sucked in a loud breath. 'You're at their house? Are you fucking insane?'

'It wasn't like I had a choice in the matter: I was unconscious when they brought me here.'

'*What?*' Judging by Alannah's raucous tone, smoke must have been billowing out of her ears. 'Are you saying they kidnapped you?'

'No Mum, it's not like that. They brought me here to nurse me after the fall I had. And to save me from further humiliation.' Tears threatened to resurface as thoughts of Jasper and the awful video plagued her mind.

'What fall? Why didn't the school contact me about this?'

Seeking an explanation, Neve glanced at Erik, who was eavesdropping on the conversation.

'We needed to keep the incident contained. Alerting the staff would have taken too much time… among other risks,' he replied.

'What incident? What is Erik talking about?' Alannah demanded.

Neve sighed. 'You know how Jasper took my virginity on the weekend?'

'Yes.' Her mother's voice wavered.

'He set me up. He um… drugged me and recorded the whole thing. Either that, or he used my hidden camera. Point is, he released the footage online today.'

'*The fuck?* What drug did he use?'

Pulling the phone away from her pierced eardrum, Neve put it on loudspeaker. 'I know. It horrified me too, hence the fainting spell. He gave me a potion called Rhapsody. As for the video, Erik removed it from the internet, and he deleted all the copies.'

'I swear to the Gods, I will feed Jasper to those damn dragons,' Alannah seethed, prompting a chuckle from Erik. He probably relished the idea of Jasper becoming dragon fodder. 'Speaking of dragons, I am on my way to your grandparents' house right now,' Mum continued. 'I want you to meet me there. It is our safest hideout during this war with the dragons. Your grandpa's wards ought to keep the dragons and their fire out.'

'Actually, Lady Winters,' Erik interjected, 'your daughter is much safer here with us. We can guarantee protection against the dragons. They have no quarrel with us.'

'I'm sure you can shelter her from the dragons, but is she safe from you?' Alannah scoffed.

'Neve has nothing to fear from us, Lady Winters. My sister and I are both in love with her. We will not harm her, and we will do everything in our power to shield her from the evils of this world.'

'Is this okay with you, Neve?' Alannah asked.

'Yes, Mum. I'm good here.'

An exasperated sigh slipped from Alannah's lips. 'Fine. I will ring to check on you, Neve. If I so much as suspect those twins are hurting you in any way, I will haul Erik and Elna's faerie arses over stygian coals.'

'Of course, My Lady. We promise to take good care of her.' After the call disconnected, he gave Neve a crooked smile.

'What are you thinking about?'

'All the ways we can amuse ourselves during this period of lockdown. We no longer have a pesky hymen to worry about.' Erik brushed his fingers along her inner thigh.

Neve flinched from the soft touch. 'Tickles.'

With eyelids at half-mast, Erik grinned lasciviously. 'Mm-hm. I can smell your arousal from here, sweetheart, and I haven't even heightened my senses yet.'

Neve licked her lips. 'What are you going to do about it?'

Accepting her invitation, Erik thrust his hand between her legs. 'I'm going to make you come harder than ever before.'

Hearing about Jasper's crimes against Neve shocked Alannah. Knowing date rape had played a part in his nefarious scheme further sickened her. *And he used Rhapsody of all things. What would Brendan think if he knew his designer potion was used against his own daughter? Speaking of Brendan…*

She picked up her burner phone and shot him a quick text: MEET ME AT THE ESPLANADE LOOKOUT ASAP. AND PACK AN OVERNIGHT BAG. Then she drove the short distance from the school to her designated meeting spot. After the meeting with Kieran, Liam had dropped Alannah home so she could get the cat and take her own car. From there, he had taken the armour to his parents' place. Meanwhile, Alannah had driven to the school. Her plan had been to collect Neve, then enlist Brendan's help with her conjuring work.

Brendan's reply arrived as she pulled into a parking bay. COLOUR ME INTRIGUED ;-) BE THERE IN 15.

Unbuckling her belt, Alannah reclined slightly in her seat. She whispered a few soothing words to Luna, who yowled in her carry cage. Watching the ocean's waves lapping against the beach calmed her. Losing all sense of time, she sat up with a start when Brendan tapped on her window. After unlocking the doors, she gestured for him to get in her car.

'I'm all for a romantic rendezvous with you Lana, but do you think it wise given the current climate?'

She rolled her eyes. 'I hope you've had enough time to cool down because I need your help.'

'So long as I don't have to see Liam's ugly mug, I'm sure I'll be fine. What sort of help do you need?'

'I have a shit tonne of armour to imbue for the Council's army. I'll get it done much quicker with your help.'

His eyes narrowed on her. 'You know I'm not attuned to matter or names. I can't imbue items, Lana.'

'I know, but some of the spells I need will involve your attunements. If you cast those spells, I can piggyback on them and focus on casting the others you are not proficient in.'

Brendan snorted. 'Right, because all warlocks need vests of seduction for those cold, lonely nights.'

Stifling her own laugh, Alannah shook her head. 'I'm referring to senses and nether.'

Wide eyes and a gaping mouth stared at her. 'Did Kieran seriously ask you to use nether?'

'Yeah, he did.'

'Christ. It really is the end of the world. Okay, fine. What's the plan?'

'Did you bring an overnight bag? This is going to take a few days.'

He nodded. 'It's in the boot of my car.'

'Good. Grab it, then I'll drive you to the safehouse.'

Brendan cocked a brow. 'Safehouse?'

'You'll see.'

431

After locking his own car, Brendan threw a large gym bag in the boot of her Tesla. Returning to the front passenger seat, he asked, 'Did you feel the big-ass tremor earlier?'

'Yeah. I was in the Council chambers at the time. Kieran said all the volcanoes in the southeast are now erupting.'

Brendan whistled through his teeth. 'I'm guessing the dragons will get here soon.'

'That's the consensus in the Council.'

'What's Kieran's plan?'

'For now, his priority is to get the mage community to safety. He sent Liam to help evacuate the Limestone Coast. Kieran is instructing everyone else to find warded safehouses or underground bunkers. He also has all the dwarves and conjurers building a powerful arsenal to deploy with the troops.'

'Shit! I need to call home and warn them. I know this is a big ask, Lana, but can Caleb and Bridey join us at this safehouse of yours?'

'Caleb, yes; but hell to the no for Bridey. Besides, I doubt our hosts would be willing to put her up.'

'Hosts, what hosts?'

As she turned onto Ross and Nora's street, Alannah jutted her chin forward to direct Brendan's gaze.

'Are you fucking kidding me? I doubt I'm even welcome here! Plus, the Council probably bugged their house too.'

'They haven't. I already checked.'

He huffed as the car pulled into the gravel driveway. 'Dad's going to kill me. You know that right? What use am I to you then?'

Alannah laughed. 'Are you forgetting I can commune with the dead, regardless of which way your soul travels?'

All the blood drained from his face.

'Relax, Brendan. They know you are coming, and they are fine with it.'

Brendan cast a sidelong glance her way. 'Sure, that's what they told *you*, but—'

'It'll be fine. Trust me.' Killing the engine, she climbed out of the car and ran to Nora's open arms.

'I'm so relieved you are okay!' cried Nora.

'Same here.'

Ross gave her a brief hug, frowning in Brendan's direction. 'Where's Neve?'

Brendan edged forward.

'She is staying with friends,' Alannah replied.

'Is that wise?'

She sighed. 'I'm not sure, but they are seelie fae, so at least she is safe from the dragons.'

With eyes bugging out, Brendan picked up the pace. 'What the hell? Are you suggesting Neve is staying with the Alvarsson twins?'

'Yeah, she is. It's a long story, and you'll want to be sitting down when I tell you the rest.'

Ross crossed his arms over his chest. 'So, the prodigal son returns.'

'Good to see you again too, Dad,' Brendan hissed.

Nora yanked Brendan away from the awkward confrontation and pulled him into her arms. 'We are glad to see you again, Brendan. You have no idea how much I've missed you. How much we've *all* missed you.'

Yielding to the embrace, Brendan threw his arms around his mother, hiding his face in her shoulder. Alannah could not be certain, but she thought she heard a small whimper escape the lips of one Brendan Winters, A.K.A. Lord Jet, nether-wielding kingpin of the infamous Dark Syndicate.

Chapter Twenty-One

Every part of Neve's body tingled. She wavered between sleep and a warm wakefulness, thinking only of the bodies either side of her. When her stomach growled, she attempted to get up. Failing spectacularly, she flopped onto Erik's fine form. Hours of lovemaking had rendered her legs useless.

With a groan, Erik stirred from his own slumber, smiling when his eyes fluttered open. His arm snaked around her waist. 'You are insatiable, sweetheart.'

Neve's cheeks flushed, the warmth spreading from her face in a downward trajectory. 'I'm actually hungry for food this time.'

'I suppose we should go have some dinner.'

She bit her lip.

Erik's eyes narrowed on her mouth, his thumb plucking her lip away from her teeth. 'What's wrong?'

'It's my legs. They've turned to jelly.'

He let out a boisterous laugh.

'What's so funny?' Neve asked in a defensive tone.

'Sounds like Elna and I did our jobs well,' Erik replied with a wink. 'Come on, I'll help you.'

She groaned. 'Can't we eat in bed?'

Erik gasped. 'How uncouth! Besides, it is time for you to meet my parents. You are staying here thanks to their generosity. It would be rude to snub them on your first night.'

The blood drained from Neve's face. 'Your parents? Aren't they like royalty? I have nothing to wear.'

Sitting up, Erik scooped her into his arms. 'Relax, babe. I'm sure they'll love you as much as I do. As for clothing, you can borrow anything from Elna's wardrobe. I know for a fact you are the same bra size, although she is a few inches taller, so her dresses might be a bit long.'

Neve stared aghast. *How does he know my bra size already, let alone Elna's?*

'Don't look so shocked. I pay attention to these things.' Erik yanked the quilt from Elna and slapped her bare arse. 'Wake up Sister dearest! It's dinner time.'

Rolling over, Elna gave them a brazen display of her flawless skin from head to toe. 'Mm sounds good. I call dibs on the shower.'

Erik huffed. 'Fine, but can you assist our fiancée?' With eyes locked on Neve, his voice dropped to a deep, sensual tone. 'She is a little unsteady on her feet.'

Arching an eyebrow, Elna grinned. 'Knowing how strong her gymnast legs are, we should take it as a compliment.'

Neve's cheeks turned red again. 'Sex is a very different type of workout.'

'Indeed,' Elna smirked, helping Neve to her feet.

Wearing a knee-length dress, Neve made her way to the dining room, arms linked with Erik. The strength had returned to her legs, but she still needed his moral support.

A tall man with dirty blond hair and designer stubble rose from his seat at the end of the table. He focused a stern glare on Erik. 'I am so glad you decided to join us, Son.' His attention shifted to Neve. 'And who is this? Your latest conquest?'

Erik tensed. 'No Father, this is Neve, the girl Elna and I have claimed.'

'Well, it is about time you introduced us. Come here, girl. Give us a look at you.'

Skin prickling and heat rising along the back of her neck, Neve remained glued to the floor. It took a firm prod from Erik to shift her forward. She stood before Alvar and offered a slight curtsy. 'H-hello Your Highness.'

Alvar leered, casting his gaze over her for several seconds. The intensity of his scrutiny increased the goosebumps crawling across Neve's flesh. His attention shifted to Erik. 'A bloodline mage?'

'Not just any bloodline mage, Sir. Neve is the most powerful of her generation. She is of the Winters clan, and she has the Beltane blessing.'

Nodding, Alvar returned his gaze to Neve. 'Are you a virgin?'

Erik had prepared her for this question. She maintained eye contact and used magic to glamour her aura. 'Yes, Your Highness.'

Alvar smiled. 'I am impressed. You have done well, Son. It is about time you started taking your family obligations seriously. Neve, please meet my wife, Estelar, princess of the Seelie Court.' His hand extended toward the woman sitting at the opposite end of the long banquet table.

When Neve turned, she gaped at the beauty before her eyes. A soft glow emanated from Estelar even without her aura on display. A crown of blue gum leaves and white floral buds adorned her golden hair. She even wore a long dress of blue silk that could have come from the set of a Medieval movie. 'It is lovely to meet you, dear. Please take a seat beside me.'

Neve glanced at Erik, and he nodded, so she sat next to the elven princess. Her mouth watered at the feast before her. They had covered the table with a smorgasbord: fresh fruits, salad greens, cold meats, and a range of sweet and savoury pastries. *How do they eat all this?*

Erik took the seat to Neve's left. 'What we don't consume, the servants will finish. Food never goes to waste in this house.'

Reading my mind again, huh?

He chuckled, confirming her suspicions.

'Tell me, Neve, do you love my children?' Estelar asked.

'Hmph, you know love is not necessary,' scoffed Alvar.

Estelar frowned at her husband. 'No, but it helps. Things will run smoother if they have genuine feelings.' Her gaze returned to Neve.

'Yes, Your Highness. I love them both very much.' Erik and Elna gasped in unison. The truth of her own words surprised Neve just as much. She exchanged a smile with each of them.

'I will prepare the betrothal contract for signing tomorrow,' Alvar announced in an authoritative tone. 'Who are your parents, Neve?'

'My mother is Alannah Winters. My father is…' *Damnit. Does he want to know Brendan is my bio dad, or —*

'Her legal father is Liam Winters, Sir,' Erik explained.

'Right, of course. You are a Beltane child. I apologise for failing to clarify my question.' Alvar was holding a goblet of wine over which he studied Neve for a moment before taking a sip. 'Normally I would send the papers to your father, but I understand your clan is matriarchal. Is this true?'

'Yes, Your Highness. And my mother is my current matriarch.'

'Very well. I will arrange things with her. You will stay with us, Neve. It is much safer here than with your own people.'

Neve's blood began to boil, and her rebellious side wanted to rear its ugly head, yet she swallowed hard against it. 'Thank you, Your Highness.' She picked up a mini quiche and began eating.

'That was an order, Neve, but it is cute how you think of it as an offer.'

She met his blazing eyes head on. Neve wanted to tell him where to stick it. But she kept her mouth shut, choosing to maintain a defiant glower for two seconds before she caved. *What the hell have I gotten myself into?*

Pausing at the top of the stairs, Brendan looked at his mother. 'So, what's the status of our old bedrooms?'

'Liam kept his, Neve claimed Alannah's, and we turned yours into a guest room. You may as well stay in there,' Nora explained.

He nodded. 'Where does Lana sleep?' Brendan glanced at Alannah.

The reply came from his father: 'Liam's room, of course.'

'Of course.' When he cast a sidelong glance in Alannah's direction, she shook her head subtly, so he dropped the subject. After dumping his bag beside the queen-sized ensemble, Brendan made his way to Liam *and* Alannah's room. He entered with a light knock on the door. 'Hey.'

Alannah stepped out from the walk-in robe. 'Oh, hey.'

'I was hoping you'd fill me in on what's happening with Neve before we get on with the magic work.'

'No probs. Grab a seat. I'll be a sec.' Pulling another dress from her suitcase, she tucked a hanger into its neckline and hung it up.

Perching on the foot of the bed, Brendan watched. Her firm backside shifting beneath the folds of her short, slinky skirt entranced him. 'Why have you shared a room with Liam here for all this time? Didn't your relationship sour years ago? '

With a sigh, she hooked the garment she was holding onto the rail. 'Liam insisted we keep up appearances.'

'Do you mean to imply my folks don't even know how strained things are between the two of you?'

'Pretty much.'

'Christ! Family dinners must be hard on you these days.'

As Alannah glanced over her shoulder, the light glimmered within her unshed tears. 'More than you'd think.' Returning her attention to the task at hand, she finished hanging the clothes. She approached Brendan. 'As for Neve, Jasper Rowan needs a serious arse-kicking after what he did to our girl. It seems he is living up to the Rowan name.'

Brendan's fists clenched in his lap. 'Shit! What did he do?'

'You know how Jasper slept with Neve at Erik's party on the weekend?'

He nodded.

'Turns out he drugged Neve first, then took advantage of her.'

His eyes bugged out. 'Damn that boy and his whole fucking family. Is Neve okay?'

Standing an inch in front of him, Alannah combed a hand through her hair. 'Not really. You haven't even heard the worst of it. Not only did Jasper seemingly date-rape her, but he also recorded the whole thing and put the video online.'

Brendan's blood boiled with murderous intent. Determined to do everything in his power to destroy Jasper, he began to rise. But the ground trembled, knocking him off balance. When his back hit the bed, Alannah fell with him, pressing down with the extent of her weight, meagre as it was. Brendan's arms shot up to stabilise her, and when his hands caught her hips, hot prickles crawled across his skin. Thoughts of violent vengeance fled his mind, replaced by ardent arousal. 'Are you okay?' he rasped.

'Yeah,' Alannah replied in kind. Her lids shuttered, eyes darkening as they focused on Brendan's mouth.

Scarcely conscious of the room shaking, Brendan rolled Alannah onto her back. He straddled her with his more considerable mass. Not waiting for invitations or protests, he claimed her lips with his own. Alannah was as soft and yielding as he remembered. She rewarded his rough touch with moans, spurring him on. Her musky fragrance put him in mind of the sweet, pink confectionary sticks he had devoured as a child. She was every bit as delicious and far more enjoyable to his matured palate.

As their tongues entwined, Brendan thrust against her. Black business pants struggled to contain his excitement. Alannah responded instantly, liquid lust soaking through every layer separating them. Her grip on his shoulders tightened, and her nails dug into his flesh. Flinging his head back, Brendan exhaled. 'Aaaah!' A second later he sunk his teeth into her neck, feeling her quiver beneath him. Slipping a hand between her supple folds, he brought Alannah to climax within seconds.

When he stood to unfasten his belt, Alannah's eyes shot wide open. 'Wait! Not yet.'

Brendan's brow furrowed. 'Are you for real? I know you want this as much as I do, Lana. Your body and soul are screaming for it.'

Alannah sat upright and took a deep breath. 'I know. And I do, but we shouldn't. Not yet.' She licked her lips. 'There is a tonne of work to do. If we start fucking now, I doubt we will stop anytime soon.' Reaching out for his hand, she offered Brendan a sly grin.

Laughing, he took her hand and pulled her up against his pounding heart. 'You're not wrong. We have years to catch up on, after all.' Toying with a lock of Alannah's hair, he tucked it behind her ear. He caressed her cheek, sparking a blazing inferno in her eyes. 'That kiss? Wow! You literally rocked my world.' Brendan cringed as soon as the words left his mouth. 'Shit! Did I really say that?'

Alannah bit her lip.

'What?'

A smile beamed from her. 'Well you are a dad now.'

He laughed. 'Right. Free ticket to Lame Punsville. Speaking of which, you were still filling me in on Neve's situation before the earth tremor… distracted us.'

She sighed. 'Indeed. Can we sit?'

Unwilling to relinquish contact yet, Brendan tugged her down into his lap. 'Go on.'

'So yeah, the sex tape got released on the internet, but Erik removed it. He didn't want word getting back to the rest of the Seelie Court about Neve losing her virginity. He and Elna professed to loving Neve. They want to keep their claim, which means doing everything in their power to hide the truth.'

He shook his head. 'Jasper is a spiteful little twat. I'd love to put the kid on trial for the shit he pulled, but you and Neve would need to be on board.'

'I want to, but the timing sucks. We are on the verge of a global war that could end life as we know it. Let's talk about it if we all pull through, okay?'

'Fine. Can you at least tell me what Jasper drugged Neve with?'

Alannah tensed. 'Rhapsody.'

Bile surged up Brendan's oesophagus, and he swallowed hard. 'Fuck! Are you sure?'

'That's what she said it was, and I've never told her about the stuff or your involvement in making it.'

Knowing he had a small part to play in the ruination of his own daughter freaked him the fuck out. 'Lana, there is a chance whatever Jasper gave Neve was a seelie knock-off. Their shit is far worse than what the Syndicate have been peddling. I need to contact Jacob and find out who was dealing at that party. Genuine Rhapsody shouldn't even be on the street now.' He dialled Jacob's number, but the call went straight to voicemail. 'Fuck! I'll have to try him again after the ritual.'

Liam felt a strange sense of duty to a woman he should not be seeing let alone entertaining sentiment for. Yet there was no holding him back from paying a final visit before his departure. He grabbed the surfboard from his car and headed down the concrete ramp, onto the soft sand. A gentle breeze wafted across the ocean, sprinkling light droplets of water over his face. There was not much swell to speak of, so he would need to create his own, but it was of little consequence. He was not out for a pleasure surf.

After a few minutes of floating on his board, Saoirse's delicate face peeked above the surface and smiled at him. 'I wasn't sure you'd come back after last night, but I'm glad you did.' She leaned in close for a kiss, but Liam backed away, prompting her to frown. 'What's wrong?'

'We can't do this anymore, Saoirse. You know I have a wife.'

She huffed, bringing her bare breasts a little above water. It was not the distraction Liam needed. 'A wife whose soul belongs to another. Why do you still fight this? We would be good together, Liam. You know it as well as I do.'

'Because I am a fool. I still love Lana, and I refuse to give up on her while she still needs me.'

Tears pooled in Saoirse's eyes. 'Then why come to see me at all? You keep sending me mixed signals, and I'm not sure my heart can take it much longer.'

Glancing down, Liam focused on a patch of seaweed gliding past. 'I'm sorry. I needed to see you one last time. I'm about to leave town on a Council mission, and with war dawning on the horizon I'm not sure I'll get to see you again. I…' He looked up into her shimmering, aqua eyes. 'I wanted to say goodbye.'

'Oh.' Her eyes had grown wide, and she drew her trembling bottom lip between her teeth.

'I need to know if your offer of accommodation still stands. I understand if it'll be too—'

'Of course. You and your family are still welcome if you need to seek sanctuary at any time during the war. You need only get my attention with a lightning bolt, and I'll come meet you.'

'Thank you. It means a lot to me.'

She forced a smile. 'And if the situation with your wife changes, you know where to find me.'

'Please don't hold out hope for us. It may never happen, and I don't want you putting your life on hold for me.' A single tear slid down her cheek, and Liam reached out to wipe it away.

Grabbing his hand, she pulled him closer. 'If this is goodbye, can we have one last kiss?'

He sucked in a breath through clenched teeth, unsure what he should do. Releasing his breath in a sigh, Liam shifted his weight on the surfboard. He invited her to sit beside him with a pat of his hand. Saoirse beamed as she slid gracefully in place beside him, wrapping her tail around him. Her tall, slim body fit perfectly with his. Thinking this might be the last time he touched her made his heart ache. Their lips collided in unbridled ferocity. Heated blood coursed through his veins, rushing south of his waistline. He grunted. *Mm, I wish I knew what it was like to be inside you.*

Saoirse gasped.

Crap, did I say that aloud? When Liam looked into her eyes, he saw them focus somewhere behind him. He heard the clicking of a camera and spun round to challenge their voyeur.

'Liam?' Connor's jaw dropped. The diving camera clicked once more as he lowered it into a bag within his motorboat. 'What the hell dude?'

Liam glared. 'I could say the same for you. What are you doing with those photos? Are they for your own perverted use, or are you working the cryptid porn market now?' He started moving the surfboard closer to Connor's boat, preparing to fight the jerk.

Raising his hands, Connor shook his head. 'Neither. It's my job to study and care for marine life. I came to see if the merfolk required aid during the impending war. I didn't expect to find this….' A scowled marred his scruffy face as he gestured toward their intimate embrace. 'Does Alannah know you've been practising breaststroke with Fish Features here?'

A growl slipped from Liam's lips as he clenched his fists. 'Show some fucking respect. Saoirse is a good person.'

Connor's brow furrowed. 'Oh, I'm sure she is, but she is not the woman you swore to remain faithful to.'

'My love life is none of your business, so don't go sticking your nose where it's not wanted.'

'Alannah is one of my best friends, so it damn well is my business. I won't stand by and watch another man ruin her.' The motor roared to life, and Connor took off at break-neck speed toward the beach.

'Shit! I don't really have time for damage control.' *I guess I'll have to make time, for Lana's sake.* He glanced at Saoirse. 'I'm sorry, but I have to go now.'

She nodded and dove into the water.

Sitting upon the cushions in the ritual room, Alannah grasped Brendan's hands and closed her eyes. Amidst a backdrop of flickering candlelight and incense, the atmosphere charged with magic. Vivid memories of better times brought on by Brendan's touch filled her mind. She could feel him inside her head, reading her thoughts, watching the video reel. Rather than expel Brendan, Alannah drew him in deeper, crossing the bridge into his own mind. Still new to mind reading, she was thankful for his willingness to let her in. '*It is time.*'

She conveyed her message using their mental connection.

Brendan commenced his visualisation. His demonic form chained Alannah to a boulder in the pits of the underworld and ravished her. It was the same imagery she had used to channel nether for the first time. Because of her seat on the Council, Alannah's connection to the Celestial element was always open. As soon as Brendan connected to the stygian element, power surged through them both. It flash-flooded her magical conduits: a sensation akin to a saline drip rushing through her bloodstream, yet this felt ten times stronger. Her eyes shot open, locking with his. *'You feel that?'*

'Yup. Feels fucking amazing.'

'I expected to feel more power through our connection, but this is something else. How is it possible?'

'I have my theories, but I'll share them later. You have more mana to channel yet.'

She smiled and focused on drawing the power of the primordial from her sunstone ring. Years of practice made this a simple task, but she did not expect the extra surge of power to wind her.

'Christ! Are you okay, gorgeous?' Brendan quaked.

After catching her breath, Alannah nodded. 'I'm not used to this much power. How are you handling it so well?'

Brendan shrugged. *'This isn't my first rodeo.'*

Alannah's brows arched above her wide eyes.

'Hey, try to focus. I'll explain later.' Brendan squeezed her hand. *'Let's get on with this job for now.'*

'Okay,' she agreed. With the necessary mana flowing through them, Alannah touched each piece of armour. She imbued them with all the spells Kieran had requested. Thanks to the boost, Alannah completed the job in a fraction of the anticipated time. Days of work took a couple of hours. Good thing too, because Alannah's muscles ached by the end of it and her eyelids drooped. Glancing over the fruits of their labour, she shook her head. 'I can't believe we managed to finish them all so quickly. This expediency is gonna blow Kieran's mind.'

Brendan sighed. 'Close the circle, Lana.'

'Oh right, sorry.' She completed the final stage of the ritual and collapsed on her back.

Moving close beside her, Brendan tickled her neck with his hot breath. 'You okay?'

'Yeah, just tired. I should go to bed, but I'm also dying to hear your theory.'

He rose to his feet. 'Head to my room and cast a soundproofing ward if you can. I'll be there in five minutes.'

'What are you doing?'

'Making us some coffee.'

Alannah followed him out of the cellar with a smile. Being with Brendan, working magic with him, felt good. A sense of normality verging on hope was returning to her life. *It's almost like he never left.*

The ward was up by the time Brendan entered, carrying two cups. He placed them on his bedside table before sitting next to her on the mattress.

She eyed the steaming hot brew. 'Is one of those for me?'

'Yup. But I want something first.' He grinned.

Clutching a hand to her chest, Alannah let out an exaggerated gasp. 'You're holding my coffee for ransom? You wicked man!'

A sinister gleam sparkled in Brendan's eyes. 'Spend the night in bed with me and I'll redefine wicked for you.'

With her jaw dropping, heat pooled in her core. 'Brendan…'

'I know you're exhausted and frankly so am I. I'm not asking about tonight, but soon. What I want is the truth, Lana. Tell me if I'm wasting my time, or if there is hope for us again.'

Her chest rose and fell with short, rapid breaths and a manic heart. 'I... I don't know what's possible after... everything. But I can tell you I still love you. And I'm sure you know how much my body wants you.'

Brendan inhaled deeply. 'Thank you.' Leaning forward, he brought his forehead into contact with hers. 'My feelings for you never lessened Lana. I don't think it is possible to fall out of love with you. I need you in my life again, consequences be damned.'

'What consequences?'

'I'll get to those in a moment, but first I need to explain a few things. Oh, and here.' He handed her a cup of caffeinated heaven.

A loud knock at the door startled Alannah, and hot coffee spilled across her lap. 'Ah, fuck!'

'Alannah, sweetie, are you in there?' Nora called out. 'You have a visitor.'

'What the hell? Who could that be at this time of night?' Brendan mused.

Chapter Twenty-Two

'Connor? What are you doing here?' Alannah opened the door wider, stepping aside to allow him entry into Brendan's room.

Freezing mid stride, Connor paled, his eyes widening at the sight of Brendan sitting on the bed. 'What the hell?' His eyes darted to-and-fro, settling on Alannah. 'I had heard rumours of his return, but I had no idea you were seeing him.'

'Dude, I'm right here,' Brendan called across the room.

Connor's gaze remained fixed on Alannah.

'Things are… complicated. I'm not sure there is time to go into it all with you at the moment. I appreciate your concern, Connor, but you needn't worry about me. How about we focus on the reason for your visit?'

He nodded. 'Actually, my concern for you is what brought me here.' When he finally moved into the room, Alannah shut the door. She perched on the end of the bed, gesturing for him to continue. 'I was working late tonight, and I saw something out at sea you should know about… I don't know how long this has been going on… I didn't even realise it was him at first…'

'Please cut the cryptic crap and tell me,' Alannah insisted.

Connor handed her his camera. The image on the small screen was hard to make out. From what she could tell it was a pair of merfolk kissing. 'I'm not sure what you are trying to show me.'

'Scroll to the next photo.'

Alannah gasped as everything became clear. 'By the Gods!' *Has Liam given up on me?* Her chest grew tight and painful.

Peeking over her shoulder, Brendan whistled through his teeth. 'Looks to me like Liam took the concept of chasing tail much too literally.'

Connor snorted. 'I see a life of crime hasn't dampened your sense of humour, Brendan.'

'Far from it. Darkened it a little, but I find mirth keeps me sane,' Brendan replied, resting his chin on Alannah's shoulder. 'I take it this is news to you?'

'Quite. I knew Liam had befriended a mermaid, but he never mentioned anything like this.' Alannah handed the camera back to Connor.

Connor pursed his lips. 'I'm sorry to be the bearer of bad news, but I figured you had a right to know the truth.'

'Thanks. I appreciate you letting me know. This could be his reaction to the news of my own affair.'

With brows arched, Connor glanced toward Brendan.

'Why do you assume the worst of me, man?' Brendan whined.

Crossing his arms, Connor glared at Brendan. 'Oh, I don't know. Because you *are* the worst: a criminal, a drug peddling lech; not to mention your history with Alannah.'

'Pfft. If I'd been lucky enough to win Lana's heart back, she wouldn't have stayed married to Liam.'

Turning, she gave him a sidelong glance. 'Brendan, you know *full well* you're the reason for my affair.'

'Affair with who?' Connor asked, scratching his head.

'Tyler. My doppelganger,' Brendan replied before embarking on his explanation of mystic twins.

Connor had taken a seat on the floor partway through Brendan's tale. He leaned back against the wall next to the door and focused his attention on Alannah. 'You started sleeping with Tyler because he looks like Brendan?'

'Pretty much. Although the affair continued because the resemblance was more than skin deep,' Alannah explained.

'That's some messed up shit. And Liam knows about Tyler?'

'Yeah. I recently told him everything. We started marriage counselling and it seemed like we had made a breakthrough, but then...'

'Then what?' Both men asked in unison.

She sighed. 'Never mind.'

'So, have the pair of you reconciled?' Connor asked, gesturing from Alannah to Brendan.

'Yup—'

'Mostly,' Alannah replied, cutting Brendan off. They exchanged wide-eyed looks.

'I see you have some way to go yet,' Connor observed. 'Let me guess: the whole crime boss thing is a major hurdle for you, Alannah.'

She shrugged. 'Not so much. But there are other... issues.'

Connor's jaw dropped. After shaking his head, he rose to his feet. 'I should go. I'm still looking for a safe place to hide Amy before the dragons show up.'

It was Alannah's turn to stare gobsmacked. 'How did you hear? I thought Kieran was keeping it all hush-hush.'

'Jacob told me; not sure how he heard about it.' Connor and Alannah both looked at Brendan.

'What? As if I was gonna keep my friends in the dark,' Brendan retorted.

Alannah smiled. 'I had hoped you would inform them. With all the surveillance on me, I needed to be careful who I told. I'll talk to Ross and Nora, but I'm sure you guys are welcome here. Same goes for the rest of the gang.'

'Really? That would be awesome.'

'No promises, but I'll keep you posted.' As soon as Connor left, Alannah returned to her room to grab her phone.

Brendan followed her. 'What are you gonna do about Liam?'

'I'm not sure. First I want to hear what he has to say for himself.' She typed out a text to Liam: CARE TO EXPLAIN WHY CONNOR HAS PHOTOS OF YOU SUCKING FACE WITH A MERMAID?

His reply came several seconds later: I'M ON MY WAY OVER TO EXPLAIN IT NOW. SORRY YOU HAD TO HEAR IT FROM SOMEONE ELSE.

'Well fuck! He isn't even denying it.' She showed Brendan the message.

'He must figure denial is pointless in light of the evidence.' After returning her phone, Brendan made his way across the room. 'I'll leave you to it for a bit. I'm gonna try to reach Jacob again. I'm here if you need to talk about it after.'

She forced a smile. 'Thanks.'

Ensuring the soundproof ward was still intact, Brendan retrieved his 'business' phone.

Jacob answered the call after two rings. 'Hello?'

'About fucking time. Why has your phone been off?'

'Sorry man. I was dealing with family issues. What's up?'

Resting back against the headboard of his bed, Brendan closed his eyes. 'I need all the intel you can get on a Rhapsody deal that went down on the weekend.'

'There were no deals, Boss. As per your request, we ceased operations.'

Brendan sighed. 'That's what worries me. I fear this may have been a seelie fake. Is there any chance our stuff was still on the market?'

'I suppose it is possible a private dealer used his own stash. With the short supply they'd make a killing too. Mind if I ask what this is about, Sir?'

'Some dickwad drugged my daughter at a party on the weekend. The guy told her it was Rhapsody.'

'Oh hell. I'm sorry man. Is she okay?'

'I don't know. I haven't seen her much since and the seelie have her now, but Lana did speak to her on the phone today. She has not reported any side-effects yet.'

'Hm, all signs point to the seelie knockoff shit.'

'Can you do some digging and find out what she took? The kid who gave it to her was Jasper Rowan. He bought it at the party hosted by Erik Alvarsson on Saturday night.'

'Oh. That party.'

Brendan's heart began to hammer against his ribs. 'What do you mean by *that* party?'

'I don't know who ended up dealing there, but I know those kids were looking for the real deal. Elna Alvarsson contacted me. She wanted to know where she could get her hands on genuine Rhapsody. I told her we had frozen our supply, but I did give her the names of a few dealers. I'm so fucking sorry, Sir. I thought I was doing business with the Seelie Court; I had no idea she was in with Neve's circle of friends.'

Brendan did not know what was worse: the possibility Neve had taken some junk with unknown side effects or the more likely probability it was genuine Rhapsody, a drug that only existed because of him. 'Go through your list of dealers and find out if any of them were responsible.'

'Yes, Sir.'

Throwing the phone on the bed, Brendan pulled his laptop out. He opened the surveillance app connected to Neve's secret camera. It came as no surprise that the live feed was already dead, but he was able to retrieve the recorded footage. It started with Jasper pressuring Neve to take the potion. Soon after she gave in, they were fooling around. Brendan felt sickened by the whole show, doubly so knowing it was his daughter.

Brendan wanted to avert his eyes, to skip past the sex scene, but feared missing some crucial clue. Lucky thing he did. Erik entered the room without either of them aware of his presence. He snuck past the camera, slipping into the bathroom. The altered camera angle suggested Erik kept the door ajar, spying on the couple. After Neve and Jasper blacked out, Elna entered the room and Erik emerged from his hiding spot.

'Everything went according to plan,' Erik explained.

Elna sported a wicked grin. 'Excellent.' She turned her gaze to the bed. 'Gosh they make a hot couple. It'll be a pity to destroy them.'

'You aren't having doubts, are you?' Erik asked.

'Of course not! I wasn't being serious.'

'Good. Now I need to find the camera Neve hid here somewhere. You go hack into their computers and wipe the footage.' Once Elna left, it took very little time for Erik to find the camera, putting an end to Brendan's viewing.

What are those seelie arseholes plotting? What do they want with my baby girl?

Having parked his SUV in the carport, Liam read the message from Alannah and cursed under his breath. 'Damn Connor, the nosy bastard!' He did not even bother stepping inside his house. Heading around to the back garden, he jumped across the ley lines to Cailleach Estate.

His father greeted him at the back door. 'Liam? What are you doing back? I thought you'd be on your way to Mount Gambier by now.'

'Sorry Dad, I don't have time to explain. I need to speak with Lana about a private matter.'

Ross frowned. 'Does this have anything to do with Connor's visit earlier?'

'Sort of, but Connor was just the messenger. Please, Dad, give me some time to sort things out with my wife.'

'Yes, of course. Let me know if you need anything from me.'

They parted ways and Liam sprinted up the stairs. He found Alannah waiting for him on their bed. She sat atop the covers, cross legged, still in her day clothes despite the late hour. Schooling her expression, she maintained a neutral mask.

'First, let me preface this by saying how deeply sorry I am you found out this way.'

She scoffed. 'But you're not sorry for cheating on me, huh?'

'What? No! Please let me explain. It was just a kiss, Lana. I was not going to let any more come of it. I went out there to say goodbye to her, to cut all ties with her. I wasn't planning to kiss her, but she wanted a proper goodbye. I swear it was the last time.'

Alannah's brow furrowed. 'If this was the last time, when was the first?'

Drawing closer, he sat near her on the bed, but she inched away. Liam sighed. 'I met her on Australia Day, but the first and only other time we kissed was last night.'

'All those times you've been out surfing or kayaking over the last three weeks—were you meeting *her* out there?'

Liam glanced down at his fidgeting hands, hunching his shoulders. 'Not always, but most of the time, yes.' He looked back up into Alannah's eyes. He could see tears pooling in the corners, and knowing he was the cause of her grief made his heart ache. 'I didn't think our friendship would evolve the way it did. I'm sorry I let things get carried away.'

She rose in a huff, challenging him with hands on her hips. '*Why the hell didn't you tell me what was going on?*'

'*You mean like how you were always so honest about your affair with Tyler?* Give me a break, Lana!'

'At least you heard it from me!'

'And how did it happen again? Oh right, you told me I was such a lousy lay you had to seek your gratification elsewhere. Thanks, bunches!'

Snorting laughter resounded from the doorway. Liam turned to see Brendan doubled over.

'Do you mind? This is a private conversation,' Liam scowled.

Brendan caught his breath. 'Sorry, but there ain't no soundproofing ward on the room and your voices travelled down the hall. I came to support Lana. I didn't expect to hear such gold. Tell me about this mermaid, bro. Have you finally found a woman you can get wet?'

Liam heard Alannah stifle a laugh. When he spun around to face her, the mask was back up. 'What do you want from me, Lana? I'm trying here, but you keep pushing me away.'

'Do you love her?' Alannah asked.

'I don't know. I've been suppressing my feelings for her because I'm still in love with you. I refuse to give up on you, on us. When I promised I'd never leave you again, I meant it.' He glanced toward Brendan. 'Unlike this tosser.'

Brendan stormed up to him. 'You're treading on very thin ice, *Brother*. I never would have left if you hadn't put the moves on Lana when she was with me. You fucked things up for both of us, throwing my whole world into chaos. And I have a God of Vengeance whispering in my ear, so choose your words very carefully.'

'So, you finally grew a pair, huh? All it took was a life of dark magic and organised crime. How is your endarkened whore doing these days?'

Wincing, Brendan fell quiet and backed away.

'Still fucking her, hm? How does Lana feel about that? You think I don't know what you're up to, Brendan? Swooping in here, manipulating Lana so she will take you back. Yet what you fail to realise is how she has grown wise to your games. I won't let you hurt her again.'

A smug grin grew on Brendan's face. 'What *you* fail to see is this was never a game for me, and Lana understands now. I wonder whose bed she will choose to sleep in when you're away fighting dragons?' He sauntered out the room.

Liam stared at Alannah. 'Is there something you wanna tell me, Lana?'

'You mean like how Brendan and I kissed?'

His pulse kicked it up a notch. 'When?'

'Earlier today. But *it was just a kiss.*' Her mocking tone did not escape him.

'Gods! What are we doing here Lana? Our marriage has become a complete joke. Do we try to salvage what's left, or do you want to move on?'

With a sigh, she collapsed beside him. 'I'm not sure. You know how I feel about Brendan, but things are beyond complicated with him. We should spend our time apart doing some soul searching.'

'Okay. Best not to rush decisions like this anyway. Promise me one thing?'

'What?'

'Please be careful with Brendan. Don't forget he is a changed man who has fallen in with some of the vilest people to walk this earth.'

She nodded. 'I'll be careful.'

Liam aimed to kiss her forehead, but she lifted her face and met his lips with her own. Alannah climbed into his lap, letting the heat escalate between them, and before he knew it, their clothes vanished, and she was riding him.

Bittersweet, Liam thought in the dimming afterglow. *Two people, who love, but are not in love, find hollow joy in each other for what felt like one last time. Is this goodbye?*

Chapter Twenty-Three

The aroma of freshly brewed coffee drew Alannah downstairs late the following morning. Reaching the breakfast bar, she paused to admire Brendan's backside in tight jeans. A contented sigh slipped from her lips as she settled into one of the seats. The house was otherwise empty. Ross and Nora had followed Liam to help with the Limestone Coast situation.

Brendan glanced over his shoulder. 'Coffee?'

'Yes please.' *I could get used to mornings like this. They'd be better still after nights in bed with him.*

He slid the drink across the bench, remaining in the kitchen. 'I take it you and Liam patched things up?'

Alannah's brow furrowed. 'Why do you say that?'

'Oh please. I heard the pair of you going at it last night. Tell me: was the lack of soundproofing an oversight, or did you want me to listen?'

She gaped at him. 'Things just happened. I'm sorry I subjected you to the noise, but I didn't intend for you to eavesdrop. Why are you being such a jealous douche?'

Glaring at her, Brendan sipped his coffee with slow deliberation. 'After everything we've been through, you shouldn't need to ask. Did our kiss yesterday mean nothing to you?'

She tightened her grip on the coffee mug. 'No, of course it meant something. If I'm honest, it was far more meaningful than the sympathy bone I gave Liam.'

Brendan froze, eyes wide as saucers. 'What?'

'Liam and I agreed to take a break to think things over during his absence. But in our heart of hearts, we both know the marriage is over. I guess I wanted to give him a proper goodbye.'

Resting his elbows on the bench, he leaned forward with his eyes fixed on hers. 'Do you want me back, Lana?'

Sucking in a deep breath, she began to weigh up all the pros and cons in her mind. 'I don't know.'

Growling, Brendan leaned back against the cupboards and crossed his arms. 'Why are you still struggling with this? You know how I feel about you... how sorry I am for running off and making a mess of things when I thought I lost you.'

'For one thing, there's Bridey. I can't stomach the idea of you being with her still.'

Brendan exhaled sharply. 'I can't cut all ties with Bridey, not yet. There is too much at stake for such a risky move. What if I promise to stop having sex with her? Would that make you happy?'

'No.'

Fire blazed in Brendan's eyes. 'W—'

'I'm struggling to trust you again, Brendan. Your promises don't mean much to me anymore, not after you broke the big one. You swore you would never leave me, but in a moment of weakness, you did just that. I know you misread the situation, and Bridey trapped you for months because of the mistake you made. But it doesn't change what you did. What if you overreact to a similar situation again in the future?'

'I'm still here now aren't I, even after hearing you fuck Liam. You need to give me a chance, Lana. Let me earn your trust back.'

The pressure of tears swelled in her eyes, but Alannah refused to let them escape. 'I don't know how. Losing you the first time almost destroyed me. I'm not sure I could survive another of your betrayals.'

Rounding the bench, Brendan zeroed in on Alannah, cupping her chin with his hand. 'Do I need to keep repeating myself until the message sinks in? You need to give me a chance. Spend more time with me and I'll prove how much I love you.' He leaned in for a kiss.

Alannah pushed him back. 'I can't.'

'Why not?'

'Because I keep thinking of you with *her*, and… because you didn't return to me when your servitude finished.'

'Argh!' Clenching his fists, Brendan scowled at the ceiling. He lowered his gaze, looking at her with laser beam intensity. 'Why must you be so stubborn and infuriating? Quite aside from thinking you were happily married, I stayed away to protect you. So sue me for giving a damn!' Storming out of the room, he slammed the back door behind him.

'*Typical Brendan!*' she screamed after him. 'Running off when things get hard!' Alannah moved into the living room and slumped onto the sofa. *How on earth was he protecting me by staying away? Surely, I'm safer with him at my side? Not that I need protecting! Why does he have to be such an arse?*

On the verge of blowing a fuse, Brendan hopped the ley lines to the lookout, his hand trembling as he unlocked his Jag. For every step forward he made with Alannah, they took several back. *I don't know how much more of this torture I can handle.*

He took a few deep breaths to centre himself before driving. The car cruised along the windy, country roads to Jasper Rowan's house. Kieran had shut down the school, so Brendan figured the little shit's home was the best place to start. The Rowans would have warded their property against fire, like most of the country estates. They would not need to evacuate. He also had it on good authority Jasper's parents were away.

Parking on the roadside, he made a stealthy approach, ducking between almond trees. A tall, galvanised fence separated the front garden from the backyard. It posed little difficulty for Brendan. After jumping over it, he crouched down. Crawling along the side of the redbrick building, he avoided the large windows. Reaching a wooden side door, Brendan retrieved his lockpick and gained entry to the house.

By using his heightened senses, he identified two people in the house. One of them, a young girl, gossiped on the phone in her upstairs room. The other was gaming in the basement. *Perfect!* Descending the carpeted stairs, he found Jasper.

The boy was playing a gritty first-person shooter on the latest Xbox.

Brendan threw up a soundproofing ward. Then he closed the door with an audible click, alerting Jasper to his presence.

'The fuck?' Jasper spun round to face Brendan. 'Who the hell are you?'

'Someone you don't want to piss off. Unfortunately, you already have.'

As Jasper grabbed his phone, Brendan set it on fire with the snap of his fingers. Flames filled the room with a distinctive sulphurous odour.

'Ow, mother fuck!' Dropping the phone on the ground, Jasper failed to smother the flames with a blanket he pulled off the couch. He shot Brendan a wary look. 'That was hellfire, wasn't it?'

A sly grin tugged at Brendan's lips as he extinguished the fire with a wave of his hand. 'Surprise!' He moved further into the room, laughing as Jasper backed away.

'What do you want?'

'I'd like to have a little chat about respecting women.'

Backing up into the far wall, Jasper gulped.

Brendan continued to advance. 'Tell me Jasper, do you love your family?'

The kid's eyes grew wide. 'Y-yes.'

'I reckon you looked up to your father and uncle a little too much. They are both first-rate scumbags, especially Clayton. Thing is, boy, I love my family too. But you and your uncle have hurt my family.'

A lightbulb flicked on behind Jasper's eyes. 'Shit! You're Neve's uncle?'

'No, Jasper. I'm Neve's *real* father.'

The Adam's apple in Jasper's throat bobbed again. 'B-but you're *him*. The Syndicate Boss?'

'Yeah, I am. But right now, you should be more worried I am the irate father of a girl you fucked over. Don't even try to deny it. I saw the surveillance feed from Neve's hidden camera.' He pinned Jasper against the wall with a firm chokehold. The pressure allowed enough air through for the boy to keep breathing. 'The same footage you put on the internet. Do you know what the Magus Court will do to you for date rape and uploading child pornography? I bet they'll give you the cell right next door to your uncle; if you're still alive after I'm done with you.'

'I didn't do it!' Jasper rasped.

'I warned you not to deny it, skid mark. I've seen the evidence.'

'The video. I didn't release it. I swear to the Gods.'

476

Brendan loosened his grip.

'I love Neve. There's no way I'd do anything like that to her,' Jasper continued to explain. 'And I only broke up with her because Erik blackmailed me.'

'Do you take me for a fool? The video uploaded from your computer.'

'I know, but it wasn't me. Someone hacked it, like they hacked my phone and sent a message to Neve with the video link. After uploading the footage, they wiped the video from my system. I never even saw the whole thing, only what went online.'

Thinking back to the footage, Brendan realised Jasper was probably being honest. But he needed to be sure. 'Show me your aura, then tell me the truth.'

Jasper dropped all his mental shields. 'I swear I did not intend to hurt Neve, nor did I release the sex tape. I love her more than anything.' There was no sign of dishonesty showing in his aura.

Brendan released him. 'Then tell me what Erik has over you. Why did you break my little girl's heart?'

'The bastard threatened Neve's life.'

Simmering blood boiled over as Brendan refocused his rage where it belonged: *Erik Alvarsson.*

Chaos reigned supreme in the small-town streets of Mount Gambier. The cries of people trapped in burning buildings mingled with ash in the air. Those lucky enough to escape either keeled over from toxic gas exposure or left in manic haste. Dressed in a hazmat suit, Liam parted the flowing lava as he searched for the Council Chambers. Three blocks further and he found his destination: one of the few places not on fire. He ducked inside. 'Hello?'

A rugged man with a powerful aura stepped forward. 'Identify yourself!'

'Warlock Liam Winters of the Fleurieu District. I am here to lead the relief efforts. You are?'

'Councillor Johnathan Ryan, district mayor. Boy, am I glad to see you, Sir!' He stepped forward to shake Liam's hand. 'I have a few magic folk taking refuge in the basement. They are safe for the time being. Best if you focus on finding other survivors.'

'I will, but first, I need to meet the rest of my team here. I also need a space to set up a temporary hospital.'

'Right, of course. Follow me.' Ryan led Liam outside. They crossed a landscaped garden where abjurers warded the space from volcanic devastation. Gesturing toward them, Ryan answered Liam's unspoken question. 'High Magus Lane told me to prepare a space for you, so I kept the path clear between these buildings.' He unlocked a large hall. 'Will this suffice?'

'Perfect. Thank you.' Liam pulled out his radio. 'Dougherty, do you copy? Over.'

Bailey Dougherty replied immediately, 'Yes, Winters. I copy. Over.'

'Council Chambers confirmed secure. Rendezvous at City Hall. Over and out.'

'Understood. Over and out.'

Fifteen minutes later, Bailey arrived. He helped Liam's father drive the truck full of medical supplies into the loading dock. Kieran had recruited several abjurers from around the state. Each of them travelled with a warlock or shaman escort who kept the fire and lava at bay.

Liam oversaw the setup of the makeshift hospital, sending the younger healers to Ross. Then he guided the warlocks and shamans back to the

Council Chambers. 'Okay so here's the plan: I'm pairing each warlock with a shaman and assigning each partnership to a separate sector. Warlocks, let the shamans handle fire control as much as possible. Reserve your magic to back up the shamans if conflict arises. Your objective is to recover all surviving mages, regardless of blood purity. If they have injuries, bring them back here. Otherwise jump the ley lines and get them to your designated safe house. If any of you start to tire, let your partner know. When this happens, I want you both to find a safe place to rest until you are both ready to get back to work. Do you understand?'

Everyone voiced an affirmative. Bailey, who stood close beside Cara, raised his hand.

'What is it, Dougherty?'

'What if we find other magicals needing help?'

'The High Magus was very explicit in his instructions. We are not to assist any fae or cursed. The seelie won't need our help anyway. I'll leave it to your discretion with other magicals.'

Bailey nodded. 'Thank you.'

As Liam finished pairing everyone, he turned to Nora. 'Mum, you're with me.'

She smiled. 'Of course.'

Councillor Ryan knew the region better than anyone. He helped Liam assign each pair their sector. Once everyone else had left, he turned to Liam. 'There is one last spot I was hoping you could investigate.'

'Where?'

'Ground Zero. I know it is unlikely, but I still hold out hope for some of Grant's team. Will you explore the area around Mount Schank?'

Liam sighed. *Unlikely is an understatement, but if the old man thinks it's worthwhile...* 'Okay.'

When they arrived, it took both Nora and Liam's efforts to stem the flow of lava spurting forth from the volcano. Scouring the mountain's surrounds, Liam was on the verge of giving up when he spotted a cave. Rather than pooling into it as one might expect, the lava travelled in a channel around it. *Curious.* He signalled for Nora to follow as he approached the hollow. Sure enough, as soon as they entered, they did not need their magic to ensure safe footing. They both took a few moments to rest and catch their breath.

Several metres down the dark tunnel, a tall, blond man stepped out of the shadows. He illuminated the space with a mage light. 'Halt! Do not come any further.'

Liam raised his hands in supplication. 'It's okay. We have come to help. I am Warlock Liam Winters of the Fleurieu District, and this is my mother, Nora.'

'You are of the Winters clan?'

'Yes. And we are evacuating all mages from the area.'

A groan sounded from behind the man. Liam moved forward, attempting to see who made the noise, but the stranger stopped him.

'What was that?' Liam asked. 'It sounds like you have an injured companion. Please, let us help.'

The man sighed. 'Very well. I have been doing my best to heal him. His injuries were severe, and I have also been using my magic to keep the lava out of here. I would appreciate any help you can offer.'

'What is your name?'

'Hugh. Hugh Doran.' He stood aside, letting Liam pass.

'Thank you, Mr. Doran.' Liam kneeled beside the injured man and gasped. 'Tyler?'

His mother's reaction was similar when she drew near.

'What do you mean?' Doran asked.

'This man. I know him,' Liam replied. 'His name is Tyler Quirke.'

Doran shook his head. 'No. This is Danny Erling, a local warlock.'

'Gods! How many of them are there?' Liam mused. 'Explains the longer hair.'

'I'm sorry, but you've lost me. How many what?'

'Doppelgangers. First Tyler, and now this Danny fellow. They are both the spitting image of my younger brother. Something about being mystic twins. Although now I suppose they'd be triplets.'

Doran's brows rose. 'Hm… interesting. Listen, do you think you could get us out of here?'

'Of course. It's what we are here to do.' Liam offered a slight smile. He helped Doran lift Warlock Erling, draping the man's unconscious form over Doran's back.

The sky had grown darker when they emerged from the cave. Nora cast a small ward around the group. It protected Doran and Erling from the toxic plumes. Liam took point, fending off the lava. Travelling by ley lines in their treacherous terrain was bad enough. Doing so with an injured party member could prove downright deadly. The three conscious mages had to concentrate twice as hard to avoid the perils along their path.

They made it back to Mount Gambier, handing Erling over to Ross for medical attention.

Nora grabbed Liam's arm as they walked out of the hall. 'Liam, sweetie, that took it out of me. I need to rest before we do more.'

'It's okay, Mum. Go grab some shut eye.' Still buzzing with energy, Liam decided to see if his father needed anything. As he turned back toward the hospital, shouts and cries drew his attention west, to the main street. *Don't tell me the humans have started rioting.* With a deep breath, he walked closer to investigate the commotion.

Several mages were standing around staring up at the sky. Liam followed their gaze, gasping at the large silhouettes. *So, this is it. The dragons have taken to the skies.*

To be continued...

What's Next?

Thank you for reading *Winter's Mother 1*. I would be most grateful if you could show your support by leaving a rating or even a review.

Alannah and Brendan's stories continue *in Winter's Mother 2*, due for release May 2023 (hopefully)!

Keep reading for a sample…

Acknowledgements

Firstly, I want to apologise for the cliff-hanger (well sort of). Personally, I don't mind them, but I know a lot of you detest them. Thing is, this book would have been twice the size and taken another 6 months to release if I gave you both parts at once. To those of you who appreciate the excitement of waiting for the next instalment—I love you! You are my people!

Now for my long list of praise and gratitude....

I'd like to thank Jana Hoffmann for more amazing cover art. Her talent blows my mind every time. If you haven't yet, please check out her website: www.janahoffmann.com.

Felix Staica continues to impress me with his editing prowess. If you are looking for a skilled line editor, please look him up, or contact me for more details.

Much love to my hubby for his continued support in my creative endeavours. I've lost count of the number of times I considered throwing in the towel, only to get right back in the saddle thanks to his encouragement.

ACKNOWLEDGEMENTS

Much thanks to my personal assistant, Priyanka Mukherjee. She has done a marvellous job taking over the marketing side of my business so that I can focus what little spare time I have on my writing.

I am extremely grateful for my beta team. These wonderful people volunteered their time to proof-read and critique my work, helping me deliver a quality story. Thank you, Amanda Mashburn, Deborah Apodaca, Elli Morgan, Hayley Brooks (nee Mckenna), and Joshua Wake.

And a big shout out to my street team! Your reviews make a huge difference to the success of my books.

The Winter's Magic Series

A modern fantasy and paranormal romance about secrets, mysticism, empowerment, and the complexities of love.

Winter's Mother 2

True love has the power to rise from the ashes.

An ancient power awakens, and everything is burning. With humanity on the brink of destruction, the Council makes a dicey decision that puts the entire magic community at risk: they invite humans to their own farewell party.

War is raging outside, and Cailleach Estate is one of the few safehouses in the state. Things are getting awfully cosy when Alannah bunkers down with her friends and several refugees from Mt. Gambier. With cabin fevers rising, old grudges flaring to life, and lustful desires blazing, this house becomes hotter than the fires scorching the land.

But Alannah Winters detests hiding. She is a fighter. And she will do anything to protect the people she loves.

AVAILABLE MAY 2023
Keep Reading for a sample…

Chapter One

Everything beyond the mystic perimeter was burning. Fire rained in apocalyptic torrents from the mouths of three gargantuan beasts in the sky. Liam crossed the garden toward the Mount Gambier Council Chambers. Jerking his head towards the sound of someone calling his name, he spotted Bailey Dougherty beside the pub across the carpark. *Figures he'd gravitate towards his natural habitat*. He started striding toward Bailey but stopped when the warlock punk shook his head and pointed down the street. Lava continued to flow from the Blue Lake although the recently erected wards kept the magma from reaching the Council Chambers and surrounding buildings.

Bailey jogged up to him. 'On the horizon, look.' He gestured to the distant shadows flying directly for Mount Gambier. 'Looks like more of their friends are coming.'

'Shit! They must be from the southern seamounts.' Liam wished he could channel senses mana or get his hands on a pair of binoculars so he could get see the dragons clearly. 'We need to hurry evacuate the rest of this area before they get here. Have you cleared out your sector?'

'Yeah, Naracoorte's empty. Cara and I have been helping with this place.'

'Thanks, man. I better let the mayor know what's going on. Keep your eye on the sky and get me on the radio if you have any issues.'

With a nod, Bailey took off toward Cara Hughes, who also happened to be his girlfriend. Liam had paired them on purpose because their relationship gave them additional incentive to protect one another. A pang of jealousy tightened his chest as he watched them work together and for the umpteenth time that day, he wanted his wife by his side. Powerful as she was, Alannah would have more hope defeating the dragons than anyone else there. He also worried about Brendan worming his way back into her broken soul while they sought refuge at Cailleach Estate together. He disliked High Magus Kieran's decision to keep her in the reserves, supporting the war effort with her conjuration expertise, but he respected the need to protect her.

He turned away from the devastation and went back inside The Council Chambers where he found Councillor Johnathan Ryan—the town's mayor—talking to a local mage.

Councillor Ryan glanced at him with a furrowed brow. 'I'm glad you found Danny—err, Warlock Erling alive. It saddens me that the rest of Warlock Grant's team perished.'

'What about Doran?' asked Liam.

Ryan's eyes narrowed. 'Who?'

'Hugh Doran. The man who helped us get Warlock Erling back here. Tall blond guy with a British accent.'

'Hm. I have no idea who that man is. Might be worth asking the High Magus to do a background check on him. Internet is down across town so I can't exactly look up his file on *my* computer.'

Liam tensed. 'Will do. The last thing we need to worry about right now is a potential traitor in our midst.' He moved closer to Ryan and whispered, 'Can I speak to you in private?'

The mayor led him into a boardroom and shut the door. 'What's the situation out there?'

'Not good. Three dragons have taken to the skies above us and there's another thunder of them heading this way from the south. I'm not sure how many—they are too far away to count.'

Ryan heaved a mournful sigh. 'It's time to count our losses and hightail it outta here.'

He nodded. 'I'll talk to Dad about getting his patients to safety.'

'Thank you, Warlock Winters, for this and everything else you've been doing to help us.'

'I wish I could do more.'

With heavy hearts, they left the Council Chambers and trudged across the lush garden.

'It will be sad to see such beauty perish,' Ryan mused while waving his hand toward the large sinkhole dominating the garden. 'I assume the Umpherston Cave down the road has collapsed beneath the magma by now.'

'It is likely, Sir. There is only so much we can do and saving lives is our priority.'

Ryan huffed. 'But only certain lives, right? I can't pretend to like High Magus Lane's directive. Not when I have so many human friends in this town.'

He wanted to explain Kieran's reasoning: that protecting humans would only anger the dragons more. He bit his lip instead and fell silent for the rest of the walk.

Entering the hall, they found Ross tending to Danny Erling's injuries. The burns were severe but healing fast. He observed the dark circles around his father's eyes. *Dad looks as exhausted as I feel.* 'We need to go.'

Raising his brows, Ross shot him a wide-eyed look. 'We can't. Half these people are out cold, and the others aren't fit to travel by ley line.'

'We'll transport the unconscious in the truck and send each of the others with a warlock/shaman pair,' Liam explained. 'Travel along the Coorong and take regular rest stops on your journey.'

Doran rose from his seat beside Erling's stretcher. 'I will help ward the truck.'

'Um....' He hesitated, concerned by what Councillor Ryan had mentioned earlier.

'It's okay, Liam,' Ross assured him. 'Kieran already vouched for Hugh.'

Liam exhaled his relief in a gust to rival a gale. 'Fine. Mr. Doran—go with your friend and keep the others safe.'

Doran smiled. 'Of course. Oh, and please call me Hugh.'

Sensing something was off about Doran, Liam gave him a curt nod. The man was far too friendly given the circumstances.

A tempest raged within Alannah's mind as she curled up on the sofa with her fluffy white cat. Thoughts and feelings for Brendan whirled about like a cyclone. She wanted to trust him again, but she did not know how. *What the hell did he mean about protecting me? Does he want to shield me from his life of crime? Or is there something else?*

'Hey, are you okay Alannah?'

She looked up at Amy's gruff voice and forced a smile. In the chaos of her morning spat with Brendan, Alannah had forgotten about the other house guests staying with her at Cailleach Estate. Amy and Jacob had arrived in the middle of the night, just as Liam was leaving with his parents. She sighed. 'No, not really.'

The butch dwarf sat beside her on the couch. 'Worried about Liam?'

A short, bitter laugh escaped her raspy throat. 'Not as much as I should be. I was thinking about Brendan.'

Amy perked up. 'Oh shit! Really? What happened with Brendo?'

Alannah briefly debated the wisdom of confiding in Amy. They had never been especially close, but that had more to do with circumstance than the woman herself. Yet she needed someone to talk to and Cara was away helping with the volcano situation. 'Promise to keep a secret?'

'Of course, dude! I'm not a gossip queen, unlike some of your other friends.'

Ignoring the snide remark clearly aimed at Monique Lane and Jessica Ó Máille, Alannah took a deep breath and braced herself. 'I'm still in love with Brendan.'

'Well dah. That much is obvious with the way your eyes glaze over every time his name comes up in conversation. I hear he is back in town, though. Has something happened between the two of you?'

Tears trickled down her cheeks as she nodded.

'Oh hell. What did he do?' Amy clenched her fists in her lap. 'Want me to beat the crap out of him?'

Alannah snorted. 'No, but thanks for the offer. I'm upset because of lost opportunities.'

Amy scrunched her brow. 'Whadda ya mean?'

'Brendan left me all those years ago because he thought *I* betrayed *him*.' She explained how Liam had kissed her on the night Brendan announced their soul link, the way Brendan had reacted to the scene, and the Bridey related aftermath that followed. 'He still wants me, Amy. Brendan never stopped loving me, but I don't know how to trust him anymore.'

'Fuck, that's heavy stuff,' Amy admitted.

'What should I do?' Alannah sniffled and grabbed a nearby tissue box.

'You should give him a second chance.' The voice to her left startled her. Jacob slouched in the doorway with his arms crossed. 'It's only fair after the number of times you welcomed Liam back after *he* screwed up.'

'Jacob?' Alannah queried in a mumble. 'I didn't see you there.'

'They don't call me a spymaster for nothing, sweets.'

Amy scowled at him. 'How long have you been eavesdropping, Bennett?'

'Long enough to know how Alannah truly feels about Brendo.' Jacob drew closer and sat in an armchair facing them. 'That man's heart bleeds for you, Alannah. His soul aches for its other half and I'm sure yours does too. Am I right?'

She sucked in a lungful of air. 'But Bridey—'

'Can suck my cock! Seriously woman, you can't let that bitch keep him from you any longer.'

The doorbell rang, putting an end to their conversation. She sprang to her feet and frowned at Jacob. 'You should hide. I'm expecting Kieran today, so that might be him now. I can't afford to lose his favour. Offering asylum to unseelie is a sure way of doing so.'

Grinning wide enough to show his razor-sharp teeth, Jacob saluted her. 'Yes, ma'am!' He marched out of the living room and hurried upstairs toward the secret attic hidden by powerful glamour.

High Magus Kieran stood on the doorstep, flanked by two large trunks. 'Hi, Alannah. I have more armour for you to imbue.'

'Come in.' She unlocked the screen door and held it open for him as he wheeled the crates inside. 'I finished the last lot.'

'Already? How did you finish so quick?'

Leading him through to the family room, she shrugged. 'You said it yourself. I'm a powerful mage.' No way in hell was she going to admit Brendan had helped her.

Kieran chuckled. 'Modesty doesn't suit—' Stopping dead in his tracks, he stared at Amy on the sofa. 'Miss Smith? What are you doing here?'

Leaping to her feet, Amy bowed before him. 'Greetings, Your Honour. Councillor Winters was kind enough to offer sanctuary, Sir.'

'Shouldn't you be helping your parents at the forge. We need all hands-on-deck right now.'

'Apologies Sir, but my folks and I don't exactly see eye-to-eye.'

Kieran harrumphed. 'With your lifestyle choices, I'm not surprised.' The High Magus was nothing if not ultra conservative. He would never understand the kinkster scene; few pureblood mages did. 'That said, I'd still appreciate your help in the war. The dragons have appeared now, so we need to double down on our preparations.'

'*What?*' Alannah and Amy screeched together.

'Did you just say the dragons are here?' Alannah's voice trembled, revealing the panic she felt thumping in her veins.

'Not in Gaeilge Shores, yet. They are still down in the Southeast, but it's only a matter of time before they descend upon the rest of the state,' he explained.

'I'll go get the first batch of armour and take these to the cellar.' She grabbed a trunk and dragged it toward the stairs.

'I'll give you a hand,' insisted Kieran as he took the other case.

Once they reached the glamoured door hiding the ritual room from the rest of the basement, Kieran seized her wrist. 'Please tell me you aren't sheltering any other lost lambs here?'

Holding his gaze, she schooled her expression. 'No. Amy is the only one staying with me. My other friends are either helping with the war or they have their own safehouses.'

'For your sake, I hope that's true. Spending time with Brendan is dangerous in ways you can't even begin to fathom.'

The hairs on the back of her neck stood on end. Laughing it off nervously, she shook her head. 'I don't know what you're talking about, Your Honour. There's no way I'd let a villain like him back into my bed, let alone my heart.'

He cocked a brow. 'Please be careful, Alannah.'

Gulping, she turned to unlock the cellar.

Wrapping herself in a plush robe, Neve stepped out of the bathroom and crossed Erik and Elna's bedroom to look out the window. The house—a massive log cabin structure—sat nestled in the thick bushland canopy. Letting her mind drift, she spied a koala chomping on the leaves of a neighbouring gum tree. Her own stomach grumbled at the thought of food, but there was something else the koala had that she craved even more.

'You're dripping all over the floor, Neve,' Erik grumbled while glaring at her bare feet. Completely starkers, he stood tall, not the least bit self-conscious. Not that anyone would be ashamed of such a finely sculpted body and flawless golden skin.

Lowering her gaze, she glimpsed a few trickles of water trailing down her legs and splattering on the timber floor. She shrugged. 'It'll dry.' Her attention returned to the sleepy marsupial outside. 'Am I a prisoner?'

With a huff, he closed the distance between them and hugged her from behind. 'Is it so terrible here? I thought you enjoyed my company, and Elna's.' He spun her around to face him and smirked. 'You weren't complaining this morning, or this afternoon. I lost track of how many times we made you come.'

Her cheeks flushed as recent memories flicked through like a movie reel in fast forward. 'I... Don't get me wrong. The sex is amazing... a great distraction, but I miss my other friends and family. I'm not a fan of being cooped up inside too long either.'

Erik sighed and released her from his grip. 'You're not my captive, Neve. Feel free to come and go as you please.'

'But your dad—'

'I know what my father said last night, but I won't stop you. I wouldn't advise it, however. The outside world is not safe and every time you step beyond the borders of this property, you risk a toasty fate.'

'What if I hop the ley lines and only go to safehouses?'

Erik laughed drily. 'The only safehouses belong to the seelie. Your mage friends are fools to they think their wards will hold against dragon fire.'

She gasped and dashed to the wardrobe, throwing clothes on the bed in a rush to get dressed. 'Oh Gods! Mum and Caitlin! I can't let them burn—'

'Neve, wait! Don't go running off without a care for your own safety.' Erik tugged at the collar of her robe, pulling her back into his arms.

Collapsing under the weight of frustration and worry, she twisted in his embrace and sobbed against his shoulder. 'I need to do something to save them.'

'Don't worry, my love. Dad intends to help your mother if she agrees to the terms of our betrothal.'

She peered up into his impassive green eyes. 'What terms?'

'The legally binding conditions of our betrothal contract. Would you like to read it before or after your mother signs on the dotted line tomorrow?'

Realising she was gaping at him; she snapped her mouth shut and frowned. 'You make it sound like a financial transaction, as if I'm a piece of property for sale.'

'That's how marriage works in my world. From what I understand, it's not much different for most pureblood mages either. Love and happy endings are luxuries most of us can only dream of, which is why I feel so lucky to have your heart as you have mine.' He stroked the side of her face tenderly and leaned down to kiss her lips.

Erik still hadn't bathed after their day of making love and she tasted her own tang on his lips. It sent tingles through her body and stirred her core.

'And here I thought we were getting ready for dinner,' Elna remarked as she opened the bathroom door. Plumes of steam billowed around her, and a skimpy scrap of terrycloth struggled to conceal her voluptuous curves. 'Looks like the pair of you are ready to go another round.'

Tucking Neve into his side, he grinned at Elna. 'I was just easing our girl's anxieties while you hogged all the hot water.'

'Pfft. Looks like you could use a cold shower anyway, Brother dearest.' Elna glanced at the situation below his waist and smiled smugly.

He pressed his mouth against the shell of Neve's ear. 'Wake me up next time so I can shower with you, sweetheart.' His teeth nipped at her earlobe and she half-squealed, half-giggled as he strode toward the ensuite.

'Hm, I wonder,' Elna mused as the girls watched Erik disappear into the bathroom. 'Is it a puberty thing, or are you the reason for the increase in his sex drive?'

'Are you saying he wasn't this…?' Neve blushed.

'I think the word you are looking for is horny. And no—before you, he was content with far less.'

'Oh.' She fell silent and shifted her attention to getting dressed.

Dinner was another awkward affair of forced conversation and stiff formality. She wondered if things would remain this way, or if Alvar would eventually warm up to her. After placing her cutlery neatly on her plate, she cleared her throat. 'Excuse me, Your Highness. May I please read the betrothal contract?'

Alvar sipped his red wine and dabbed his mouth with a linen napkin. 'Certainly. It is wise to understand the rules, so you do not break them unknowingly.' He rang the brass bell beside his glass and asked the butler to fetch the document. 'I am confident your mother will agree to my terms. She stands to lose a great deal by refusing, so it is in her best interest.' He handed her the papers.

She felt the blood drain from her face as she read through the extensive list of conditions and her heart skipped a beat when she reached the virginity clauses:

> *During the period of betrothal, The Claimed will submit to a physical examination on an annual basis to confirm*

her hymen remains intact. This procedure
will be performed by an independent party.
    If The Claimed loses her virginity at
any point prior to matrimony, The Claimant
will lose his claim and the parties responsible
will be charged with treason, punishable by
death.

She didn't need a law degree to understand the severity of her situation. *If Mum signs that contract, I'm as good as dead when they check for my hymen. But if she doesn't sign it, her own life and those of everyone staying at Cailleach Estate will be in danger.*

Alannah awoke with a start beneath the solid mass of a man's body. She tried to scream, but a hand clamped over her mouth, and she flicked her eyes open. Within the seconds it took her vision to adjust to the darkness, his familiar musky scent filtered through the panic and seeped into her senses. The tension eased from her muscles, and she stopped struggling. Another second passed before she realised Brendan had crept beneath the covers to straddle her and heat crept across her scantily clad skin. When she attempted to question him, he increased the pressure of his grip against her mouth.

Bringing his chest flush with hers, he whispered in her ear, 'Shoosh gorgeous. Erect a sound ward first.'

She glared at him but did as he asked. 'Why couldn't you put up your own damn soundproofing?'

'Your wards are much stronger, and they even hold up if someone opens the door.'

'Oh.' The hint of a blush warmed her cheeks. 'So, what do you want to talk about?'

Brendan smirked. 'Why do you assume I want to talk? Maybe I just want to ravish you and spare our guests the embarrassment.'

She arched her brows and gave him a sidelong glance.

'Yeah okay, you got me there. I couldn't care less if they heard your cries of ecstasy, but I do owe you an explanation.'

'And you had to wake me up in the middle of the night? I'm exhausted after a full day of conjuration, and it wasn't easy to get to sleep.'

He gave her a sheepish simper. 'I'm sorry, Lana. I couldn't wait any longer.'

'Okay fine. Let me sit up first because I won't be able to concentrate in this position. I can feel your dick straining against those flimsy track pants you're wearing.'

He gave her a sly grin. 'At least I'm wearing pants,' Brendan's hand slid up her thigh as he spoke, 'unlike you. I'd forgotten how you tend not to wear panties to bed.' He tugged gently at the hem of her black satin slip before lifting it above her hip.

'Brendan.' She intended to use a threatening tone, but her warning sounded more like a whimpering plea.

'Hm, maybe the talk can wait a *little* longer.' He brushed his lips across her cheek and thrust his erection against her.

She moaned as her body shuddered and her core flooded. 'Brendan, please.'

'Please what, Lana?' He breathed the words against her lips.

'Please stop.'

'Who are you trying to convince?' His cock pressed hard against her clit.

Closing her eyes, she took a deep breath and blurted out, 'Richard.'

He scrambled away from her and sat on the edge of the bed with wide eyes.

She had never needed to safeword out with him before and it pained her to do so, but they had too many issues to resolve first. Sitting up, she leaned against the headboard. 'I'm sorry, Brendan, but I'm not ready. We really should talk first.'

'Don't ever feel you need to apologise for using your safeword, gorgeous. I'm just surprised is all.' He was panting heavily and took several seconds to compose himself. 'Is it okay if I still hold you while we talk?'

She nodded and moved across to give him space. Sitting beside her, he pulled her into his arms. Slumping down, she placed her head against his chest and listened to the frantic thumping of his heart.

A full minute elapsed before he spoke again. 'The reason I didn't return after gaining my freedom, my excuse for staying away from you all these years was fear. I'm a coward when it comes to you, Lana, always have been. Yeah, I was scared you'd reject me, but I was even more afraid of losing you to our enemy.'

'Enemy?'

'I still don't know who they are, but I'm pretty sure their identity is part of Tara's big secret.'

'Wouldn't I be safer with you here to protect me?'

He squeezed her tight and pressed a chaste kiss against the crown of her head. 'I wish it were that simple. The enemy doesn't want us to be together. Bridey made that abundantly clear.'

She tensed at the sound of the bitch's name. 'Why? And what does the she-devil have to do with this?'

'I only just learned Bridey is working for the enemy by trying to keep us apart and even spying on me. I don't know the full extent of her involvement, which is why I can't cut ties with her yet. I used to think her dislike for you was personal. When I first gained my freedom, I struck a deal with her. I was still heartbroken over you at the time, so I agreed without question.'

Painful silence followed and she prompted him to continue with a soft voice, 'What did you agree to?'

He sucked in a breath. 'To stay away from you. In exchange for her support in the Syndicate and… continued access to Caleb.'

'Fuck.' The muttered curse slipped out before she could stop it.

'Yeah, I know. I didn't intend to keep my word for long. I dreamed of ways I could sneak away to visit you in secret. But then I started unravelling the doppelganger mystery with Tyler and that threw a massive spanner in the works.'

'I heard about that stuff from Tyler, but what does it have to do with us?'

'Tyler hasn't told you the full truth of the mater because he doesn't even know. I kept my theory to myself.'

'What theory?'

'Then you went and proved it yesterday.'

Goosebumps prickled her exposed arms. 'What theory, Brendan?'

'You're my doppelganger, Lana.'

She sat bolt upright and gaped at him. 'What? How? I'm a woman, I can't be *your* doppelganger.'

He leered at her breasts and licked his lips. 'I'm quite aware of your gender, gorgeous.'

She smacked his arm. 'Quit it.'

Mischief twinkled in his eyes when they returned to hers. 'From what I understand, doppelgangers don't have to be the same sex. We are mystic twins because of your DNA. Your bio dad, whoever he was, must descend from a God of magic, probably The Dagda if he was Irish, but who really knows? That power surge we felt during the ritual yesterday—that was due to our mystical connection. I felt the same with Tyler, but it was much stronger with you, and I think that is why the enemy wants to keep us apart. Because us working together, on top of your Beltane blessing, turns us into a force to be reckoned with. Someone perceives us as a threat, and they'll stop at nothing to keep us from working together. We can't fight an unknown enemy, so until we know who they are, we must be extremely careful.'

'If we are such a threat, why not take us out before we become unstoppable?'

'I don't know. I've wondered the same thing. Maybe they have plans for us? Like how the Obsidian Cult used Tyler and me. The value of our mystic connection might outweigh the risks, but this is all conjecture because I have no fucking idea who this dickhead is, let alone how their mind works.'

She inhaled deeply and breathed out through pursed lips. 'Thanks. I understand now. I hate it, but I get it.'

'Yup. It sucks balls alright. Now that I know what really went down with Liam back then, *and* I know how you feel about me, I'm willing to fight for us. I'm sorry it took me this long to grow a pair.'

She sank back into the bed. 'Will you stay with me tonight?'

'Of course.' He held her, stroking her until she fell asleep in his arms.

Also By L. Starla

The Phoebe Braddock Books
(Taboo Romance & Forbidden Love)

I Heart Mr. Collins
From Prying Eyes
Crystal's Crucible
Undeniably Wrong
Book #5 to be Announced

Serial Fiction Boxsets

Well I'll Be Damned Season 1
The Dark Matter Between Our Hearts Season 1

About the Author

L. Starla is an Australian author who often raided her mother's shelves for any form of fiction she could get her hands on. Her first love was the horror genre, but she owes her love affair with the romance novel to her high-school English teacher, who started her on the classics. Given her earlier reading, magical realism and paranormal romance were a natural progression. Along with steamy romance, these are the genres she writes.

Starla also loves spending her spare time playing tabletop and video games, paper crafting, singing, dancing, and watching anime.

Access Exclusive Content

Join my newsletter to access free stuff like short stories, deleted scenes, fan art, and invitations to future launch events.

Newsletter: www.starlaarts.com>freebies
Facebook Group: groups/l.starlareadersgroup

Follow me Online:
Website & Blog: www.starlaarts.com
Goodreads: L. Starla
BookBub: www.bookbub.com/profile/l-starla
Amazon Author Profile: author/l.starla
Instagram: L. Starla Author
Facebook: L.Starla
Twitter: @LStarla2019